THE
GOODBYE
SUMMER

Wendy Deaman

The
Goodbye
Summer

Patricia Gaffney

POCKET
BOOKS

LONDON · NEW YORK · SYDNEY · TORONTO

First published in Great Britain by Simon & Schuster UK Ltd, 2004

This edition first published by Pocket Books, 2005

An imprint of Simon & Schuster UK Ltd

A CBS COMPANY

1 3 5 7 9 10 8 6 4 2

Simon & Schuster UK Ltd
1st Floor
222 Gray's Inn Road
London WC1X 8HB

www.simonandschuster.co.uk

Simon & Schuster Australia,
Sydney

A CIP catalogue record for this book is available from the British Library.

ISBN 978-1-84983-358-5

Printed and bound in Great Britain by
CPI Cox & Wyman, Reading, Berkshire

To the loving, gentle, dedicated staff at Brooke Grove Retirement Village, particularly those at The Meadows and at Sharon Nursing Home. Thank you for relieving my mind, and for your many, many kindnesses.

ACKNOWLEDGMENTS

Thanks again to Nurse McComas, who never lets me down.

I'm grateful to Maya Ginsberg, whose advice on music teaching was invaluable.

Thank you, Carl P. E. dos Santos, for your friendliness and expertise, and for convincing this skeptic that not all skydivers are insane.

Much affection and gratitude to Mary Alice Kruesi for Finney, the gift that keeps on giving.

And warmest thanks and love to Aaron Priest for everything.

The Goodbye Summer

1

The first Caddie Winger ever heard of Wake House was when she was helping her grandmother get her drawers on over the cast on her leg.

It was Nana's second day back from the hospital. "If I was at Wake House," she said, lying flat on the sofa and holding her bunched-up nightgown over her lap for modesty, "somebody who knew what they were doing would be doing this."

"What house? Awake?"

"Wake House. That place on Calvert Street across from the thing. The thing, where you go with papers. To get signed."

"The notary? Put your good foot in here, Nan. Are you talking about that old house with the tower and all the porches? I think it's a boarding-house."

"Before. Now it's an old folks' home."

"Oh, you don't need to go to a place like that, I can take care of you fine."

"*Ow.*"

"It's a learning curve."

Nana mentioning a nursing home, imagine that. For the rest of the morning Caddie pondered what it might mean. When the old lady across the street went dotty and her children put her in a nursing home, Nana was aghast. "Shoot me if you ever want to get rid of me that bad, you hear? Take me out in the backyard and fire away." Caddie assumed the subject of nursing homes was off-limits forever.

3

That afternoon, though, out of the blue, Nana brought up Wake House again.

They were on the front porch, Nana slumped in her rented wheelchair, resting her broken leg on a pillow on top of the low kitchen stool. Caddie stood behind her, braiding her hair. Nana had long, pretty, smoke-gray hair and, before it softened with age, a long, bony, sharp-featured face. She loved it when people told her she looked like Virginia Woolf. Nobody ever added, "If she'd lived to seventy-nine instead of walking into the river."

"What's-her-name died there," she said, breaking a drowsy silence.

"Who died where, Nan?"

"Wake House. What's-her-name, you know. Pink hair, Tuesday nights."

Hm. Back in Nana's Buddhist period, when she'd led a chanting service in the dining room one night a week, an elderly lady who dyed her hair pink had shown up occasionally. "Mrs. Pringle?"

"Inez Pringle, thank you."

"She *died* at Wake House?"

Nana shrugged. "You have to die someplace."

Caddie leaned over to see if she was joking. Her eyes were fixed on something out in the yard—Caddie followed her gaze to what was left of *George Bush in Love*. That's how she'd broken her leg, by falling off the stepladder while putting a final cowboy boot on top of her phallus-shaped, seven-foot-high lawn sculpture. Nana was an artist.

"Are you serious?" Caddie asked.

A moment passed. "About what?" Nana said dreamily.

Caddie smiled and went back to braiding her hair. How were they going to wash it? This old house had only one bathroom, upstairs, and right now Nana couldn't stand up at the kitchen sink for longer than a minute or two. Maybe one of those dry shampoos, they were supposed to . . .

"About Wake House? Damn right I'm serious. Call 'em up, find out how much it costs to stay there."

Her next pain pill wasn't for forty minutes. She'd broken her leg in two places, but luckily the breaks were simple, so her recovery was supposed to be long and tedious but not tricky or dangerous. The pain made her irritable, though. That's all Caddie could think of to account for Nana's sudden interest in recovering anyplace except the house on Early Street she'd lived in for fifty years.

"Wake House. I even like the sound of it."

"You do?" It made Caddie think of a funeral home.

"It's not like one of those places, it's not a mick . . . mick . . ."

"McNursing Home," Caddie guessed.

"This place is going to the dogs."

"Our house?"

"The whole neighborhood. It's not even safe anymore."

"Yes, it is."

"No, it's not."

Caddie stopped arguing, because she never won, but Nana was exaggerating. Early Street might not be what it used to be, not that it had ever been that much, but it still had decent, hardworking families with fairly well-behaved children, plenty of old-timers rocking out their afternoons on the shady, crooked front porches. Crime was still pretty much in the vandalism category, boys breaking things or writing on things. It was getting older, that's all. Everything got older.

"Wake House," Nana resumed. "I bet it's got an elevator. Ramps, wheelchairs with motors. People giving you massages."

"Oh, boy."

"I'm a senior citizen, I deserve the best. This place is a death trap."

"Only about half an hour till your next pill, then you'll feel better. Want me to play the piano? You could listen through the window."

"Look it up in the yellow pages. Better yet, take me to see it—I always wanted to go inside that place. It's not just for old folks, you can get well there, too. Conva . . . conva . . ."

"Nan, I know you don't want to, but if you would just go *upstairs*, this whole thing would be a lot simpler. I really think."

"No way."

"You'd be near the bathroom—you know how you hate that climb up the stairs four or five times a day. You could sleep in your own bed instead of the lumpy couch. You wouldn't have to move every time one of my students comes over for a lesson. You could have a bell or a whistle, and I'd come up anytime you needed something, I wouldn't mind a bit. It just makes so much more—"

"*No.*"

"But why?"

"I told you, I'm not going up there."

"But why *not*?"

"Once you go up, you never come down."

"Nana, you only broke your *leg*."

"That's it, I've made up my mind. Wake House. I used to know the family, you know."

Maybe Caddie could take one of Nana's pills for the headache she was getting. "You knew the Wakes?" Her back cracked when she arched it to stretch out the stiffness.

"Well, not knew as in *know*, as in sit in the parlor and drink tea and eat cucumber sandwiches." She cackled; she cracked herself up. "The whole town knew the Wakes. The old man owned the Bank of Michaelstown. It used to be on the corner of Maryland and Antietam."

"It still is."

"Yes, but Wakes don't own it anymore. They were the big cheeses around here, like the, the—Hyannisport—"

"Kennedys."

"Kennedys, till the old man lost all the money. After that they just disappeared. Dried up and blew away."

"Well, anyway—I still think if you'd go to bed and not move for about two weeks, your *own* bed, it would give you a good start. On healing. Remember, the doctor said—"

Her grandmother stuck her thumbs in her ears and wriggled her fingers while she went *pbbbbbb* with her lips.

"Well—*honestly,*" Caddie said, offended, then saw the two boys out on the sidewalk. Neighbor kids; she knew their faces but not their names. They stopped in front of the house, arrested by Nana's raspberry. One had a skateboard slung over his shoulder, the other had a silent boom box; like little men coming home from work, Caddie thought, only with toys instead of rakes or picks on their shoulders. "Hi!" she called out, with a cheery smile, waving. "How're you doing?"

"Miniature thugs," Nana said too loud.

"Hush." They already thought old lady Winger was a witch. "How's it going?" Caddie called gaily. "What's happening?"

The one with the skateboard finally lifted his hand in a belligerent half-wave.

"Have a good day!"

They jostled each other, swaggering off down the sidewalk.

"Nana, *why* do you—"

"Hoodlums."

"You don't even know it's them."

"If it's not, it's one of their com . . . you know, com . . ."

"Comrades. Compatriots."

George Bush in Love wasn't Nana's only artistic creation in the front yard, not by a long shot. It was starting to look like a playground out there, or a wax museum. Her most attention-getting artworks were *Earthen Uterus* and the long, cylindrical *Passionate Ones United.* Mysterious additions that infuriated Nana and mortified Caddie appeared on or near the sculptures in the night, things like scattered sanitary napkins or used condoms; once somebody hung a toilet seat over the scrap metal head of *Fecund Goddess*. The sculptures weren't popular on Early Street, but they were legal—the neighbors had found that out after a lot of complaints to the police, the city council, the Neighborhood Watch.

Finney, Nana's Jack Russell terrier, scratched at the screen door to come out. "Okay," Caddie told him, "but only on your rope." Otherwise he'd take off after anything that moved.

"Jane, put him up on my lap."

"Sure?" She'd long since stopped correcting Nana when she called her by her daughter's name—Caddie's mother, who'd been dead for twenty-three years. "Won't it hurt your leg?"

"You kidding?" She knocked on the fiberglass cast under her denim skirt. "Can't feel a thing."

"You know, if you went to a place like Wake House, you probably wouldn't be able to keep Finney," Caddie said, lifting the dog onto her grandmother's lap. He was only two and a half and still a holy terror, but if Nana petted him, he'd sit still for hours.

"Maybe, maybe not. Inez said they have cats." She stroked the dog's silky ears and kissed him on top of his head. "Now, listen to me, Caddie Winger. You're . . . oh, shoot."

"What?"

"How the hell old are you?"

"Thirty-two."

"I knew that."

"Course you did." She finished with her grandmother's hair, gave her a quick hug, and came around to sit on the porch rail. The sun felt good on her back. Spring was finally getting started. She batted a bee away. It was a soft, shimmery-blue afternoon, and the neighbors' yards were sprouting tulips and azaleas and dogwood blossoms. In Nana's yard the sculptures made of dirt were sprouting bright green, spiky-soft grass, like Chia pets.

"We went to the movies on your birthday," Nana recalled.

"Yes."

"Now that is a fine thing, going to a movie with your grandmother on your birthday."

"I thought you liked it." Caddie had worried a little about the profanity; it was a gangster movie.

"It was okay. I give it one thumb up. But that's not the point." She frowned, trying to recall the point. "The point is, when's the last time you went out on a date? A real date, not violin practice with that Adolphe Menjou guy."

"If you mean Morris, he was my stand partner in the orchestra, and anyway, he's gay."

"*That's* the point. I'm holding you back. I see it all now, it came to me in the hospital."

"Boy, you must've been high on those painkillers." Caddie laughed weakly. "Because that's ridiculous."

"Look at you. It's my fault."

"What's wrong with me?" She had on her gray pants and her black sweater, which was speckled with Finney's little white hairs. But everything in the house was speckled with Finney's hairs, it was like they were coated with an adhesive.

She should never have asked, because Nana squirmed in her wheelchair, searching for a more comfortable position, and proceeded to tell her what was wrong with her. "You don't look like other girls. I've been watching a lot of tube lately, I know what I'm talking about."

"Soap operas in the hospital, that's not—"

"You don't put yourself out. You're invisible. Look at your hair, it doesn't have any *oomph*. Blondes have more fun, but not if they don't even try. Are you having fun?"

"I'm having plenty of fun."

"How tall are you?"

Caddie sighed. "Five eleven."

"Five eleven!" she exclaimed, as if this were brand-new news. "Five feet eleven inches tall, and look at you. Sit up straight, make your shoulders go back. Let's see your bosoms, I know you've got some."

"Yikes!" Caddie jumped off the rail and whirled around, turning her back on her grandmother. "Quit picking on me," she wailed, laughing along with Nana's wheezy *haw-haw*. "What's gotten into you?"

Funny, though, that Nana would use the word "invisible." When Caddie was little, pretending nobody could see her had been her favorite game. And later, like a song hook in the back of her mind had been any version of *I could've fallen through the floor,* or *I wished the earth would open up and swallow me.* Maybe Nana was right; maybe she'd succeeded so well that at last nobody *could* see her.

"Nothing's gotten into me, I've seen the light. I'll go to Wake House and you go to a whatchamacallit, garden apartment, handsome men hanging over the balcony looking down at the girls in the swimming pool. Everybody's single, nobody's got a job."

"No more TV for you."

"You think you'll be lonesome. That's why you're against it." When they focused, Nana's eyes could look unnervingly shrewd. "You've never been on your own, so you're scared."

"I have, too. Graduate school, when I got my music master's."

"Two years," she said dismissively, "and you didn't go very far away, did you? How'd you like it?"

"Fine. I liked it fine."

"I bet."

"What does that mean? What does 'I bet' mean?"

"I bet you had the time of your life."

"I did not. I mean . . ." She forgot what side she was arguing on. Nana's lined old face sagged. "Caddie, honey, I'm the old lady,

10

not you. I'm the one who's supposed to not want anything to change."

"That's not right." She wrapped her arms around herself. "I want plenty of things to change. About *me*, though—I don't see why *you* have to do anything."

Caddie didn't get the joke, but for some reason that tickled her grandmother. She went into her wheezy laugh again, *haw-haw-haw*, bobbing Finney up and down on her lap. "Oh, me." She pushed her knuckle under her glasses to wipe away a tear. "I'm only talking for a couple of months, you know."

"Oh. A couple of months?"

"While my leg heals. I can't even pee down here."

"That's what I've been saying, that's why going upstairs makes so much more—"

"Lord, I'm tired all of a sudden. Wheel me inside, honey, I have to lie down."

No more was said about old folks' homes, and Caddie was pretty sure the subject was closed. She gave Nana her pain pill and got her settled on the couch, then went in the kitchen and tried to be quiet while she chopped onions for a casserole. Her grandmother confused her with her talk of leaving, but no more than she confused herself. What did *she* want? Normalcy, she'd have said, her unsuccessful goal since about age ten. And Nana was offering it to her, at least temporarily, a chance to be *really* invisible. She could bring a friend home and not have to worry that her grandmother would invite what was left of her nudist club over to join them, or that she'd have finger-painted Coptic symbols on the front door, or dyed Finney beige for fun. Caddie wouldn't want to fall through the floor. Being by herself was nothing compared to that. Anyway, you didn't have to be alone to be lonesome.

They had a quiet dinner. Nana watched *Jeopardy!* while Caddie did the dishes and tidied up, fed the dog. When she went in the living room to get Nana ready for bed, she found her with the telephone on her lap, dialing.

"Who are you calling?"

"Sh." She pressed the phone to her ear with her shoulder and held up her left wrist. "Good thing I put this on"—she flicked a rubber band—"because *you'd* sure never've remembered."

"What?"

She put a finger to her lips and screwed up her face, listening. "Oh, for Pete's sake. Well, *this* doesn't bode well."

"Who is it?"

She cleared her throat and spoke in her message-leaving voice. "Hello, this is Frances Winger. Please call me back at your earliest convenience." She gave the number and started to hang up. Changed her mind. "And frankly, even if this is the business office, I think you ought to have a human being at the helm over there, not a machine. Even at night."

"Nana, who are you calling?"

"If you're a *home,* you should be *homey.*"

"Oh, boy."

Nana hung up decisively.

"How'd you get the number?" The phone book was in the kitchen.

"Information." She wore a smug smile. She plucked at her skirt, arranging it over her cast just so. "We'll go there tomorrow, check the joint out."

"Wake House."

"Wake House."

"And it's just temporary?"

"Just temporary. Did I tell you I used to know the Wakes? Well, not know as in *know* . . ."

2

Nana had to have all her art supplies with her, *all* of them, so it took a whole day and about seven trips back and forth in Caddie's old Pontiac to move her into Wake House. "Wish I could help," she'd say every time Caddie staggered into her sunny, spacious, second-floor room with a box of engraving tools or an armload of canvases. Wake House had an elevator—Nana had been right about that, thank goodness—but it also had six steps between the sidewalk and the front walk, four more up to the wide front porch. By late afternoon Caddie was on her last legs.

"Go home," Nana told her. "Put your feet up, have a drink. *Hey*." She sat up straight in her wheelchair. "Do they serve booze here? We never even asked."

Caddie blew a damp fall of hair out of her eyes. "I've only got a few more things to bring in." One more, actually: Nana's nude, life-size, papier-mâché statue of Michelangelo's *David*. She had to have it, even though she used it only for a hat rack. Caddie had been saving it for last, hoping the front porch would be clear of witnesses by now. Half a dozen elderly Wake House residents had been monitoring the whole moving-in process since morning, and they all had kindly, welcoming smiles and eagle eyes.

"No, you go home, I mean it. I didn't even do anything, and *I'm* exhausted."

"You met people—that's tiring."

13

"I met a hundred people," Nana agreed. "Can't remember a single one's name. Except those two gals—"

"The Harrises," Caddie guessed, and they laughed together. Mrs. and Mrs. Harris were seventy-something ladies who lived on the same floor but never spoke a word to each other because—according to Claudette, the activities director—they used to be married to the same man. The late Mr. Harris.

"And Lorton," Nana recalled, "somebody Lorton, him I remember because he's the only one who's older than me. He's a hundred and ten."

"I've seen lots of people who look much older than you."

Nana grunted, blinking drowsily. Her eyes looked clear gray, almost transparent in the glare of late-afternoon sun.

"Wouldn't this be a good place to set up your easel? In front of these pretty doors." Lovely old French doors leading to a tiny balcony over the front yard and Calvert Street. "I bet the light's perfect here practically all day. For painting."

"Quit talking, I'm trying to doze off."

"Oh! Okay, I'll come and get you around six, then. Brenda said that's when people start to gather in the blue parlor before dinner, a little get-together every night."

"No, thank you. I want to go down on my own steam, eat dinner, and go to bed."

"Well, I wasn't going to stay for dinner, just the little get-together. To help, you know, sort of get you settled—"

"I don't need any help."

"But it's your first night and I just . . . I thought I'd slip out right before the meal." The busiest time, when Nana was in so many people's capable hands, food in the offing, everything a little bit hectic. So she'd hardly even notice Caddie was gone.

"No, slip out right now. *Get.*" She turned her chair around to face the sun sliding down behind the glass doors.

"Oh, well. Okay, then." Nana's thick gray braid hung down in back, light against the black of the wheelchair. Caddie gave it a gentle tug. Her grandmother wasn't much for hugging. Caddie leaned down anyway and put her lips on Nana's soft cheek. The backs of her eyes stung right before they filled with tears.

Nana saw. "Well, for the Lord's sake." She found Caddie's hand and gave it a hard, jerky shake. "How silly can you be. I'll probably be home in a month."

"I know."

"I'm a fifteen-minute drive away."

"I know." She wiped her face. "So I'll call you as soon as I get home, okay?"

"*Caddie . . .*"

She laughed. "That's a joke."

Nana punched her on the arm. "Go, goodbye. Do something crazy while I'm out of the way. Go wild. Kick up your heels while you've got the chance." She dropped skeptical eyes to Caddie's shoes: sensible black flats. "Try, anyway."

"I love you, Nan."

"Likewise. Oh, and another thing, don't miss me. That's an order."

"Don't miss you?" She laughed, but her grandmother wasn't smiling. "Sorry," Caddie said softly, "that I can't promise." She blew Nana a kiss and backed out of the room.

The entrance hall, like the rest of Wake House, was a sort of good-natured jumble of grand and gone-to-seed. It had flocked peony wallpaper; blackish, shoulder-high wainscoting; and a chandelier looming over everything like a big, dusty bunch of grapes. More lights in sconces lined the walls above brown-painted benches that looked like church pews. Pocket doors on either side led to identical parlors called the Red Room and the Blue Room. You went to the Blue Room for arts and crafts, exercise class, bridge, house meetings, things like that. The Red Room was the formal parlor; you had to be quiet in there, read a book, play checkers or chess, entertain sedate visitors.

Caddie was crossing the hall—the scuffed parquet floor was so creaky it sounded like little firecrackers exploding under her feet at every step—when Brenda Herbert came around the corner from her office. "Caddie!" She had a hearty, booming voice, as if a microphone were pinned to her lapel. "All moved in? Poor thing, you must be worn out. Sorry we couldn't give you more help, but I had no idea how much—how many—I do hope there's *room* for everything," she finished tactfully, planting herself in front of Caddie and folding her arms. She owned Wake House. She was round-faced, solid-bodied, a widow; Caddie had never seen her in an apron, but she seemed like the kind of person who'd feel at home in one. "How is Frances?" she asked, wrinkling her forehead in concern. "Is she all right? Settling in okay?"

"Fine! Great! She loves it already. I think she's going to fit right in. I really do."

She didn't like the way Brenda patted her on the arm and softened her megaphone voice to say, "Oh, dear, I hope so, I do hope so."

"No, really, she's going to be *fine*." She said that too fervently, but Brenda had the wrong idea about Nana. "She's *eccentric*," Caddie had already tried to explain several times. "She's always been like this, this is how she *is*," but the skepticism in Brenda's face never really went away. "Anyway," Caddie reminded her, "it's just temporary— till her leg heals. The doctor didn't give a time, he just said it'll be longer than usual because of her age."

"Well, even if it takes a year," Brenda said in a dry tone, "we can be sure she won't run out of art supplies."

Thumping footsteps sounded on the wooden front porch. An old man with thick glasses and wild, Albert Einstein hair stomped inside the house. He had on baggy-kneed trousers and a bow tie. His body bent forward at the shoulders in a predatory hunch, like a half-plucked but still dangerous bird, and Caddie was glad when he ignored her and dove straight at Brenda.

"So now the plan is to freeze us out? Eh? I thought it was to *burn* us out when you painted the damn windows shut."

"Ah, Cornel. Good day to you, too."

"You think it's a good day? You think so? You must not live on the third floor. You must not've been standing in the shower at seven-thirty this morning."

"Oh, dear."

"Seven-thirty A.M. You think it's unreasonable to expect the hot water to last till half-past seven in the morning?"

"Sorry, Cornel, there must've been a run on showers this morning."

"That's not the problem. The problem is the boiler. You got ten people trying to wash at the same time, and you got a boiler big enough to heat water for eight."

Brenda held her ground when he bent even closer. She said, "Well, I guess we all—"

"I can *hear* Mrs. Brill, and I happen to know she stands under that shower for fifteen minutes every damn day of the week. What's a woman that age got to wash off for fifteen minutes? And she's not the only—"

Brenda cut in jovially, "Look who's here, Cornel, we have a new resident, I know you're going to enjoy her so much, she's an *artist*. Cornel Davenport, this is Caddie Winger, her grandmother is *Frances* Winger, she's upstairs but you'll be meeting—"

"You're new?" Cornel said accusingly, looking Caddie up and down. "Christ almighty, they're getting younger every day. What do we do, charge double if they're under fifty? This makes three now—"

17

"No, it's not me—"

"And if you ask me it brings down the tone of the place. No offense, and not that it had such a high tone to begin—"

"*Not her,* Cornel," Brenda raised her voice to say.

"What's that?"

"Her *grandmother.*"

"Oh. Grandmother. Which one's this?"

"Caddie," Caddie said. "Pleased to meet you."

They shook hands. His was dry and hard. He had such thin lips; if they were smiling, it was hard to tell.

"Cornel's one of our oldest residents," Brenda said, "almost a charter member of Wake House."

"Yeah, and fifty cents'll get me a cuppa coffee. *Sleep* House, that's what we call it."

"He's also our resident grump."

A tall, frail-looking boy in wrinkled blue pajamas shambled around the corner from a corridor Caddie hadn't noticed before. He stopped when he saw them. "Oops. Company," he mumbled. The suddenness of halting must've thrown him off balance: he took two backward steps and smacked against the wall, causing a framed aerial photograph of Wake House to fall off its nail, strike the parquet floor, and break. Glass shattered.

Cornel laughed, a surprisingly pleasant sound. "This is Magill," he told Caddie, "he's one o' the young ones—we got two. We like him, though, he gives old age a good name."

"Don't move," Brenda instructed when Magill, who was barefooted, stretched out one of his thin legs as if he meant to step over the glass. Was he drunk? He had a black eye and a livid bruise on his left temple. And he wasn't a boy at all, Caddie saw, he was a grown man; beard stubble shadowed his gaunt cheeks, and a piece of bloody toilet paper was still stuck to a cut on his chin.

"No, stay put," Brenda ordered over his muttered apologies,

rushing over to take his arm. "Watch out, honey, be careful. This way, look at your feet." She kept one arm around his waist and one on his forearm while she led him over to where Caddie and Cornel stood under the chandelier. He had on kneepads, the kind skateboarders wore. Had he been skateboarding? In his pajamas?

Cornel said, "This here's Caddie something—"

"Winger."

"She's dropping off her grandma. We got almost a full house again."

Magill reached up to straighten his hair, which was black and shoved up on one side like a cardinal's crest, flat on the other. "Hi."

"Hello. It's nice to meet you."

"Nice to meet you. I'm sure your grandmother will like it here."

"I'm sure she will."

He had a slow, sweet smile. Or maybe it was sly. "Make sure she stays on Brenda's good side, though," he said confidingly. "Otherwise . . ." He turned his head and made a quick, furtive gesture toward his swollen and bloodshot eye. "Kind of a hothead. I know, you'd never think it. And usually she's fine, but you just don't want to cross her."

Caddie stared at him with her mouth open.

A whoop of laughter exploded from Cornel; he rocked with it, leaning forward to slap his thighs.

Brenda rolled her eyes, chuckling in sympathy.

"Oh," Caddie said, so glad it was a joke. "Oh, I see."

A phone rang somewhere. "Sorry, 'scuse me," Brenda said, and dashed off down the hall.

Caddie told Cornel and Magill she was happy to have met them, and they said the same to her. They made an odd couple, she thought, glancing back from the front porch. They stood in the hall

19

to watch her go, the older man with his arms crossed and his legs braced to bear the weight of the younger one, who leaned against his shoulder and cocked his eyebrows at Caddie, smiling the sly, sweet smile.

3

Nana had been on a sort of quasi-macrobiotic diet ever since she'd read somewhere it would increase her life span by seven to nine years. But only if she started it in her twenties; she'd missed that part, and Caddie hadn't had the heart to point it out. Driving by the local supermarket on her way home from Wake House, it occurred to her that yin and yang were now the cook at Wake House's worry, not hers, and she could eat anything she liked. She went in and bought half a pound of salmon, some fresh dill, a huge baking potato, salad makings (including tomatoes, which, macrobiotically speaking, never went with anything), and a pint of her favorite ice cream, chocolate almond, which she never got at home because Nana had diverticulosis and couldn't eat nuts. She'd cheer herself up by having a feast. With wine. And some magazines—all she had at home to read were improving books. Kick up your heels, Nana had said. Go wild. Well, okay, Caddie thought, opening the car windows and turning the radio up loud. If I must.

She had shut Finney up in her bedroom so he wouldn't be underfoot while she moved Nana's things, then forgotten to let him out on the last trip. As soon as she opened the door, he bolted between her legs, down the hall, down the stairs, and started on one of his circular tears, hall, dining room, kitchen, living room, around and around until he ran out of breath. Then he started barking.

"*Good* boy," she told him when he did his long, relieved business on the grass between the street and the sidewalk in front of Mrs.

21

Tourneau's house. Say what you would about Finney's bad habits, and he had a million, at least he was housebroken.

The same mini-revelation she'd had driving past the grocery store came over her again as she was deciding what music to put on while she made her dinner, her feast. She could play anything. Jazz, for example. Nana hated it, so she made cracks about it; the more progressive the jazz, the more sarcastic the cracks. *Ha!* Caddie thought, with an airy feeling in her chest, and put on *Bitches Brew*.

She listened to her phone messages while she uncorked her nine-dollar bottle of sauvignon blanc. Larry Fish's mother had canceled his violin lesson; she'd forgotten his appointment with the orthodontist tomorrow. "Grrr," Caddie said to the dog. "That's against the rules." She sent flyers out every few months, clarifying the cancellation policy: forty-eight hours minimum. Try getting Mrs. Fish to pay for that missed lesson, though. "There goes thirty bucks," she told Finney. Oh, great—was she going to start talking to the dog? The rest of the messages were requests to reschedule, one legitimate cancellation, and Rayanne Schmidt calling to report she'd spilled Dr Pepper on her electric keyboard and now she was afraid to turn it on.

Might as well go all out and eat in the dining room, Caddie decided. It looked a little sad, one lonely place setting at the head of the table. But she and Nana always ate in the kitchen, and she was setting new precedents tonight. Breaking with tradition. What the heck—she'd light candles, too.

Her grandmother had probably finished dinner by now. If she hadn't gone straight up to her room, she might be sipping tea and chatting in one of the parlors, making new friends. People who weren't afraid of Nana really liked her. Would she like them, though? There were two elderly old-maid sisters, Bea and Edgie Copes, who'd brought an African violet to Nana's room this morning, a little welcoming present. "I hope you two aren't married to the same man," Nana had greeted them, and they tittered like young girls. Caddie thought they were charming, but when they left, her grandmother had pronounced them "too sweet."

Should she call Nana now, just to see how she was doing? No—no, she decided, they were better off on their own tonight. Learning to do without each other.

The phone rang. *I knew it*, she thought, *I should've called first.*

"Hey, Caddie. Can I ask you—what do you think of Angela Ann Noonenberg?"

"Angie?"

"Yeah, it's me. Angela Ann—how does that sound?"

"Well . . . good, it sounds very nice. Is that your name?" Angie was Caddie's best violin student, and still only a junior in high school.

"No. Okay, what do you think of Angela May Noonenberg?"

"Um . . . well, which one is your name?"

"Neither, I don't have a middle name. Mom thinks I should have three names, but I don't know. You know, for the *pageant*. I told her she should've thought of that about seventeen years ago."

"So you'd just add a name?"

"Sure, you can do it easy, you just start using it, writing it on all your stuff, and pretty soon it's like grandfathered in or something. Mom says it's perfectly legal."

Angie had been Miss Apple Blossom Festival last fall, and before that Miss Junior Grape, but she and Mrs. Noonenberg, a former beauty queen herself, had bigger things in mind, beginning with Miss Michaelstown next December. "But I don't understand," Caddie said. "Why do you need three names?"

"Mom thinks it'll give me a better chance, either that or being named Heather. There've been two Miss America Heathers since '95. But Mary Ann Mobley's the most famous of all time except for Vanessa Williams, so we're thinking three names is the way to go. So which do you like, Angela Ann or Angela May?"

"Angela Ann, I guess. My middle name's Ann."

"It is?"

"Catherine Ann Winger."

"Wow, I never even knew that. Okay, Ann, that's settled. Okay, listen, you're gonna be mad at me on Wednesday."

"Uh-oh." She held the phone with her shoulder so she could chop a scallion. "I know it's hard to practice this time of year, everything's starting to——"

"Yeah, no, not that, I've been practicing okay, I mean fairly okay, although this piece is really *hard*."

"Slow and steady." Angie had chosen "Meditation" from *Thaïs* for the talent portion of the pageant, and it was a challenge for her.

"Right, although how this music could get any *slower*—but no, remember what we talked about last time? Towards the end? About my fingernails!"

"Oh, yes. You said you were going to cut them."

"Yeah, but if I cut them now they'll look lame for the prom. I'll cut them right after, okay? The very next day, out they go. Okay?"

She cleaned off the cutting board and started on a mushroom. "Fine, but this is a critical time, don't forget. You're beginning a new, important piece——"

"Which I already don't even like."

"——and you want to begin it correctly. If your nails are too long, you're going to internalize poor technique and then waste time unlearning it. But it's up to you."

"*God,* I *hate* when you say that."

She laughed. "Well, sorry." Angie had been taking private violin lessons with her for almost four years; there wasn't much about her dramatic teenage life Caddie didn't know. "What's wrong with 'Meditation'? Last week you thought it was perfect."

"It *is*, it's just so, *God*, sappy or something. Okay, I gotta go, I just wanted to ask you about Angela Ann, so—okay, ciao."

"Ciao."

Students like Angie were what made teaching a joy. Adults could bring a lot of satisfaction, too, but Angie was one of her few students under eighteen or so who came to her voluntarily, not because their parents made them. She might not be a prodigy (if she were, Caddie wouldn't have anything to teach her), but she had real talent, definite professional potential. All she needed was focus.

When dinner was on the table, Caddie unfurled a napkin, a *cloth* napkin, over her lap and sat up straight. *To me,* she toasted, eyeing her reflection in the dining room window. And to Nana. She wasn't allowed to miss her, but she hoped her first night was going beautifully.

Mmm, the salmon was perfect, if she said so herself, and the dill sauce she'd whipped up without a recipe was superb. She was a good cook, she just didn't get to practice much. When Nana wasn't eating macrobiotically, she liked old-fashioned food, fifties food, lots of plain, starchy casseroles made with condensed soup. It would be fun to try some new recipes while she was away.

She sighed, moving a piece of potato from one side of her plate to the other. What was she doing, anyway, sitting by herself in romantic candlelight in the dining room, acting as if she was worth it? Now that she wasn't starving, she felt silly. And bored. Dinner conversation between her and her grandmother might not be riveting, but they talked about how their day had gone, gossiped about Caddie's students; Nana always had a peculiar take on something in the news. They'd lived together for almost all Caddie's life, but they'd never gotten like an old married couple, silent and uninterested, or so in tune with each other's deepest feelings that words weren't necessary. Nana *loved* to talk. And Caddie, who was shy with everybody, wasn't shy with her, so eventually her grandmother got to hear just about everything she was thinking. In a thousand ways Caddie hadn't begun to appreciate—but she guessed she would soon—they depended on each other.

Fine, but she wasn't going to sit here and mope about it. That was the point of this nice dinner, and she *was* worth it. Dr. Kardashian had harped on that the whole two years she'd been able to afford him. "If you aren't kind and loving to yourself, Caddie, who else will be?" It all went back to her mother, was his theory, whose abandonment behavior had inculcated a pervasive sense of unentitlement. Too bad he didn't know a cure.

Except for being kind and loving to herself. Which she decided to put into practice by skipping the dishes, lying on the sofa, and reading her fashion magazines while she ate ice cream out of the carton.

She always felt older than the women in women's magazines. Not smarter, definitely not, she felt like a twelve-year-old compared to them—but in her outlook, as if she were from a different generation. She didn't even understand the language. Who were these people who thought about what shade of brown their mascara was? Who studied the ever so slightly different shades of beige in the artful photos of foundation smears and little mounds of powder? Caddie almost always thought the girl in the Before picture looked better than the one in the After.

She was a sucker for the quizzes, though. She took them all, the personality tests, the face-shape tests, the body language tests. She always came out Nature Girl or Miss Sensitive, Best Friend, Mother Earth, never Sex Goddess or Big Flirt or Bitchin' Babe. Her body mass index was twenty-one, which was thin, but try getting any sympathy for being too thin. You were a voice crying in the desert.

"What is your best feature?" There was always a questionnaire about that. If you thought it was your eyes, you should "play them up," presumably with new shades of mascara. Caddie thought her large, innocent-looking blue-gray eyes were her best feature on the basis of one comment, "You have pretty eyes," from a boy she'd gone out with in college. So she'd asked Nana, "What do you think of my eyes?" and she'd answered, "You've got Winger eyes. We all look dazed."

As for her worst feature, she had as much body anxiety as the next person, so the list was long: big feet, veiny hands, freckles, fair skin that wouldn't tan, dirty-blonde hair that just hung there, small breasts, not enough butt. She could go on. Supposedly men never even *saw* the flaws women obsessed over, at least that's what all the articles claimed, and as proof they'd quote actual men saying things like, "I personally *like* seeing a girl's panty line, I think it's sexy."

She got up, restless. She felt like doing something, changing something, and it was too late to call up her hairdresser and tell her to cut everything off. Not that she would have, anyway. Impulsiveness wasn't one of her vices; she even corrected people who said "Moderation in all things" to "Moderation in *most* things." But she was in the oddest mood tonight to take a positive step toward *something*.

This room. Nana's living room. Caddie hated it. She couldn't sit down on the couch without first having to move Paulo and Francesca, life-size stuffed dolls her grandmother had made on the sewing machine, and she couldn't let a student in the house without first making sure Nana hadn't arranged the dolls in suggestive postures. *Out.* She scooped them up and carried them upstairs. Let them do whatever they liked on Nana's bed till she came home.

That was easy. The fireplace screen would be harder, because it was the chrome grille of a 1979 Cadillac El Dorado her grandmother had scavenged from a junkyard. It still had dead bugs stuck to it, or the desiccated stains dead bugs had left long ago, and Caddie wasn't allowed to clean them off because they were the "best part." The grille was a heavy, awkward armful, she got stuck turning the corner between the kitchen pantry and the basement steps, but she did it, retired the monster to a corner by the furnace. She'd put a big, frilly fern in its place, or some coleus, something light and colorful and *alive*.

Next: Nana's paintings, weird sculptures, and religious icons on the walls and tables and on top of the piano. Caddie didn't have enough things of her own to replace them, but even flowers would be an improvement. And she did have a few pictures and prints she'd bought while she was in graduate school and had her own little apartment. They were in the attic—she went up and got them, dusted them off, and brought them back down. Tomorrow she'd hang them on the off-white walls. Get some pillows for the couch to replace the dummies. Bring in some of the peonies blooming in the side yard. She could see it already, and it was going to be so much better. Luckily the carpet was as neutral as the walls, so the room could accommodate styles as opposite as hers and Nana's.

But that was assuming she *had* a style. Maybe she didn't, or only a style by default: anything that wasn't Nana's (flamboyant, attention-demanding, sort of willfully peculiar) was hers (quiet, conservative, so understated it was mute). She had an image in her mind of a scale between them, and it was up to her to keep it balanced. Or a see-saw, and she had to weigh more on her side or Nana would shoot her up in the air, like the big, older kid who tosses you up and you're stuck there until he grins and flexes his knees and sends you down fast, *wham,* your whole backbone vibrating from the blow. . . . Anyway, Caddie's job was to balance her grandmother's eccentricity with her ordinariness, and it had been that way for as long as she could remember. *Look, the Winger family is okay, because I'm not crazy! She is, but I'm not!*

Most women acquired their personal styles by watching their mothers when they were young, then either copying or rejecting their mothers' styles when they grew up. What Caddie could remember of her mother was skimpy: she'd worn hippie clothes and smoked cigarettes; she'd always tapped her foot or drummed her fingers or jogged her knee up and down; she'd had long blonde hair she let fall over one eye, and Caddie always wanted to pull it back like a curtain so she could see more, unveil the secret. But her mother hadn't been around much, and she'd died when Caddie was too young really to understand her *style*. After that she'd had only Nana's style to observe. She'd rejected it, she was *still* rejecting it, but she hadn't replaced it with anything interesting of her own.

But it was early days, and she was making a new start. She didn't have the knack for living alone yet either, but it was only her first night. The *Michaelstown Monitor* ran personal ads every Friday afternoon. She got the paper, retrieved her pen, poured herself a second glass of wine—for courage—and sat down by the phone.

The code didn't mystify her anymore; she knew what a DHM was, a GWF, an SPBM. She read the personals every week, and once in a while she even felt tempted to answer one. She never had, but if she was ever going to, tonight was the night. *Action.* "I'm all about change," she told Finney, who twitched in his sleep on her lap. "I am a wild woman."

Too bad the women always sounded more interesting than the men. Were they just better writers? No question, writing ads was an art form, but it was more than that. The men went on about their height and weight, the height and weight they wanted from the women who responded, the age range they would tolerate, the personality type they had to have. Whereas women seemed kinder and more open-minded. Easier to get along with. Here was an SWF who was "brainy, witty, sensual and spontaneous, loves entertaining, works/plays hard, comfortable in jeans and sequins." Wouldn't she make a cool friend? A lot more fun than this guy, seeking "clean SWF with high morals, no dependents."

Slim pickings this week. This one sounded the best: "Attractive SPWM, self-supporting, good conversationalist, serious but fun, enjoys politics, long walks, old movies. ISO intelligent woman who likes same, with whom to spend time and enjoy life."

With whom. Wow.

If she thought about this for longer than ten seconds, she'd chicken out. She got her credit card out of her purse—two dollars and twenty-nine cents a *minute*—picked up the phone, and dialed.

"Hello, this is Byron," a deep, prerecorded voice said. "Thank you for answering my ad. Please leave a message and tell me a little about yourself. And don't forget to leave your number so I can call you back."

Yikes, she was supposed to give her phone number to a total stranger? Well, if that was how it worked . . .

"Um, hi, I'm Caddie. Hi, Byron. I thought you sounded very nice in your ad. I was hoping we could talk and, you know, see how we, um, are together . . . I've never done this before. Ha, that's proba-bly what they all say! I guess I should say what I look like, that's what . . ." That's what men always wanted to know. "I'm five eleven. I'm on the thin side. Slim. Slender. I have sort of blonde hair, streaky blonde, down to my shoulders . . . blue eyes . . . I have good posture. Oh, I'm thirty-two. I'm also self-supporting, like you, so—and I have my own car. I'm living alone at the moment . . . I'm easy to get along with, I think, no real . . . um, demands or anything." She heaved a deep, silent sigh.

"I'm just looking for a nice guy, you know, somebody to hang out with. Till we get to know each other. And then, well, whatever. Long-term relationship, that would be fine with me. That would be *great*." Her laugh sounded nervous and silly. Time to stop talking; she didn't like the sound of herself any more than Byron was going to. She left her number and hung up.

"Agh!" she screamed, and Finney shot up in the air. She had to catch him and console him before she could resume, in a softer voice, "*Agh, agh, agh.*"

Never again, she'd rather go to a singles bar. She'd rather be rejected for stupid things like small breasts and no butt than hang herself with her own words. *Good posture!* "I'm all about personal humiliation," she told the dog, and took him out for his last walk.

Unbelievably, the phone was ringing when she got back. She raced to it and tried to say "Hello?" without sounding breathless.

The unmistakable voice of Byron, low-pitched and slightly nasal, like an Englishman but without the accent, said, "Hello, is this Cattie?"

"Caddie, yes, hi—Byron?"

"I hope I haven't called too late."

"No, no, not at all. How are you?"

"I'm well, thanks. You said this is your first time answering one of the ads?"

"It is, yes, and it's kind of nerve-racking. I'm not even sure what you *do*."

"It's an artificial socializing mechanism, true, but at the same time it's pretty civilized, I think. You can avoid a lot of the rough-and-tumble in the beginning, save quite a bit of time."

"Yes, I'm sure that's true."

"Dating is intrinsically messy, just an awkward construct by nature. I've never felt in any way demeaned by the personals process, never thought it tainted me as 'desperate' or anything of that sort."

"Oh, no, of course not." Not *him,* obviously. It was different for her, though, she *was* desperate. "Have you had a lot of success, then?"

"Well, that depends on your definition of success. If it's marriage and happily ever after, I'd have to say no."

"No, I wasn't—"

"If it's the quiet companionship of two intelligent, seeking people who may or may not be kindred spirits, then the results have been

31

somewhat more encouraging. So tell me, Carrie, what do you do for a living?"

"Caddie. I'm a music teacher. I teach piano and violin."

"I see."

"And what do *you* do?" She felt giddy from nervousness; she wanted to giggle; she had to stop herself from adding "Brian?"

"I'm in management consulting. I design systems for expenses and inventory control for small businesses."

"*Oh*. That sounds interesting."

"What are your hobbies?"

It was like a job interview, but with a black screen between her and the interviewer. "Um, well, music, of course, I love to listen to all kinds. I used to be in the Michaelstown Community Orchestra, I played second violin, but I had to drop out—"

"I enjoy music, but I'm pretty much tone-deaf, you may as well know. Where are you in the sibling hierarchy?"

The sibling hierarchy . . . "Oh—I'm an only child."

"I see. I'm the eldest of three."

"Do you believe in that, birth order and so forth?"

He huffed out his breath. "Most certainly I do."

"I've never thought about it much, but I'm sure it's very revealing. Of character and . . . stuff. What are your hobbies?" She squeezed her eyes shut, a habit when she wished she were somewhere else.

"I enjoy antique car shows. I have a barbed wire collection. I play handball and golf. Now, let's see . . ." He seemed to be ticking items off a list. "You said you currently live alone?"

She'd felt disingenuous about that, afraid it might've sounded as if she were temporarily without a live-in boyfriend. Which would certainly send the wrong message. "Well, actually, I live with my grandmother, but she had an accident and she's gone to recuperate in a home. For a few months. So I'm on my own *now*."

"Ah. You live with your grandmother, and you're thirty-two?"

She didn't like Byron very much, might as well admit it, but she particularly disliked the way he'd phrased that question. "How old are you?" she countered. "In your ad, you don't say."

"Thirty-nine. Just."

There was a pause. She didn't have any other questions, and she was pretty sure he didn't either.

He cleared his throat. "I've found it's better to make a clean, quick break when there seems to be, as they say, no chemistry, so—"

"Oh, I think that's best, too," Caddie broke in, "just get it over with." The end was coming up fast, and she was *not* going to be dumped by Byron. This was a two-way breakup. "It's really been nice talking to you, though. Good luck and everything. I hope you find—"

"Yes, indeed. Bye."

She put her head in her lap and moaned quietly for a while. It could've been worse, he could've been a stalker. He still could be, in theory, and this was how he threw his victims off, by rejecting them. But something told her she was safe from Byron for the rest of her life.

She went to bed early, but she couldn't sleep. Nana didn't snore or mutter or get up and down in the night, so the house shouldn't have sounded so weirdly, unnaturally quiet. Every random creak made her start. Finney, too. He lay with his head on her shin, blinking at her in the moonlight. "You miss Nana, don't you? Want to go see her? One of these days?" He scooted up and pushed his head under her arm. "But they have cats. *Cats*," she repeated, to test him, and sure enough, his ears cocked. "I'll have to call Brenda first to clear the way. They have rules. *Rules*." Nothing.

Oh God, oh God, she was going to turn into an old lady who talked to her dog. "Go sleep in Nana's room," she ordered, edging

Finney off the bed with her hip. "Go on. You're not allowed up here anyway." He hit the floor with an offended thump, his nails making a skittery sound when he trotted out of the room. A few minutes later he tiptoed back in and hopped up on the foot of the bed so gently she had to open her eyes to make sure he was there.

She lay still, taking deep, slow breaths, pretending she was asleep. So he wouldn't think she was a pushover.

Some first night. She'd done all right on her own, she guessed, indulged herself, altered her personal space, made a few good resolutions for the future. Where she'd fallen down was in the reaching-out-to-others department, the part she couldn't control. She watched moon shadows creep up the wall, heard the snap of her digital clock when P.M. turned into A.M. "Don't miss me," Nana had commanded her. Truthfully, she wasn't doing too hot in that department, either.

4 "They're starting this big memory book," her grandmother called to say one day after she'd been at Wake House for about two weeks. "Everybody has to write out their life story, tell how it was back in the good old days. 'We Remember' or some such thing. They're going to keep it on the table in the front hall."

"I know," Caddie said, "I was there when Brenda suggested it, don't you remember?" Cornel, the grumpy old guy, had wanted to call it "We Can't Remember."

"Well, of course I do, I was there, too, wasn't I? So I want you to type one up for me when you get time. Make me sound important."

"Type one up?"

"It doesn't have to be long. But not *short,* either. I'm seventy-nine years old, I've got a history."

"So just . . ."

"When I was born, where I went to school, my accomplishments. Like an obituary, except I'm not dead."

"Um, okay, I guess I can do that."

"How come you're not over here by now?"

"No, remember, I'm coming tomorrow."

"Tomorrow, that's right. Well, too late now anyway, never mind."

"Too late for what?"

"Today this preacher comes over, not a real one, a 'lay preacher,'

35

calls himself—now I'm thinking why didn't *I* do that, become a 'lay preacher' when I was young, that's something I'd've been good at, a natural, I probably missed my calling."

"So the lay preacher came—"

"Preacher came, and he gathers everybody around for Bible study, fine with me, *but*. Guess what, I open my book, and turns out I've got my Koran instead of my Bible."

"Uh-oh."

"Caddie Ann, you'd've thought I let loose a basket of snakes. Especially Mrs. Brill, that one with the walker, she almost had a coronary. Christians have very little sense of humor, I'm sorry to say."

"So you want me to bring your Bible?"

"No great rush, just if you remember."

"How are you? How's your leg today?"

"Leg's fine, everything's fine. I've got to go, Susan wants to use the phone."

"See, if you had your own phone—"

"What do I need a phone for? Bye—don't forget my history."

"Morning," Caddie paused in the front hall to say to Magill, who was lifting hand weights in the Blue Room. "Have you seen my grandmother?" At least she assumed it was Magill. He wasn't wearing knee pads today, but he had on a huge, bright orange football helmet with his baggy pants and oversize T-shirt. To protect his head in case he fell, she assumed.

"Nope. Susan?" he raised his voice to say.

Caddie hadn't seen Susan in her wheelchair by the window, listening through headphones to a tape player. She and Magill were the two "young ones," although Susan looked at least forty. She was a librarian, according to Nana; she was recovering from a stroke;

she had a boyfriend named Stan. She waved to Caddie and slipped the headphones off.

"Hi."

"Hi, Caddie."

"I'm looking for my grandmother. Have you seen her?"

Susan nodded, then said something in her thick, lispy voice Caddie couldn't quite catch.

Susan gave a crooked smile and went back to her tape.

"Oh, okay. Thanks!"

"She, um . . ." Caddie drifted closer to Magill, embarrassed because she'd pretended to understand when she hadn't, not wanting to hurt Susan's feelings.

"She went to Hershey," Magill said.

"Hershey?" That's what she'd thought Susan had said. "Hershey, Pennsylvania? How come?"

"Field trip, Cornel and Bernie, Bea and Edgie, Frances. They're touring the chocolate factory."

"Wow." How . . . all-American. "Well, how about that, I've been stood up. After I went and wrote Nana's biography for her." She held up the manila folder she'd put it in.

"Thoughtless," Magill agreed.

She leaned against the piano, out of his way. "Are you going to write one? For the memory book?"

He shot her a glance, as if he thought she was kidding. "Uh, no."

"Why not? You're a resident—why don't you write one?"

He hoisted his rusty silver weights behind his head, up and down, knotty muscles coming and going in his stringy arms. He smiled and didn't answer.

"I could write it for you," she said on an impulse. "My grandmother's turned out pretty well. If I say so myself." She tapped the folder invitingly. The truth was, she was curious about him. "Want me to?"

"Sure, go ahead."

"Really?" He didn't look serious. "Okay, what do you do?"

"Nothing. No, wait. Today I got my shoes on by myself. Look, perfect bows, no Velcro for me." He stuck out a running shoe—but then he had to grab the edge of the windowsill to keep his balance.

"I mean before you came here." Before his accident. It happened about fifteen months ago, and it was some kind of *skydiving* mishap, of all things, but the details were off-limits. Nobody talked about it, and that by itself was strange; after the state of their health, the main topic of conversation among Wake House residents was each other.

He went back to doing curls, flexing the ropy tendons in his forearms. "Engineer."

"What kind?"

"Biomechanical."

A skydiving biomechanical engineer. "How old are you?"

He sent her some kind of look, but it was hard to tell what kind because of the football helmet. It wasn't like her to be so intrusive. The pretense that this was for "We Remember" made a good cover for pure nosiness. "Thirty, thirty-five," he said. "Around in there."

She laughed. "Around in there?" His body was so thin and wobbly, it made him look younger. "Do you work for a company?"

"I had my own company. Have. Had."

"What do you make? Did you make?"

"Feet."

"Feet? Feet?"

"Feet, legs, hips, pelvises. Mostly feet."

"Oh, you mean artificial limbs?"

"Orthotics." He put the weights down to take a drink from his soda. No, not soda, one of those nutritional drinks they advertised on TV for old people, supposed to give you energy or a new lease on life or something. He must drink it for the calories. According to Nana,

38

food didn't mean anything to him since the accident. He'd completely lost his sense of taste.

"Um, are you from Maryland? A native Michaelstowner?"

"Are you?"

"Yes, I was born right here. I grew up on the west side—do you know Early Street?"

He shook his head.

"Where do you live?" she asked.

"Here."

"Just till you get well. Where's your home? I just thought maybe we went to the same school or something. We could have friends in common."

"No home anymore. This is it." He pushed off from the wall and walked away.

She was afraid she'd upset him—she was relieved when he just went over to help Susan change the tape in her tape player. Susan spent most mornings doing speech and physical therapy to learn how to talk and walk again. The sessions left her so tired, she kept quiet and still the rest of the day.

"Is it okay?" Magill asked her. "Loud enough? Sure?"

"It's perfect," Susan answered, smiling at him.

"You're never going to let me write your biography, are you?" Caddie asked him when he came back. "Because I don't even know your first name. Some biography."

She was glad when he took off his football helmet, even though it had flattened one-half of his hair and made the other half stick up like a rooster's crest. At least now she could see his face. "Yeah, well," he said. "One's enough for me." When he bent down to pick up his weights, he missed; he had to try again with one eye closed. Besides everything else, he had bad depth perception. He could play cards with Cornel, but not checkers or chess. Once, Caddie saw him walk into a door.

"One's enough? Like Cher?" It was fun to tease him. He tried not to show that he liked it, but he did. She wished she knew the secret about him, the mystery.

Thump, step, step. Mrs. Brill paused in the hallway on her way out.

"Good morning, Mrs. Brill," Caddie and Magill called to her in unison. Magill put his weights on the windowsill and stood up straight: Mrs. Brill brought out everybody's best behavior. She lived across the hall from Nana. A white card on her door said in neat black ink, SUNDAY SCHOOL TEACHER, RETIRED, and that was all Caddie knew about her. She had on white gloves today, and black-and-white spectator pumps with a matching purse that swung wide from her wrist each time she pushed her metal walker. She pulled back the left sleeve of her polka-dot blouse. "Good afternoon," she corrected, tapping the watch face.

"Good *afternoon*," they echoed, and she started off again with a push of her walker. They heard her on the porch, *thump*, step, step. *Thump*, step, step.

"Where does she go?"

"Just walking," Magill said. "I think."

"She's very dignified."

"She scares the hell out of me."

Caddie looked at her own watch. "Wow, I didn't know it was so late. I have to go, I've got a twelve-thirty lesson."

"Uh . . ."

She paused in gathering up her things.

He dug something out of the back pocket of his voluminous trousers, which hung dangerously low on his hips; she could plainly see the elastic top of his shorts. "Just something," he muttered, handing over a plastic box.

A CD case. "For me?" She opened it. It was blank, no writing on the shiny disc inside. "What is it?"

40

"You said you didn't know anything about electronic music. You wished you could hear more, so you could find out if you liked it."

That's right, she had said that. They'd been talking about music, she and Magill and Miss Edgie Copes, and Caddie had mentioned she liked every kind of music except techno, but only because they never played it on any of the local stations and she never got to hear it. "Did you make it?"

"Yeah, it's nothing, stuff off the computer. I burned it."

"I didn't know you liked this kind of music."

"I don't, it sounds like noise to me. You listen and tell me what I'm missing."

"Well, thank you very much. I will."

"You're welcome."

"Was it a lot of trouble? I hope it didn't take a long time to make."

"I only had to cancel one important business trip." He smiled with one side of his mouth.

"Thanks again, that was really nice. I'll listen to it tonight. Well, bye. I'll probably see you tomorrow."

He didn't reply. Maybe he didn't hear; he'd put his football helmet back on.

Caddie started to leave, then paused, uncertain, in the foyer. She still had her grandmother's biography for "We Remember." She ran upstairs and put the manila folder on Nana's bed, where she'd be sure to see it.

Frances Marguerite Winger was born right here in Michaelstown on September 29, 1924. Her father was a conductor for the C&O Railroad, and her mother was a professional seamstress who also sang and played the organ in the choir at St. Alban's Episcopal Church on Reister Street.

Frances had one older brother, Frank, but he died in 1930 of rheumatic fever.

Frances was a good student, and after graduating from Michaelstown High School, she went on to Peterson State College and earned a B.A. in art (1944). That same year she married Charles Eliot Buchanan, an army first lieutenant, who died tragically but bravely in Guam without ever seeing their child, born six months after his death.

For the next thirty-five years Frances taught art in almost every grade in the county school system. She was active in the Landmark Society, the Triangle Women's Club, and the Michaelstown Garden Club, of which she was president for two terms.

In 1980, Frances's only child, Jane Winger, a singer and musician who used the professional name Chelsea, died in an automobile accident. She was thirty-one years old. She left one child, Caddie, whom Frances raised with as much love and care as if she were her own daughter.

In the early 1980s, when other women her age might've been thinking about retiring, Frances's life took a new, exciting turn. She gave up teaching and began a career as an independent artist. Perhaps taking a page from her mother's book, her earliest medium was needle and thread, with which she constructed large needlepoint samplers with interesting and unusual messages. One of the largest of these, *Women Take Back the World*, was displayed at the Michaelstown Arts Festival of 1984, where it won second place in the sewing and crafts category.

Later in the 1980s, Frances was instrumental in the founding of EBFA, Essential Body Fluids for Art, at first a local movement but eventually national, with members from as far away as Ohio and Virginia. Adherents of EBFA had a rich, complicated aesthetic, but to oversimplify, they basically believed that true art should include as many of the essential body fluids as possible, preferably all seven.

Frances's restless artistic spirit took her next to mixed media and collage, followed by an energetic period of photo-realism. But in 1995 she found her true and most satisfying artistic niche. "It was an accident," she says with characteristic modesty. Accident—maybe. One day in the early spring while checking on the status of her side yard compost heap (since her youth, Frances has been an avid and creative gardener), she noticed her clipping and leaf pile had taken on an odd formation. "It was definitely two faces in profile, one talking, one listening. They were human, but they were also part of the ground. Earth people communicating."

Thus was born Earth People Communicating, Frances Winger's new and completely unique grassroots artistic medium, a form of expression she would explore tirelessly, along with other projects, until an unfortunate accident put her active art career on hold. Today, striking evidence of her work in the form of living sculptures can be seen on the lawn of her home at 823 Early Street in the heart of Michaelstown.

It hasn't always been an easy road Frances has followed. Her work has been misunderstood, even denounced. But she always meets her critics with tolerance and good humor. When neighbors dismissed her earthy creations as "dirt" or eyesores, she always took it in stride, smiled, and shrugged, and never once considered filing a countersuit. Live and let live is Frances's motto. "Life is short," she likes to say. "You only get one, and if you waste it worrying about what other people think, you're an idiot."

5

Caddie had entertained a private fantasy of Finney becoming Wake House's therapy dog, but it died the first day she brought him. In hindsight she could see it was a bad idea from the start, but Nana had kept pestering her to bring him, Brenda had said it would be all right as long as they shut the cats up in the office first, and Caddie had a picture in her head of a docile, grinning, blood pressure-lowering Finney being pulled onto lap after lap of delighted Wake House residents sitting around in the Red Room. She'd forgotten that, except with Nana, Finney was docile only when he was sleeping.

He had a new leash, the kind that extended for fifteen feet or so when fully unfurled; you held it by a plastic handle and pressed a button to make it shorten, *zip*, like a vacuum cleaner cord. Caddie hadn't quite mastered the mechanism herself yet, and Nana couldn't figure it out at all. The first thing Finney did was wind the leash around ancient Mr. Lorton's legs four or five times as he was making his turtle-paced, hunched-over way back to the parlor from the bathroom. Luckily, he stayed on his feet, but Caddie couldn't help thinking what if it had been Magill.

After they got Mr. Lorton untangled, Finney grabbed hold of Cornel's foot in its leather bedroom slipper and wouldn't let go. People thought it was funny at first, and even Cornel had eked out a smile with his turtle lips and made a joke about what a ferocious dog that was, a pint-size pit bull, better watch out, and so on. Finney looked harmless—that's what threw people off. He weighed seventeen pounds. He was all white except for one brown eye and two black spots on his back. He looked like a child's toy. One of his tricks was lunging at you when you were walking fast—say, trying to get to the phone before it stopped ringing—and latching onto your shoe like a lobster. You ended up having to drag him across the room with you because he would *not* let go, he *was* like a pit bull— and Cornel wasn't a bit amused after he figured that out because the joke had gone on too long.

"Damn dog, get him off me, Caddie, tell him no, would you? Get *off*. . ." He ended up kicking his slipper off so Finney could have it. Unattached to a foot, though, Finney had no interest in it.

Caddie wrestled the leash from Nana and reeled him in. Peace reigned for one minute; then Susan rolled her wheelchair into the room. Finney had seen Nana's wheelchair before, so why he went into a fit of shrill, ear-splitting barking at the sight of Susan's, Caddie couldn't imagine. Susan shrank back against the vinyl seat, gaping in fear and trying to make the chair go backward, but her left arm was weaker than her right and in her distress she made it turn in a circle. Finney took that as a provocation and began to make fake lunges at the wheels, barking and snarling and showing his teeth. "Finney!" Caddie shouted about fifty times. Every time she almost had him, he squirted away.

At last, he wound his extension leash so many times around Susan's chair that he had to stop or choke to death. Caddie was hoping for the latter, but he halted, winded and panting, head down, hackles raised. "He's not like this," she kept saying as she unhooked him, shoved him into Nana's arms, and got his leash untied around the chair wheels. "He's a really nice dog." No one objected when she suggested to Nana that they take him up to her room for a private visit.

*

"Mrs. Tourneau says to tell you those peonies are finally blooming."

"What peonies?"

"Remember the peonies you let her dig up and plant on her side? At least three years ago, and all they did was send up leaves. Well, this year they've finally got flowers."

"That's nice."

"We had a good program on Saturday afternoon," Caddie went on. "Remember, I told you we were playing the Vivaldi concerto? Well, we had to change it at the last minute because the first violinist came down with food poisoning. So instead we did 'Spotlight on Chopin,' but it went fine."

"Mmm," Nana said dreamily. She looked half asleep in her chair, with a dozing Finney in her lap, getting his little white hairs all over her skirt. Seeing them together like that, relaxed and content, Caddie couldn't be sorry she'd brought him, even though he'd disgraced himself.

"Lessons have been going pretty well. So far only one person's called to cancel for the summer, so that's good. So far so good. And I have two new students, so as of now it's a net gain—a little boy for piano and a lady for violin. She just got a divorce and she's changing her life. She says her husband always told her she was too old to learn the violin, so now she's showing him."

"Ha," Nana said. "Show him."

"So I think we're okay, I think everything's going to be fine . . ." She tapered off, didn't say "with the money situation this summer," because—why bring it up at all?

"You get your new cast tomorrow, don't forget. A canvas thing you can take on and off—won't that be nice?"

"Yep." Nana put her head back and closed her eyes. She fell into naps so easily these days.

Before she could drift off, Caddie said, "You like it here, don't you, Nan?"

"I told you I do."

"I know, but do you still?" She hadn't said it in a while, and she'd been here almost four weeks. "You can come home anytime, you know. Just say the word. Even for a visit."

"Why would I want to come home? You come to see *me* every day. So I have everything. Oh, honey, I'm just so glad you thought of this place. *Thank* you." She reached over and squeezed Caddie's hand.

Well, that answered that question. Anyway, why wouldn't Nana love it here? Something was always going on, a class or a game, a conversation, a field trip in the ratty old van with WAKE HOUSE ELDER CARE & CONVALESCENCE still visible under a fresh coat of paint—Brenda had the name covered up when the van got too old to be a good advertisement for the house. Nana got plenty of stimulation, much more than she had at home with just Caddie and the television. Her biography in "We Remember" had sparked interest in her life as an artist, and she'd agreed to give a talk about it for the Gray Gurus— or the Golden Geezers, as Cornel called it—an informal lecture series in which anybody who'd had a particularly interesting job or taken a fascinating trip or had some unusual knowledge could give a presentation on it to the other residents. Nana was more excited about this than she let on. Her lecture was weeks away, but she was already writing down notes and gathering her materials.

"What about you?" Nana asked. "What else new and exciting have you done besides change everything around in my house?"

"I should never have told you about that." Nana was kidding, sort of, but she never missed a chance to bring up what Caddie had done to the living room. "Well, I'm learning a new Beethoven, the Sonata Number Seventeen—"

"*New and exciting*, I said. Have you called up any more men in the sex ads?"

"The personal ads, and no, I haven't. Once was enough."

"Caddie Ann—"

"Did you know twenty-seven million Americans live alone? And the median age of the whole population is thirty-five? I read that somewhere. So I'm definitely . . . I'm in the whatchacallit."

"Mainstream," Nana said, sighing.

"What's this?" Caddie picked up a snail shell from the windowsill. "And this." A dry twig and, next to it, pieces of a speckled blue eggshell. "What's this stuff?"

Nana sat up straight. "That's for my project. Be careful, don't break anything. Put that down, Caddie, it's fragile."

"Sorry. This is your new art project? How exciting." Nana had been hinting about a new work, something *big* taking shape in her mind, but Caddie hadn't been sure if it was real or not. Sometimes her grandmother's art schemes stayed there, in her mind, never actually bore fruit in a material way. If this one was already taking form in twigs and eggshells, that was a good sign. Nana was always happiest when she was making something.

"It's a monument," she said. "To oldness. To age. It will symbolize the courage and beauty of elderliness. It'll have 'longevity' in the title. That's all I can say right now."

"How will it—what form will it take?"

"Well, I don't know that *yet*. It'll be a construction. It'll have to be big, representational."

"You mean it'll look like something?"

"Not necessarily. It will have *representatives*, I mean. Of everything that's old."

"Everything?" Another global project. Nana's art was so *inclusive*.

Through the window, Caddie saw a black taxi stop at the curb in front of the house. The driver jumped out, came around, opened the rear passenger door, and stuck his hand in to help somebody out. A woman swung her legs out, nice legs under a knee-length cherry-red skirt, and stood up. She had on a straw hat with a wide brim; Caddie

48

couldn't see her face until she leaned back against the car to look up at the house. Just for a second, it felt as if they were looking right into each other's eyes. The woman said something to the driver that made him laugh. She laughed, too, and Caddie heard one ringing, agreeable "Ha!"

"Nana," she said excitedly, "I think it's the new lady, the one who's taking the tower suite. The room you wanted, remember? I bet it's her—Brenda said she was coming today or tomorrow." The tower suite was a beautiful, round-walled bedroom with its own sitting room, but it was already taken, reserved, when Nana moved in. It would've been too expensive, anyway.

Nana wheeled her chair over and peered down with Caddie.

"Doesn't she look nice? Where are your glasses, can you see? She looks young." Relatively; middle sixties, Caddie estimated. Around here, that was a whippersnapper. Brenda said her name was Dorothea Barnes. She was a widow with no children. She came from somewhere on the Eastern Shore, but she'd grown up here, Brenda said. She was coming home. "Barnes," Cornel had been saying suspiciously for days. "Barnes. I don't recall any Dorothea Barnes." He'd grown up in Michaelstown, too, and he thought he knew everybody.

There went Brenda, hurrying down the front walk to greet the new arrival. She had a lot of luggage; the cab driver kept pulling boxes and suitcases from the trunk and piling them on the curb. She saw Brenda and went toward her, holding out her hands. She greeted her that way, shaking her hands warmly with both of hers, smiling and tilting her head to listen to Brenda's welcoming words.

"Doesn't she look nice?" Caddie said again. "It'll be good to have a new person here, then you can feel like an old veteran." Although, actually, one of the things Nana liked best about Wake House was that she was the new kid; she got a lot of attention that way. "Not that you won't still be the—Nan? What's wrong?" She looked funny. Guilty.

"Nothing."

"Finney! Where is he? Did you let him off the leash? Oh, *Nana*." He was gone, his leash in a coil on the floor, and they'd stupidly left the door open. "He went downstairs, I bet—he probably smells those cats."

"I'm coming, too," Nana said. Caddie started to push her chair, but Nana said, "I can do it—you better go!"

She took the stairs, Nana took the elevator. From the last landing, Caddie could see Cornel, Bea and Edgie Copes, and one of the Harris wives loitering in the front hall. Even Mrs. Brill had pulled her chair in the Red Room closer to the archway for a better view.

"What a *beautiful* porch," came a musical voice from outside, over the racket of manic barking. "So pretty. It's just the way I remember it."

A lot of things happened at once. Brenda bustled through the front door holding a suitcase in each hand, calling back, "Oh, yes, it's lovely out here on warm evenings. Sometimes the whole house gathers—"

Cornel's voice cut her off: "Look out, get that dog. Where's Frances? Caddie, would you *please*—" Finney shot through the door, whirled around, and began to bark louder, high, excited, hysterical-sounding barks that could vibrate your eardrums and rattle your teeth.

"Finney!" Caddie shouted, starting down the half flight of steps. Fur stood up in a line down the middle of his back; you'd think he lived here and the UPS man was at the door. "Finney! Stop it!" Dorothea Barnes came in next, followed by the taxi driver, loaded down with more suitcases. "Oh, what a cute dog," said Mrs. Barnes. She leaned down, put out her hand, and Finney bit her.

"*Ow!*"

Caddie clattered down the rest of the stairs, horrified. Everybody gathered around, Brenda, Cornel, the cabdriver, Mrs. Harris, Mrs. Brill. "How bad is it? Are you bleeding? Did it break the skin? Does it hurt?"

Finney quit barking, began to wag his stubby tail frantically, trying to undo this.

Caddie pushed through the crush of worried people around Mrs. Barnes. "Oh, no, oh, I'm so sorry—he's my grandmother's dog but I brought him, it's my fault—are you all right?"

"Fine." She looked pale, though. Her hat was askew, mussing her silver-gray hair. She had dark, high-arching eyebrows, startled Vs above clear blue eyes. She was trying to smile, but it was a shaky effort. She held her right hand in her left—the middle finger was turning purple at the nail.

"Did it break the skin?"

"Oh, I don't think so. Just a bruise."

Someone said "rabies." Somebody said "rabies shots."

"He's had his shot," Caddie rushed to say. "It lasts three years—he's only two!"

"I'm *fine*." She reached out to Caddie's shoulder and gave it a soft press with her good hand. *"Really."*

"Sit down," Brenda urged. She looked ill, probably imagining lawsuits. Dorothea Barnes let herself be led over by Brenda to the church pew under the coat hooks along the wall. Cornel offered to get her a glass of water. Mrs. Harris said she'd call the doctor.

"I am really quite all right." She looked up at them all and gave a shivery laugh. "I was startled, mostly. That wasn't quite the welcome I was expecting!"

Caddie started apologizing again, but she waved it off, insisting she was fine. The crisis was over. Finney had gone into the Red Room to be alone. Caddie looked around for Nana.

She was huddled in her wheelchair by the elevator. She had her

51

mouth covered with the fingertips of both hands and she was wide-eyed, pressing back into the vinyl seat. Caddie hurried over to her.

"Nana? Hey, it's okay. It's over, everything's fine."

"Are they going to put him to sleep?"

"Finney? *No.*"

"They have to kill them to look at their brains."

"They what?" Caddie touched her, tried to take her hands from her face, but Nana was frozen. Her fear infected Caddie—she'd never seen her like this before.

Caddie felt a hand on her back. It was Mrs. Barnes. "Hi," she said to Nana. Somebody had wrapped a handkerchief around her finger; she folded her arms to keep it out of Nana's sight. "I'm Thea. Thea Barnes. How are you?"

Nana couldn't speak, only stare at her with round, worried eyes.

"You know what, I think I just scared him. I bent down too fast, that's what happened. He's a lovely dog."

Nana took her hands away. "He is. A lovely dog. I don't know why that happened—he's never done it before."

"Well," said Caddie. No point in going overboard.

Mrs. Barnes held out her good hand.

Nana took it. "I'm Frances Winger," she said cordially.

"Hello, Frances."

"Nice to meet you."

"It's nice to meet you."

Nana's relieved smile turned crafty. "Did you bring anything old?"

6   The offices of CAT, Creative Animal Therapy, turned
     out to be one room over a candle and incense shop on a
one-way downtown street. Finney was afraid of the slippery wooden
steps; Caddie had to pick him up and carry him to the second floor.
She could hear talking on the other side of the frosted glass in a door
at the end of the hallway, so she opened the door and peeked in. A
man at a desk heaped high with scattered papers, files, and folders
swiveled in his chair and gestured for her to come in.

He was on the phone. "No, we're nationwide, we've got over
eight hundred CAT teams around the country, but the training for
the volunteers is always local. Through workshops with licensed
instructors in each . . . that's right, and then at headquarters they
coordinate the volunteers with facilities in their own communities.
No, this is just a regional office. Small. Um . . . well, me." He put
his hand over the phone, said "Hi, have a seat, I'll just be a minute,"
and went back to his conversation.

There wasn't a seat, not unless she moved a basketball, a pair of
running shoes, and a bag of kitty litter from the only other chair in
the small, cluttered office. Finney was pulling her around to all the
corners anyway, sniffing everything, as nervous as if he were at the
vet's. He must smell other animals. He dragged her over to where
several plaques and certificates in frames were tacked to the wall.
Service awards, outstanding citizen citations, training certificates.
All for Christopher Dalton Fox, except for the ones for Christopher

Dalton Fox's dog, King, who had several plaques of his own for animal citizenship and community service. Christopher was the man behind the desk—she recognized him from all the photographs of him and King in chummy poses with various groups of people and other dogs.

One caught Caddie's eye in particular because it was obviously taken in a nursing home. A real one, not like Wake House; the residents were feeble and old, many in wheelchairs. King, a large, beautiful dog, maybe a shepherd except he was fluffier, sat on a long sofa between two frail old ladies, and all three were beaming into the camera with the same calm, gentle, beatific expression. *There*, thought Caddie. *That's* what she'd wanted, that kind of animal-human bonding. It looked almost spiritual. Why couldn't Finney be like King?

Christopher Fox got off the phone. "Hi. Sorry about that." He stood up and came around his desk. "You must be . . . uh . . ."

"Caddie Winger."

"Good to meet you. And this must be Finnegan." He went down on one knee and patted the other. Caddie looked down at his bent head, admiring the clean part in his streaky blond hair, lighter than hers and almost as long. It fell around the sides of his face in bright, tawny waves. She thought of a golden retriever, that russet-yellow color, the fur just bathed and brushed.

Finney came to him instantly, nubby tail vibrating, sniffing his hands, his shoes, his crotch. "Sit," Christopher said in a firm voice, and Finney did. It wasn't exactly a miracle; he'd heard the command before. Heard but rarely obeyed it, especially if no dog biscuit reward was involved. "Lie down," Christopher said next, but Finney had reached his limit. "Sit" was all he could do, and he was tired of doing that. He jumped up and licked Christopher on the nose.

"He's being very good, actually," Caddie said. "He wasn't this good on Tuesday."

"You said he bit someone."

"Nipped. Bit, yes. He bit her."

"A stranger, someone he didn't know?" Under Christopher's slow, petting hands Finney flopped over on his back and stuck his feet in the air.

"Wow, he really likes you. Yes, it was a woman he'd never met before, a nice older lady, she wasn't doing anything except trying to pet him. Do you know Wake House? It's a sort of assisted-living place on Calvert Street."

"Wake House." He shook his head. "That's one I don't know."

"It's not a real nursing home, and it's very small, only about a dozen people live there. I was hoping they would like Finney and he could become their sort of, you know, therapy dog."

When Christopher Fox smiled, a small crease deepened at the left side of his mouth. He had greenish eyes behind rimless glasses, and they twinkled, as if she'd said something funny. "Jack Russells are great little dogs, but most don't have the temperament to be companion or therapy animals. Too much energy. And they're a little on the stubborn side. Unless you find a way to make it worth their while, they'll always do what they want to do."

"Oh, gosh, that's true." It felt natural to kneel down across from him on the other side of Finney. "That's exactly what he's like. He loves to sit in my lap when I'm reading or something, but if I *call* him to come sit in my lap, he just looks at me."

"That's a J.R."

"And if I'm playing the piano and I *don't* want him to sit in my lap, that's the only place he wants to be."

"You play the piano?"

"I'm a teacher. Piano and violin."

"Really." He sat down, folding his long legs and resting his hands on his knees. "I can play 'Für Elise' and 'Chopsticks.' "

She laughed. "How long did you study?"

"Four years, and I hated every second."

"Your parents made you," she guessed.

"No, my sisters played, so I wanted to, too, not taking into account that they had *talent*. My folks were saints to put up with it for so long. Money down the drain."

"At least you wanted to. I have students who'd rather peel their skin off than take music lessons."

"That must be a drag."

"It's when I really hate my job."

"When do you love it?"

"Oh, when they master something and go on to the next level, a new book or a new piece. When they're excited and proud of themselves."

"What do you do when you get a kid who's completely hopeless, no aptitude for music whatsoever?"

"I've never had one. Well, a couple of times I've had kids with learning disabilities."

"Do you tell them to find another outlet for their creativity?"

"No, I wouldn't, that would be—I'd never discourage anyone who really loves music."

"You must be a good teacher."

"I'm . . . yes, I think I am."

He combed his hair back with his fingers and smiled at her, as if he agreed. He had the kind of good looks you didn't notice so much at first, but gradually his perfectly shaped nose came into focus, and the way his eyebrows tapered together in the middle in a neat line of golden-brown hairs. He wore a plaid flannel shirt with the sleeves rolled up to show the long stretch of muscles and tendons in his forearms and the gracefulness of his wrists. His long, strong hands.

She was going to think about him after today, Caddie realized. When they said goodbye and she went on her way—assuming he couldn't help her turn Finney into a therapy dog, a hope she was coming more and more to see as deluded—Christopher Fox would stay in her mind for a while, maybe a long while, as an example of the kind of man she was never going to have. She didn't resent it—she certainly didn't resent him. People fell into classes, and you were allowed to pick who you wanted to be with from certain categories but not from others. Men like Christopher Fox were not in Caddie's selection range.

"Has Finnegan ever had any obedience training?" he asked.

"Not that I know of."

Christopher's face changed when he turned his attention to Finney, went from friendly and open to serious and searching; his professional face, Caddie assumed. He held the dog's chin in his hand and looked into his huge, almond-shaped brown eyes, and she wondered what he could see, how deeply he could go. All she ever saw there was the most deceptive innocence.

"Is there any hope?" she asked humorously.

"Always." He gave Finney a pat on the neck and stood up. How graceful he was. Caddie scrambled to her feet, feeling silly for the second or two she was on the floor without him. He was taller than she was; in fact, standing up, her eyes were on a level with his mouth. "Would you be interested," he asked, "in taking the training to become one of our volunteers?"

"Oh! Really? With Finney?"

"Probably not with Finney. For him I'd recommend some enlightened obedience training, but to be certified as a therapy or visitation animal he'd need much more than that. Even if he had the temperament for it, and I'm afraid he doesn't, you'd be looking at at least six months of training with one of our teams."

"Oh. Well, then, I guess that's that."

"Not necessarily. CAT always has more animals than volunteers. If you're interested, you could enroll in a training program and borrow one of our dogs. Or cats, or guinea pigs. Cockatoos. We even have a chicken."

"A *chicken*." Her mind raced while Christopher told her about the chicken, Estelle, how gentle she was, what wonderful companions chickens could make. Did she want to do this? Did she have time? She tried to imagine herself in a cancer ward or a rehab center, a hospice, ministering to the ill or the dying with a borrowed golden retriever. Was she the sort of person who could do that? What if she wasn't and she had to pretend she was?

"It's a big decision," Christopher said, nodding his big, handsome head with understanding, and she liked him better than ever—if she wanted to say no, he had already forgiven her. "Shall we talk about it some more? Do you want to find out what's involved?"

"I'd like to do that, yes. Definitely."

"Good. Would you be free for dinner?"

"Dinner?" She was only partly successful in keeping her voice within a low, unamazed range. "Tonight, you mean?"

"If you're free." He took off his glasses, an intimate gesture in the small room, or so it seemed to her. "I'll tell you about the work we do, and you can decide if it might interest you."

"I'd like—yes, I'm free. I think, I'm almost positive. No—I forgot, I've got a lesson at seven. Oh, I'm sorry." Too good to be true. She'd known it all along.

"How long does it last?"

"An hour."

"Eight o'clock, then. Or would that be too late for you?"

Was this a date? He had such an open, interested face, and he'd been nice to her since she'd walked in the door. He wasn't being any nicer now, and his warm, handsome smile didn't look any more interested. Maybe it wasn't a date.

"Eight's perfect." She said it brightly and casually, as if being invited to dinner by gorgeous men on short acquaintance happened to her every day. "Where shall we meet?"

Christopher snapped his fingers, and Finney, who'd been exploring along the baseboard behind his desk, came trotting over, bright-eyed and attentive, ears cocked. Christopher bent down to retrieve his leash and pressed it into Caddie's hand. "Anywhere you like. Or I'll pick you up—would that be all right?"

She was cautious about men, as a rule. But she only gave Christopher Fox's question a second's consideration. "I'll write down my address for you."

He took her to a German restaurant in the east end, the only end of Michaelstown that could remotely be called trendy. He must have called ahead; the hostess seated them at one of the window tables, screened from the view of sidewalk pedestrians by red-and-white-checked café curtains. They both ordered beer instead of wine, Caddie because she liked beer, and also because she thought it made her seem more like a fun person, somebody who was easy to please. She'd spent much too much time deciding what to wear—a white T-shirt under her long khaki jumper—and she'd felt a little disappointed, actually a little silly, when Christopher had picked her up wearing the same clothes he'd had on this afternoon.

"I come here fairly often," he told her. "It's pretty good, and it's only a couple of blocks from my apartment." He lived on the first floor of a three-story converted town house, and it was a good deal because he had the whole fenced-in backyard to himself. He and his staff used it to train the dogs and volunteers for the visitation teams.

"How many people are on the staff?"

He smiled down at the beer stein he was rotating in circles on the tablecloth. "*Staff* might be a slight exaggeration. I don't even have an assistant. What I have is team leaders, and the number fluctuates as people come and go. The organization's very spread out, and of course the real work goes on out in the field. I could probably operate from a laptop in my living room, but don't tell headquarters that."

"Where's headquarters?"

"Ohio."

The waitress came. Caddie ordered Wiener schnitzel. Christopher took his time deciding, asking the server how the broccoli was prepared tonight, if the sausage was homemade. He ended up ordering four appetizers, all with specific instructions for their preparation, including how much tarragon he wanted on his new potatoes. She would've worried that he was too finicky, that he was going to be a prissy, difficult man, except for the way he jollied the waitress into enjoying herself while he made his selections, charming her into a real investment in how much he was going to like his dinner.

She still didn't know if this was a date, and it made her nervous. Except for music, every subject she knew anything about sounded silly or boring when she framed an introductory sentence in her head. She hadn't been on a real date in so long, she'd forgotten how to talk, that was the problem. She'd gotten used to thinking of her life as flat and straight, not metaphorical; everything just was what it was, nothing stood for anything else. While Christopher talked, she tried to think of her life as a series of stories, looking for one that might make an interesting topic of conversation. She had a new student, a middle-aged widower who wanted to learn show tunes on the piano because he thought that would make him more popular in the singles club he'd just joined. Was that a good story? Or was it just gossip, trivial people-news that wouldn't interest Christopher because his conversation was on a higher plane?

"Most people know on some instinctive level that animals are good for our health, but it's only in the last twenty-five years or so that we've been studying it, proving the phenomenon scientifically.

We know that loneliness is at the root of a lot of illnesses, and we know that people over sixty-five who have pets go to the doctor a lot less often than people without pets."

Caddie nodded, although she hadn't known that.

"It's good to be able to back up what we do with data, but once you've observed a well-run pet visit at a hospital or a nursing home or a psych unit, you don't need any more proof. It's right there in front of your eyes." He leaned forward on his elbows, ignoring his dinner. Candlelight sparkled on his glasses and made his eyes dance. "I've seen folks come back almost from the *dead* because a dog put his head in their lap. Disoriented people, people sick with pain or hopelessness, crazy people, violent, disconnected—you can see their *eyes* clear. An animal is such a pure thing, Caddie, it's got no motivation except to be with these people, and they know it. It breaks through. Touch. That's all they want. Bring a dog into a roomful of old folks, everybody's in their own little world, it's fifteen or twenty separate brains on autopilot. Bring that dog in—something happens. People start talking, first to the animal, then to each other. They even sing to it. The dog or the cat, whatever it is, unlocks memories, associations. Everybody has a story—all of a sudden there's community."

"It's wonderful."

"Trust. The animal has no agenda, it just wants to lick your face, hear your voice. Barriers these people have erected against the outside world come crashing down without a fight, and it's just warmth and two-way gentleness. The innocent animal-human bond. It's powerful, it's beyond words. Deeper than words."

"Wow," Caddie breathed. "What wonderful work. You must find it so satisfying."

"There are frustrations, too, of course. Nothing happens as fast as you'd like it to. People resist out of ignorance, so you have to start from page one all the time, educating and reeducating—it's frustrating."

"I can imagine."

He sat back suddenly and took off his eyeglasses. "Is this boring?"

"*No.*"

"I'm sorry, I get on a roll and forget this isn't the most important thing in everyone else's life, too."

"It's not boring at all! You're so lucky to have work that means the world to you. How did you get into it? How did you start out?"

He'd grown up in Iowa on a farm, so there had always been lots of animals around the house, cats and dogs, birds, guinea pigs, rabbits, a duck, and, once, a llama. But especially dogs—dogs were his passion. He was the baby, with three older sisters who spoiled him. One was a lawyer now, but the other two were veterinarians, and that's what he'd wanted to be, too. In college he did a little too much partying, though, and when it was time to go to grad school in vet med, his grades weren't good enough.

"I ended up with a degree in business I didn't know what to do with. I backpacked in Europe for a year, came home, worked a couple of dead-end jobs. I started going out with a woman whose brother trained dogs to be companion animals for handicapped people, and he took me on as an assistant."

That ended when the relationship with the sister ended, but by then he'd acquired one-year-old King, who'd flunked out of the brother's assistance dog school for being too "scattered."

"By then I'd heard about CAT, which had a chapter in Columbus, where I happened to be living. I signed up to be a volunteer, took the training with King, and became a visitation team leader. For no pay—I paid the rent by working in the accounting office of a big insurance firm, which I hated. I was praying for the day I could quit. Which I did when CAT hired me to be chapter coordinator for the eastern region—thirteen states and the District of Columbia. So that's my life story."

"But what do you *do?*"

"I open chapters, get them up and running and independent enough so they can be administered from headquarters instead of on-site. Then move on to the next place."

"How long have you been here?"

"A couple of weeks."

"How long does it usually take to get a chapter going?"

"Depends. I've done it in a month, I've done it in six months. Lot of variables."

"Michaelstown is so small," Caddie noted, dispirited.

"But there's a lot of opportunity here. It's small, but it's in the center of a bigger region we haven't organized yet. We're hoping to use Michaelstown as a base for establishing a number of satellite chapters."

"Wonderful," she said. Christopher smiled knowingly. She blushed. They finished drinking their coffees in a pleasurably self-conscious silence.

They were the last to leave the restaurant. "Too bad it's too late to take a walk," Christopher said, opening his car door for her. "I could use one—I ate too much." He patted his hard, flat stomach. "Show-off," Caddie said, and he threw back his head and laughed. She blushed again, this time with delight.

They drove through the all-but-deserted streets with the radio on low to a classical music station he'd preprogrammed into his selections. A good sign, she thought. *Another* good sign. On the west side of town, the pretty shops and renovated town houses gave way within a block or two to less attractive buildings and more haphazard zoning. More bars. The commercial section of her neighborhood was a single intersection of one- and two-story convenience marts, a couple of taverns, a store for uniforms and trophies, a Chinese takeout. It wasn't very dangerous, but every year it got a little seedier. She saw it through Christopher's eyes, how low and gritty and squat everything looked. At least her street still had plenty of trees on both sides, big green maples in their full spring glory. There was nothing like leaves to hide a neighborhood's imperfections, especially at night.

Christopher coasted the car to a stop in front of her house and turned off the engine. He angled his body toward her, throwing one arm across the steering wheel, one over the back of the seat. She turned to him, happy to block his view of Nana's shadowy, lumpen lawn sculptures with her head and upper torso. If he'd noticed them earlier when he'd picked her up, he hadn't said, but in the dark he might've mistaken them for shrubbery. It didn't really matter, but she wasn't up to explaining *Birth Canal* to him on their first date.

If this was a date.

"Well," he said, "what do you think?"

"About what?"

"Becoming a volunteer."

"Um, well, I think it sounds . . ."

"Scary."

"Yes. Because . . ."

"You're not sure you'd be good at it."

"Yes." It was good to have her reservations articulated for her.

"Here's something I tell all the volunteers, Caddie. *It's not about you.* As soon as that sinks in, the pressure's off. There's a lot to being a good visitor, I won't minimize it, but at the same time, most of it boils down to common sense. But where the real action is—you're not there. It's between the animal and the client. The dog and the little old lady, the cat and the bald kid with cancer. You're just the person on the other end of the leash."

"I see. Yes, that's helpful, but the thing is . . ."

"Time."

She laughed. "You have to quit reading my mind!"

"You're not sure you can fit in a new responsibility."

"Yes, time is definitely—I'm thinking of taking a part-time job at Winslow's this summer, because I'll probably be losing some of my students for the holiday—music teaching is a seasonal business, believe it or not."

"What's Winslow's?"

"The music store downtown. I worked there last summer, and I'm almost sure I can this summer if I want to."

"Okay." He was smiling, not at all disapproving. She couldn't have stood it if he'd tried to make her feel guilty about this. If he'd pressed her at all, she'd have agreed to anything, the way she did with charity solicitors on the telephone.

"And another thing," she felt bold enough to admit. "I'm not sure I'd be any good as an animal handler anyway. To tell you the truth, dogs never do what I say. I'm not forceful. They ignore me."

"All of them?"

"Yes."

"Turn around and look the other way?"

"They turn their backs on me."

"It must hurt your feelings."

"It's devastating."

The light from the streetlamp cast interesting shadows on his broad, reassuring, Midwestern face. She smiled at him, feeling safe and accepted, not judged. He was so easy to talk to. She didn't want this to end yet, she wanted to sit in the close, ticking car and talk and talk, establish herself in his mind as a viable person, someone he might be interested in.

But he was turning away, unbuckling his seat belt, unlocking his door. "You haven't met the right dogs, that's your problem. You don't know how easy this could be if you were paired with the right animal."

He got out of the car and came around, opened her door for her. They ambled up the walk, and she forgot to be embarrassed about the sculptures when he suddenly said, "What are you doing Saturday afternoon?"

"Oh, I have lessons. All day. Saturday's my longest day."

"Sunday?"

"Sunday. Sunday I'm not doing anything."

"Meet me in the park. About two o'clock, is that a good time?"

"Two, yes, two is great."

"If it doesn't rain, you'll see King in action."

She took her bag off her shoulder to fumble in it for the key, and also to hide her expression, which she imagined was confused. Even now, when it was almost over, she couldn't be sure what sort of evening they were having, business or social. About dogs or about them. "Thanks so much for dinner," she said, trying for a breezy tone to cover all the possibilities. "I really enjoyed hearing about what you do, what your job is like."

"Don't rub it in."

"What?"

"That I monopolized the conversation."

"You didn't!"

"I'm not really like this. Your fault, you're too good a listener."

She'd heard that before. She never felt especially complimented by it, since people who were good listeners usually weren't very good talkers.

"Next time," Christopher said. He brushed the backs of her fingers with his. "I'll shut up and you can tell me all about yourself."

"Oh, well. I'm not that interesting."

"I disagree." He caught her hand and swung it between them—a chummy, lighthearted gesture, she thought, until he lifted her hand to his mouth and kissed it. Then everything fell into place. Like playing computer solitaire, you put the last king up and all the cards flapped down in triumphant spirals. The end. *Want to play again?*

She moved into his open arms. They exchanged the lightest of kisses, more of a caress with their mouths than a kiss, but they lingered over it, drawing the moment out. Caddie felt dizzy, disembodied. "Night," Christopher said, and she whispered it back.

She put her key in the lock, and that was the end of romance. Finney went berserk—he must've had his ear to the door, listening for metal on metal.

Christopher chuckled and stepped back. They waved, and she went in the house, closing the door fast so the dog couldn't escape.

If she did what she wanted to do, which was dance around the living room, Finney would *never* stop barking, so she sat on the second-to-last step of the staircase in the dim hall and petted him until he settled down, got over his frantic gladness. "That's Christopher, yes," she told him while he sniffed her shoes, her hands, her face. "Yes, Christopher. You like him, don't you? Me, too. We like Christopher, don't we? Yes, we do."

And he liked them. Christopher Dalton Fox. What a wonderful name. She felt euphoric. Very likely things would not work out, he'd realize they weren't meant to be, or she'd find out he had a wife in Youngstown, something would happen to spoil it. But even so, she'd always remember this moment, when he was just a memory and she could contemplate all that had been and might be. "It's perfect right now," she told the dog, "right this minute. Even if it's as good as it's going to get."

7

"One and *two* and one and *two*—that's it—one and *two* and one and *whooo!*"

Claudette, the activities director, bent over and slapped the floor with her palms, miming that she was winded. She wasn't, Claudette was tireless, a machine, but she had worked herself into quite a sweat disco dancing to Madonna.

The men of Wake House never joined in the exercise class she led on Tuesdays and Thursdays in the Blue Room, but they never missed it. Even if they were late, they always came slinking in eventually— as Thea Barnes said, like cats hearing the can opener. It wasn't the music that drew them, and Caddie didn't think it was the sight of a lot of old ladies hopping around in their socks, waving their arms in time to "Like a Virgin." It was Claudette.

Nana cackled, taking it all in from her wheelchair by the wall, wriggling her toes at the end of her new canvas cast in time to the beat. Her red toes: Claudette had painted her nails for her in arts and crafts. "Look at Cornel," she said to Caddie over the music. "Is that drool on his chin?"

She peered over at Cornel in alarm. "No, I don't—oh, ha." Good joke. Grouchy old Cornel, who complained about everything, wasn't complaining about Claudette in her skintight bicycle shorts and one of those tank tops with the bra built in. He was spellbound. So was Bernie, his roommate, a burly, sad sack of a man who usually looked like a basset hound. Right now he looked like a basset hound on point.

Thea Barnes, who was doing slow stretching exercises by herself in the corner, heard Nana's crack and laughed, "Ha!" the same uninhibited belt of laughter Caddie had heard from the window on the day Thea arrived.

"I should be doing those with you," Caddie said, moving closer. "You're so limber. Do you do yoga?"

"I used to dance—ballet. But I've got terrible arthritis in my big toe, so now I just stretch." She looked like a dancer in her black leotard under a full, calf-length skirt. The gold scarf she'd tied around her head drifted over her shoulders when she bent or swayed, following her graceful movements.

"I know I should jog or something," Caddie persisted. "I don't really do anything."

"You don't need to, you're so slim."

"Well, I do walk the dog a lot . . ." She winced. Sore subject.

Thea grinned, waving her hand. "All healed. Look, not even a bruise."

"You were so nice about that."

"It was nothing! Forget it."

"I didn't tell you—I took Finney to a dog trainer. He said he's beyond hope."

"Oh, dear."

"His name is Christopher Fox—the trainer. He works in town." Caddie ran her sandal along the edge of the rug. "He's very nice."

Thea lifted her dark, expressive eyebrows.

"Actually." Caddie laughed, self-conscious, keeping her eyes down. "We've started going out."

"Oh, how *lovely*."

"It is," she agreed.

"What's he like?"

"He's . . . oh . . ."

Thea clapped her hands, delighted. "She's *speechless*. You'll have to bring this man over so we can get a look at him."

"I was thinking I would." How funny to be telling Thea about Christopher when she hadn't even told Nana yet. "He's got a *beautiful* dog, a perfect dog, much better than Finney."

"Well, you know, it's not really the *dog* we want to meet."

Caddie grinned and examined her cuticles.

"Are you blushing? I'm sorry," Thea said, laughing, "I shouldn't tease. Poor Caddie, I'm afraid you're our designated élan vital."

"Your *what?*"

"Our vital spirit. We're too old for lives of our own, so we have to live through *you*."

She made a face. "Oh, boy. You're in big trouble, then."

"No, you're our heartbeat, we're counting on you."

"I think you should get a new vital spirit."

"Too late, you're it!" Thea's gray eyes danced with a warm, knowing fondness that startled Caddie and set her at ease at the same time. It was so nice to be teased with affection; it felt like a friendly touch or a compliment. For some reason she felt closer to Thea than their brief acquaintances warranted, and if she wasn't mistaken, Thea felt the same.

"Okay, people," Claudette called out, "let's slow it down a little! How about something from the olden days? Pair up!"

"*Well*," Thea said from the side of her mouth. "I think she could've phrased *that* a little more tactfully."

Caddie held out her hand. "Want to dance?" Claudette had put on "Don't Be Cruel," and the Copes sisters, Bea and Edgie, were doing a creaky, slow-motion jitterbug.

"Not me." Thea wriggled her foot in its black ballet slipper. "Damn toe." She lowered her voice. "Uh-oh. Caddie, look."

"What? Oh." Bea and Edgie had paired up, but the Harris wives, the only ladies left on the floor, had not. In fact, they'd turned their backs on each other, and now the second Mrs. Harris, a regal, silvery-haired lady whose first name was Doré—"as in do, re, mi, fa," Nana liked to say—was leaving, striding out of the room in her mauve warm-up suit, not a hair out of place after all that exercising.

Thea rolled her eyes. "It's so tiresome. I have to sit between them in the dining room."

"I got stuck between them once, and it was awful. They really can't stand each other."

"Believe me, I know."

One day, after Nana had been at Wake House for about a week, Caddie had come out on the front porch and found Mrs. and Mrs. Harris sitting in two chairs, with a third, empty chair between them. Without thinking, she'd taken the middle chair. At first it seemed as if they were having a normal conversation, but that was because it took her so long to notice that the Harrises only spoke to *her*, never to each other. She'd heard that about them, of course, but it didn't seem possible; she hadn't quite believed it. Maxine, the original Mrs. Harris, said something about Caddie being a music teacher and how much she, Maxine, had always loved music. "It surely does soothe the savage beast," she said with a sniffing laugh, "and there's times in my life I'd've been a beast without it."

Mrs. Doré Harris was a sharp, careful dresser; she always wore outfits, slacks and sweaters that matched, necklaces that went with her earrings. That morning she'd had on a filmy white blouse with a black bow at the throat, a wide, droopy bow as big as a telephone, a real fashion statement. She was from the South, and she had a low, buttery accent that didn't always sound perfectly sincere.

"Now *that's* a frightenin' thought," she'd leaned closer to Caddie to say, putting a finger in her *Good Housekeeping* magazine to hold her place. "Imagine the *beastliness* o' some people if they *didn't* have music." She gave a tinkly, ladylike laugh. "But of *co*-us, the correct quote is savage *breast,* not *beast.*"

Maxine started a light drumming with her heels on the floor. She was older than Doré, heavyset, with graying, bowl-cut hair and squared-off bangs like Mamie Eisenhower. "Of *co*-us," she said— Caddie had flinched, realizing she was mocking Doré's accent—"of *co*-us, some people can only *say* 'breast' because they've never *had* any breasts and are flat as pancakes."

Doré might or might not be flat-chested, it was hard to tell because of the black bow. But what a thing to say! Caddie waited, horrified and fascinated, to hear how she would answer.

"Id'n it funny, Caddie, how some people who've let themselves *go* can't resist makin' fun o' people who've kept themselves *up*. Or it *would* be funny if it wadden so pathetic."

"What's funny, Caddie, is people who don't *know* they're pathetic."

"Now that is certainly the truth," Doré said, forgetting to be indirect. When she remembered, she reached over and patted Caddie on the arm, to indicate she'd been speaking only to her. "The ones who don't know they're pathetic ah truly the most pathetic of all."

"My goodness, I'd better go get Nana ready for our drive," Caddie had said, and she ran for her life.

"Claudette should've known better," Thea said now, watching the exercise class break up early—not enough dancers.

"Caddie?" Nana called over, fanning her chest with a pinch of her "Oh my God, I forgot to have children!" T-shirt. "Bring me a glass of water, would you? Watching all that jumping around's made me thirsty."

"How about you?" Caddie asked Thea.

"No, thanks, I'm fine."

Coming back from the kitchen, Caddie paused in the high-ceilinged hall to gaze around at the church pew benches along the wall, the shaggy ferns on pedestals, the dusty chandelier overhead. Gone-to-seed Victorian genteel, that's what Wake House was. J. P.

Morgan, if he was slumming, could be standing on the dark staircase landing, blocking the rose light from the stained-glass window, jingling change in his pocket. All the floors slanted and the doors closed by themselves, because there were no right angles anymore. The outside was still imposing, with its black mansard roof and puffy, three-story brick tower on one side, and at least it had never been "modernized" like some of its neighbors on Calvert Street. The best feature, everybody agreed, was the porch stretching across the whole front and one side; a wide, airy, perfect porch, lined with rocking chairs and gliders, exactly the sort of porch an old folks' home ought to have.

Caddie paused to look at the line of framed black-and-white photos on the wall—including the one Magill had broken on Nana's first day, now repaired. Three generations of Wakes posed in formal and informal groups on the lawn and front steps of the family mansion. Old man Wake was always at the center, growing whiter, plumper, and more distinguished as time went by. Then the Wakes were gone, and the other photos were of more recent, less grand incarnations, as the house became a boarders' hotel, law offices, a school for therapeutic massage, a day spa, and back to a boardinghouse. And now, "elder care and convalescence." Caddie didn't care for the lesson, the perspective on time the photographs conveyed. She'd have liked Wake House, *this* Wake House, to last forever, and it wasn't going to. Nothing did, and here was the proof on the wall.

"Caddie!" Bea Copes called from the couch in the Blue Room, where she and Edgie had collapsed on the sofa, fanning their faces with their handkerchiefs. "Caddie, come and see us!" She should've brought *them* glasses of water. She brought Nana hers and went to see what the Copes sisters wanted.

They didn't look alike. Edgie was fluffier, a more feminine sort of woman than Bea, who reminded Caddie of the farmer's wife in the Grant Wood painting. And yet she'd have guessed they were sisters

73

without being told, if only because their voices had the same cadence, and they spoke with the same rural Maryland accent. And something else, too, a deference in their postures, the way their bodies inclined toward each other to talk or to listen.

"Sit!" Edgie urged, patting the place next to her on the sofa. She looked like a wilted flower in her damp, light green shirtwaist and her cottony yellow hair. She was the flighty, fidgety younger sister in Caddie's mental shorthand, the decorative one, while Bea was older and more serious and practical, the one who took care of business.

"We want to ask you a question," Bea said, taking off her glasses to polish them on her sleeve. Her eyes had that pale, whitish ring around the irises that old people got sometimes, but they were still handsome eyes. She was tall and rawboned, with long limbs and knotty joints. Caddie loved to watch her walk. She threw out her legs in a funny, jerky way that was graceful and ungainly at the same time.

"We *loved* the history you made of your grandmother," Edgie leaned toward her to say.

Uh-oh. Were they going to ask her about the seven body fluids? Cornel had, and so had Mrs. Brill, and she couldn't tell them. "Ask Nana," she'd said. She just couldn't bring herself to say the word "semen" or "urine" to these nice old people. And certainly not "vaginal secretions."

"I can't write anymore, you know," Bea said.

"Arthritis," Edgie explained. "She used to be able to type a hundred words a minute. Taught her*self*."

"Plus I can't *see*. So we—"

"Whereas I've got all my faculties and I *still* can't write," Edgie said.

"You can write, you just can't *spell*," Bea said. "Now, Caddie, we need to ask you a big favor. We're so *old*, we're the last ones to go—"

74

"In our generation."

"In our generation; all our brothers are gone, we were the youngest of the six, and now there's nothing left but nieces and nephews."

"But plenty of *them*," Edgie said, counting on her fingers. "There's four of Edward's, three of Jack's, three of David's, and Bernard's one."

"And don't even start on the *greats*."

"They don't keep up, the greats, although David's girl Sarah does visit once in a while, as does Buster, Bernard's boy. Say what you will about Buster, he never forgets us at Christmas."

"*Anyway*," Bea said. "Point is, they don't really *know* us, these young ones. And not that we're all that interesting—"

"Speak for yourself."

"But someday they might want to know about their family, things the boys didn't pass on because they didn't know, being too old—"

"Or didn't care about, being boys."

"And so—we were wondering—if you might have time to write down a little history of us if we told it to you, Edgie and me. For 'We Remember,' and for our kin."

"It wouldn't be very long," Edgie cautioned.

"Oh, no, it would be *short*. Just the highlights."

"Such as they are."

"There's hardly anything to say."

"Just something for them to have after we're gone."

"I'd be glad to," Caddie said. "I'd like to."

"Really? Are you sure?" Edgie sat up and clapped her hands. "But you're so busy. We'd understand if you wouldn't have time, we surely would."

"No, truly, I'd like to. I'm free right now—want to do it now?"

"Out on the front porch," Bea said, "it's cooler," and they all got up and went outside.

"Papa had dairy cows and some chickens, but he wasn't a real farmer, not full-time. He did other jobs to keep the family, machine repair and being the deputy sheriff of the county."

"Bea, tell about that time—"

"One time he kept a prisoner in our barn for two nights on account of a rainstorm that took out the bridge over the creek between our house and the lockup in town. Oh, my, that was something."

"We huddled in the bed both nights and didn't sleep a wink. He was a colored man," Edgie lowered her voice to say, Caddie wasn't sure why, maybe because of Mrs. Brill, although she was nowhere in sight. "I don't believe, looking back, he'd done much more than get drunk, but we were scared to death he was going to bust out and murder us in our beds."

"It was in those times when you heard such stories, you know," Bea said. "Then, too, we were a couple of right silly girls."

"Tell her about the time the two—"

"One day two ladies came to our house, which was a piece out of town, not isolated exactly but plenty rural. They knocked on the front door, and Mama answered."

"I expect we were about six and ten years old at the time this happened," Edgie said, "somewhere in there."

"Edgie and I were in the kitchen making poppy seed cakes when one of these women comes in. She was older than us but not as old as our mother—"

"Maybe twenty," Edgie estimated.

" 'Oh,' she says, 'your mama sent me back to get a drink of water. I've been walking.' Well, that didn't sound right to me for some reason. Not that Mama wouldn't have let a complete stranger waltz in and have a glass of water, she certainly would have, and fed them, too—"

"It wasn't the Depression yet, but we did have hobos come to the house once in a while asking for a quarter or a job or something to eat."

"Our mother was a soft touch," Bea said, with a sweet, remembering smile.

"Oh, she surely was."

"But something was not right about this woman in the kitchen."

"Bea knew it before I did."

"She had funny eyes, and she was dressed wrong, not like she was poor and she'd been walking. She had on a red coat, I remember. She looked around with little darty eyes like she'd never seen a kitchen before—"

"But really she was casing the joint."

"And she got her water and went out. 'Thanks,' she said, and sailed out the door. Well, I don't know why, I truly do not, but I told Edgie to stay put, and I followed her. Sure enough, she didn't go back down the hall to the front door, where I could hear Mama out on the porch talking to somebody else—this is the first I knew there were two of them—sure enough, this first lady ducked into our dining room!"

Edgie took Bea's arm and squeezed it with both hands. She pressed her lips together, determined not to interrupt, but she widened her eyes at Caddie, as if to say, *Isn't this exciting?*

"Why, she's after the silver, I thought to myself, and took off down the hall hollering for Mama. Just when I got there, I saw the other lady—"

"Who turned out to be *her* mother, the first one's—"

"Edgie, now, don't spoil it—"

"Okay, but call them 'mother' and 'daughter,' Bea, so she'll know who's who."

Bea took a deep breath. "The *mother* of the first one—anyway, I saw her give *my* mama such a shove it bruised her hip, she pushed her right up against the gateleg table in the hall and darted past, into the dining room, where the other one was. I yelled or screamed or something—"

"Which is when I ran in," Edgie said, "when I heard all this commotion."

"Next thing you know, the daughter is waving a *knife* at us, yes, a *knife*—"

"Huge!"

"And the mother—who, by the way, looked like our aunt Clarice, I mean the most respectable person you could imagine, she looked like she'd come to sell you the Bible—"

"Which when you think about it is what they should've said to us in the first place. Glass of water," Edgie said in disgust.

"Anyway—the daughter has got this big shiny knife pointing at us and the mother is pulling out the drawers in the oak breakfront and stuffing her pockets with silverware!"

Caddie made exclamations of amazement.

"*Well.* I don't know what came over Mama," Bea said. "She—"

"The sweetest, gentlest soul. When we were bad she couldn't even spank us, or the boys either. Just didn't have it in her."

"Papa's coat was hanging on a hook in the hall alongside everybody else's. I told you he was the deputy sheriff. Well, that day he was out in the field—"

"She means the *fields*, he was out doing farmwork."

"Yes, and so there was his gun in the holster under his coat."

"Can you *imagine* a man leaving a loaded pistol by the front door in this day and age? With six children?"

"But these were different times—"

"That's what I'm saying. Back then we didn't think a thing of it."

"Edgie, I am almost done telling this story. When I'm through, you can start over and add all your interesting comments."

Edgie sat back and made a key-turning motion over her lips.

"*Any*way. Our sweet, soft-hearted mama pulled the gun out of that holster like she was Deadeye Dick. 'You put down that knife!' she yells to the two in the dining room, with her voice shaking, and you can believe that's what they did. You never saw two such scared women in your life—unless it was me and Edgie! Mama made them to lie down on the floor, and she told me to go in the parlor and call up the sheriff. Which I did, and then we waited."

"And waited."

"Lordy, it felt like two days before he came driving up the lane in his black car, but I expect it was only about twenty minutes."

"The longest twenty minutes of my life," Edgie declared.

"And mine. I will never, ever forget it. What my mama looked like with that silver pistol in her hand."

"Papa said he was going to retire and let *her* be the deputy."

They leaned against each other, chuckling, shaking their heads. Sitting next to Bea on the squeaky glider, Edgie's feet didn't quite touch the ground, so her sister was the one who got them going every now and then with one of her long, jointless legs. "Hush," Bea said suddenly. "Caddie, don't move. Is that a hummingbird? Over the rhododendron. There, right there."

"No, honey, it's a bee," Edgie told her.

This was going to take longer than Caddie had thought. She looked down at the notes she had so far for the Copes sisters' biography. They wanted only one for both of them, not two separate histories. "Born 1917, 1921, Point of Rocks, Maryland." So far, that was it. She didn't mind, but each time she asked a question, no matter how factual she made it—What did your father do? What kind of a house did you grow up in?—the answer turned into a story.

So next she asked, "How old were you when your mother died?" That was a subject that always interested Caddie, when people's mothers died. Hers had when she was nine. When she was younger, she'd liked to borrow pieces of other people's stories for a while, using their details to fill in the gaps of her story, which was thin and paltry and not satisfying. You could use the experiences of other people like thickener, she'd found out, tablespoons of flour to stiffen a watery soup.

"Edgie was nine, I was thirteen." Bea sat back and gave the glider another push with her foot.

"Was it sudden?"

"No."

"It was to me," Edgie said in a soft voice. "Her name was Labelle—isn't that pretty? Labelle Ida Rostraver. She had all six of us before she was thirty-five."

"She had cancer of the ovary. She was sick the whole winter, and in April she died. She was only forty-four."

"April the third, the day after Bea's birthday."

They looked down with gentle, forlorn faces, gazing at the same spot on the peeling porch floor.

"You must've missed her a lot," Caddie said.

"We still do," Edgie said. "People think you get over things just because you get old."

"Papa lived to ninety-six," Bea said. "We were with him when he passed, holding his hand, talking to him. Of course I'll never forget that, but what I remember like yesterday is the morning he came into our room and told us our mother was gone." She stuck one finger under the lens of her glasses to wipe her eye. "Broke my heart. Before or since, that was the saddest time of my life, and I'm eighty-six years old."

Edgie said after a moment, "I have a different memory. That time she called us into her room."

"Oh, yes."

"I knew she wasn't well, but not that it was so bad. We had to be quiet in the house, but she never fussed at us if we weren't. When I'd sneak in her room, she always acted glad to see me. I remember her smile. She always put her hair up, but after she got sick she wore it down, and it was so lovely to me. Yellow hair. She'd let me brush it for her. I swear I don't know why, but I just never *knew* how sick she was."

"You were too little," Bea said.

"Yes, but I should've known better than I did. That day—Bea, you recall that day when she told us what might happen."

"Yes."

"She asked us to get up in the bed with her. That was a treat—I half expected us to start playing a game. She told us sweet things I don't want to say out loud, don't want to start crying. But about how much she loved us, you know, how happy we'd made her. How glad she was . . . well, cripes." She gave a laugh while she dug a tissue out of her skirt pocket. "I'm ashamed to say I hated God when she said He might want her up there with Him in heaven soon. Selfish old man, I thought. Take somebody else, don't take my mama." She sniffed deeply and blotted her cheeks. "Isn't this something, now, this many years later. Don't think I'm a silly old woman, Caddie—"

"I don't."

"Well, you *are* a silly old woman," Bea said.

In the quiet that settled over them, Caddie heard a high, tinny sound, almost like a voice.

"That's my watch," Bea said, chuckling at her expression. "It talks. Tells me when it's time for my pills."

"I'll go get you some water," Edgie said.

"Let me get it," Caddie said.

"No, you sit still." Edgie hauled herself out of the glider with both hands, making an exaggerated grunting noise to disguise her difficulty. "Bea, tell her about the time we won the trip to New York. Two rubes in the city. We saw Vaughn Monroe!" she called from inside the house.

Bea smiled at Caddie. "We've had good lives, in spite of acting

81

like a couple of water spigots today. Don't forget to put that down in the history, Caddie. That we've been happy."

"I won't."

"But lately, I feel like I'm spoiling the last little bit of it."

"How do you mean?"

"I *worry*. I just worry and fret all the time about what's going to happen next. That's no way to live, but I can't help it. Every time I go to the doctor, it's something else that's broken down. How much longer can I stay here? You know Brenda's already filed for a waiver to keep me—she's not licensed for the kind of care I'm getting, what with all the medicines and restrictions and the special diet for my diabetes and this and that." She softened her voice. "I just don't know what Edgie's going to do if something happens to me. I don't know how she'll get along without me."

"Oh," Caddie said, "nothing's going to happen to you." The silliest, most cowardly thing she could have said.

Bea treated it the way it deserved and ignored it. "Life's been good to us for so long. If I have to go in a real nursing home—"

The screen door slammed. "If you have to go in a real nursing home, I'm going with you." Edgie handed her sister a full glass of water and sat back down beside her. "That's all there is to that."

"Do you regret anything?" Caddie asked after Bea had swallowed down four or five pills from a white plastic box with so many compartments and different-colored pills, it looked like a honeycomb. "Do you look back and wish you'd done anything different?"

"No! I'm not sorry about anything. Are you, Bea?"

"I wouldn't do a thing different. So many people have passed on, loved ones have left us behind—that's the hardest thing to bear at our age, but that's what life brings you, sure as God made little apples, if you last long enough."

"Now, Caddie, don't think all we can talk about is people who've died and gone. Bea, quit talking about death. Tell about Buddy's second wedding to that preacher girl. Our favorite nephew married a lady minister out in a wildflower meadow, and it didn't last six months!"

8

Early on Friday, two students called within ten minutes of each other, both claiming they had a cold and couldn't make their morning lesson. Something must be going around, but it was hard to imagine what on such a warm June day, flowers bursting out everywhere, hazy sun burning off the dew before Caddie could finish her coffee. She looked out across the greening sculptures from Nana's rocker on the front porch and realized she had the whole morning free.

For years she'd been meaning to take up some healthy physical pursuit, and watching Thea do her yoga exercises the other day had given her new resolve. Wake House was a fifteen-minute drive, so probably . . . about a three-mile walk, give or take. Nothing to it. She finished her piece of toast, put on shorts and tennis shoes, told Finney to behave himself, and set off to visit Nana.

How pathetic, she used to think—had thought as recently as a few weeks ago—that she was thirty-two years old and her favorite pastime was visiting old folks in a home. She'd reminded herself of one of those women in thoughtful, depressing novels about English spinsters, repressed women who trudged gallantly from one grim day to the next until the last page, when, usually, they died. She read these books because they made her life seem like Mardi Gras in comparison.

Now everything was different—she didn't see herself as pitiful anymore. She could interpret her daily visits to Wake House as normal, kindly meant, simply another facet in a well-rounded person's social repertoire, because her life had proportion again. She was a regular person. She was Caddie Winger, and she had a boyfriend.

Christopher Fox. Christopher Dalton Fox. She set her feet down on the concrete sidewalk in rhythm with each stately syllable. She wasn't compulsively writing his name in a notebook, but in other ways she was feeling, possibly behaving, like an infatuated ninth-grader. She'd seen him two times since their dinner at the German restaurant, and they were both definitely dates, no guesswork required. On Sunday, a spectacular day, the most beautiful day of the year, they'd romped in the park with King, the perfect dog. Half collie, half German shepherd, King didn't even need a leash, and he didn't respond to commands from Christopher so much as read his mind. Compared to King, Finney was a foaming lunatic in a strait-jacket in an asylum for the criminally insane.

Who was handsomer, King or his master? They had the same tawny, soft, floppy hair that blew in the breeze like a woman's hair in a slow-motion shampoo commercial. Christopher had long, beautiful hands, and Caddie loved to watch them disappear into King's golden fur when he ruffled the whitish patch under his collar or pulled gently on his velvety ears. *Christopher's hands.* Last night he'd taken her to the movies, and she'd sat in the dark beside him feeling as if she couldn't fully exhale, as if she had a pleasant excess of air inside and it was causing her to levitate.

She'd never been courted by anybody like him before. She couldn't think of anything about him she would change. Tonight he was taking her to a softball game. A softball game. Already she loved the mundaneness of their dates, the bland, unimaginative whole-someness of sitting on a hard bleacher seat and ordering a hot dog and a plastic cup of beer. It was frightening to contemplate how closely Christopher resembled the kind of man she'd always wanted, so she was trying not to think about it. She was tricking herself by feigning casualness, like Finney when she had a toy he wanted. He'd look the other way and pretend he couldn't care less, then pounce on it when she lost interest. She hoped her act was more convincing than his.

She had sore feet by the time she got to Wake House. And a sunburned nose. She went straight to the kitchen and gulped down a glass of water without stopping. Three miles was a lot harder than she'd expected, especially on a day as humid as this. She took off her shoes and socks and went in search of Nana.

She wasn't in her room. She wasn't on the side porch, not in either of the parlors, and she wasn't in the backyard. She might be in Magill's room; she was fond of him, and Caddie had found her there more than once. But Caddie felt a little reluctant to look there today, considering what had happened the last time she'd knocked on Magill's door.

Actually, she hadn't knocked; the door had been ajar, so she'd just pushed it open and taken a single step in. Magill, sitting at his desk, working at his computer—she thought—had jumped out of his chair like a man with a hot foot, whirling around so fast he lost his balance and started flapping his arms, falling, falling, finally collapsing on top of his bed. *What in the world*—she'd started to go to him, then she'd processed the image on his computer screen: naked ladies, cheerleaders, having their way with a hairy, muscular, happy-looking young man in a locker room. She could tell they were cheerleaders because of the imaginative ways in which they were using their pom-poms. Magill's horrified face made her giggle, but the action on his computer monitor made her blush. She mumbled something: "Oh, sorry, should've knocked," and Magill, spread-eagle on the bed, picked up the pillow and dropped it on top of his head. She left.

So she approached his ground-floor room with caution now, but before she even got close she heard the stagy, unnatural rhythm of soap opera dialogue blaring through the closed door. Along with everything else, Magill's *hearing* was supposed to have been affected by his skydiving accident. She knocked, waited. Knocked again louder.

He opened the door.

"Hi."

"Hi."

She could swear he looked guilty again. She started to back up, but then she saw Nana half sitting, half lying on his bed with her foot on a pillow, watching the small TV across the room. Holding a plastic glass in her hand.

"I only gave her a swallow, a thimbleful, I made it almost all 7 UP."

Caddie came all the way in. The room smelled like cigarettes and booze. "You gave my grandmother a *drink?*"

"A little Seagram's, a *spot.* She saw me pouring it and asked if she could have some. What could I say?"

"No?" She wasn't really upset, but he looked so defensive, she felt she ought to be. "I wish you hadn't," she said crisply, "it'll only put her to sleep. And what if Brenda finds out?" Drinking was forbidden except on special occasions.

Magill reached around her and slammed the door. He had on regular clothes today, not sweats or pajamas, and his knee pads but no football helmet. He used the furniture for help getting across the room to the bed, first the desk, then the top of a chair. That probably didn't have anything to do with alcohol, though; any fast movement could send him sprawling.

"Hey, Caddie," Nana said, just noticing her. "Come over and sit. We're watching our story." She patted a place between her and Magill on the bed. "Zander just found out about the baby, what's-her-name's baby, this girl right here. What's her name?"

"Laura," Magill mumbled, sounding sheepish. He moved his legs reluctantly, and Caddie sat at the bottom of his rumpled bed. He and Nana lay side by side with their backs propped on pillows, cozy-looking, a couple of old pals.

"I didn't know you two had a story."

"This girl's pregnant but she couldn't tell Jason because she thought he loved the other one, Rachel," Nana informed her. "Shh, listen."

A slick, shiny, blue-black-haired, distraught young man in shirt-sleeves and a vest was telling a blonde girl, "Laura, for the love of *God*, why didn't you tell me? Darling, darling, did you think I'd be angry? Oh, sweetheart—"

Laura began to sob. Whenever anybody cried, in life or on screen, Caddie cried, too. She had to blink fast and swallow down a sympathetic lump when Zander and Laura embraced, both of them crying now in extreme close-ups, mashing their faces against each other, holding on so hard it looked painful. Stirring music swelled and a commercial came on.

"That's not how it was when I told my boyfriend *I* was pregnant."

Caddie reached for the remote control and pressed the mute button. "What, Nana?"

In the sudden quiet, her grandmother's long, crinkly face registered surprise, as if she'd startled herself, too. "Sometimes I think I've already told you."

"Told me what?"

"You're illegitimate."

Magill brought his fist to his mouth to clear his throat.

"Oh," Caddie said with an artificial laugh, "I already knew that." She sent Magill an apologetic glance. *Sorry. Family laundry.*

Nana pushed up from the pillow and looked at her more closely. "Jane, I meant Jane. I should've told *her*."

"My mother?" Caddie gave another chagrined hiccup of a laugh. "No, Nan, *I* am. I'm Caddie," she reminded her.

Nana shook her head sadly. "Oh, honey, Chick and I never did get married, and then he went and died."

Chick? "You mean Grampa Charles? No, he was killed on the last day of the war, World War Two, remember? He got all those medals for bravery. He was your husband."

Nana made a face by squeezing her eyes shut tight and rolling her lips back over her dentures. "Too handsome," she said in a stage whisper. "That's what got me."

"He was," Caddie agreed. She'd seen his picture. One of those man-and-car photos, her grandfather leaning against an old Dodge with his legs crossed, cigarette in his mouth, a sexy shock of black hair in his eyes. She'd never seen a picture of him in his army uniform. Never seen any of his medals for courage, either.

"He mowed the lawn at the college," Nana said. "Junior gardener, he called it. We started up that spring I got my teacher's certificate. Pretty spring. I always blamed it on the azaleas."

"What?"

"I never told your mother, and I should've."

"That what?"

"I fell in love, that's what."

"You and Chick—Charles—"

"Chick Buckman. You should've seen him walk. That was one man nobody could resist, especially from the back."

"Chick Buckman? Then who's Charles Buchanan?"

Nana made a grinding sound in the back of her throat. Her eyes watered. "Haaaa," she said fondly, nudging Caddie's hip with her good foot.

"But—so then—what, Nan, he died?"

"I heard he did, yes, some years later. He left town the day after he found out about the baby. Not like Zander." She reached for the remote and turned the sound back on the TV.

Caddie took it from her and turned it off. "Wait. You didn't marry him? He left you pregnant? My *grandfather*?"

"Yes, yes, yes, and now I don't want to talk about it anymore. I should've told you before. I wasn't *ashamed,* I just never got around to it. Give me that thing, honey, it's starting."

"But you—you made up the name Buchanan? You just pretended to be a war widow . . ."

"Till I took back my own name and said to hell with it. It was after Jane died and there was no reason to keep pretending." She turned to Magill, who was staring at the silent TV screen in perfect stillness. "So that's two whatchamacallits of fatherless girls."

"Generations?" His face was a study.

"Two generations of bastard daughters in a row. Poor Jane and then poor Caddie. The sins of the mothers. Caddie's father, we don't even *know* who he was. A fine man, though, I'm sure." She grabbed again for the remote. Caddie held on; after a tug-of-war Nana yanked it out of her hand and punched the sound back on.

Wow. The things you learned.

Magill got up. He went over to the bureau and pulled a pint of whiskey from the top drawer. "Want to sit outside for a while?" He wagged the bottle invitingly.

Nana had her arms crossed over her bosom, staring at the TV with fierce attention. She was through talking.

"Sure," said Caddie. And a drink, too. It wasn't every day you found out you were the second generation of bastard daughters.

Magill's room was on the first floor, so his French doors, unlike Nana's, weren't locked or painted shut. They led onto a small porch with a stone floor and a sagging overhead trellis, vine-covered. He had the best room in the house, even better than Thea's tower room, Caddie thought, because he could walk right out into the grassy side yard whenever he liked. The only furniture on the porch, though, was one chipped white wrought-iron chair and a matching table. After some polite wrangling, Caddie took the chair and he sat on the table.

Sounds of hammering overhead broke the sleepy afternoon quiet. A roofer, nailing shingles that had blown off last week in a storm. Something was always falling off Wake House. Caddie watched Magill pour whiskey and 7 UP into clear plastic cups, swish them around, add a little more booze to his cup, and push hers over to her. "To interesting news," he said in a neutral voice. They drank.

Fat bees drifted over their heads, looking for a nesting place in the flaky wood lattice. The same windy rain that had blown off roof shingles had blown away the petals on a white dogwood tree in the yard, and now they lay rotting on the grass, turning brown. Magill spoiled the sweet smell of honeysuckle by lighting up a cigarette. "Are you okay?" he asked casually, tapping ash against the side of the table. "Not upset?"

"Because of Nana and . . ." Whoever.

"Chuck Bickman."

"Chick Buckman. No, not upset. I'm surprised. I'm *amazed*. It's something I would never have known about if she hadn't just told me, if she hadn't been watching Zander and Laura. It makes you wonder." What other secrets Nana was keeping. Maybe not even on purpose, just out of forgetfulness.

"I don't think I've ever known a bastard before," Magill observed.

"It wasn't so bad. When I was little, I just told people my dad was dead." She would think about this later: When they were children, she and her mother had told their playmates the exact same lie about their fathers, and the only difference was, her mother had thought it was the truth.

"You have no idea who he was?"

"My father? Not really. My mother was a singer, back in the

seventies. All I know, because it's all she ever told Nana, is that he was somebody in the band. But the members changed every few months, so that wasn't much help."

"What was the band called?"

"Oh, different things. They never got famous. Red Sky, that was one of their names. My grandmother went to see them once. She said they were pretty good." Nana had met a guitar player named Bobby, a drummer named Patrick, a handsome, sweet boy—she said she wished it was him, but Caddie didn't look a thing like him—and another boy, the bass player, but she said it couldn't be him because he was black.

"Why do you think she didn't tell you about Chick Buckman before?" Magill wondered.

"I don't know. She said she never got around to it, but that's . . ."

"It couldn't have been much fun being pregnant with no husband in Michaelstown in the 1940s."

"No," Caddie agreed.

"So she invents a dead one, and there he is. Years go by, he's not doing any harm. She was a teacher, right? It's the conservative fifties, she's Mrs. Buchanan, respectable widow—"

"Until my mother died. Right after that, Nana told me our name was going to be Winger," she remembered.

"No reason to keep pretending."

"Except she *did* keep pretending, even to *me*."

"How old were you when your mother died?"

"Nine."

"Well."

"I know, but—why not tell me later? When I was older?"

Magill shook his head. "Must've been complicated."

Very complicated. A lot of things had changed, not just Caddie's last name, when her mother died. Nana only had six years to go before she could retire from teaching art, but suddenly she'd given it up and started making her own strange art. She'd turned into a sort of bohemian, a look that blue-collar Early Street didn't exactly embrace. Neither did Caddie, who, as always, only wanted to blend in.

"My mother and my grandmother didn't get along," she told Magill. "I think Nana was too strict. Believe it or not. They fought all the time and my mother rebelled, and finally she left home for good."

"Joined a rock-and-roll band."

"I guess after she died, Nana decided she could stop being this super-respectable person she thought she needed to be to set a good example for her daughter."

"Where were you all this time? When you were little. Where'd you grow up?"

"Here. I grew up here. With Nana."

Magill waited for the explanation.

There wasn't much of one. "My mother—I guess she couldn't take care of me and be a singer, too. She had to move around a lot. So, that's how that worked. Why don't you ever use your first name? I still don't even know what it is."

He tilted his head and narrowed his eyes on her, processing the change of subject. She hadn't managed that very smoothly, but she didn't like talking about her mother, it was like approaching a hole in the ground loosely covered with camouflaging brush and sticks. Some things you just knew better than to go near.

"Henry," Magill said. "That answer your question?" With two loud zips, he unfastened the knee pads from around his legs.

"Henry. That's all right, it's a good name. What's wrong with it?"

He picked up a stick that had been leaning against the table and began to peel the bark off, squinting his eyes against smoke from his cigarette.

"But you always just use one name. 'One's enough for me,' you said that day in the parlor. Remember? You were lifting weights."

"Was I drinking?"

"What?"

"Sounds like something I'd say if I was drunk. Get some cheap sympathy."

"No, you were drinking Ensure. I think." Maybe he'd spiked it, though. Bourbon and Ensure, like an eggnog. "Do you always . . . nothing. Never mind."

"Go ahead."

"It's none of my business."

"Ask."

"Do you always drink during the day?"

He kept his eyes down, intent on the stick. "Only if I've been to see my therapist in the morning. That always drives me to drink by afternoon."

"Oh. I guess you went this morning, then."

"No, last Wednesday."

"But . . ."

He was kidding. He kept a straight face but let his blue eyes go sly, and finally he smiled, confirming the joke. She hadn't quite known how to take Magill at first, but now it was simple: You just kept in mind that everything was a joke to him. And if he happened to say something bitter or serious, he *pretended* it was a joke, and you had to play along.

"Lieberman," he said. "Isn't that a great name for a shrink? Dr. Lieberman. He hates it when I call him Fred."

"So of course you do."

"Yeah, but only when he gets on his favorite subject."

"Which is?" A personal question, but she could tell he wanted her to ask.

"How much of what ails me is in my head."

Well, that was certainly getting to the heart of it. She wanted to know the answer to that question, too. She imagined everybody did, especially Magill.

"What I don't get is what difference it makes," he said, banging the stick against the top of his running shoe. "What if I'm a world-class hypochondriac? So what? Just because you're psychosomatic doesn't mean you're not crippled." He grinned, then lapsed into morose silence.

She'd heard something, an awful rumor about his accident. Secrets didn't keep for long at Wake House. "The woman in the picture," she said softly, "in your room, that photograph on your dresser, is she . . ."

He lifted his head and looked at her.

"She's very pretty," she finished, losing her courage.

He put his elbows on his knees and his hands over his ears.

She looked like she was funny, the girl in the picture. Like she would enjoy making you laugh. She was wearing pajama tops and leaning against a magnet-spattered refrigerator with a quart of milk in her hand. She had tousled brown hair and a wide, toothy mouth, squinty, dancing eyes. How could he bear to look at that picture? Caddie would've kept another one on her dresser if she were Magill. A soberer one, not smiling. Not so alive.

"She was a schoolteacher," he said, still with his head in his hands. He had a funny way of speaking sometimes, as if he had to take care with every word or it might come out garbled. Everything was clear, but it sounded like an effort. "Second-grade teacher. The kids used to hang on her like . . . balls on a Christmas tree. You couldn't pry them off."

He straightened up to take a long pull from his drink. "She used to do accents, German, French, Yiddish. She'd crack the kids up telling these long, silly stories. Sometimes I'd drive over, try to see her when she was outside, supervising recess. But I couldn't get near her, the kids wouldn't leave her alone. They just, you know. They loved her."

Caddie smiled, but Magill wasn't looking at her; he didn't see. "What was her name?" she asked.

"Holly."

"Pretty."

"She didn't want to go up with me. I wouldn't let it go. I kept telling her about the rush, how she'd never know anything so intense, if she did it once she'd be hooked for life. Do you want to know how it happened? It was her birthday."

"No. I'm sorry. I don't."

"Sure? Lieberman does. His mouth is watering." He kept his eyes on her in a fixed stare, smiling a small, not nice smile. His gaze seemed to shift back and forth between her and a scene playing inside his head.

"Don't tell me." With all her heart, she didn't want to hear how Holly had died, not the way he would tell it to her now, in this mean mood she'd never seen him in before. "Why do people skydive?" she asked. "I would never, I mean, I don't understand it. Why in the—"

"I'm so *fucking* sick of that question." He ripped a strip of bark from the stick in one violent pull and stood up. She was afraid he'd stumble, but he was steady on his legs, glaring off to the side while he clenched and unclenched his jaws. He punched his thumb against the end of the stick, gouging the pad of it with the sharp point.

"What was your life like before?"

He cupped his ear. "What?"

"What was your life like before the accident?"

"I can't remember."

"I bet you can." But then she had a thought. "Oh—you mean you have amnesia?"

He peered at her, his eyes incredulous. Then he burst out laughing. She was so relieved, and his laughter sounded so *real*, just pure, tickled mirth, she had to laugh with him. Soap opera organ music soared through the open door from his room just then, and they looked at each other and doubled over. Amnesia! Magill had to drop back down on the table to keep his balance. He had a rolling, carbonated kind of laugh she'd never heard before and couldn't resist. When they finally groaned to a stop, he wiping moisture from his eyelashes, they were their old friendly selves again. No, much better.

"What was my life like. I was an engineer, I told you. I had a little company. Employees."

"That's right. Orthotic devices. How did you get started doing that?" It seemed so strange, like choosing to be an undertaker. But Caddie had always had a secret horror of amputation, people's missing limbs, stumps, stubs. It shamed her, how much revulsion she would feel at the sight of some poor person's artificial leg or mechanical claw of a hand. She counted it one of her pettiest failings.

"My father stepped on a land mine in Vietnam and lost his leg from the knee down. He walked around on a clumsy, painful prosthesis for years, then he invented a better one. Eventually he designed the prototype for the first Full Speed Feet foot. He wasn't even an engineer, he was a cabinetmaker."

"Full Speed Feet."

"The foot line we make. We do the full range of lower-extremity orthotics, but feet are our specialty."

"Do you have a . . . a factory?" She was trying to picture the work environment of a company that made feet.

"Sure. It's small. Ever heard of Kinesthetics, Inc.?"

"No. I don't think so. Maybe," she added thoughtfully when she saw he was disappointed.

"Hold on." He got up and went inside, came back with a folded brochure. "Here. By the way, your grandmother's asleep."

She was expecting a picture of a flesh-colored artificial foot made out of rubber or plastic or something, but this . . . it looked more like a pair of grass clippers. It was a dark gray metal contraption with bolts and springy, odd-shaped parts at the base and two long, arching prongs at the end. Toes?

"This is our basic model, the Pacesetter. We also have a child's foot called the Running Start, another for athletes, the Mach Run. They're all patented FSF feet."

They could be customized, she read, to fit almost anyone's weight or activity needs. Their polycentric design and multiaxial function provided outstanding durability, comfort, and a more natural, noiseless gait.

Noiseless. She couldn't help it, that gave her a queer feeling. "It's so high tech. This is what you put in your shoe? Don't some people want something a little more . . . I know they never really *look* real, but—"

"This is the innards, Caddie, the part that's engineered for loco-motion and joint alignment, weight distribution, functional foot drop, equilibrium. It goes—" He flipped open the brochure. "It goes inside a foot shell. Like this."

"Oh!" Here was the kind of fake foot she'd had in mind. "Oh, I see, it goes *inside.* And this is flexible, the shell thing? All right, I get it. Well, this isn't . . . it's really . . . it's interesting." *This isn't as creepy as I thought it would be*, she'd almost said.

She turned to the back page, which had a photograph of "Our R&D Team," four smiling, friendly looking young people, three men and a woman. "Your staff looks—" She peered more closely. She put her fingertip under the chin of one of the men. "Is that *you?*"

Magill rubbed his whiskery cheek, raised his eyebrows.

"Is it? Gosh, you look really . . ." Healthy, with color in cheeks that weren't sunken and flesh on a neck that wasn't stalky. Confidence in shoulders that weren't so bony they poked through his shirt like coat hangers. He was smiling the same slightly sly, off-center smile as always, but without the self-mockery in his eyes to make it suspect.

"The point is, we make some of the most progressive lower-limb orthotics in the world. The Running Start is a hell of a foot, I wish I had a picture of it. It's the first time some of these kids have ever walked on anything halfway approaching a real foot. Now all of a sudden they can run and play and jump, they can rotate, they're stable, they don't get exhausted. Their parents write us letters, Billy played soccer for the first time in his life, Katie's gait looks completely natural, nobody even knows she's wearing a prosthesis."

He kept talking, the longest she'd ever heard him at one time, speaking with animation and no irony, telling her why the Running Start was revolutionary and explaining the biomechanics of something new, a foot he'd been working on before his accident; he wanted to call it Roughshod, it would be super-tough, athlete amputees would wear it for long-distance and rough-terrain hiking.

"Is your father still working?" she asked when he paused. "Still inventing things?"

"He died about four years ago."

"Oh, I'm sorry. And now you run the company?"

"What's left of it." He tilted his head and closed one eye to stare at her.

"Do you have a mother?"

"Sure. What do you think, I hatched?"

"I meant, is she living?"

"She lives in Phoenix with her new husband. Which is fine with me, I have no *issues* with it." He smiled, but he sounded tired; he and Dr. Lieberman must've gone into that pretty thoroughly. "She's got a new life and I'm glad for her," he said, rubbing his forehead hard. "Nothing but glad."

"Okay," Caddie said, and they lapsed into silence. "She must worry about you, though."

"This is how you get 'em to tell you all the gory details. Right? You just keep chipping away."

"Who?"

"Your subjects. I hear old man Lorton wants you to write *his* life story next."

"My subjects." She laughed. "Actually, I don't say much of anything, I just write down what people tell me."

"You're good at it."

"Thanks."

"You were probably good in English. I was terrible. Twelve years of lit classes and I only remember two things."

"What?"

"Sympathetic characters and concrete detail."

She thought of Christopher: four years of piano lessons and all he could play was "Für Elise" and "Chopsticks." She handed Magill his brochure back. "How long do you think you'll have to stay here?"

As soon as she asked, she was sorry. He straightened up from his friendly slouch and turned away.

"I know, I'm sorry, but I don't understand—why can't you work? Couldn't you . . . if you just . . ." Sat still and didn't move, closed one eye, told other people what to do, explained exactly what he wanted to those nice-looking people in the photograph . . .

"Do you think I'd be here if I could work? Something's wrong with my *head*. I'm an engineer, a designer, I'm supposed to invent things—my *brain's* scrambled, I can't draw a line with a straight edge. I can't *see* things, images on a computer look like nothing, it's just meaningless lines—"

"Well," she interjected, because that wasn't true, she happened to know. "Unless it's cheerleaders."

She wanted him to laugh, but he started away, moving jerkily out into the bumpy, grassy yard. He got about ten yards, using his stick to take furious whacks at dandelion heads as he went, before he staggered to a stop. He swayed, bracing his knees for balance, then gave up and sat down hard on the ground.

She walked out to him, careful not to hurry. When he saw her he fell over backward, holding his temples and squinting up at the sky, which she imagined was spinning. She stood over him. "Are you okay?"

"Go away. Take your grandmother and vacate my room."

She sat down, folding her bare legs and blowing a dandelion seed-pod off her knee. "I walked all the way over here from my house, aren't you impressed? I am, except now I have to walk all the way back."

"Take a cab."

"No, I'm on a health kick."

"You're fine."

She pondered whether or not that was a compliment. "Nana has a new art project. It's on . . . well, it's hard to say."

"Oldness."

"Oh, you heard."

"She wants all my old cigarette butts."

"I don't understand why it always has to be *all*. Is it still art if you don't pick and choose?" She plucked a clover shoot out of the ground and pulled the leaves off one at a time, letting them fall in her lap. She nibbled the stem. Magill was shading his eyes with one hand, looking up at her. "Too bad," she said, wistful, "you can't make a prosthetic device for your poor head."

He smiled.

Christopher had nice lips, too. Fuller than Magill's; the bottom one was downright pillowy. "I have a date tonight," she said.

"Oh, *good* for you."

"He's a therapy animal expert."

"I know."

What a wonderful job, so sunny and happy, so perfect for

Christopher. "I met him through Finney," she explained, and told Magill about Christopher's cramped little office and the mission of CAT. She told him about King, the wonder dog.

"I'm more of a cat person." He folded both arms over his eyes.

"They have cats, too. They have everything, even horses, even chickens." She told him about Estelle. "I'm thinking of taking the training. Not with Finney, I guess he's hopeless, but I could borrow a dog. Christopher says I could even borrow King after I go through the program. I think it would be really worthwhile, something I could do in my spare time. Everything changes when you bring a dog into a room full of sick people, even if they're just sick with— *especially* if they're just sick with loneliness. They forget all about themselves. They love the dog, and it's really love, not just *oh, how cute*. Sometimes it's the first time they've communicated with anything in a long time. All of a sudden they're back in the world. In the moment. And it lasts, it starts relationships with the other people, I mean it doesn't just stop when the hour's over and the dog leaves. It keeps going. A beneficial cycle."

All she could see was the top of his forehead and his pressed-together lips; the rest of his face was hidden under his ropy forearms. Under his T-shirt, his spiky rib cage rose and fell with his breathing, dropping off to an alarmingly concave belly. If he were six feet lower, he'd be a skeleton in the ground.

She shook that thought away. "Are you going to sleep?"

"Yes."

"First Nana, now you—I might as well go home." She pulled a grass blade and tried to whistle on it between her thumbs. She leaned back on her hands and looked at a buzzard circling high up in the clouds, or maybe a hawk. A grasshopper jumped on her knee. She brushed it off and stood up.

"Okay, well, see you."

"Have a nice time tonight with Timmy."

"Christopher. Who's Timmy? Oh." Lassie's boy. "Ha-ha, very funny."

He smacked his lips, ostentatiously readying himself for sleep.

"Don't lie there for long. Don't go and pass out, you'll get sunburned."

No answer.

She made a face he couldn't see because his eyes were closed, and set off on her long walk home.

9

This is what I missed in high school, Caddie thought, jumping up when Christopher did to cheer somebody's leaping catch of a fly ball to center field. Beer sloshed from her cup onto her thigh, and she just laughed. It was a warm, buggy, sweaty night with the smell of popcorn and dust in the air, heat lightning in the distance. The Beavers were beating the Trolls by fourteen runs, nobody was taking the game seriously, and everything was funny.

"I've never done this before!" she dared to tell Christopher, who put his arm around her back and leaned closer to hear. "I've never been to a softball game. Or a baseball game, or football!"

He had a way of looking amazed when she told him things like that, things he'd apparently never heard anyone say, and then looking politely thoughtful. She wished he would tell her what he was thinking, even if it was *Where did you come from, Mars?* But he just opened his eyes in amazement, then pursed his lips in thought, as if filing the information away for later.

"I was in the orchestra instead of the band," she tried to explain, but he just grinned, ran his fingers into her hair at the back, gave her head an affectionate shake, and went back to watching the game.

Oh, well, he wouldn't understand anyway. In high school he'd have been one of the players on the field, or else he'd have been sitting on one of these hard, splintery bleachers surrounded by his attractive, confident friends, speaking the foreign language Caddie had never mastered, performing the social rituals she couldn't duplicate. Except for music, adolescence for her had been one long personal embarrassment. She'd never held that against the favored ones like Christopher, though, or even particularly envied them. It would've been like envying gods: pointless.

The Beavers hit six more runs in the seventh inning and the game ended, or collapsed. Christopher steered Caddie out on the field and introduced her to his friends, Rick and Toby, Wesley, this was Keith, here was Glen—she lost track of names when their wives and girlfriends joined them. They were all on their way to a bar on the west side, Hennessey's, they went there after every game, were Christopher and Caddie going to join them? "Want to?" Christopher asked her, but that was only a formality, and before she knew it she was sitting on a sticky bench in the corner of a loud, crowded tavern, trying to shout a pizza order over an endless Allman Brothers song on the jukebox.

Toby was the chef at a restaurant in town, Rick was Christopher's landlord, Glen's wife, Phyllis, was a team leader and dog trainer at CAT, Keith—Caddie couldn't hear what Keith said when he explained himself, but she nodded and smiled and pretended she did. She'd never really liked loud, noisy bars, having to strain to hear and shout to be heard. It came to her now that the appeal wasn't the ambiance anyway, it was creating your own little island of intimacy in the middle of chaos. Pressing her arm against Christopher's arm, enjoying the cup of his hand on her thigh, feeling his warm, beery breath on her cheek—it was like watching a violent summer storm from the safety of a screened-in porch, cozy and exciting at the same time. This is how real people live, she thought, this is what they do all the time. Everything that must be prosaic to them, the pretty neon liquor signs glowing over the bar, the wafting palls of blue cigarette smoke, the long line of variously shaped rear ends on the bar stools, seemed exotic to her tonight. This was good clean American fun, and she was like a new immigrant from some third-world country, dazzled and over-whelmed and hoping to fit in.

When she excused herself to go to the ladies' room, Phyllis went with her. They stood beside each other at the mirror, repairing their faces. Phyllis said, "I love that lipstick shade, Caddie."

"Thanks."

"Is your hair naturally straight? God, I've always wanted straight hair. Mine curls up like a party ribbon in this humidity."

Phyllis was lovely, copper-haired, porcelain-skinned, dainty as an elf. When she left, Caddie stared at her reflection, trying to see herself as a stranger would, somebody as petite and cute as Phyllis, for example. Her hair had no style, just hung long and lank from a side part; she was constantly throwing her head back to get it out of her left eye. Did having no hairstyle make her look like a hippie, a sort of earth mother? Could that be her image to Phyllis and the others? To Christopher? She'd dithered for an hour over what to wear tonight and finally chosen, for reasons that seemed completely inexplicable now, a long black tunic of Nana's over a short plaid skirt of her own, and sandals. What did this look mean? What *was* she in this outfit? She'd walked out of the house feeling leggy and fun, but under the fluorescent ladies' room light and in the metaphorical shadow of small, stylish Phyllis, all she could see were flaws. Including the fact that the hem and pushed-up sleeves of her black tunic were covered with dog hair.

But Christopher smiled at her from all the way across the room. "Hey, you." He stood up to let her squeeze back into her place on the bench, and for the two or three seconds he held her tight against him, her back against his front, all she felt was chosen.

They held hands under the table. He caressed her bare thigh in the most thrilling, matter-of-fact way, as if they were already intimate. "Would you like to dance?" he said in her ear. There was an area about six feet square near the jukebox where one other couple was dancing, or, rather, swaying, not even moving their feet. The current song was a theatrical ballad by a singer Caddie disliked—she thought Christopher was joking or being ironic, that dancing to it was his way to make fun of this over orchestrated love song. But once in the circle of his arms, pressed against him and easily following the fluid slide of his long legs wherever he moved her, she could tell he meant it. Felt it, was *into* the sentimental lyrics and the woozy tune—and from that moment on she loved the song. How wrong she'd been about it. It was simple and real, it told the truth, and she'd been not only snobbish but cynical not to see that before.

Christopher's whiskers prickled her cheek. He turned his head, and they danced with his lips in the hollow under her ear, she with her eyes closed, because when she opened them the room spun. The song ended, and in the interval of quiet before the next one, they kissed. *People are watching us*, she thought hazily, not caring. Christopher rested his forehead on hers and smiled into her eyes. "Caddie Winger," he said, like a revelation, and she thought, *This is real. Wake up, Caddie, it's happening to you.*

When he told them they were leaving, his friends looked knowing and not surprised. And *glad*, Caddie imagined, affection for them welling up in her. She had their approval, and also, right now, their interested speculation in her love life, her sex life. She didn't blame them. She felt fascinating and unexplored, full of potential. A little like an exhibitionist. What she and Christopher were doing was public foreplay, and she liked it.

She'd met him at the ball field, so they had two cars. "Follow me home?" he said in the parking lot, with another of his devastating smiles. There had never been much mystery about how this evening would end, but just the same it was lovely to finally have everything confirmed and out in the open. Now she had only to obsess about *how* it would be, not *if*.

But first they had to walk King. He met them at the front door of Christopher's first-floor apartment with no barking, but if he remembered Caddie from before, he gave no sign, had eyes only for his master. "Hey, big guy. You miss me? Hi, fella," Christopher greeted him, ruffling his ears and thumping him on the back. They strolled behind King along the quiet sidewalks of Christopher's neighborhood, holding hands, pausing each time the dog did his dignified business. King was so well behaved, he didn't even need a leash. Would Christopher think she was a bad owner for not worrying about Finney's walk? He didn't say anything about it, so she didn't either.

His apartment wasn't what she'd expected. She'd imagined him living in a messy, all-male sort of place furnished with thrift-shop furniture, everything a little shabby and run-down because he had more important things on his mind than housekeeping. She'd actually fantasized about cleaning the place for him, adding subtly warm, womanly touches he wouldn't notice right away, but when he did they'd make him smile.

Instead, everything was spare and tidy as a monk's cell, much, much neater than her house, and the style he'd chosen was *modern*. *Never* would she have guessed that. He liked metal and glass furniture, everything angular and either black and white or gray, and rush mats for rugs on the gleaming bare wood floors. Abstract art on the walls! He took her into the kitchen to open a bottle of wine, and he had a little machine for it, a stainless steel stand; he put the bottle on it and pushed down on a lever to uncork it. He hung his wineglasses upside down from a wooden rack under one of the cabinets. He had a bread machine. He had a set of those heavy gray pots and pans she had given up looking at in kitchen catalogs because she would never be able to afford them.

"Christopher, this place is amazing! Did you do it all yourself?"

He chuckled as he poured wine into two huge, bulblike glasses. "Do you like it?"

"It's just—I never thought—yes, I like it, it's just not what I expected! It's so . . ." Grown-up or something. But she was re-adjusting fast, deciding it suited him perfectly, mentally slapping herself for assuming he'd live in some grungy, grad student's garret kind of place. He had too much self . . . self-regard, no, self-esteem . . . the word wouldn't come to her.

He gave her a glass, and they toasted. "To us," he said, looking into her eyes. She was too shy to say it back, or too superstitious, but she clinked glasses with hope and enthusiasm.

In the living room, she was about to sit down on the white leather couch when he took her wineglass from her and set it on the glass-topped coffee table. She'd never cared for that gesture in the movies—what if the woman *wanted* her drink, she'd think—but when Christopher did it, it made her heart pound in anticipation. He put his arms around her. He was the best kisser she had ever known, he brought out skills of her own she'd never even suspected. He ran his hands up and down her sides and pressed his leg between hers, backing her up against the couch. He got his hand under her short skirt and pulled her up close against him. She started to lose her breath. Would they—would they make love right here, like this? She'd never done it standing up. Her knees started to quake. Christopher broke away and took her by the hand.

Oh, the bedroom—that was better anyway, she wasn't disappointed—

"Let's take a shower." He flicked on the bright fluorescent light and pulled her into the bathroom.

"Okay." She stood motionless, too startled to do anything but watch him pull the clear plastic curtain back and turn on the water, fiddle with the temperature until he had it to his liking, take down fresh towels and washcloths from a shelf over the toilet, open a new bar of soap. When he pulled his shirt over his head, she blushed and slipped her sandals off and started to unbutton her blouse.

Was this romantic? She couldn't tell. Maybe this wasn't

foreplay at all, just practicality. Like two guys in a locker room. They were sweaty from the game and smoky from the bar, and that must matter to Christopher. Of course, he'd want them to be clean and fresh for their first time together—who wouldn't? This was natural, not odd, she felt sure, although it still seemed wrong to strip in front of him without touching. Something as scary as nakedness ought to be accomplished, at least the first time, with as much affection and reassurance as you could manage, shouldn't it? Maybe not, though, if you had a perfect body. And Christopher did.

It was hard to look at him. Impossible not to—he took up the whole room, or that was how it seemed, with his long thigh muscles and his chest and his hard abdomen and his body hair and his testicles. His feet. "Wow," Caddie said sincerely, proud of herself for not giggling.

He noticed she'd gotten stuck, or else he read her mind and knew she wanted help, support—he picked up her hand and kissed it very sweetly. He kissed the top of her shoulder, then reached around and unhooked her bra. She stole a glance at his face. He didn't say "Wow," but he did flare his nostrils a little; that was a good sign. He stuck his finger in the waist of her skirt and tugged gently. "Hurry," he said, gave her a peck on the lips, and stepped into the shower.

Okay. She was starting to get his romantic rhythm. It was every man for himself, no mollycoddling. She got out of the rest of her clothes, folded them in a neat pile opposite Christopher's neat pile on the sink counter, and got into the shower with him.

Where they just washed themselves, separately, taking turns under the spray. They didn't even talk much. He was all business. He did look at her with what she hoped was friendliness and admiration while he lathered his hair with shampoo, but by then she was so unsure, all she could think about was whether she ought to wash *her* hair.

But then, thank God, he finished with his hair, wringing it out till it squeaked, and he kissed her. As soon as he did, everything was fine. She forgot what she'd been worried about. Forgot everything, in fact, except that it was a miracle she was here, naked in the shower with the most exciting man she'd ever met. "This is so nice," she murmured against his mouth, stroking his slippery skin, curving her hands over the muscular bulge of his buttocks.

"Mmm," he agreed. "Let's get out."

Maybe he just liked keeping her off balance. As soon as she got used to one thing, he started doing another. She watched him blow-dry his hair while she dried herself off with one of his thick, soft towels and then wrapped it around herself. What now? Would they brush their teeth? He pulled up the toilet seat, and she left the room.

King, who had been lying in the hall in front of the closed door, got up and followed her to the bedroom. She patted his noble head, but she had the sensation he was monitoring her movements more than keeping her company. "Hi, big dog," she said in a cozy voice, trying to win him over. "This is a great room, isn't it?" She liked it better than the living room; the textures were softer, wood and cloth instead of chrome and leather. She heard water running and located a miniature fountain on the windowsill, one of those electric stone-and-copper deals she'd seen in Nana's yoga catalogs. Why, it was charming, what a pleasant, restful sound. Zenlike.

She went to the dresser to look at the pictures—it was covered with framed photos of Christopher and King, Christopher and other dogs, Christopher and a ferret. Here was one of Christopher and three women; they looked so much like him, she knew they were his sisters. They'd spoiled him, he joked. If so, Caddie couldn't blame them. What a lucky life he'd led, being the youngest in a family who adored him, looking the way he looked, loving and being good at satisfying work that truly helped others. She could've envied, might even have resented someone who led a life that charmed. But for some reason he was inviting her to share it with him, and resentment was the furthest thing from her mind.

She almost didn't hear him until he was behind her, sliding his arms around her waist. They smiled at each other in the mirror. "We look good," he said, pressing his cheek to her temple. "Don't we?"

He looked good. Her hair was damp and straggly and she'd lost most of her makeup in the shower. Maybe he liked that, though, the wholesome look. He was from the Midwest.

"Let's get in bed," he whispered in her ear.

She nodded, shivering.

But first he lit candles, a fat, fragrant one on each bedside table, a row of white ones beside the gurgling fountain on the windowsill. They turned the heavy bedspread down together. He took off his bathrobe, she took off her towel.

It had been a long time since she'd been with a man, even longer with one she cared much about. She couldn't relax. She felt overwhelmed, overstimulated by all Christopher's *skin*, the warm and the cool places, hairy places, indescribably soft places. And all hers for the taking, which made her shy and inept. "You okay?" he murmured between kisses. The candlelight shadowed his cheeks and gleamed on his broad forehead. "Anything wrong?"

"*No*. It's—this is great, it's just—you know, the first time . . ."

He drew back, horrified.

"For us—the first time for us!"

He dropped his forehead on her chest and sighed out his breath. "Oh, thank God."

She started to laugh, helpless giggling, and after a few seconds he joined in. That felt so good, like the most intimate thing they'd done together yet, it almost cured her of her nerves.

"You scared the hell out of me." He started all over, taking little bites of her jaw, her neck, moving down to her breasts. She slipped her fingers into his hair and let herself drift. He was a wonderful lover. He made her feel masterful and natural, as if she knew what she was doing. He found condoms in his bedside drawer. She wanted to preserve the moment when he came inside her, commemorate it, make it last, because nothing she'd done with a man had ever felt this important. She made him stop so they could kiss—but then it was over, time moved on. She forgot about preserving things in the heat of her gathering excitement. Christopher was a groaner. She was shocked, then thrilled by his guttural, free, heartfelt grunts of pleasure. He buried his face in her hair. She held tight, and in the instant before she might have approached an edge, might have gotten close to a place to jump off from, she saw King.

He was standing next to the bed, his head inches from hers, peering at her with alert brown eyes and a judicial expression. Wagging his tail very slowly.

She wanted to tell on him, *Look what your dog is doing!*—but it wasn't the right time. And just then Christopher ground his teeth and let go, driving into her with enough force to push her shoulders against the headboard. Such a release! She felt complimented and proud.

"That was incredible," he sighed, collapsed on her. He turned her, holding her from behind, his warm breath on the back of her neck. "Are you good?"

She smiled. "I'm good."

He sighed, relieved. "Yes, you are. You are damn good." He kissed her behind the ear.

Her heart swelled. She wanted to tell him what it had meant to her. "Your dog was looking at us," she said instead.

"Hmm?"

"Not like this. He was closer." King had curled up across the room in front of a wicker and bentwood rocker, and he was blinking his avid eyes with exaggerated sleepiness. "Much closer. I mean, he was really *watching*."

"Hmm."

He fell asleep while she and King stared at each other. It ought to be easy to stare a dog down, but King won. Caddie shut her eyes first and didn't open them again. She felt like Rebecca, and King was Mrs. Danvers.

When she woke up, the clock on the bedside table said twelve-thirty. Yikes! Finney! Oh, but she didn't want to get up yet. Christopher was all warm and golden, lying on his side in a loose, sexy sprawl. What fun it would be to kiss him awake and see what happened. No, she had to go home. She would look at him for a minute, and if he woke up because of mental telepathy, her mind calling to his, it would be fate. She peered at him between his eyebrows, which might've twitched. She stared hard at his temple. *Wake up, Christopher.*

She sighed and got out of bed. So much for mental telepathy.

Dressing, she stared at herself in the bathroom mirror, the same way she'd stared at herself in the ladies' room at Hennessey's, this time trying to reconcile the kind of woman a man like Christopher would want to be with and the kind of woman she looked like right now. What was confusing was that she looked exactly like herself; she looked the way she looked when she got up in the middle of the night to pee or something. She had stupid hair. Her teeth were crooked, her lips were too thick, and her smile was asymmetrical. She disliked the whole lower half of her face. Nana used to say a man would sleep with any girl who had two legs and a vagina, and the two legs were negotiable. But that couldn't be it, because Christopher wasn't that kind of man.

What did he see in her, then? She liked animals. He liked music. He was in a new town; he had friends, but probably not too many. Maybe he was lonely?

Those were possibilities, but deep down she had a better hunch. There was something real between them. There, it was out—she'd been too superstitious to put it in words before. It was just starting for him, but she'd felt it from the start, a true chance at connection, a genuine relationship. Love.

She made a face in the mirror, like knocking on wood. She'd almost given up on it ever happening to her, she'd seen herself as marked, excluded because of circumstances from the community of lucky ones who met other normal, ordinary people and made it work. *If I'd had a regular family*, she would think. *If I'd had a mother who stayed, if I'd had a father, if I'd lived in a regular house. If Nana hadn't been so crazy.* But look—Christopher didn't care about any of that, he liked her the way she was. It was enough to make her think better of herself.

"Are you leaving?"

She turned, startled. He filled up the doorway, sleepy and tousled. "I have to. I have to let Finney out," she said virtuously, "he's been in all night."

He yawned and rubbed his eyes, rubbed his bare chest under his bathrobe. "I'll miss you." He put his arm around her as he walked her to the front door. She felt let down and realized she'd been hoping he would come home with her. But that was silly, he'd have to get dressed, they'd have two cars again, not to mention the problem of King.

"Let's do something tomorrow. Supposed to be nice. How about a picnic?"

"I can't. Saturdays are my busiest," she reminded him. *Tomorrow*, though—he wanted to see her *tomorrow*.

"How about tomorrow night?" he said. "It can be late. Come over and I'll make you dinner."

"Oh, lovely. But you come to my house, I'll make *you* dinner." What would she make? Something romantic and sophisticated. She'd have to get a magazine.

"No, you come here, it's better. Besides, you'll be tired, and this way you won't have to do anything."

"You talked me into it." She hugged him, touched and grateful. They kissed good night. He made it so sweet, she pulled back to look into his eyes, see if the same tenderness she felt was in them. It was . . . she thought it was. She framed his face with her hands. "I had the most . . . I had a very nice time." If she said what she was really thinking, she might scare him off.

"Me, too, Caddie. I'll call you in the morning."

She went out briskly, striding down the walk with her arms swinging, to show she wasn't a clingy sort of person. She couldn't resist a look back from the sidewalk, though. His dark silhouette looked tall and straight in the doorway, and handsome even from here. King stood at his side with his ears cocked, watching her go.

10

Mr. Lorton told Caddie she'd better hurry up and write down his life story before anybody else's, winking at her to make sure she got the joke. So they set up a time and a place, right after breakfast one morning in the Blue Room. He sat in the big easy chair with his cane between his knees, his feet barely touching the floor. His two flesh-colored hearing aids made his ears stick out on either side of his bald, freckled head. "What I'd like is for you to write it but make it sound like me. Put it down just like I'm saying it to you, not fancy or anything, but fix up the grammar and whatnot. Can you do that?"

"I'll try. If you don't go too fast."

He gave a wheezy laugh, twinkling his eyes at her. "Too fast is not a problem, believe you me. Well, you ready?"

"Ready."

My name's Charles Micheaux Lorton and I was born in Fairfield, Pennsylvania, so long ago it doesn't make any difference. I get tired talking about my age. After you hit ninety, it's about the only claim to fame you've got, and people run it into the ground. Oh, well, I'm ninety-seven, but let that be the end of it. And don't ask me the secret to my longevity. Which I'd say is moderation, but nobody wants to hear that. They either want some peculiar regime

117

like yogurt and deep knee bends three times a day, or else they want to hear how you smoke a big fat cigar and drink two martinis every night. I've just lived like a regular fella, tried not to get arrested, offend anybody, or draw too much attention to myself. That approach appears to be working.

My father was a blacksmith, a horse trainer, a mechanic, an amateur boxer, and a bartender. My mother was the church organist at Otterbein Macedonia Lutheran Church. They had two babies before me who both died, and after me they had my sister, Alice, and my brother, Floyd. We lived in various towns in southern Pennsylvania, which is still pretty country, and then in 1917, when I was nine, my father got shot trying to bust up a fight between two drunks in a tavern. He died eight days later of blood poisoning. After that, we moved to Frederick, Maryland, because my mother had family there, and that's where I finished growing up.

I had a wild streak when I was a young fella. Nothing like now, of course. We were innocent babes compared to what goes on these days. I won a car in a card game, a 1920 Ford Depot Hack, which was a kind of a station wagon fitted on a Model T chassis to haul passengers and luggage to train stations. This one had seen about all the depot hacking it was ever going to, but it had enough life left that I got plenty of speeding tickets tooling around Maryland, West Virginia, Virginia, Pennsylvania, and D.C. Course, back then speeding meant you were going thirty-five instead of thirty. I remember one time I got in a race with my best friend, Buster Flanagan, on what used to be the two-lane road to Gettysburg but is now U.S. Route 15. Buster had an old Oldsmobile, I believe it was a 1915 Model 42 Roadster, that had also seen better days, but he thought the world of it, was always challenging me and my Ford to the point where I got fed up and said okay, let's go. Of course, this was an illegal enterprise, and we had to have it during the day on account of Buster's car's headlights had gotten smashed in a previous accident and he didn't have the money for new ones. Well, we get to going side by side up what's now the turnoff to Libertytown but back then was nothing but woods and cow fields, and we come to that leftward curve, which to this day is too sharp, they need to iron it out. We're pushing forty, neither one giving ground, we're neck and neck all the way when all of a sudden Buster can't turn his Olds any sharper, and instead of rounding that curve he side-swipes my Ford and runs us both off the road. I flipped over and landed in the ditch, his car kept going and slammed into a tree, and neither one of us got a scratch. But about two minutes after Buster climbed out of his wreck and came over to see if I was alive or dead, that Oldsmobile caught on fire and blew up. Boom! You never saw anything like it. Except us trying to tell the police about how a herd of deer ran out on the road in front of us and we oversteered—both of us, mind you—over-steered and ended up in the rough. They didn't believe a word of it, but they couldn't prove otherwise so we got off scot-free. Except Buster, whose heart was broke; he'd still be mourning that old Oldsmobile today if he was alive. He died in 1959 of cirrhosis of the liver.

I didn't inherit my dad's mechanical bent, but I liked working with my hands, and my first good job was odd-job man to a house builder. After that I got into the carpenter trade. Which went bust as soon as the crash hit, rendering me and most people I knew unemployed. What growing up didn't cure of my former wild ways, the Depression did. I got by out of the kindness of a Mr. Abel C. Brooks, good friend to my mother's sister's husband. Mr. Brooks owned the ACB Hardware on what used to be Potomac Street in east Frederick. He gave me a job cleaning up and stocking, which turned into selling, then ordering, billing, and inventory, and eventually everything else, and in 1935 Mr. Brooks retired and offered me the business on terms so favorable I was just able to swing it. I stayed in the hardware game for forty-plus years, and retired in 1981 at age seventy-three.

Military-wise, I was 4-F because of my feet, so I volunteered in the civil defense and served as an air raid warden, 1942 to 1944, then chief air raid warden for Washington County, 1944 to VJ Day. I took a little ribbing, some people not considering that proper military service for an able-looking man, but I took pride in it and did as good a job as I could, and you notice the Germans never did bomb Frederick, Maryland.

I thought I'd end up a bachelor because until I was thirty-nine I never met a girl who could put up with me for long, or else me with her. I wasn't that particular, I just wanted someone down to earth and kind of heart who thought a little better of me than I deserved. Good looks wouldn't've hurt anything. Well, one day I'm helping the wire mill delivery man unload fasteners off his truck and the dang fool drops a keg of 16-penny nails on my foot. Broke it! I'm hollering like a baby, never been in such agony before or since, so he shoves me in the truck and drives me to the hospital. And there she was. I used to say it was the shot she gave me for the pain that disordered my brain and made me fall so hard, but that was a joke, I'd say it just to needle her. "Nurse Stanley," it said on her collar, and I had to pretend I was dying in order to get her to tell me her first name. Sarah. She said it laughing. She was so pretty, with yellow hair and light brown eyes, but Sarah saying her name and laughing is what made me fall in love.

It took a good deal of persistence, but finally she consented to a date and I took her to the Maryland Hotel to hear the Lewis Tranes Orchestra. She wore a green dress with a white collar and a matching jacket. She told me I was a good dancer, that was her first compliment to me, and that's when I knew for sure she wasn't only pretty, she was a most sweet and tenderhearted liar. We got married five months later.

I don't know what she saw in me, then or in all the forty-one years we had together. I can say in truth I never let a day go by without thanking the Lord for her, and although she's gone now I still do. If I made anything of myself, if I did any good or served any purpose, it's because of Sarah.

We had Daniel first, then William two years later with lots of complications, and after that we couldn't have any more. They were wonderful boys, and that's not just prejudice. They looked like Sarah, for one thing, brown-eyed blonds with her same soft nature and heart. Daniel died in Vietnam in 1969, age twenty. That's all I got to say about that, because even though so many years have passed since I lost my boy, it hurts exactly the same. Sarah's the only one I could talk to about it, and her not that much. She used to poke and prod me to open up, but even for her I couldn't do it. I still can't.

William's a good boy and he lives in Spokane, Washington, don't ask me why. He's an engineer, works with airplane parts and such. Says he's about to retire. He's got kids and his kids have got kids, but I never see them, they're too dang far away. We talk on the phone some.

So now I'm an old man, older than anybody I've personally known, and it's the most peculiar thing you can imagine. Inside I'm myself, same as always, and outside I'm this crippled-up old shell of a guy. By nighttime I'm used to myself, but when I first wake up in the morning and see that wreck in the mirror, there's a minute when I can't recognize him. "Who the hell are you?" I say, as I try to shave around all the wrinkles without cutting my chin off. Seems like I was in a car race with Buster a couple of years ago, not almost eighty. Wake House is a fine place and everybody's nice to me, and I'm a lucky man in that nothing much hurts except the usual, what you might expect, but I've got to say this is never how I pictured ending up. I only have one big regret, and it's that Sarah went ahead of me. I wish I could've gone first, it would've been more in the natural order of things.

But here I am, and if God's forgot about me, there's nothing to do but make the best of it till he remembers. Here's the part where I'm supposed to say something wise, I guess. I don't have any advice for anybody. Love the ones you've got while you've got 'em, because you never know how long that'll be. Stay on the level, try to treat everybody fair and square, because your name's worth more than your money. That's it. I wouldn't do anything different, and that's about as much as a man can hope for.

On Wednesday afternoons Claudette always led a game in the Blue Room, Pictionary or Trivial Pursuit, or sometimes a game she just made up. This day it was "Name That Friend"—Caddie vaguely remembered playing a version of it with girls in her dorm back in college days. You took turns being the guesser, and you had to figure out who the others were talking about when they answered questions like, If this person were a flower, what would he or she be? What color is this person? He/she is the sort of person who . . . fill in the blank. No doubt Claudette's object was to bring the residents of Wake House closer by exploring in creative, free-form ways how they really thought of each other. The possibility of pitfalls must never have entered her mind.

Everybody was there except Susan, whose boyfriend had taken her out for a drive, and Mrs. Brill, who had an eye doctor appointment. Somehow Caddie got talked into joining the circle of players, she wasn't sure how; one minute she was sitting with Nana on the sofa, thumbing through an old AARP magazine, and the next she was trying to decide what kind of vegetable Mr. Lorton was.

Thea came into the parlor after the game was in full swing. Everybody stopped what they were doing to greet her—"Hello, Thea," "Hi, Thea, where've you been?" "Thea, come sit over here." She was sorry to be late, sorry to interrupt the game, she'd just watch and not say anything—*No, no*, they wouldn't have it, she had to play, she would be so good at this—Cornel and Bernie shot out of their chairs and insisted she sit, sit right here, come over and sit down. "Thank you, thanks, I believe I'll just squeeze in here with Frances and Caddie." Nana moved her leg in her cast a little further down on the coffee table, Caddie moved the other way, and Thea sat down between them.

She always wore a faint, citrusy perfume, very lively and distinct, not like the powdery, old-fashioned scent the other women wore. She didn't dress like them, either. She wore jeans and a man's white shirt tied in front, she wore capes, berets at cocky angles, tight black capri pants with a long, bulky sweater. When the weather was nice, she went barefooted. "What's she think she is, a beatnik?" Caddie once heard Mrs. Doré Harris ask no one in particular after Thea had left the room. Nobody answered, nobody even nodded or said "Hmm." They liked Thea. If Doré didn't, Caddie was pretty sure it was because until Thea came, *she* was the youngest and prettiest of the ladies at Wake House.

Thea patted Nana on the knee. "You said you'd wake me up," she whispered. "I was just going to close my eyes for a second, I *told* you."

She made it sound conspiratorial, as if Nana had colluded with her in some fun but naughty adventure. Nana hadn't quite made up her mind about Thea ("Too young, and there's nothing the matter with her. What's she doing here?"), but she couldn't help smiling and shaking her head back at her. "Sorry," she whispered, shrugging, drawn in in spite of herself.

"Look at you," Thea said, turning to Caddie, "there's something different about you today. What is it?"

Caddie widened innocent eyes and opened her hands to show they were empty. *I might be in love*, she thought. Could Thea tell?

"What are we doing?" she asked in a murmur, leaning against Caddie's shoulder. "I don't understand the game."

No wonder. People were going around the circle saying things like "Thornbush" and "A holly tree with prickly leaves" and "A dead one!" Caddie whispered in Thea's ear, "Edgie has to guess who the mystery person is. It's one of us. If they were a tree, she just asked, what would they be. You take turns and go around—"

"So it's Cornel?"

Caddie covered a laugh with her hand. "How'd you get it so fast?"

They snickered together, looking over at Cornel, who was scowling around, not pleased with the picture of himself people were painting. He knew he was "it"—Claudette passed around a slip of paper with the name of the person each new guesser had to guess— so Cornel had to answer questions about *himself*, and either be honest and searching or pretend he was talking about somebody else to throw Edgie off. "Sturdy oak," he answered to the tree question.

Next Edgie asked, "What kind of *car* is this person?" and Bernie, Cornel's roommate, called out, "Hearse!" to general amusement. Somebody said "Model T," somebody else guessed "Rusty old Studebaker."

When Thea's turn came, she paused thoughtfully, a finger on her lips. "One of those cars that's been in a garage for the last forty years or so. Somebody finds it, and under all the dirt and grime there's a perfect vintage . . . something or other. A classic Cadillac. A Rolls-Royce."

Cornel blushed. Caddie wouldn't have believed it if she hadn't seen it.

Edgie finally guessed him—Caddie thought she'd known for a long time but enjoyed dragging the questions out—and Claudette sent around the next slip of paper. "Magill," it said, and Edgie's sister, Bea, was the guesser. "Complete the sentence," she said. "This is the kind of person who—"

"Shouldn't be here," Edgie answered promptly.

"You just want to hug," said Maxine.

"You just want to belt one," said Cornel.

Caddie thought for a second. "Makes me laugh."

Magill's turn. He had on baggy khakis and a gray T-shirt, and whoever had cut his hair last had taken too much off the sides. He looked like a POW. Pensively, rasping the whiskers on his unshaved chin, he said, "Bears an uncanny resemblance to Antonio Banderas."

Bea guessed him after the first round.

The next piece of paper said "Doré Harris." *Uh-oh,* Caddie thought. What kind of tree was this person, asked Bernie, the guesser. A tall, stately elm, someone said; somebody mentioned Japanese maple.

"Ginkgo," Maxine Harris answered with relish. "One of those

messy trees that drop their sticky leaves all over and make a nuisance."

Everybody made a point of not looking at Doré.

What kind of car?

"An Edsel," Maxine said.

What kind of jewelry?

"A choker."

What kind of person?

"The kind you better not turn your back on."

Doré got up and walked out of the room.

It almost ended the game. Awkward, embarrassed, fascinated silence fell; even Maxine looked a little shocked at herself. But pretty Claudette said, "Well! Plenty of names left, shall we keep going?" She pretended so well that nothing was amiss, people decided to believe her.

Another slip of paper went around, and Caddie read her name on it. The article of clothing she most reminded people of was a long, flowered skirt. Her tree was willow; three people said so, although two said sapling. Magill said a white dogwood tree—she liked that. Thea said, "Is mountain laurel a tree? I'm saying mountain laurel, because it's shy and blooms in the dark. It cheers up the forest."

Old Mr. Lorton was the guesser this time. Caddie thought he knew who it was already—they'd gotten pretty well acquainted when she'd written his "We Remember" piece—and he just wanted to keep the game going. "Fill in the blank," he instructed in his gruff voice—he had to clear his throat constantly. "This is the kind of person who . . ."

"Wears flannel pajamas," Maxine said. "I bet."

"Catches bugs and lets 'em go outside." Cornel pulled his mouth sideways to show he didn't think that was much of a compliment.

"Tips too much," said Bernie. "Never got a speeding ticket."

"People can talk to," said Edgie.

"People can ask a favor of," said Bea.

Magill sat with his elbows on his knees, hands loose and drooping between his spidery legs. "Laughs at your jokes whether they're funny or not. So you won't feel bad."

Caddie said, "Your turn, Nan."

"Hm?" She looked again at the name on her slip of paper. "What's the question?"

"This is the kind of person who . . ."

"This is the kind of person you clean your language up for when they're around."

All the men nodded.

Caddie was still smarting from flannel pajamas. "Loves to dance," she blurted out. "And sing in the shower. Really loud."

Thea went last. She looked down, smoothing the edge of the sofa with her hand. "Makes me wish for something I used to wish for all the time, before I got so old." She looked up, smiling. "That's all I'm saying, or you'll guess."

Mr. Lorton said he thought the person might be Caddie.

She sat still, trying to concentrate on the next person to guess but really replaying everybody's impressions of herself. No surprise that people liked her and said what they considered—she wasn't so sure—nice things about her; sometimes she felt like the house mascot, or as if she had eight or nine brand-new doting grandparents. It was nice to be clucked over—she never had been before. Thanks to Nana and Thea, they knew about Christopher, and now she couldn't have a conversation, not even hi, how are you, without being asked, "How's that new boyfriend? Taking good care of you, is he? When are you bringing him over so we can get a look at him?"

In a way, her life was perfect right now, because—it just occurred to her—really, she was living *two* lives: a child's and an adult's. The child had this big house she could come to any time she liked, full of kind, sympathetic parent figures who truly wanted the best for her, and meanwhile the adult had the most exciting lover she'd ever known, a wonderful, deepening relationship, and a sex life, a sex life that just . . . took her breath away. It was all so *sweet*. This was the best summer of her life. She wasn't exactly happy—how could you be happy when you were in love? It was too nerve-racking—but she was on the right track. Definitely moving in the right direction.

"Okay, people." Claudette stood up. "That's it, we've done everybody. That was fun, wasn't it? Okay, so for next week, I want you all to be thinking about your *best memory* from childhood. Everybody gets to tell their very best memory from when they were little—that's the game. Okay? Okeydoke!" She started clapping, a signal the game was over, time for people to get up and go on to their next activity.

"I'm going up to lie down for a while," Nana said.

"Need some help?"

"Nope."

Cornel came over and plopped down on the sofa. He'd taken pains with his wild, platinum-colored hair today, slicked it down with water or maybe even hair cream; Caddie could see the fine comb tracks in the shiny surface. He had bad posture, always hunched over and in your face, as if he might attack you. He was almost six feet tall, but he had no flesh left, just stringy muscles clinging to his brittle bones. His disposition was terrible, she'd never known anybody so crabby and sour. "Best memory," he growled, rubbing the shiny knees of his trousers. "Yeah, that's what I wanna hear, everybody's best memory. Can't wait."

Thea faced him, crossing her legs. She had on a pleated skirt, stockings, and loafers, and Caddie saw Cornel's critical eyes travel up and down her legs, which were still in excellent shape. She wrapped her hands around one knee and cocked her eyebrow at

128

him. "What would you rather hear, everybody's *worst* childhood memory?"

"*Haw*," he went, his version of a laugh. "Hell, yes, that'd be all right, wouldn't it? Going around the room telling our most miserable memories. Then you'd have something."

He looked so tickled, Thea laughed, too. "Cornel, what is your best memory? Tell it right now, because I don't expect we'll be hearing it next week."

"Damn right. Nobody's business." He'd scoffed at the idea of telling Caddie the story of his life for the memory book, too; "Wait'll I'm dead for my damn obituary" was the way he'd put it. "What's yours?" he demanded, pointing his chin at Thea.

Caddie sat back, out of their line of sight. She felt in the way.

"Oh, you'll have to wait. I'm a team player and I don't want to repeat myself."

"Haw." He ran his thumbs up and down behind his suspenders, tilting his head, squinting his eyes. Thinking. "Okay, I got mine. Want to hear it?"

"Why, I do, I surely do."

"It's the time my brother and me got stuck in the schoolhouse all night in a snowstorm."

"How old were you?"

"Ten, and Frank was eight. We'd stayed late to help Miss Kemper clean the stove. Wasn't a punishment," he wanted her to know, "it was a reward."

"For . . . ?"

"High marks and good behavior. Well, it started to snow around lunchtime, but in those days, of course, they didn't close school down because a few flakes fell."

"No, indeed. We were made of sterner stuff."

He eyed her, not sure if she meant that sincerely or not. "Anyway, Miss Kemper lighted out quick when it started to pile up, and we did, too, in the other direction, but before we got too far Frank fell over a log hid in the snow and sprained his ankle. Well, home's another mile and a half away, so we limped back to school, which was locked, so I crawled in through the cloakroom window and opened up for Frank."

Cornel was one of those people whose mouths form a little dot of spit in the corners the longer they talk. He took care of it by a quick sweep inward with his thumb and forefinger every now and then.

"Somehow we got the stove going again—good thing, because otherwise we'd've froze to death. Turns out it's a blizzard we're having. Foodwise, Miss Kemper's desk was a bust, not even an apple. We looked everywhere, every desk, every sweater pocket in the cloakroom, and all we came up with was four pieces of horehound candy, some redballs, and a Rocket toffee bar."

"Oh, I remember Rocket toffee bars," Thea said.

"I told stories to keep Frank from getting scared. Well, keep *me* from getting scared, too. We fell asleep sometime on our coats in front of the stove, hanging on to each other like a couple of bear cubs. Afraid and all, but excited, too. Wondering what was going on at home, how they were taking our absence. Well, about daybreak our dad busts in with his red face and his snowy hair, just a-*roaring* at us. Frightened us out of our wits."

He sat hunched over, contemplating his wrinkled hands, a faraway look in his eyes. He looked up when Thea said "Well," in a polite, uncertain tone.

"Well, see—" He cleared his throat harshly. "It's a good memory because he was so damn relieved. We cried and carried on, apologizing and explaining and justifying, but inside, we had this perfect kind of . . ."

"Joy."

"Well, anyway." He rubbed his cheeks, embarrassed by "joy." "Our big, scary papa had to shout to keep from crying in front of us, and we liked that. Liked being rescued and screamed at and pummeled and hugged . . ." His bony shoulders shrugged, nonchalant, under his pressed white dress shirt. "I just liked it. Never forgot it."

"No."

He tightened his lips. "Course, they're all dead now, Frank at age twelve in a stupid accident. They're all gone."

"And *your* family . . ."

"Dead. My wife and my son, Frank Junior." He used the sofa arm to stand up. "So what good does a happy memory do you?" He looked angry, duped.

"Oh, happy memories are nice enough," Thea said before he could make a solitary dramatic exit. "As long as we don't have to stop making new ones, that is. *I* for one am not through making memories."

"Hmph." He stood, indecisive. "Going outside. Nice day. Wanna sit with me?"

Was he inviting both of them or just Thea? Caddie had that third-wheel feeling again.

"In a minute," Thea answered. "I have to ask Caddie something."

"Right." Cornel saluted them and stalked out.

"Sheesh, what a grouch," Thea said, smiling after him. "Why do we put up with him?"

"Because he's sweet, deep down. Plus—I think he's got a crush on you," Caddie whispered.

"Oh, pooh." She laughed and flapped her hand. Either she didn't believe it or she was so used to men having crushes on her it didn't impress her. "Here's what I wanted to ask you—are you all booked up with students this summer?"

"No. Summer's my lightest season because everybody goes on vacation. Why? You want to take lessons?"

She was kidding, but Thea wasn't. "Yes, I do. Piano."

"*Really?*"

"Well, it's now or never. When I was little I wasn't interested, and when I grew up there wasn't time. Now there's nothing but time, and nobody I want to teach me but *you*."

"Oh, how fun! I'd love to. I'd *love* to."

"You are the *sweetest* girl," Thea said, and kissed her on both cheeks. "I absolutely adore you."

Mrs. Doré Harris didn't want Caddie to write her biography for "We Remember," she wanted to write it herself, "an *auto*biography," and have Caddie type it up on her computer. "I believe I'll write it in the third person, though, so it'll sound more *authentic*. Don't you think? And you can turn on that spell-check thing, but I bet you won't find a single mistake. Spelling's always been my forte."

Mrs. Stewart R. Harris was born Doré Arnette Sloan on April 2, 1927, in Spartanburg, South Carolina, the only daughter of Bynel and Eunice Sloan. Mr. Sloan distinguished himself over a long career in the wholesale feed and grain trade, and Mrs. Sloan, an accomplished musician, floral arranger, and amateur watercolorist, was also famous for her unique cooking and gardening skills, which took many prizes in local fairs and contests.

Doré was a lively, attractive, studious child with many friends and interests. Her best subjects were spelling, grammar, and math, so it's no surprise that upon graduation from Robert E. Lee High School she decided to go into the secretarial line of work. But she was also anxious to see more of the world, so when she was nineteen she moved to Washington, D.C., where she worked briefly for the phone company, honing her clerical skills. In 1948, she took a job as secretary-receptionist in the office of Dr. Drew McDonald, a noted podiatrist in the suburb of Wheaton, Maryland. Doré worked for Dr. McDonald until 1950, when the two became engaged and got married.

After a honeymoon in Miami, Florida, the couple moved into their new home in the Springfield section of Wheaton, where they particularly loved to entertain around the in-ground swimming pool. Doré was active in the Garden Club, the Welcome Committee, the Neighborhood Beautification Auxiliary, and the annual Springfield House Tour. In 1952, the couple gave birth to their only child, a beautiful daughter, Estella Doré. In 1956, Dr. McDonald was named Podiatrist of the Year by the Montgomery County Podiatry Association, and he was feted that year at the state convention in Annapolis.

In 1959, the couple separated, and in 1961 they were divorced.

Doré remained in the Springfield home for the next seven years, occupying herself with motherhood, neighborhood projects, and volunteer work, as well as trips to Paris, France; Vancouver, British Columbia; Reno, Nevada; and New York City.

In 1969, with Estella away at school (Shepherdstown College, Shepherdstown, West Virginia), and in search of a quieter, more contemplative life, Doré moved to Damascus, Maryland. There, to make herself useful and give meaning to her days, she took a part-time job at Nawson's Jewelers. In a short time she was promoted to assistant manager. More surprising still, a year later she became affianced to Clarence "Bud" Nawson, and the couple were wed on June 4, 1971.

Doré continued her volunteer and community activities in Damascus, and also enjoyed success and some acclaim as a model for the Mrs. & Older line of clothing at Jewell's Department Store. The Nawsons enjoyed vacations in Puerto Vallarta, Mexico, and Las Vegas, Nevada.

Tragically, their happiness was short-lived. In 1974, Bud, a lifelong smoker, was diagnosed with lung cancer, and in three months he was dead.

Grief-stricken, Doré sold the store and moved west again, this time to Michaelstown, where she bought a condo on Marshall Street and set about rebuilding her life. Never one to remain idle for long, and even though finances were not a problem, she soon found meaningful work in the accounts department at Harris Recreational Vehicles on Route 15. There the friendliness and camaraderie of her coworkers acted like a tonic on Doré's downcast spirits. She took up ballroom dancing, studied French at night at Boormin Community College, and renewed an old, neglected passion, Japanese flower arranging.

Fate took a surprising twist in 1978. Having vowed never to remarry, Doré could hardly believe it when she found herself falling in love again. Stewart R. Harris swept her off her feet, and after a short, whirlwind courtship, the couple flew to Acapulco, Mexico, where they became man and wife.

"With Stewart, I found what my heart had been searching for. We were a purely blessed union. I had never known such happiness, nor will I ever again. He was my Galahad, my Lancelot."

Stewart wanted to name their new Airstream, a wedding present, after his bride, but Doré insisted on calling it *Excalibur*. In it they took many an idyllic road trip, and Doré now has seen every state in the Union except Alaska, Hawaii, Vermont, Maine, and New Hampshire.

And so life passed in a happy glow, and as the couple's golden years beckoned, Stewart began to think more and more about retirement. They planned trips—Stewart had never been to Europe, unlike Doré—and joked about what he'd do with himself if he weren't selling RVs. In preparation for their new life, Doré finally retired from the Women's Auxiliary of the Michaelstown Key Club, where she had served for many years on the planning committee and one year as treasurer. Best of all, they bought their dream house: a four-bedroom split-level on three and a half semiwooded acres in the Tortoise Creek Hills subdivision.

And then, on June 4, 1988, thirteen days shy of their tenth wedding anniversary, tragedy struck again. While cutting the lawn on his riding mower, the John Deere Cadet Doré had given him for his combination birthday/housewarming present, Stewart suffered a massive heart attack. Paramedics were summoned, but to no avail. He passed away next to the lane of Leyland cypress trees he had planted along the driveway just one week before. Doré was kneeling by his side, holding his hand. His last words were, "Dodo [an endearment], I'll see you in heaven!"

"The rest isn't important," Doré says. "To tell the truth, I barely remember the nineties. Without Stewart, my soulmate, who loved me more than any man ever had or ever could, my life withered on the vine. Material possessions meant nothing to me, nor do they mean anything to me now."

Doré has been at Wake House since 2001, when heart trouble made living on her own too dangerous. Would she do anything differently? "What a question!" she says. "Who wouldn't? And yet, I do feel as if my life had a purpose, an arrow pointing me in one direction and one only: toward

Stewart Harris. If I had a second chance I would try to find him sooner, for it's when I met Stewart that my real life began. And his, too, I believe. True love is a fragile, rare thing, but we had it. Romeo and Juliet, Othello and Desdemona, Elizabeth and Mr. Darcy, Gatsby and Daisy, Ross and Rachel—I would add to that list Doré and Stewart Harris. Yes, I would! We had a love for the ages."

11

Thea arrived for her first piano lesson late on a Wednesday afternoon, and as she was coming in the wide-open front door, Angie Noonenberg was going out. Caddie introduced them. Afterward, Thea tossed her pocketbook on the living room sofa and exclaimed, "Oh, my, what a beautiful girl. Those *eyes*."

"I know. Too bad she's mad at me."

"Why?"

"Artistic differences." She explained about the Miss Michaelstown contest next December. "Angie's my best violin student, and now she's decided she doesn't like the piece by Massenet we've been practicing for the last six weeks, it's not *fun*. She wants to play . . ." She laughed; she could still hardly believe it. "She wants to play a *bluegrass fiddle song*. And sing!"

Thea laughed with her. "Well, what's wrong with that?"

"Oh, no, not you, too! But it's her decision, all I can do is advise her. Today I won, but who knows what she'll decide when the time comes."

Angie had been secretly practicing "Man of Constant Sorrow," the twangiest of twangy country tunes, and today she'd played the solo break and sung the song a cappella for Caddie for the first time. "Just *listen*, okay, just try to hear it with an open mind," she'd begged, then launched into a performance Caddie could truthfully tell her afterward was *soulful*. Angie had a pretty voice, but for "Man of

Constant Sorrow" she flattened it down to the thinness of ribbon, changing the lyric to "maid" and singing through her nose. With a lot of feeling, though—Caddie couldn't deny that Angie sang and played her bluegrass tune with more enthusiasm and emotion than she played "Meditation."

"I'm just disappointed," she confessed to Thea. "We've been together a long time. I've been watching her grow. She's got real talent, and I hate to see it go this way."

"But if she really *wants* to play the fiddle."

"I told her the judges won't take her seriously. She's going up against girls singing opera and dancing ballet. I told her the baton twirlers never win."

"Is that true?"

"I don't know. But it ought to be. Well, anyway—here you are."

"Here I am. Caddie, those lawn sculptures—I couldn't believe my eyes."

"I know. There's nothing I can—"

"They're fantastic, I *love* them."

"You don't."

"They're *wonderful*, so inventive and free. I recognized the one called *Birth Canal* from Frances's description. Aren't you proud of her? I think she's a phenomenon."

Caddie searched Thea's face to see if she was pulling her leg. "She's one of a kind," she agreed, inwardly wondering how Thea would like Nana's sculptures in *her* front yard. "Well, shall we start?"

Thea pulled up her shoulders on a deep inhale and patted her heart. "I'm nervous."

"No, this is going to be fun. Come and sit. Really, nothing but fun, that's why we're here."

"Yes, but have you ever taught a complete know-nothing before? Not a child, I mean a grown-up, a *fossil*."

"Beginning adults are easier to teach than kids. It's their idea, they've come willingly, they really *want* to learn. You don't read music at all? We're going to start very simply. Don't panic. This is the book I like to use for adult beginners, but if you don't—"

"Caddie . . ." Thea touched middle C with one of her pink-painted fingernails. She looked smart today in white slacks and a canary-colored blouse, her hair pulled back from her face with pretty combs. "At the risk of being as big a pain in the behind for you as Angie . . ."

"Uh-oh."

"I've been thinking about this since you said you'd teach me. I'm an old lady, I don't want to play the scales or learn music theory, I don't want to work my way up from 'Little Bo Peep.' "

"Oh, Thea." She could see trouble coming.

"Honey, I'm sixty-nine years old, I'm never going to be a real piano player. All my life I've wanted to play one song, sit down and entertain people with *one* song."

Oh, boy. "What?"

" 'Maple Leaf Rag.' "

Caddie put her head in her hands and wailed.

"I know! I know it's hard, but believe it or not, I'm musical. I can pick out melodies by ear, and I can already play the top part with one finger. If you'd just show me the chords on the bottom—"

"Oh, Thea! Do you know how hard it is to play ragtime?"

"I *do*."

"It sounds easy, but it's not, it's as hard as classical music for a beginner. You might as well say, 'Caddie, I just want to learn Beethoven's Ninth, that's all I want to play.' "

"Now, that is an exaggeration."

"Okay, but almost. It's the rhythm that's so tricky, you have to play a march tempo with your left hand and a very complicated syncopated beat with your right. Honestly, you could hardly pick a more difficult piece."

"But you could simplify it for me."

"There are simplified transcriptions, yes. All over the place."

"I really want to play it, and I've got nothing but time. I'll be the most conscientious student you ever had. Teach me."

"You don't look anywhere *near* sixty-nine years old."

Thea put an arm around her waist and hugged her. "Don't sidetrack me—will you teach it to me? Please?"

Caddie kept shaking her head, but then she laughed, helpless. "Okay, I'll try."

Thea clapped her hands.

"But *why*, of all the songs—"

"Because I love it! It peps people up. As soon as you hear it, you start tapping your foot and smiling. I want to learn it before I get so old I can't see the keys."

Caddie was getting excited in spite of herself. "I can make a recording, a simplified version you could listen to over and over, get used to before I show you how to play it. I've never taught without music before, I'm not even sure how we'll do it. How does it go? I don't even know what key it's in. A-flat? It's got four sections, they all do, rags, almost all, and they repeat." She hummed a few notes— "No, that's 'The Entertainer.' How does it go?"

Even Thea couldn't remember how it started. She put her hands over her ears. "Wait, hush, let me think."

They came up with it at the same time. "Bum bum—do-*do*-do-do-do—"

"Do-*do*-do-do-do!" Caddie played the first four measures with her right hand, and they burst out laughing.

"You see? It never fails!"

"You're right, it's happy music. But I can't play any more without the sheet music, I really can't." So there wasn't much more they could do at Thea's first lesson. "Would you like to have some coffee?" Caddie invited, and they adjourned to the kitchen.

Thea spotted an envelope from Wake House on the counter and tapped her fingernail on it. "You got one, too."

"Brenda's letter?" It had come yesterday. She apologized over and over, but the bottom line was, rates at Wake House were going up. "It's worse for you, Thea—you've hardly been here a month, and she's raising the price."

"Sounds like it's unavoidable. Repairs for staying certified, that kind of thing. Last week it was squirrels in the chimney, this week the roof leaks. Always something."

"I know, but still. It's a hardship."

"Are you and Frances . . ."

"We're okay. I worry about some of the others, though."

"Caddie, look." She froze in front of the window over the sink, pointing. "You've got a Baltimore oriole on your feeder. Oh—he flew away. Did you see him?"

"No. Well, wings, I saw something."

"They're getting so rare, and they used to be everywhere." She sat down in Nana's old chair at the scratched white metal table, and Caddie thought how natural she looked there, comfortable and relaxed, as if she were in her own kitchen. How long had it been since Caddie had had company, somebody in the house who was a friend, not a student?

"Are you a birder?" she asked. "Nana was, sort of. I put food out, but I don't pay much attention to who's who."

"Not me—Will was the bird-watcher. His lifelong hobby. He was so keen, and he knew *every*thing." She had wistful gray eyes that crinkled at the corners, even when she wasn't smiling. "I think of him all the time, but seeing a bird, oh my, just about *any* bird, that's a guaranteed memory."

"Will was your husband?" Thea nodded. "Did you lose him recently? I was thinking it had been some time."

"It was two years ago in February. February the eighth."

"You miss him a lot," Caddie said shyly, setting their cups on the table, sitting down in her old chair. "How long were you married?"

"Four years."

"*Oh*. Oh, I thought—"

"He wasn't my first husband. And we lived together for a couple of years before we got married." She sipped her coffee pensively. "He was nothing like the kind of man I ever thought I'd marry, but for the time we had together I'd never been happier. Which shows what I knew."

"What was he like?"

"Younger than me. Not too much, six years. And not successful, not in the way most people define success. The way *I* defined success—he was nothing like my first husband, in other words. Or my father, or my grandfather, the men in my life I'd always used as models."

"Thea," Caddie interrupted, "I could write your biography. You could talk to me just like this, and I could write it down for you."

"That's sweet."

"Want me to? It'd be fun."

"Oh, but then I'd have to reveal all my secrets."

"You keep secrets from *me*?" She mimed shock.

"Only the ones you don't need to know." Thea's smile was more tender than jocular. "Anyway, I'm too young for a biography! You'd have to keep updating it."

"You are, much too young. Do you have a picture of Will?"

"Not with me, I've got one at home." She gave a wondering laugh. "At *home*, listen to me."

"Does it feel like home already? It does to Nana, I think. Your room is fabulous." Thea's tower suite had the sun all day from three windows set deep in its graceful, rounded wall. "You must feel like a princess."

"Maybe one that's a little long in the tooth."

"Why did you come to Wake House? If I may ask," Caddie thought to add. "You're younger than anybody. You're healthy, you could be independent if you wanted."

"I'm getting macular degeneration in one eye."

"But still—"

"And arthritis in my toe, I told you. Don't laugh, it's disabling. I have to wear old-lady shoes or I hobble around like a cripple. But at least it's my toe and not my thumb—then I couldn't play 'Maple Leaf Rag.' "

"Seriously," Caddie pressed.

"Seriously." She sat back in her chair. "The house was so sad without Will. The nicest thing Carl, my first husband, ever gave me—he was a banker, a pillar of the community, we didn't suit at *all*—was our vacation home in the settlement. It's not very big or fancy, but it's old and lovely, and it's on the prettiest little creek. Heron Creek—near Berlin on the Eastern Shore. I went to live there after the divorce, and eventually I hired Will to dam up a little piece of the creek so I could swim there. That's how we met."

"How romantic."

"He was a handyman. That's how I found him in the want ads, under 'Handyman.' Oh, my, there wasn't anything he couldn't fix. Or make." She slid one finger around the rim of her cup, her face dreamy. "It started with me taking coffee out to him and talking with him while he worked. We were both divorced, but his was friendlier and his ex-wife had just died. So he was sad. He had a daughter, but she was married and living way out in Phoenix. Still does."

"You were both lonely."

"Well, *I* was. Will had more outlets." She laughed. "After he dammed up the creek, he built me a garden shed. Oh, you should see it, it's a work of art. Then it was bookcases for my bedroom, then a new chimney. When fall came, he went back to his *real* job— selling woodstoves and solar heat panels. *And* he was a poet."

"Goodness."

"I'd never met anybody like him, needless to say. He didn't care a thing about money, had no ambition except to enjoy his life—that's what drove wife number one crazy. 'It goes by so fast,' he'd say, 'I can't sleep through any of it.' That was his philosophy. One day we just drove up to Atlantic City and got married. Ha! He proposed to me in a poem. Oh, we were like teenagers. He made our wedding rings."

"Oh, Thea."

"I told you he could do anything."

"It's beautiful." Caddie had admired it before, an unusual ring of heavy, twisted gold.

"We had nine perfect years, which is more than lots of people get. The last one wasn't so good—he got cancer, and it killed him. 'You see?' he'd say. 'I told you it goes by fast. I didn't want to have to *prove* it to you, though.' " Her smile was full of melancholy.

"After he was gone, I waited two years—that's what they say, don't do anything, take no drastic steps after you lose your spouse for at least two years. And I found I couldn't stay in the house without him. So here I am, I've come home. This is the town I grew up in, you know."

"Where, what street?"

"I'll take you by it sometime, my aunt and uncle's house—I went to live with them after my mother died."

"How old were you? When your mother died?"

"I was nine."

"Oh, Thea—"

"But that's another story. A *long* story. Hey, you're worming my biography out of me!"

"I wasn't trying to, honest. But, Thea, I was nine when my mother died, too."

"Were you?" She looked at her with warmth and interest and no surprise. "Then we have something sad in common." She stroked her finger lightly over the top of Caddie's hand. "Remember that game we played? The one where we had to describe each other?"

Caddie made a face. "When I found out I'm the kind of person who wears flannel pajamas and never gets a speeding ticket."

"Oh, did that hurt your feelings?" Thea chuckled. "When it was your turn, I said you made me wish for something again. Something I used to wish for, but then I got too old. Do you know what it was?"

Caddie shook her head, but she did know. She hoped.

"Carl and I wanted children so badly, but in those days there weren't as many miracles as there are today, so—we just couldn't. And now look. In my old age, my *golden years*, look what I've found. I hope that doesn't embarrass you."

"No. No." Caddie kept her gaze on their touching hands, not quite able to look Thea in the eye. It hardly ever happened that she got her heart's desire. "I feel the same," she said in a murmur. "I didn't have much of a mother. She was a musician. Always leaving. Always . . ."

The phone rang.

"I didn't call in the middle of a lesson, did I?"

It was Christopher. "Hi, no, it's fine. I have company, though."

Thea made a knowing face. She pointed to herself, pointed to the dining room door, started to get up.

Caddie walked over, pulling the tangled phone cord tight, and pressed her back down. "It's my friend Thea, from Wake House. We're just having coffee, sitting here having such a nice—"

"I only have a sec," Christopher interrupted. "I've got an appointment. Just wanted to make sure we're still on for the weekend before I make the reservation."

"We absolutely are."

"You canceled what you had to cancel?"

145

"Yep." Nine lessons, three on Friday afternoon, six on Saturday. Rescheduling had been a nightmare.

"Excellent."

She could hear the smile in his voice. "Excellent," she repeated, grinning like the Cheshire cat.

"Okay, then we're on."

"Who's driving? I don't mind driving."

He laughed heartily. "That piece of junk? No, thanks, I'll drive."

"I resent that—my car's a classic."

"Classic piece of junk."

She started giggling and couldn't stop. This was how most of their phone conversations went, at least on her end.

"Drive it over to my place tonight, though," he said in a different voice. "I'm dying to see you."

"Well, I don't know, what if it broke down? Maybe I shouldn't take the chance."

She wanted to keep on teasing him, but he had to go. "See you tonight," he said, and hung up.

"That was Christopher."

"I gathered," Thea said dryly. "Are you going on a trip?"

"I'm so excited—we're going to Washington for the weekend. He's only been once, when he was a little boy, so I'm going to show him around."

"I am *dying* to meet this man."

"I'll bring him to Wake House soon—he wants to come. He'll probably bring King—that's his dog I told you about."

"The perfect dog for the perfect man."

"Oh, Thea. Wait till you meet him." She gave a tight-shouldered shrug of excitement.

"Is this getting serious?"

"I don't know! *I'm* serious. Oh, God, I'm so . . . I finally get what they're talking about in love songs." She blushed. "I mean, I always *got* it, but now—I'm *having* it."

"Ah, that stage. You never forget it. What's he like, this Christopher?"

"Well . . . he's very handsome."

"Of course."

"He's serious, but he's also funny. He's a really *good* person. His whole life is like one long good deed, and that makes him happy. I think people who love what they do are so lucky, don't you? It's what *makes* them good. You can't be mean or unkind or nasty if you *love* your work. Anyway, that's my theory."

"Don't you love your job?"

"Well, sometimes. And I'm pretty good at it—that's satisfying."

Thea put her elbow on the table, chin on her hand. "What's missing?"

Caddie hesitated. It was easier to talk about Christopher.

"What would you be if you could be anything?" Thea asked.

She laughed. "Regardless of skill, you mean."

Thea shrugged. "What would you be? Still a musician?"

"Oh, yes. It's my only talent."

"Well, what kind of musician? If you could be *anything*."

She laughed again—to show in advance that this was all a joke. "Okay, I have this fantasy. That I'm singing the blues in a smoky jazz club. You know, Billie Holiday, Peggy Lee. I'm a lounge singer!"

Thea didn't laugh. She narrowed her eyes. "Oh, yes, I can see it. You in a slinky black dress with that blonde hair—stunning. Do you sing?"

"Not like Billie Holiday! Ha! No, and anyway, pop music isn't for me, I'm completely classical, that's the kind of person I am. It's all I know, and really, it's all I want to know. It suits me."

Thea raised a skeptical eyebrow.

"Plus I get terrible stage fright," she confessed. Might as well tell Thea everything.

"Stage fright? Really?"

"I used to play the violin in the Michaelstown Community Orchestra, but I had to give it up. Terrified."

"Why?"

"I don't know! I wasn't even *first* violin. I just—" She gave a mock shudder. "I'm too self-conscious, and then I get scared. So I just don't play in front of people anymore."

"What a shame. Do you know why Henry took up skydiving?"

"What?" The question was so unexpected, she couldn't think.

"Do you know why Henry took up skydiving?"

"No. Why?"

"Because," she said distinctly, looking straight into Caddie's eyes, "he was afraid of heights." She got up and carried her cup to the sink. "My cab's coming. I'd better wait by the door so I can see it."

Caddie followed her out to the hall, frowning. She didn't much care for parables. If Thea had advice for her, she wished she'd just come out and say it.

"So you're going to simplify my song, right?"

"Yes, I'll either find or make a very rudimentary version, and I'll tape it, record me playing it. Probably in a different key, something easier than whatever it's in. For some reason I keep thinking A-flat major."

"And you're going to record it *slowly*."

"Very slowly. Dirgelike. And we'll use that for our starting point. I have no idea how this is going to work—I hope you won't be too disappointed, Thea, if it doesn't. But I have to tell you, you've chosen one of the worst songs in the world for your one and only song."

"But it *is* going to work! You worry too much."

"But I think it's wonderful that you want to learn it, I really—"

148

"You mean, *at my age*."

"Yeah. No—I mean——"

"I agree with you, I'm very admirable." She leaned against one side of the screen door, Caddie leaned against the other. "And this is only *one* thing I want to do. I've got a whole list."

"You do? What else is on it?"

"Well, one thing, I definitely want to smoke weed."

Caddie's eyes bulged.

Thea laughed gaily. "I do! Everybody in the whole world has smoked pot but me, and I want to try it. You don't have a dealer, do you?"

"A *dealer*?"

"Or know of one?"

"Sorry."

"I know—I'll ask Magill."

"Good idea," Caddie said, chortling with her. "He's probably got a secret stash in his room."

"Or a plant."

The taxi pulled up.

Thea got halfway down the walk, turned, and spread her arms wide. "How," she called back, "*how* could you not love these sculptures? Look at them!"

"I have. Every day for years!"

She shook her head. "Bye—thanks for the lesson. If I don't see you before the weekend, have a *grand* time in Washington."

"Oh, I will."

Thea cupped her ear.

"I'm planning to!"

Dolores, Mrs. Brill's youngest daughter, drove up from the Washington suburbs once a week to visit. When she heard Caddie was writing down Wake House residents' life stories, she asked if she would mind writing her mother's. Caddie said yes, gladly. Mrs. Brill talked about the weather, about flowers, and about the food at Wake House—if it was good; if it wasn't, she said nothing—and she sympathized with other people's physical ailments but wouldn't discuss her own (which must be numerous, since she was forever going to some doctor's appointment or other). What she never talked about was her personal life, and Caddie was curious. And "Sunday School Teacher, Retired" was a pretty skimpy biography—she was sure she could do better.

They sat out on the front porch on a clear, sunny day, Mrs. Brill, Dolores, Caddie, and Dolores's seven-year-old daughter, Keesha. Caddie planned just to jot down notes while Dolores chatted with her mother, drawing out dates and major events of her life, but pretty soon she could see things weren't going to be that easy.

"Mama," Dolores began, "when were you born?"

"Now, I don't see why anybody needs to know *that*." Mrs. Brill had a daunting way of holding her head back and looking down at you through thick glasses that magnified her eyes and made them seem closer to the lenses than they really were. And she always looked like she was either on her way to church or just getting back.

Dolores didn't look like her at all. She was a thin, nervous woman in her early fifties, with smart gray eyes and the longest fingernails Caddie had ever seen. Today she had on white capri pants and platform shoes, and a soft perfume that smelled like lilacs. When she turned her head, rows and rows of beads in her hair clacked like dice. "Uh-oh," she said, crossing her legs and setting her chair to a fast rock. "Question number one, and we're stuck already."

Mrs. Brill hesitated, then gave a regal shrug. "September the fifth, nineteen and twenty."

"She's a Virgo," Dolores told Caddie.

"Well, *that* I don't hold with. What I am is a *Baptist*."

"What was your maiden name?" Caddie asked.

"Dwiggins."

"And your first name?" She'd never heard it, she realized; nobody called Mrs. Brill anything but Mrs. Brill.

"Eula Bernice."

"Tell where you were born and so on, Mama," Dolores said, "don't make her drag it out of you."

"Alamance County, North Carolina, a little town called Ossipee."

"And you were the seventh of nine children," Dolores prompted, "and your father was a preacher. The fire-and-brimstone kind."

"He was a minister of the church," her mother corrected, with a frown. "We were all in the choir, all nine of us. Papa farmed, too; not tenant land, either, he owned his own plot and raised vegetables and chickens. We all went to school and were expected to do well, and we did."

"Except for Uncle Clay. And Aunt June."

"I won't hear ill spoken of the dead." She put one hand on her walker, as if to remind everybody she could get up and go anytime she wanted.

"Well, shoot, Mama, you're the last one. If we can't speak ill of the dead, we can't speak ill of anybody."

Keesha giggled.

Mrs. Brill turned her intimidating scowl on her granddaughter, then smiled.

"You lived in Ossipee till you were ten," Dolores prodded, "then what?"

"Well, it was the Depression, people couldn't make a living doing what they used to do, so we moved, all of us except my sister Martha and my brother Tom, who were both married and had families by then. The rest of us moved up north to Wilmington, Delaware, and Papa gave up preaching and found work in a factory that made ready-to-install windows."

151

"Was it hard to leave home?" Caddie asked. "Or exciting?"

"It was hard, because I dearly loved that farm. Seemed to me like everybody was happy there and living a godly life. I think back on that time now and it feels like paradise."

"And Aunt Calla," Dolores said softly.

"My sister, the nearest in age to me, the one I was closest to, she got a lung disease the first year we were in Wilmington, a dirty, filthy city, and she passed away. Twelve years old. So you could say it was hard leaving home." She pressed her wrinkled lips together and reared her head back further.

"Mama, tell about the time you saved the little white girl on the pony."

Keesha, who'd begun to fidget, sat up at that. "You saved a white girl, Neenie?"

"You didn't know that about your old granny, did you? No, I'll tell that story later, honey, it's not the kind of thing I want for this history Caddie's doing."

"Oh, Mama, why not? It's just *exactly* the kind of thing *I* want for it."

"Maybe, but it's not your history. Besides, if Caddie wrote down every little thing that happened to me, we'd be here a week."

"But this wasn't a little thing. Caddie, when she was eleven, she saved a little girl's life—the girl fell off her pony and Mama found her and carried her two miles to the hospital in a wagon. She got a reward from the family, and it was even in the newspaper. It's a *wonderful* story—"

"Which I will tell my granddaughter one of these days when I'm feeling up to it. Now, the next event that happened was my first marriage, and the less said about *that* the better."

"What? But you haven't even mentioned being in show business yet!" Dolores's hair beads rattled in protest.

"In *show* business," Caddie said in amazement. Mrs. Brill?

Even Keesha knew about that. "Neenie, tell about the lady you used to sing with."

"Oh, well, that's nothing much. I had a brief singing career with my friend Ruth Nash. It was the early 1940s and we called ourselves the Melody Sisters. The most famous place we ever played in was the Sweet Club in Harlem, which of course nobody ever heard of nowadays. Then in '44 I got married to K. C. Meecham, a bass player, and had my first child the next year. End of my singing career. We had three more children, and then we had a parting of the ways. Ruth got sick and died of TB in 1948."

Dolores folded her arms. "This is the most—*discreet*, the most *boring*—"

Mrs. Brill gave a loud, threatening cough that silenced her.

"I worked as a maid for three different white women while I raised my children, and in 1952 I got married to Lewis Johnson, a milkman, who had two young children of his own. We moved to Baltimore because he had people there, and I had my last child in 1953."

"Me," said Dolores.

"That was another marriage that didn't work out, my last—"

"Meaning I never saw my father after I was five years old," Dolores said with some bitterness.

"My last, I swore, and I went through the sixties and seventies very happily without benefit of male companionship."

"Did you have any other jobs?" Caddie asked.

"Well, since I had five children under the age of thirteen plus Lewis's two, I guess I did. Different things, I sold Avon, magazine subscriptions, once I sold Kirby vacuum cleaners." She started counting them out on her fingers. "I was a cashier at a lunch counter, I worked at a dry cleaner's. Salad girl in a restaurant till my feet gave out, then I did phone solicitations. Then, in 1963, I went on disability."

"At least tell her how that happened," Dolores said.

"An accident."

Dolores sighed. "She was working as an elevator operator in an old office building downtown and the elevator dropped from the second floor to the basement."

Keesha came back from examining a spiderweb behind the glider. "Did you get hurt?"

Mrs. Brill's prominent black eyes softened behind her glasses. "Little bit, mostly my knees."

"Were you scared? Was anybody else with you?"

"I was all by myself and scared half to death. One thing I learned, it doesn't do any good to jump up and down—you remember that if you're ever on a falling elevator."

"Did it hurt when you landed?"

"Goodness, child, what do you think? It hurt like about if you jumped off the top of this building."

"Did you pray?"

"I surely did. Not a very long prayer." She winked at Caddie. "Like this: Oh, Lord—*bam!*" She chuckled and rubbed her knees. "Well, then time went on, and I met my third and last husband, Mr. Marcus A. Thompson."

"A for Aurelius," Dolores contributed. "Time went on? You left out seeing Martin Luther King Jr., you left out Lloyd's death—that was her second child—"

"I'll come back, just let me get through to the end first."

"She has a *plan*," Dolores said to Caddie, making a sarcastic face she was careful not to let her mother see.

"The third time's supposed to be the charm, and when you get married again at sixty-two, it better be. Mr. Thompson was a retired bus driver—"

"And she called him that," Dolores said in a soft voice, so as not to interrupt the flow, " 'Mr. Thompson,' the whole time they were married."

"A retired bus driver, a very handsome, sharp-dressed older man I would not have given the time of day to if he hadn't been a deacon at my church."

"Where you taught Sunday school," Dolores put in.

"Yes, I certainly did, for nineteen years. Didn't retire till 1989. What was I saying?"

"Mr. Thompson was a deacon," Caddie said.

"Yes, and so when he invited me to come have coffee after service and school was over one Sunday, I said why, yes, I would, although ordinarily I would not have had any truck with a man who looked like he did or took such care with his dress."

"Why?"

"Red flags to a bull. I had married two good-looking men, and I did not want a third, not at my age. But Mr. Thompson, who had recently lost his wife of fifty-one years, was sewed from a different cut of cloth entirely. Mr. Thompson was a gentleman."

"*And* he was seventy-six," Dolores mentioned.

"But fit and spry, not decrepit one bit," Mrs. Brill defended, "and a hardworking man to boot. Dedicated. Saw his wife through her last illness like a saint. We courted very slowly—well, for our age it was slow, half a year—and when he finally popped the question I said yes."

"Where were you?" Caddie thought to ask. "When he proposed."

Mrs. Brill reared her head back. "Where were we? Well, gracious, we were in the graveyard, if you want to know. The man put flowers on his wife's grave every Sunday, and I'd taken to going with him."

"He proposed to you in front of his wife's grave?" Dolores said, round-eyed. "You never told me that."

"I didn't think a thing of it. Didn't seem peculiar to me, seemed natural. We got married on May the eleventh, a raining-cats-and-dogs day, and took the train up to New York City for a honeymoon weekend. That was a time, oh my." She got a hankie out of the sleeve of her dress with fumbling fingers.

"We had three good years before his health began to fail. Peaceful, soft time. I'm blessed for that, and still grateful. But his heart, his lungs, his blood, they all let him down, seemed like all at the same time. He had a sister in Michaelstown, Juanita, who'd just lost her husband, and she said come on out here, the two of us women could take care of Mr. Thompson better than me alone with my knees in Baltimore, so that's what we did. We lived in her house on Acorn Street, me and Mr. Thompson on the first floor, until he passed away in 1994. His sister two years later. I ended up here, and there endeth the story. Just in time," she said, blotting her cheeks with the handkerchief, "because I am about parched dry. Lamb, run inside and get me a big, tall glass of ice water."

Keesha stared at her with wide, worried eyes, as if she'd never seen her grandmother cry before.

"Run, child."

Keesha ran in the house.

"Are your other children nearby?" Caddie asked after a respectful moment. "Or scattered all over?"

"Mostly scattered. That's the way it is with children nowadays."

Dolores looked like she could say something about that.

"Lloyd, my second child, passed away thirty years ago. He was only twenty-three. That's still my life's biggest sorrow, to this day."

"How many grandchildren do you have?"

She worked her lips, thinking. "Eight."

"Nine," Dolores corrected. "Clarence and Virginia had another girl two months ago."

For a moment Mrs. Brill looked shocked. Had she forgotten? Or had she never known? Then her face went stony.

"Mama was awfully strict," Dolores said softly, quickly. "I was the

156

baby, so I missed most of it. Compared to the others, I was spoiled."

"What? Speak up, I can't hear what you're saying."

"I was just—I was trying to explain why there's some friction, you know, Mama, between you and Clarence and you and Belinda—"

Mrs. Brill took a sharp breath and drew herself up. "That is family business. I won't have that written down. *I won't have it.*"

"I won't write it," Caddie said quickly.

"She could just put 'estranged,' " Dolores said. "She should put *something* in to explain why you've hardly seen your own—"

"Dolores, now, that will be *enough*."

Keesha came out on the porch, holding a brimming glass with both hands. "It's nice and cold, Neenie."

"Thank you, lamb pie." She took a few gulps and set the glass on the arm of her chair.

Caddie sensed the silence might go on forever unless she broke it. "What sort of songs did you and your partner sing? You and—" she looked at her notebook—"Ruth Nash."

"All kinds. People think all black people can sing is blues or gospel, or nowadays rap, but we sang beautiful, tuneful songs, some written by black people, some written by white people. Ruth played the piano and I played the banjo and the ukulele, and our theme song was 'Goodnight, Sweetheart.' We loved all kinds of music. People would tell us we'd never get anywhere if we didn't specialize, but we didn't want to settle down to one style. We liked jazz, country, pop, swing—blues, yes, and gospel. We liked a barbershop quartet, and you can't get much whiter than that."

"No," Caddie agreed. "But then you gave it all up for a man," she said, hoping Mrs. Brill wouldn't take offense.

"Yes and no. I knew Ruth from the time I was sixteen; we were best friends, just did everything together. Such dreams we had, oh my goodness. For a couple of years, 1941 and '42, smack in the middle of the war, of all things, it seemed like they were all coming true. But Ruth took up some bad ways, habits she didn't have it in her to shake, and we started to lose what we had. Innocence or whatever you want to call it. We were so young."

She sighed and slipped her arm around Keesha's waist. "Well, wasn't anything else *to* do then except marry K.C.—who was not altogether a bad man, I don't mean to say he was, and we had four wonderful children together. But he came from New York City and I came from Ossipee, North Carolina, and never the twain shall meet. Lord help us, Caddie, aren't we about done?"

"Life lessons," Caddie said hastily. Mrs. Brill was rubbing her knee as if it ached. "Words of wisdom to pass on to your descendants. Or—what would you change if you had it to do over again?"

"Gracious me, just because you get old doesn't mean you get smart."

"You've *always* been smart," Keesha said.

"Child." She laughed and gave her granddaughter a squeeze. "What are you angling for, another candy bar?"

"Life lessons." Dolores eyed her mother with interest. "I'd love to hear what you'd do different."

"I'd raise me some more sweet grandbabies like this one." She and Keesha put their foreheads together and mashed noses.

"What else?"

"Hmm." She sipped some more water. "Let me think."

"Would you skip Lewis Johnson entirely?" Dolores asked, arching an eyebrow.

"Sakes, of course not. First of all, then I wouldn't have you. Or Belinda or Lewis Junior—those are my stepchildren," she reminded Caddie. "But second of all, just because they didn't last doesn't mean I wouldn't marry both those two men again. But I don't hold with thinking up things you'd do different, anyway. The Lord gives us just the one life, and we do the best we can with it. Which to me means living by the commandments and trying to put a distance between us and sin. Faith, hope, and charity, and the greatest of these is charity—that's my favorite teaching. I suppose my papa didn't preach it often enough in his church all those years ago, but they were different times. You learn it over your life, and the closer you come to the end, the clearer it gets, all the rest just fades away. Love and forgiveness, that's what it comes down to."

"I'll tell my stepsister," Dolores murmured.

"What's that?"

"I said, tell about seeing Sonny Liston. And Martin Luther King—Mama took the bus down to Washington to hear him give his 'I have a dream' speech, Caddie."

"Indeed I did. Gave me the chills. If you want to talk about famous people, I once saw Eleanor Roosevelt, too. Do you know who that is, Keesha?"

"No, ma'am."

"A great, great woman. *Unappreciated* woman." She wiped the condensation from her glass with her handkerchief. "I always felt in tune with her, myself. Connected under the skin, even though Mrs. Roosevelt was a white lady."

12

Soon after their return from the weekend in Washington—which was idyllic, magical, *rapturous* as far as Caddie was concerned—Christopher stopped calling.

She didn't think much of it at first, didn't even particularly notice, because he'd already told her he was in a crazy time at work; a lot of things that had been in the planning stages were coming to a head all at once, and he was the only one who could deal with them. Caddie sympathized and admired his dedication all the more. His office was criminally understaffed. Except for Phyllis, the woman she'd met that night at the softball game, Christopher was the only paid employee at the Michaelstown office of CAT, and he was already doing the work of at least two people.

One of the nicest things that had happened over the weekend was that Christopher had let his hair down, so to speak, and confided to her what he really wanted to do with his life. It was their last night, and they were having dinner in a restaurant near the hotel when he told her: he wanted to be a national spokesperson for the CAT cause.

"You mean, not work with dogs anymore?" *What a waste*, she'd thought, *what a loss!* But she was thinking too small. He'd explained it to her, how much broader his influence could be and how many more people he could reach if he put his energies into public relations. Headquarters was all for it; in fact they'd been grooming him for a bigger role for some time. They wanted him to spearhead a new public awareness campaign that would be nationwide and start next year. It would mean a lot of media exposure, and not just print interviews but radio and TV, too.

Caddie was impressed, then enthusiastic. "Absolutely, you'd be fabulous. You're so articulate and smart. And passionate and committed. I can't think of anybody who'd be a better spokesman than you. Oh, I can just *hear* you on NPR. Christopher, you could be *famous*."

"The point isn't to be famous, Caddie, it's to draw attention to issues of fund-raising and grant money and grassroots educational programs. Growing the organization."

He might disapprove of being famous, but he was ambitious, she knew from his intensity when he spoke of his prospects. In fact, that was what they'd mostly talked about while they were in Washington, approaching it from different angles and perspectives, but always coming back to the subject of Christopher's professional future. He'd had a good time—she was sure, because all weekend she'd monitored his happiness and well-being like an ICU nurse. So when it first began to sink in that he wasn't calling or returning her calls, she knew it wasn't because of the weekend. Good, because if it wasn't the weekend, it wasn't *them*. But then, what?

Wednesday turned into Thursday. Could he be out of town? No, because late in the afternoon, thank goodness, she finally reached him at his office.

"*Hi*," she said, letting a note of amazement harmonize with the gladness, a vocal invitation to explain why he'd been all but mute for four days. "How *are* you? What's been happening?"

He sounded harried, but as soon as she heard his voice she calmed down. Oh, everything was fine. She pictured him at his desk, holding the phone to his ear with his shoulder while he sifted through files and papers. Her Christopher, the same as always, and she'd been an idiot to get so worked up. "Hi," he said, "yeah, it's really been nuts around here, everything coming down at once."

"Well, I *figured.* I've missed you. Are you all right?"

"Yeah, fine, just incredibly busy."

"Sure. Sure. Well, would you like to do something? Come to dinner tonight or something? I *can* cook, you know." He never came to her house; they always ate at his place or went to a restaurant.

"No, sorry, it's impossible tonight. I'm snowed."

"Oh, okay. Well, maybe one night over the weekend. Hey, I could *bring* you dinner," she realized. "You have to eat sometime, and that way you wouldn't waste time—"

"Let me call you, okay? It's so hectic right now, I can't plan."

"That's fine, I love spur of the moment. Well, so. How are you? I've been playing some of the CDs you lent me. I love the Saint-Saëns especially. It's really—"

"Caddie, I can't talk right now."

"Oh!"

"I'll call you."

"Okay!"

"I'll call you as soon as I can."

"Great."

That was on Thursday. He didn't call that night. She skipped her usual Friday morning visit with Nana in case he called then, but he didn't. Not on Saturday, either. She couldn't believe it; if one of her students hadn't called to reschedule a lesson, she'd have thought her phone was broken. She spent Saturday evening reconstructing everything they'd said to each other—which was almost nothing—since he'd dropped her off six days ago, kissed her goodbye on the front porch, and driven away, promising to call. "I'll call you." He'd said that after she'd told him what a lovely time she'd had, the *best*. He'd agreed—"I had a great time, too, Caddie. *I'll call you.*"

Sunday morning, she woke up with a headache. Rain sluiced down the kitchen window from a stopped-up gutter, and on the bird feeder a thrush or a sparrow or something huddled under the slanted roof, pecking at damp seed. She was washing the greasy popcorn pot from last night's dinner, not thinking about anything, when all of a sudden she turned off the water and reached for the phone, hands dripping. Christopher's number rang four times before his machine picked up.

"Oh, hi, it's me. Caddie. Just calling to say—hi, hope you're fine. Call when you get a chance. See you. Bye."

Maybe he was on his way over. Sunday morning—he was probably either out walking King or on his way over. "I look awful!" she said to her reflection in the watery window, and she ran upstairs to get dressed. She put on jeans and the dark green blouse he'd admired once. She washed her face and put on lipstick. "Bleck." She looked like a corpse with a red mouth. She wiped the lipstick off.

She took Finney out, hoping he would take care of his business among the sculptures in the yard and scamper right back inside; that's what he usually did when it rained. But not today, oh no, all he wanted was to drag her behind him down the sidewalk, and he didn't mind strangling himself to do it. She'd come out without her umbrella; by the time they returned from a trip around the block, she was as soaking wet as if she'd taken a shower in her clothes. Drying Finney off with a smelly old towel, the thought came to her that she might've just missed Christopher. He'd had exactly enough time to arrive, run up to the door in the rain, knock, get no answer, race back to his car, and drive away.

She waited fifteen minutes, plenty of time for him to get home. Then she dialed his number again.

No answer. She didn't leave a message.

Wake House was quiet, practically empty downstairs, and no one was on the front porch because of the rain. She waved to Cornel in the Red Room and started for the stairs, but just then Brenda came into the hall from her office, heading for the kitchen. She had a wrench in one hand and a plunger in the other. The plumbing was always on the fritz somewhere, and unless it was a major breakdown, she was the plumber.

"Hey, Caddie. Looking for Frances? She went to church. Good thing, because the elevator's acting up. I've got the man coming any second."

Caddie paused with her foot in midair on the first step. "Nana went to church?"

"Yeah, Claudette took her in the van with Bea and Edgie and the others. Mrs. Brill, Bernie—"

"What church?"

"Unitarian."

Ah.

"It's the only one they could agree on."

"Is Thea here?"

"She's sleeping." Brenda looked wistfully out at the gray day. "Isn't it a perfect day for a nap?"

So then Caddie didn't know what to do with herself. She'd have tidied up Nana's room, but she'd been forbidden to touch anything—so had the cleaning staff; they were only allowed to change the sheets and clean the bathroom—so there was no point in going up there.

Magill—he must be here. Except when he went to see Dr. Lieberman, he was always here.

Through his open door, she saw him lying in bed with the covers up to his chin. "You asleep?" she whispered under the sound of an old movie on his TV set.

He smiled even before he opened his eyes. "Caddie. Hey." He hoisted himself up by the elbows. "Come on in."

"Just for a minute, I have to— Oh, no! What happened to you?"

Through his shaggy hair, she could see a bandage over his right eyebrow half covering a swollen, plum-colored bruise. He had a black eye, too. "Yikes, what did you *do*?"

"Fell. It's not interesting." He patted the side of the bed. "Sit."

"How? Where?"

"Second-floor landing. Missed a couple of steps, *whap*."

"Why didn't you take the elevator?" She sat down on his bed gingerly, in case he'd injured parts she couldn't see. "I bet you weren't wearing your helmet, either. What else did you hurt?"

"You left out, 'Were you drinking?' Then you'd *be* Brenda."

"Yes, but she's probably worried about a lawsuit."

"And you're worried about me." When he lifted his eyebrows hopefully, he winced.

"Well, look at you. Look at all this *food*." The tray on his bedside table hadn't been touched. "How are you going to get well if you don't eat?"

"Where've you been? I haven't seen you in a month."

"You saw me last week. What else did you hurt?"

"Nothing, my knee. How was your weekend with Timmy?"

She studied her fingernails. "Great. We saw the monuments, went to some interesting restaurants. Walked around." She met his eyes for a second, then looked away. "It was great."

"What went wrong?"

"Nothing, I told you. Don't call him Timmy."

"You don't look so good."

"Thanks. Look who's talking." Both of his eyes, not just the black one, were bloodshot. The pillow had pushed his hair up in patches, and the disreputable beard stubble on his cheeks made him look more unstable than rakish. Thea didn't believe his problems were physical, or not all of them. She thought he'd shut down his senses after the accident to punish himself. That's why he couldn't hear sometimes, couldn't taste or smell his food, literally couldn't see straight—he thought he belonged in prison, she said, so he'd made one out of his own body.

"What good does making yourself sick do?" Caddie blurted out.

"What?"

She looked down, afraid she'd crossed a line. "I just want you to . . . straighten up." She laughed, to show she knew that sounded unsympathetic but that she meant well.

He didn't smile back. "Oh, thanks. I'll be out of here tomorrow. I'll straighten up and be on my way."

"Sorry."

"No, thanks, thanks for the advice, this is great. Hey, when I think of all the time I wasted on Lieberman when I could've come straight to Caddie Winger."

"I just—I know you've got guilt feelings, but—"

"Look, don't psychoanalyze me. I can hardly afford one shrink."

"I'm sorry," she said again. "I wish you weren't here. That's all, I wish you were in your factory making feet."

He slid down on the bed and pulled the sheet over his head.

"Don't do that."

"So what went wrong with you and your boyfriend?" With each word, the sheet puffed up under the narrow wedge shape of his nose. "Trouble in paradise?"

She turned away. On the television, two women in shoulder pads were exchanging staccato bursts of words. Outside, rain plopped in heavy, stolid splashes on the concrete floor of the porch, puddling in the cracks and gurgling in the leaky gutters. Caddie sighed, feeling dreary and wilted.

Magill pulled the sheet down to his lips. "What happened?" he said in his normal voice, not the sarcastic one.

She took a long time answering, thinking of ways to phrase it. But then she just admitted, "I don't know. I have absolutely no idea."

"Sometimes guys . . ."

"What?" *Tell me,* she thought, *give me the answer.* At the same time, though, she had no hope that somebody like Magill could know what was going on in Christopher's mind.

"Sometimes we act like jerks. Women don't even have to do anything to make us feel, you know . . ."

"What?"

"Crowded."

"I *didn't* do anything. I didn't *do* anything. Just the *opposite.*"

"Okay, okay."

She and Christopher had stayed in bed late on their last morning, reading the papers and eating room service breakfast. Caddie had showed him a feature on married couples having their golden anniversaries—because it was interesting, it had the wedding photos right next to pictures of the same couples today. "Before and after," Christopher had called them, and she'd had to agree; it was both fascinating and appalling to see what time had done to the natty, hopeful, sweet-faced brides and grooms. Some were completely unrecognizable, but most were simply vague, bleached-out versions of their younger selves. They'd turned white. Their close-mouthed smiles weren't jaunty or cocky anymore, as if faith in the future was something else they'd run out of in fifty years.

"Imagine being with the same person for *half a century,*" Caddie had marveled. "I'm not even sure it's *natural.*"

"My grandparents have been together longer than that," Christopher had said, sounding proud.

"Do they still like each other?"

He'd thought for a second. "Not much." They'd laughed.

"You see? People shouldn't have to promise each other their whole lives. If we lowered our expectations, we wouldn't have to disappoint each other."

"So you're against marriage?"

"In its present form," she'd declared. "We should have renewable contracts, every five years."

"What about kids?"

She couldn't tell how seriously he was taking this. But she wasn't saying it to please him, hadn't been trying to paint a picture of herself as an independent woman with no hidden designs on his freedom. She'd been trying to confide something it was hard for her to admit, something she'd never even told anyone before: she *was* against marriage. Not because it wouldn't be grand—how wonderful to be one of the old ladies in these pictures in the newspaper, standing beside one of these bald, portly, doughy old men, still going strong, still holding hands on the way to their certain future. It was just that that kind of permanence wasn't for her. Winger women lived their lives without long-term partners, and Caddie fit comfortably in the family tradition.

"Kids," she'd said. "That's a problem."

"Don't you want children?"

She'd looked into Christopher's clear green eyes, searching for a hint to what he wanted her to say. She wasn't cynical about men, far from it, but she'd had a feeling this was a trick question. Still, what could she tell him except the truth?

"Not really. I mean . . ." She'd started to equivocate, then gave up. "No, I don't. I'm not cut out to be anybody's mother. Some people are, some aren't. I'm not."

Was that the right answer? He had three sisters; his grandparents had been married for over fifty years; he came from Iowa. Of course he wanted children.

"What about you?" she'd said, reaching for her cold coffee cup, feigning extreme offhandedness. "You probably want five or six kids."

"What makes you say that?" He'd started on the sports page; he was losing interest in the conversation.

"Because you'd make such a great father."

He'd nodded slowly. "I would. But I don't want kids, either. It's too bad—the ones who'd make the best parents never want children."

She'd felt flattered—he must be including her in that assessment. She'd wanted to ask why he thought she'd make a good mother, but she'd wanted to seem nonchalant on the whole subject even more. So she'd let it drop and started the crossword puzzle.

"The guy's an ass," Magill said. "Forget about him."

"No, he's not."

"Yeah, he is."

"No, he's not. All he did was not call me."

"I rest my case." He folded his hands over his stomach.

She smiled. "Silly." It was tempting to go on, get more sympathy, but she refrained. "I should go. Do you have any dope?"

"Say what?" He sat up on his pillows.

"Dope, grass. Do you have any marijuana? It's not for me."

"Who, then? Christopher? No, I don't, what do you take me for? Do I look like a dope dealer?"

She almost laughed, since the answer to that was absolutely *yes*. "No, not Christopher, somebody else. I don't want to say who."

"Someone I *know*?" He looked shocked, then intrigued. "Who?"

"I'm not saying. Never mind, you don't have any, so forget I asked."

"Who is it?"

"Nobody. I'm not telling."

"Frances?"

"My *grandmother*?" She burst out laughing.

He rasped his chin whiskers in a thoughtful, calculating way. "Okay, I know somebody. All I have to do is make a phone call."

"Oh, great. Well—will you?"

"Happy to. On one condition."

"Uh-oh. No—"

"You have to tell me who wants it."

"No! No fair."

"No deal."

"Blackmail! Okay, I'll tell you, but you won't believe me." She paused for dramatic effect. "It's Thea."

"Thea." Magill's face spread in a slow grin. "I believe you. And now I've got another condition."

She drove by Christopher's house on the way home. Not exactly on the way; technically it was a mile and a half out of the way. The rain made it hard to see whether the lights were on behind the closed blinds in his front window, so she turned at the alley and drove around the back. What if he was walking King in the backyard or taking out the garbage, what if he saw her? She'd die. But the rear of his first-floor apartment was as shuttered and dark as the front, and his car wasn't on the concrete pad beside the fence.

Maybe he was out of town. A family emergency, something so urgent he hadn't had time yet to tell her about it.

Since Thursday?

She spent the evening practicing her violin. She was working on Dvořák's Romance in F minor, but she found it echoed her achy mood too closely, she couldn't stay with it for long. She began to play the intense, insistent first movement of the A-minor concerto of Vivaldi; she'd learned it for a long-ago recital, and she still loved to *dig* into it, that urgent six-note repetition. But tonight it sounded more anxious than joyful, and she had to abandon that, too.

An irritating melody had been running through her brain for days, since Angie's last lesson. She found herself fingering the first few mournful notes of "Man of Constant Sorrow." Angie wanted to play the song wrong, anyway, jolly and rollicking, singing along, almost like a jig—Caddie wasn't sorry she'd talked her out of it. If you were *going* to play it, play it without double stops. Single notes only in a hopeless, yearning circle. Make the tune hard and bitter, mountain music, primitive and sad and slow. She half hypnotized herself with the plaintive melody; there seemed no way to end it, it kept rounding back and starting over. Angie was crazy to think this was a good song for the pageant. It was much too sad. It was tragic. Caddie finally ended it by setting her instrument down.

The house was so quiet. "Too quiet," she said to Finney, who followed her from room to room like a little white ghost. People talked about dogs being attuned to their moods, exhibiting canine empathy when they were blue or depressed, nudging them with their paws, licking tears from their cheeks. Finney wasn't that kind of dog, usually. Humans were useful to him for food, play, petting, and walks, and as long as you provided enough of those your mood was irrelevant to him. Tonight he wasn't himself, though. He wouldn't leave her alone. She touched his nose to see if it was hot. No; but still, it seemed more likely that *he* was sick than that he knew *she* was. Sick in the heart.

She hadn't been lonely in a long while. Weeks. She hadn't had this tightness just below the chest that wasn't pain, exactly, more like nothing, an empty pocket of air at the center. *I'm by myself again.* Worse now, because she thought she'd been rescued.

In Washington she'd been so brave, speaking right up to strangers, waiters and shopkeepers and people like that, in the bold, arch, humorous way she admired so much in others. Being with Christopher had given her the courage, made her feel assured and strong, as if she were anybody's equal. It was like being drunk. On the street, glimpses she caught of herself and Christopher in store windows had made her feel proud because they were so obviously a couple. Everything added up, like a math problem or puzzle pieces fitting together. Completion, a mystery solved.

She had some over-the-counter sleeping pills. She took two, knowing they'd make her feel groggy in the morning, and went to bed early. But the pills just gave her anxious, unsatisfying half-dreams. She got up at eleven and made some herbal tea. She stared at the phone. Christopher liked to go to bed early.

She called him anyway. "Leave a message at the tone," he recommended.

"Are you there? Are you out of town? Christopher, if you're home, would you call me? I've been worried that something's wrong. Um, everything's fine here. It's Sunday. Night. I was just thinking about you. Hoping you're not mad or something. If you are, would you call and tell me? Okay, well. Sorry if that's—paranoid," she said hurriedly, and hung up.

"Call him," Thea suggested.

"I *have* called him. He's either not there or else he's not answering."

"Then go knock on his door. Caddie, you have to find out. You'll make yourself sick if you just sit here and do nothing."

"We don't have—we haven't been having the kind of relationship where I do the calling. You know, the initiating. It just started out that he was the one, so now—if I do, it's too . . ."

"Well, that's silly. Aren't you a liberated woman? I thought you modern girls called men up at the drop of a hat."

"Anyway, I have called him. I can't reach him."

"And nothing went wrong over the weekend, you didn't have a spat—"

"Nothing. It was almost perfect."

"Almost."

"Well, nothing's perfect," Caddie said practically. She didn't want to think about that one little moment—and certainly she couldn't tell Thea about it—the only possible culprit she could imagine. "*Christopher's* perfect, though. I still want you to meet him. Oh, I hope you can."

"I'm dying to. How long have you been seeing him?"

"About five weeks."

"Are you in love?"

"Oh . . . it's so soon."

"Do you think? I fell in love with my first husband in one night. He took me to see *On the Waterfront*. I had blonde hair then, lighter than yours, and he said I looked like Eva Marie Saint." She laughed. "Naturally, I was a goner."

"When did you first tell him?"

"You mean, that I loved him? We were on a picnic. We were lying on an army blanket, I remember, looking up at the sky through the tree leaves. Holding hands. He said it first. Then me."

"How long had you known each other?"

"I don't remember exactly. Not that long, though."

"Weeks?"

"No . . ."

"Months?"

"I suppose. Why?"

"Oh, Thea," Caddie burst out, caution gone, "I'm afraid I did something. To scare him away—I think it's because of what I said."

"Sweetheart. If you told him—"

"I did. I said it, the last night. But so softly, and I thought he was asleep!"

It had to be that, those murmured words she couldn't hold back. They'd just made love, and she'd felt so fragile inside, so tender and moved, she'd cried a little. Christopher had seen her tears, but he'd only smiled, hadn't said anything. He'd just pulled her into his arms, and soon after he'd fallen asleep. That's when she'd said it: "I love you," on a soft exhale of breath.

"He must've heard me," she said miserably, "and it was too soon. No, it was, I shouldn't have said it."

"But Caddie, if you felt it—"

"I scared him away."

"I don't believe it, not from what you've told me about him. Christopher would not do this."

"I don't know, I don't know." If only she'd kept quiet. But the words had sounded so daring and bold. She'd never said them to a man before, and she'd wanted to for so long. Now that she finally had, she'd ruined everything. "I am such an *idiot*."

"No, you're not. Call him," Thea said. "Call him, because I'm not going to fear the worst until I hear it from your lips."

She waited until her last student left. Christopher's machine came on, and she was stumbling through another awkward, pretend-carefree message when he suddenly picked up. "Hello?"

"Christopher? Hi! It's me! Where've you been?"

"Hang on a sec."

Waiting through half a minute of squeaky, muffled quiet, as if he had his hand over the mouthpiece, she had time to worry that his "Hello" had sounded impatient, maybe even irritated. How many messages had she left for him in the last seven days? She'd lost count.

"Hi," he came back on to say. "Sorry about that, I had to finish something."

"Are you working?"

"I'm always working. How are you? What's up?"

"I'm fine, I—I've been worried about you. Did you get my messages?"

"Yeah, I was going to call you."

"Oh."

"I've been really busy, I just haven't had a chance."

"Oh."

"Everything okay with you? Anything new?"

Her mind went blank. She couldn't think of anything new. There must be no point to this call, then; she was only interrupting his work. What was happening?

"You sound funny," she said finally. "You don't sound like your-self." What she meant was, they'd never had a telephone conversation like this. Always before, they were playful on the phone, even sexy; in truth, she often felt more comfortable talking to Christopher on the phone than she did face-to-face.

"Yeah? Who do I sound like?"

She tried to laugh. "Somebody who wants to get off the phone."

He didn't say anything.

She waited through an excruciating silence with her eyes shut tight. "Are you angry with me for something?"

"No, I'm not angry. I'm preoccupied. I told you, I've got a lot on my mind."

"How's work going? How's—"

"It's busy."

"Would you like to come over? Take a break?" Stupid, he *never* came here, he didn't like her house. "Or I could go over there," she said when he didn't answer. "If you like. Whichever."

He took a deep breath, a reverse sigh. "It's not a good night."

She couldn't say anything for a full minute. He didn't help her. She put her hand on her throat and asked, "Are we breaking up?"

Another long, unbearable silence, and the answer in it was obvious.

"What happened?" She had to whisper to get that out.

"Nothing happened. Caddie, it's one of those things."

"It's because of what I said, isn't it?"

"What? What did you say?"

"Nothing."

"Look, it's . . . it's just that we don't have that much in common. I mean, when you think about it, we have nothing in common."

She slumped. It was true. She'd known it all along. "I thought we were having a good time, though."

"We did. No, it was fine. It's just, I think maybe it meant more to you than me," he said, and finally his voice sounded kind, not cool and impersonal. But the change wasn't consoling; it just made it impossible to argue. "It's a bad time for me to have a serious relationship. It's not your fault. And I think it's better to break it off clean rather than drag it out."

"Yeah." *But what if I hadn't called?* she thought.

"Caddie? You okay?"

"Yes. Fine."

"I'm really sorry. You've been great."

She hiccuped a laugh.

"I hope we can still be friends."

She had to pull the receiver away from her ear for a second. "Yeah," she got out. "Me, too."

"Oh—Caddie?"

"Yes?"

"You can keep the CDs, but you know those books I lent you? On dog obedience and companion animal training? I'm going to need those back. Sorry to ask, but—"

"Okay. I have to hang up now."

"Right, okay." Now there was life in his voice for the first time. She was a load off his mind. "Well, Caddie, you take care."

Years ago, in graduate school, she'd had a cat, Abigail. A scrawny, mostly gray alley cat a child in the neighborhood had foisted on her, but she'd grown to love it. One evening Abigail crawled home, sick and injured, bleeding from the mouth; she'd been hit by a car. Caddie rushed her to the vet, who'd kept her overnight. In the morning, he'd called. "I'm so sorry," he'd said in the gentlest voice, "Abigail didn't make it. We made her comfortable, but she was bleeding too much inside. She died about six o'clock this morning."

She'd wanted so much to thank the doctor, who was kindness itself, but she'd been unable to speak because she was crying, and that had embarrassed her. She'd had to hang up without saying a word. Not even goodbye.

This was like that, only worse.

13 Before Caddie could put the Pontiac's brake on in front of Wake House, Thea waved to her and started down the steps. Right behind her came Magill—with Cornel holding on to his arm. Cornel? Why was *he* coming? Oh, brother.

Bea and Edgie Copes sat in their side-by-side rockers on the front porch and called out over the railing, "Woo-hoo, Caddie!" On either side of them sat the Harris wives, ignoring each other as usual. Maxine waved her church fan; Doré acknowledged Caddie with a nod of her perfectly permed head. "Have a nice time!" Bea called out, and Caddie smiled and waved through the window, feeling guilty.

They'd all swallowed the cover story: she was having a very tiny student music recital in her home tonight. She'd be having others later for similar small groups, but to this first one she could only invite two people (which was completely absurd, and yet nobody had questioned it). Well, apparently she'd found room for a third: Cornel shambled down the walk looking even grumpier than usual, dressed in blousy seersucker pants and a powder-blue golf shirt. Between him and Magill, it was hard to say who was supporting whom; Magill had problems with his balance, but Cornel, much as he denied it, had arthritic hips, and on bad days they made him take short, mincing steps, like a woman in a too-tight skirt.

"Did you make the score?" Thea asked, still six feet from the car.

Cornel cringed. "Shhh!" he said, which made Magill laugh, which made them both tip dangerously sideways against the stair rail.

"I made the score," Caddie assured Thea once she was in the car and buckled up. She looked so pleased and excited, Caddie had less trouble hiding her own dismal mood than she'd thought she was going to. She'd considered canceling the pot party, postponing it till she felt better, whenever that might be, because it could hardly have fallen on a worse day in her life. But now she was glad she hadn't. It might even cheer her up. She'd been miserable for two weeks, each day as wretched as the last, no differentiation, no distinction. Until two days ago, when everything had gotten immeasurably worse.

"And you didn't have any trouble?" Thea asked her.

"No trouble. I was born for the doper life."

Magill's dealer buddy, a balding, clean-cut young man named Chip, had come to the house yesterday, right in the middle of Caitlin Birnbaum's piano lesson, and he and Caddie had made the exchange on the front porch: a little plastic baggie inside a paper sandwich bag for ninety-five dollars in cash. "This is highly excellent stuff, I can personally recommend it," Chip had told her. "You want to sample it first, that is no problem whatsoever." She'd whispered that that wouldn't be necessary and wished him a nice day.

"I'll write you a check when we get to the house," Thea said happily, patting her pocketbook. "Why don't you put the top down, Caddie? I haven't ridden in a convertible in I don't know how long."

"It's stuck, it doesn't go down anymore. Rust."

"You people have completely lost your minds," Cornel grumped, settling himself in the backseat. "How's it going to look if you get caught? Have you thought about that? It won't be so funny when you're behind bars. And you," he told Magill, "you won't be wearing that smirk on your face when you're a jailbird."

Magill caught Caddie's eye in the rearview mirror. "Cornel's the designated narc."

"Laugh, go ahead, you'll be glad when *one* of us is sober," Cornel said darkly.

"Straight," Thea corrected, "not sober. You're our straight man."

He kept it up all the way to Caddie's house, warning about bad trips and drug busts and reefer madness. "Cornel," Thea finally turned around in her seat to say, "Caddie can take you back to Wake House right now if you're going to spoil this for the rest of us."

He scowled and shut up.

Magill couldn't get over the sculptures in the front yard. The sun was going down, glowing orange between the dark leaves of the oak tree in Mrs. Tourneau's yard, casting shadows that added length and a little dignity to *Oppression* and *Earth Mother*. He had a cane tonight, and he used it to navigate around Nana's grass-blooming earthworks and metal contraptions. "These are amazing," he marveled. "Incredible." Thea had seen them before and Cornel wasn't impressed, so they left Magill wandering in the yard and came inside with Caddie.

She put them in the living room and went to get drinks. "This is pretty nice," she heard Cornel say on her way out. "Feels good to be in a real house, doesn't it?" Funny; she'd thought the beauty of Wake House was that it *was* a real house.

When she came back, Magill was sitting cross-legged on the floor, rolling a joint, with Thea beside him and Cornel looking on from a superior distance in the armchair. She set a tray of glasses, snacks, soft drinks, and a pitcher of iced tea on the coffee table. "I have booze, too, if anybody wants a real drink."

"Got any cold beer?" Magill asked.

"Yes."

"Me, too," said Cornel.

"That sounds wonderful," said Thea.

"Oh, okay." So they were drinking. She returned the soft drinks to the kitchen and came back with beer.

"What's that noise?" Thea asked after everybody had toasted.

"I don't hear anything," Magill said.

180

"Yeah," Cornel noticed, "like a bird chirping."

"Oh, it's Finney," Caddie said. "I locked him in Nana's bedroom. I can let him out if nobody minds."

Nobody minded.

"He should be fine since you're already here—it's when strangers come to the door that he goes nuts."

She went upstairs to let him out. He hardly spared her a glance before tearing down the hall, down the stairs, yipping, squeaking, a whitish blur of excitement. By the time she got back to the living room, he was wriggling on Thea's thighs in uncontrollable delight, leaving a blizzard of hairs on her skirt.

"Should we have some music?" She went to the stereo and leafed through the CDs currently scattered on the shelf. She put on a Brahms symphony, but after a couple of seconds she turned it off. "That's not right," she said, talking to herself. "Something lighter. I guess."

Magill came over to help. He'd cleaned up for this night out; he wore a pressed shirt and a nice pair of gray slacks. They were both too big for him, though, and the worn place on his belt was a couple of inches away from the current notch in the buckle. But still, he looked tidy and clean-shaven, and he might even have gotten a real haircut instead of letting Maxine cut it for him.

"You look very nice tonight," she told him.

"I like your hair that way," he mumbled.

"Oh." She had to touch her hair to remember how she'd combed it. Behind her ears with two barrettes. "Thanks."

"So what have you got that's really decadent?"

"Decadent?"

"For Cornel." He ran his index finger along first one stack of discs, then another. "Nothing. Absolutely nothing. Is this what you listen to all the time?"

"What's wrong with it? Not all the time."

"What's in here?" He squatted down and opened the cabinet under the stereo. "Aha. Your secret stash. Why do you keep the good stuff down here, Caddie? It's not . . ."

It's not pornography. That's what he was going to say, she was sure. She watched his ears turn pink and concentrated on not laughing.

"Bessie Smith. Sippee Wallace, Ma Rainey, Jelly Roll Morton. Memphis Minnie?"

"She's good," Caddie said, defensive for some reason. It *was* almost as if he'd stumbled on her secret collection of erotica.

"Who else . . . Eubie Blake, Koko Taylor. Alberta Hunter." He turned an old Etta James disc over and read from the back, " 'Hot Nuts, Get 'Em from the Peanut Man.' " He grinned up at her. "Play this. It's perfect."

She shrugged. "Fine, I'll put on a whole stack. There's nothing the matter with the blues."

He straightened up, using the edge of the shelf for balance. "That's for sure." He was looking at her with a sweet, intent expression, as if seeing something new, some intriguing facet he hadn't suspected. She'd revealed too much, she felt obscurely, and she wasn't even sure how. Or, for that matter, what. She shrugged again, signaling indifference, and stacked the CD player with music.

Cornel got up and closed the curtains over the front window. "For security," he told them.

"It's going to get hot," Caddie warned. It already was hot. She had an air conditioner in her bedroom, but down here only a fan.

"Anybody can stand on your porch and look right in. I for one don't want to get arrested tonight." Instead of going back to his chair, Cornel plumped himself down next to Thea on the floor, knees cracking. His pant legs rode up to show hairless white calves above shiny black socks.

"Cornel, why won't you let me write your biography?" Caddie asked him.

"Because I'm not dead yet. I told you."

"I bet you've had a very interesting life."

"Not that interesting."

"Or I could interview you—just ask questions, and you could answer the ones you wanted."

"That's an idea," Thea said. "Why don't you, Cornel?"

He looked dubious and flattered at the same time. "I'll think about it," he begrudged. "Meanwhile, can we get this foolishness on the road?"

"Yes, let's." Thea's eyes danced with anticipation; she was almost rubbing her hands together. She had on a flowered sundress that bared her freckled arms and chest, the kind of dress Doré Harris said nobody over sixty should wear. "Women past a certain age ought never to reveal their arms," she'd once told Caddie, in an obvious reference to Maxine, who'd been sporting a sleeveless blouse that day. "Even in summer?" Caddie had asked. "Not if she has any personal pride."

"You look beautiful tonight," Caddie said to Thea impulsively.

"Why, thanks. I wanted to come as a hippie, but I don't have any bell-bottoms." She had on gold hoop earrings, though, gypsy earrings that made her look reckless and carefree. No wonder Cornel couldn't take his eyes off her.

Magill struck a match and lit the tight, fat joint. Took a hit.

"Is that how you do it?" Thea took the cigarette from him in her fingertips. "Hold it in for a while before you blow it out, right?"

"If you can," he said, exhaling. "But take a small puff the first time, just a little, otherwise it'll make you cough."

"I used to smoke cigarettes," she said. "I quit in 1968."

"I quit in 1969," Cornel said interestedly, as if this gave them a special bond.

"Just a little puff," Magill warned again.

Thea brought the joint carefully to her lips and inhaled. Her eyes bulged; she looked as if she was strangling, but she managed not to cough. "Aagh," she exclaimed on the exhale, "it's so *harsh*, not like tobacco at all. Let me try another puff."

Magill sat back and laughed.

"What else do you call this besides a joint?"

"Doobie, jay. Spliff. Joystick, roach. Twist."

Cornel was scowling like a vulture but missing nothing. "Sure you don't want to try?" Thea asked, holding the joint out toward him, waving it invitingly.

"Positive."

"Could be your last chance."

"Good."

She shrugged and took another hit, very expert-looking now, holding the smoke in her lungs for a full five seconds before blowing it up at the ceiling. "Here, honey," she said, handing the joint to Caddie. "Your turn."

The loose paper crackled and sparked; Caddie tapped the long ash into the ashtray and started to take a drag. But then—"No, you know, I don't think I want any, not right now."

"*One* sensible person," Cornel said.

"Maybe later. I have a little headache. It's nothing—maybe later."

"I thought so," Thea said, reaching over to touch her arm. "Thought you weren't quite yourself tonight."

"Sure?" Magill said. Caddie said she was sure, and he took another toke.

"Okay." Thea straightened her skirt over her legs and draped her hands over her knees, yogi style. She stared ahead, alert-faced. "I don't feel anything. Shouldn't I be getting paranoid?"

"Not quite yet," Magill said consolingly.

"I've been wanting to try this for years."

"Why?" Cornel demanded.

"Because." She looked at him in perplexity. "It's a new experience."

"Hmph."

"I like the way it looks, too. I like the way you hold the cigarette and the way you hiss the smoke in through your teeth." She stroked her hands over her knees. "Mmm," she said on a drowsy but intense sigh, "I think it's hitting me." She leaned back against the sofa and stretched her legs out. "I love this music. Who is this, Caddie?"

"Hoagy Carmichael."

"What's it feel like?" Cornel wanted to know.

"A little strange. But dreamy. Disconnected. Time, something about time . . ."

"It becomes groovy," Magill said, and he and Thea started to giggle.

Caddie and Cornel smirked at each other.

Magill lay down on his back. He tried to haul the dog up on his chest, but Finney was more interested in the cheese and crackers on the coffee table. "Now what are *we* supposed to do," Cornel groused to Caddie, "just sit here and watch?"

That set Magill and Thea off again. Caddie was enjoying the way Cornel's craggy face softened when he looked at Thea. The conversation meandered in a familiar, stoned way. Caddie thought of a boy she used to go out with in college, Michael Dershowicz, whose idea of a good time was getting high and listening to heavy metal music. They'd lie on top of his dorm room bed and listen to Megadeth and Annihilator while he described to her the *geography* of the music, explaining it like architecture, like a painting. He could *see* it, he'd say, and they would have long, abstract, artificially intense debates—he stoned, she straight—over what color the notes were right here, this section, or what shape, what personality. She'd enjoyed those conversations, but she hadn't been tempted to try pot herself. If she was ever going to, she couldn't think of anyone she'd rather do it with than the three people in her living room tonight.

"Oh, I'm having a good trip." Thea scooted over and lay down beside Magill. Immediately Finney ran over and licked her in the face. "Oh, bluh." Her stomach bumped up and down with laughter.

Cornel put his fists on the floor. "Oh, hell, give me some of that spliff."

Thea and Magill sat up in astonishment, which caused Finney to scuttle back in alarm and bark at them. "Really? You're going to try it?"

Cornel pointed at Caddie. "If I go haywire, you're responsible. You're the one who has to calm me down, get me to the hospital if it comes to that."

He looked so serious, she couldn't laugh. "I will, I promise. Don't worry."

"I can do it," he snapped when Magill started to light the half-smoked joint for him. "I know how to light a damn cigarette."

"Not too much."

"I know, I know." He took a deep drag and went into a violent coughing fit.

Magill lost it. He laughed so hard, he fell over backward. Caddie poured Cornel a glass of iced tea, but he couldn't stop coughing long enough to drink it. Thea patted his back. That didn't help either, but he liked it.

"What the hell is that," he said when he could talk, "dried horse manure?"

"You have to take tiny little puffs," Thea told him, like an old hand. "Drink some tea and then try again."

"But watch out for madness." Magill definitely looked stoned, loose-jointed and slack-grinned. "I think it's improving my balance. I'm gonna get Lieberman to prescribe it for vertigo. Sure you don't want a little toke, Caddie?"

"Maybe later."

"You okay?" he asked in a quiet voice.

"Fine, I'm fine. I think I'll just . . ." She gestured toward the stereo and got up.

Because of Christopher, everybody at Wake House had been treating her with extra kindness and consideration. It was awful. She didn't care about Thea knowing, but she wished she hadn't gone on and on about him to Magill. How stupid that had been, she saw in retrospect, how uncharacteristically self-confident. Arrogant, practically: *Look at me, I have a boyfriend.* She *hated* it that he felt sorry for her now. Not just him, they all did, but she minded Magill's pity more than the others'.

She'd never had her heart broken before. She'd had two weeks to get over it, but nothing much had happened, she still felt buried alive. She'd wasted a lot of time on false hope, imagining different endings, imagining Christopher coming to his senses. Each time the phone rang her heart would stiffen and leap up, like Finney for a ball in the air, and each time it wasn't Christopher she'd feel flooded in personal humiliation. When she heard the sound of a car slowing or stopping in front of the house, or in front of Mrs. Tourneau's house, or across the street, the same wave of stupid hope would gush up and send her to the window, where the same shame and disappointment would swallow her back down.

At night she lay in bed and remembered dear, trivial things—like how pretty his hair was, how it always smelled like shampoo. The day he'd gotten so mad at her for not telling him sooner he had a poppy seed in his teeth. His habit of watching only two TV channels, the all-news one and Animal Planet. His plaid flannel bathrobe, how it looked tied around his waist in the morning. His beautiful smile, so sincere, so blindingly white.

She meant *nothing* to him. It must be true, but she still couldn't *believe* it, because she'd had no warning, no bad memories to look back on and reinterpret as danger signs. In one phone call, he'd pulled the rug out from under her. She was still falling, hadn't hit the bottom yet, so how could she recover? Today she couldn't think at all, today was a wash as far as recovery went. She'd been in a fog since morning, some kind of protective haze making everything blurry and unreal, like the wrong glasses.

"Let's play a game," Thea suggested.

Cornel groaned. He was sitting up stiff as a plank with his arms around his knees, eyes wide, facial muscles tense. If anybody could will himself to stay straight, it was Cornel.

"You, too," Thea said, leaning against his arm. He went even tighter for a second, then relaxed. "Everybody." Thea was getting that croaky, hoarse, marijuana voice. "Name three things you want to do with your life before you get too old."

"I'm already too old. *Ow.*" She'd poked him with her elbow.

"I'll start. First, I want to dye my hair red. I do," she insisted over the laughter, "I've wanted red hair all my life."

"What was it before?" Caddie asked. Before it went a soft, shiny silver-gray.

"Oh, brown, just a sort of light brownish brown."

"Your hair's fine," said Cornel. "Leave it be."

"Nope, I'm dying it red. Not fire engine red," she said, leaning over again and putting her face right in his face, so all he could do was grin. "A nice reddish-blonde, the old-lady version of red hair."

"You go, girl," said Magill.

"Caddie, you come with me when I get it done."

"Okay."

"What's the second thing?" Cornel was liking the game better now.

Thea got to her feet with a slow, wobbly grace. "Play ragtime!" Laughing, she went to the piano, plopped down at the bench, and banged out, over the music already playing on the stereo, the two introductory bass chords and the first two right-hand measures of "Maple Leaf Rag."

"Wooo, my fingers aren't working. This afternoon I had them going together, top and bottom." Her laughter erupted again. She bent over and touched her forehead to the hands she still held on the keys "Oh, my goodness, it's kicked in. Whose hands are these?"

"She plays it pretty good," Cornel told Caddie, "on that piano at the house. She practices all the time."

"*All* the time," Magill confirmed.

Thea stuck her tongue out at him. "It sounds better there than here because that piano's out of tune. Honky-tonk. *That's* my problem, Caddie's piano's too good." She swayed on the bench, chuckling with merriment, infecting the others with her silliness. "Caddie, you play something now. Come on."

"Yeah, play something," Magill said.

"Maybe later," she said. "Okay, that's two. What's the third thing?"

"Oh, I have lots of things." Thea ambled back over. "Well, the main one is, I want to go to Cape May in October."

"What for?"

"The birds," Cornel guessed. "The fall migration."

"*Yes.*" Thea's surprise and pleasure made him color. "Have you been?"

He shook his head sorrowfully, as if he hated to let her down. "I like birds, though."

"Oh, so did Will. They were his favorite hobby, practically a passion. He'd ask me every year to go with him to see the fall migration on the flyway, the East Coast flyway, but something always came up and I'd put it off." She smiled sadly. "So we never went."

"Not your fault," Cornel said gruffly. "Not something to feel guilty about, Pete's sake." His frown didn't look natural; his eyes had a hazy, unfocused swimminess he was trying to correct by scowling. Thea put her hand on top of his absently. That cleared his vision.

"It's not guilt. It's more like . . ." She paused for a long time. "A correction." She gave the word a stoned vehemence, then shook her head. "I do *not* want to get maudlin." No, no, they all agreed, leaning toward her. "But when he was dying, he told me it was one of his regrets, that I'd never gone with him to see it. It meant something to him." She laughed, dashing a tear out of her eye. "This is not right! I'm not sad, I feel *happy* tonight. And it's not the end of the world that I never went with Will to see the birds at Cape May, even *he* didn't think that. I just use it, I've made it a thing, a marker, a . . . oh, I can't think of words."

Magill reached over and squeezed her foot inside her white flat.

"It *stands* for all the things I wish I'd done that I didn't, that's all. Anyway, I'm going. That's my third thing, I'm going to see the birds at Cape May next October. Okay, I'm finished. *Henry*. You go."

Thea was the only one who called Magill by his first name. He was still on his back with his hairpin knees bent, gazing up at the ceiling. He'd taken off his shoes and socks. Finney lay curled up in the crook of his arm, and they wore similar drowsy, comfortable, satisfied expressions. "I forget the question."

Caddie reminded him. "Things you want to do before you die."

"Before you get too old," Cornel corrected.

"Get too old," she said quickly.

Magill's amused grin faded slowly. "Get my life back," he said in a monotone. "That's what I'd like to do."

Nobody spoke; the Ike and Tina Turner song on the stereo sounded too loud all of a sudden, too crass and unconcerned.

Cornel cleared his throat harshly. "Well, if you want it, you can have it. All you gotta do is take it." He didn't feel as unsympathetic as he sounded, Caddie knew that. But he looked mean to her just for a second, like someone who couldn't fit much compassion inside himself anymore because getting old had made him smaller.

Magill speared a pack of cigarettes from the pocket of his shirt without disturbing the dog, shook one out, and lit it. Finney hated smoke; he scrambled up and jumped on the couch, blinking his eyes and looking put out.

"How did it happen?" Thea asked. "The accident."

Caddie turned to her in alarm. Why would she ask him that now? His hand holding the cigarette stopped halfway to his lips. He stared at Thea through the smoke, first in disbelief, then something else. Caddie thought it looked like panic. "Does anybody need anything?" she asked. "More beer? I could make popcorn."

"How did it happen?" Thea repeated, softer, not taking her eyes from Magill's. She nodded, sending him a message. "Tell us if you want to. It's as good a time as any."

He kept looking at her, wouldn't drop his gaze. It was as if they were hanging on to each other while she guided him across a cliff edge, urging him to look at *her*, not *down*. If only Cornel would say something cynical or dismissive or snotty right now, it might head off what Caddie could see coming. Nothing had changed, she still didn't want to hear this story. Maybe she was a coward, but how could it be anything but hurtful? Cornel sat hunched over his beer bottle, absorbed in scraping the label off with his thumbnail. No help.

Magill shut his eyes. Caddie felt as if she were on an edge, too, waiting for him to decide. She could see it going either way, but it seemed more likely that he would say something funny or mocking now, then roll to his feet and stroll out to the kitchen for another beer. She could see his Adam's apple rise and fall when he swallowed. He put his hands on his upraised thighs, gripping the ropy muscles. "I took her up for a tandem dive from fourteen hundred feet. It was her birthday," he said, and Caddie closed her eyes, too.

14

"A tandem jump is the safest dive there is. Nothing can go wrong. You're harnessed together, back to front. I've done hundreds, thousands. I was a jumpmaster, I *taught* it."

Thea, kneeling beside him, put her hand on his shoulder. Just that, but Caddie saw how it steadied him, kept him from veering off into something dark, some form of self-recrimination it would be hard for him to come back from.

"It was a perfect day. June the fourth. Blue sky, white clouds. Holly was okay on the ground, nothing but excited, acting like a kid. But as soon as we took off she got scared. Waiting for your turn to jump is always the hardest, it doesn't matter how many times you've done it. There were nineteen of us packed like sardines on the twin-engine, and we were second to last. Last was a guy named Mark Kohler, a level-eight student, two jumps away from his A license. He laughed at Holly when she cried."

She cried. *Oh, God*, Caddie thought. Holly cried. She kept her eyes closed tight, because then it was like hearing confession. Magill was the penitent and they were the priests.

"She was so scared." His voice went down low, became rough. "She was laughing and crying, yelling, trying to psych herself up. She kept saying, 'What have I done?' I told her, 'Relax, relax, you're gonna love it, relax so you can *feel* it,' trying to get her loose, trying to *wake her up* so she wouldn't miss the whole thing with her eyes

192

shut. I told her—I told her nothing bad would happen. I swore it. Then we jumped.

"Free fall was perfect. We dropped two miles in less than a minute, and she never stopped screaming. But she liked it, she really loved it, she gave the thumbs-up, she . . . tried to kiss me, but her cheeks were flapping in the rush of the air, she couldn't make . . ." He made a guttural sound Caddie couldn't bear to hear, a laugh that came so close to a sob, he couldn't talk at all for a minute.

"You can't hear anything but wind during free fall, but once you open your canopy everything goes dead quiet. It's like hang gliding, just you and the blue air and the incredible earth coming up slow. It's not like flying—it is flying. So beautiful you forget to breathe. You're excited, your heart's pounding, but it's like being in a trance, too. I like it better than the dive. Free fall's just a way to get to that place. That peace."

He stopped again, and Caddie thought, *Finish it. Please, I just can't stand this.*

"Mark, the guy, the AFF student who jumped behind us—his girlfriend was filming his dive from the ground. He did—he did a hard turn to impress her. Make it look good. Dramatic. He forgot us, forgot where we were, he didn't see us, we were a hundred feet from the drop zone and he didn't see us. His turn made him fall too fast. He fell into our chute. He's wrapped up like a mummy, trailing yards of red and white nylon, and the three of us—three of us hanging from his student chute because our main's collapsed. I . . . I . . . I cut away. We weren't going to make it. I cut away the tandem chute and pulled the reserve, but there wasn't room. Wasn't time. You should never, you should never cut your main that close. But we were coming in so fast. I did it. Holly hit first and she died. Under me. She died. I don't remember anything. Mark Kohler broke his ankle."

The music had stopped. Caddie wanted it back because the

silence was horrible. Cornel was making a little cup in the carpet with his thumb, hollowing it out with pinch-faced diligence. He looked shocked and miserable, and he was as helpless, as useless as she was. They both inhaled with hope when Thea shuffled over on her knees, closer to Magill's limp body. But then Caddie was afraid she was going to embrace him, wrap him up in her arms like a baby—he wouldn't like that, he'd hate it. She heard herself blurt out, "It wasn't your fault."

Just as she feared, his lips went flat. "I don't feel absolved." He still had his eyes closed. Two tears had rolled into his hair on either side when he'd said, "She died." The tracks still glistened, untouched.

Thea didn't embrace him. She bent to him and put a kiss in the center of his forehead. He opened his eyes. She said something very soft—Caddie couldn't hear it.

She wanted to *do* something, but she couldn't move; she felt stuck, not able to unwind her arms from around her legs and stand up. *It wasn't your fault*—what a ridiculous thing to say. What would it feel like to believe you had stolen someone's life? Someone you loved, who trusted you. Who was innocent.

Magill sat up, and after that she could move, she wasn't frozen anymore. He was holding the sides of his face and smiling so painfully, a taut spreading of his lips. But he was coming around. What had Thea said to him? Was it good that he'd told them the story? Did he feel lighter now, as if fresh air had blown away some of his sadness and shame? Or did that happen only in books?

Cornel did something brilliant then. Not on purpose, she didn't think, but it saved the day. "Is it me," he said crankily, "or could anybody else eat a horse?"

"Let me make something," Caddie offered. "I could at least open a can of soup, I have chicken noodle, bean with bacon—or toasted cheese sandwiches, how would you like that? Or, I know, bacon and eggs."

"Mmm," they said, nodding appreciatively but not looking up from the leftovers they were devouring. Thea and Cornel had fallen on a plastic container of beef stew like refugees; they hadn't even heated it. Magill was standing over the sink scooping in cold rice as if it were haute cuisine. The kitchen was filled with the sounds of chewing and swallowing, satisfied humming, forks scraping, lips smacking. Caddie found that funny but also faintly nauseating. She boiled water for tea—nobody wanted any but her; they were sticking with beer—and nibbled on a carrot stick. She didn't even want that, but she wanted attention on herself even less.

"So that kid yesterday," Magill said with his mouth full, "that was your grandson, Cornel?"

He grunted yes.

"I didn't even know you had one. Where does he live?"

"Richmond."

Caddie hadn't known, either. Cornel was widowed and now childless, but yesterday a sweet-faced, tired-looking blonde woman and an eleven-year-old boy had appeared on the front porch at Wake House, looking for him. The boy was Zack, the woman was Donna; she was the widow of Cornel's son, who had been killed in an automobile accident in 1999. That surprised Caddie, too; Cornel spoke of his son so infrequently, she'd assumed he'd been dead for years and years.

"What's his name?" Magill asked. He'd been on his way to physical therapy and had seen Cornel's family only as he was leaving.

"Zachary." He snorted. "What a name. There's no Zacharys in the family, I tell you that, ours or hers. Coulda been worse, though, coulda been *Jason*. Coulda been *Alex*."

"All lovely names," Thea said mildly. "What is the matter with you?"

"Get this, if it was a girl they were gonna name it *Courtney*. Hah!"

Thea just rolled her eyes. "Donna's a darling. We had the nicest talk."

"She's all right."

"She said they have a nice house down there. Pretty little house in the suburbs."

Cornel shrugged, scraping stew gravy from the bottom of the bowl.

"She said she'd love it if you'd move down there. Be closer to them."

"Yeah." He shoved his chair back and stood. "I'm still hungry. Mind if I just . . ." He opened the refrigerator and bent inside. "Tell you what she really wants. Wants me to *move in*. Can't you picture that?"

Magill had moved aside so that Caddie could put dirty dishes in the sink. He looked tired, she thought, but not worse, not drained or unhappy or regretful. Thank God. She wanted to stay near him, or say something to make him smile, send affection to him without embarrassing him. She leaned back against the counter and hooked her hand over his shoulder. As if she just needed a place to put it and his shoulder was the closest perch.

"I certainly can picture it," Thea exclaimed. "Why wouldn't you? What a perfectly lovely idea."

"Perfectly lovely idea," Cornel mimicked, backing out of the refrigerator with a container of cottage cheese and a jar of olives. "We eat these?"

Caddie thought about Zack, a weedy, wispy boy in baggy clothes, pale hands clutching a computer game he'd rarely looked up from except for quick, shy glances at his mother. He'd spoken only once in Caddie's hearing. Donna had been telling Cornel about how Zack was having a little trouble in school this year, in fact he'd gotten a D in English and would be taking remedial reading in summer school. He was a whiz at math, though, she'd added quickly, reaching over to ruffle his crew cut—which had made him pull away. But then he'd darted a sideways look at Cornel and asked hopefully, "How 'bout my dad? Mom didn't know—did my dad do good in math?"

Cornel had lowered his bushy brows and glared at him for an unnaturally long time. Caddie had been afraid he wasn't going to answer at all, but then he'd snapped out, "*Well*, did he do *well* in math. I don't remember, it's too long ago. Quit playing fool games on that machine, that's all you need to do. Read a damn book for a change."

Poor Zack recoiled, looking stunned, as if the family cat had suddenly scratched him. Donna said in a bright tone, "Oh, I bet he was, Daddy was good at everything," and Cornel started to squirm in his rocking chair. Caddie saw him bare his teeth in a clumsy try at a smile, an apology, but too late, Zack had already ducked his head and gone back to his game. She'd been searching for a resemblance, a feature grandfather and grandson had in common, and finally she saw it. They had the same knack for shutting people out behind ferocious scowls.

"Why wouldn't you go live with them if they *want* you to?" Thea asked, plucking an olive out of the jar. "What would hold you back? I can't even imagine." She leaned toward Cornel, both elbows on the cluttered kitchen table, resting her chin in her hands. When she turned her full attention on him like that, it always discombobulated him.

"Because. Then I'd be dependent. What do you mean, why can't you imagine? Who'd want to be a burden to their own relations? Me, I'd rather be dead."

"Well, that's ridiculous. Sometimes we help the ones we love, sometimes we need their help. It's a cycle. What could be more natural? Didn't you love taking care of your family? But you'd rather *die* now than let them take care of you. It's a kind of arrogance, isn't it?"

He blinked in shock, then rallied. "Hell, no. Taking care of an old fart is nobody's idea of a good time, old age makes sure of that."

"Oh, age is just a number. What if a year had fourteen months instead of twelve? Then I'd be . . ." She turned to Caddie and Magill. "How old would I be?"

"Old age." Cornel curled his lips as if they were swear words. "It's a lot more than a number. It's losing body part after body part. Everything goes, it's one damn kick in the teeth after another. One—"

"Fifty-nine," Magill said. "Multiply your age by twelve-fourteenths, which is six-sevenths, six times sixty-nine—"

"Old age," Thea said, "isn't any different from any other age. It's still *you*. I feel like I'm the same age I've always been!"

"Really?" Caddie said.

"It's still a surprise when I hear somebody call me old. And when I look in the mirror—" She made a humorous expression of horror. "But I'm always young in my dreams. Isn't that odd? In dreams I'm my old self, my *real* self."

Cornel was staring at his clawed hands. "Getting old is for the birds. Time sneaks up on you like a . . . like a mugger. Look at these. I used to have a man's hands. Now I got hair growing outta my ears, I'm cold all the time—"

"But underneath—"

"Can't eat this, can't eat—"

"But underneath, you're still a boy, aren't you? Don't you feel that? Cornel Montgomery. Did they used to call you Cornie?"

He smiled in spite of himself.

"I love being alive," Thea declared. "I love it more, not less, the older I get. I'm still a girl under all these wrinkles. I'm still burning bright, and everything's still a mystery—I never want to leave, I'm just getting started!"

Everything was still a mystery to Thea, *too*? Caddie didn't know whether to be encouraged by that or demoralized.

"That's because you *feel* good," Cornel said. "You're in your *young* old age. Wait'll you get to your *old* old age, wait'll everything starts to go. All it takes is one little stroke, one little fall and you break your hip, bingo, into the nursing home. Diabetes, you go deaf, you can't drive anymore, quadruple bypass. Prostate, cataracts, knee replacement. Hiatal hernia. Joints hurt, can't sleep, can't pee. Canes, walkers, ugly shoes—"

"But—"

"We're invisible," he kept on. "I'm an *old man*, that's all I am. Nobody looks at me, I might as well be smoke. Young people think we're fools, they laugh in our faces."

"That's not true."

"Donna's the one who's a fool. Me in Richmond, what a joke. I *would* rather die than drag down my kin. One of these days I'll be wearing diapers—and she's not even *blood* kin."

"Zack is," Thea argued. "Did you ever think you might be able to help *him*? Maybe that's why she wants you down there, because her son needs a man, a *father*."

"What's a boy that age want with an old man? Hell's bells, I don't know a GameBoy from a *Playboy*."

"Why are you so ashamed of being old? It's life, Cornel, it's nature! You could help them, they could help you. What's undignified about that?"

"I don't want to be dependent. Period, the end. Wake House, that's the last stop before the nursing home. I *hope* I die there. Those are the lucky ones, the ones that don't wake up in the morning. Bernie told me the same stupid story about his lumbago three times yesterday."

"*Dependent*—you make it such a dirty word! If I had any family at all, if I had *anybody* and they wanted to take care of me, do you think I'd say no?"

"That's fine, but you're—" Cornel sucked in his breath. "Oh no, don't do that, now."

"I'm all right." But she was weeping, tears slipping down her cheeks in quick streaks, spreading dark plops on the bosom of her dress.

Cornel was beside himself. He half stood, half crouched over her, moving his hands in ineffectual feints in Thea's direction, almost touching, then jerking away. "Listen, don't pay any attention, that was all bull. I get going and can't shut up. Don't cry."

"I'm not." She stood up. "It's this *grass*. Is this what it does, Henry? I'm sorry, I never meant to get like this."

"No, *my* fault," Cornel insisted. "It's that pot, you're right. I got on a tear and couldn't shut up! I'm not like this usually."

That made Magill laugh. Cornel sent him an urgent *help me out* look.

"Are you all right?" Caddie said, coming close to Thea.

"I am perfectly fine. Let's go in the living room." She slipped an arm around Caddie's waist, as if to cheer *her* up—and just that quick, Caddie felt like crying, too. Oh, to hang on to Thea and burst into tears, snuffle on her shoulder while Thea held her like a mother and patted her on the back and crooned, "There, it's all right, everything's going to be fine." And she hadn't even smoked anything.

"Caddie, do something for me," Thea said, giving her waist a squeeze. "A favor."

"Name it."

Thea steered her over to the piano before she could think of resisting. "Play something. Play anything at all."

"What? No. *Hey*—" She tried to laugh during a push-pull moment, a subtle but actual physical struggle with Thea before she had to give in, only to avoid embarrassment, and sit down on the piano bench. "Thea—you know how I am. Not so good at this—"

"But not tonight. Not with us." She went behind Caddie and put her hands on her shoulders. Support or coercion? "What would you play right now if you were by yourself?"

Something incredibly depressing, Caddie thought, running nervous, uncertain fingers over the thighs of her jeans. "This is no fair. Anyway, I'm not in the mood."

Thea leaned over, put her cheek next to hers. "Please, please, please. I'm begging you. Play something by Billie Holiday."

"Billie Holiday," said Cornel, coming over to stand next to Thea, "she was good. I thought you just played classical. You know any Dinah Shore?"

She felt silly. What was she afraid of? Turning into her mother, the musician, Dr. Kardashian said, giving her mother too much power over her, something like that; all his theories about Caddie's stage fright had something to do with her mother. Her way of handling the problem was to surrender, just not play in public anymore. So simple, and it worked perfectly: no more sweaty palms, faintness, or nausea, and somehow the Michaelstown Community Orchestra had managed to get along without her.

Magill, half draped over the long top of the piano, watched her with interested eyes. "Play something you love," he suggested. "Close your eyes and pretend we're not here."

"Yeah, but you *are* here." Looking and listening. She ran one hand over the keys, indecisive. If she played one note, they'd have her.

"We'll sing along," Thea promised. "Do you know 'My Funny Valentine'? Play something you like, and we'll sing."

"Oh, people always think they know the words, but they don't," Caddie said bitterly. "They know the chorus or the line with the title in it and nothing else."

"I know the words to everything," Thea bragged. "If it's old enough. Come on, try me."

This was a lose-lose. She flexed her fingers, played a few random chords. "Okay, okay. I'd just like to say I hate this." She hunted a safe key for "My Funny Valentine" and started to fiddle around with an intro. People forgot what a sad song it was. If she *were* alone, she might've chosen it tonight. She kept her eyes on her hands and tried to give in to the slow, drifty melancholy of the piece, tried to forget herself. Thea sang with her for a little while, then hummed, then stopped completely, leaving her on her own. Of course.

Caddie liked her voice, she just didn't like anyone else to hear it. She made it to the break and thought, *I can plow on now.* Like those people who walked on burning coals. Faith in something or other got them to the other side, but she'd use common sense. *I might get burned, but I won't die. Public performance is not fatal.*

Clapping and compliments. She emerged from a grim, fuguelike state with Thea shaking her shoulders, pummeling her on the back. "*Wonderful*, oh, *Caddie*, I had no idea you could sing like that. Play some more."

"Pretty damn good," Cornel judged. "You know 'Blue Moon'? How about 'After You've Gone.' "

"Oh, that's a good one." Thea started to sing it but stalled after the first line.

Caddie's cheeks burned with her excruciating pleasure and embarrassment. It was idiotic, but she was close to tears *and* laughter. She glanced at Magill, who was looking at her in that weird way again, as if he didn't know who she was, or she'd suddenly turned into her own twin. "Fantastic," he said softly, and she started to get up—she couldn't stand it, it was too much—but Thea pressed her back down.

" 'Dream.' Play 'Dream' for me, Caddie."

"Okay."

She got through that. Then "It Had to Be You" for Cornel. Magill asked if she knew any Dusty Springfield, and she played "Breakfast in Bed."

"Hey, you're good," Cornel said, sounding amazed. "I heard this gal at the Holiday Inn once. She was okay, but you're better."

Caddie put her hands together in pretend-gratitude, but truthfully, she was thrilled. "Gosh, if I'd known you guys were going to be such *pushovers*." Each song was a little easier than the last. The sensation that she was beating something, at least starting to get over a stupid, years-long hurdle right now, *right now*, made her feel breathless, and also as if she were sitting beside herself, observing. It was probably the company—what wonderful, kind friends she had, they were the next best thing to being alone, this probably wasn't a duplicatable experience—but *still*. What a high.

"I'll play one more, but I'll have to bring it way down, so it's not going to sound like the original. Be warned. But it's the only *happy* Billie Holiday song I know. But I'm an alto and she had that sweet, almost, you know, childish—"

"*Play* it."

She played "Miss Brown to You." She was hoping they'd sing it with her, but of course nobody knew the words but her. Thea and Cornel clapped along, though, when she came to the long piano solo at the end, so it was almost like having a jazz bass accompaniment. This was a *great* song. She grinned up at Magill, who was practically lying on the piano with his chin on his folded arm, smiling back at her. "Play it again," he said as soon as she finished, and she laughed and started over.

Thea's hands suddenly went tight on her shoulders. Caddie stopped. It came again—the doorbell.

"I *knew* it." Cornel shot up on his tiptoes, elongated with panic. "I'll take the fall for you," he promised Thea, moving her toward the sofa. "Don't say a word, you're an innocent bystander."

Caddie got up slowly, feeling dazed. Who could it be? Thea said, "I'm sure it's nobody, Cornel," but she looked spooked, too. Magill was sliding the ashtray and the joint makings under a chair with his foot. The room still smelled like pot, though. It was after ten o'clock on a Saturday night; nobody ever knocked on Caddie's door at this hour. Could Mrs. Tourneau have smelled marijuana through the open windows and called the cops? *Would* she have done that? The bell rang again.

Caddie shook her head at the three pairs of eyes staring at her in various degrees of alarm, smacked her hands on her thighs, and went to see who it was.

Christopher.

15

Christopher, standing there in the yellow porch light. In his pleated khakis and maroon polo shirt and his gold-rimmed glasses. He took his hands out of his pockets and smiled, dipping his head in the shy, self-deprecating tilt she loved. "Hi."

Finney, ecstatic, hurled himself against the screen, trying to scratch it open with his paws.

"Christopher."

"How are you doing?"

"Fine, I've been all right." She didn't know what she was saying. She couldn't believe he was here, looking so normal, like this was nothing, not a miracle, standing on her doorstep and smiling at her through the screen.

"May I come in?"

"Yes, sure, come in," and she opened the door and backed up. Finney threw himself on Christopher's knees when he crossed the threshold. He said "*Down*" once, and the dog obeyed. Incredible.

"I, um, have some company," she said, in an agony of self-consciousness, waving toward Thea, Magill, and Cornel in the living room. All three were sitting down, innocent but avid, craning and peering into the dim hall. "You've never met them. Come in and I'll intr—"

"I can't stay. I came by for those books."

She stared at him stupidly.

"You said you'd return them." He smiled, forgiving her. "I guess it slipped your mind."

His dog books. He'd come for the dog-training books he'd lent her. Everything that had lifted up inside dropped back down, back into place. Her face was burning; that was strange, because it felt as if all her blood had drained to her feet. "Yes, I did, I forgot, I'm sorry. But I know right where they are—I'll go get them." Should she introduce him anyway? She couldn't think. "Um . . ."

"Hello," Thea said musically. "You must be Christopher."

He cut his eyes at Caddie in a funny way, almost accusatory, and she thought, *Were we supposed to be a secret? Was I not supposed to tell?* But he turned his charming smile on Thea, slipped his hands back into his pockets, and sauntered into the living room. Caddie said, "Well, I'll just . . . ," and ran upstairs.

In her too-bright room, she sat on the bed while her heart slowed. It came to her that, as intimate as they had been with each other, Christopher had never been up here, never seen her bedroom. Good, because it looked ludicrous to her, a girl's room instead of a woman's, with its pink-and-white-striped wallpaper, the narrow bed and the stringy white rug, the child-size closet. She embarrassed herself. She was angry with Christopher, but how could she blame him for moving on? Her life was as stunted as this room.

That he would come today of all days—did it mean something? Nana believed in signs, so Caddie didn't on general principles. But this was too close, too much of a coincidence not to imply—something. She hesitated to call it a connection. That would be pathetic and self-deceiving, and yet, why would he come *tonight* unless it meant something? She leaned over and held her face in her hands.

Footsteps on the stairs. *Who?* Thea—Caddie let out a slow breath, realizing that's who she wanted it to be. Of all people.

Thea paused in the door, took one look at her, and sat down on the bed beside her. "Is it that bad?" She stroked a wisp of Caddie's hair back from her forehead. "Just give him his damn books. The sooner he's gone—"

"Oh, Thea. Guess what I've gone and done."

"What?"

"Can't you guess? I thought you'd know by now."

Thea looked into her eyes, and the light dawned. "Oh, baby."

"Right. Exactly."

Thea made a sound, a perfect mix of shock and sympathy, and slid her arms around her.

Caddie rested her head on her soft shoulder, inhaling the musty smell of pot in her hair. She wanted to stay like that, never move again. "Should I tell him? He doesn't want a baby. Oh, God, I don't know what to do."

"Are you sure? Did you go to the doctor?"

"No, but I took the test yesterday and it was positive. So I got another one today, and it was the same. But I still can't believe it. We were always so careful." It must've happened that time, early in the morning, when they'd both been half asleep and started to make love without any protection. She was the one who'd remembered before they did much. But they must've done enough.

Thea shook her head sadly. "It can happen so easily. For some people."

"Life is so damn *unfair*." She felt as angry for Thea, who'd *wanted* a child, as she did at herself. "How could I be so stupid? I'm too *old* for this."

"I don't think there's an age limit on it. Until, of course, there is."

"But I'm supposed to be a *grown-up*. I just feel so . . ."

"Don't. It just happened, and you'll get through it. I know it feels like it, but this isn't the end of the world."

"Oh, boy, it feels like it."

· "But it's not. Too many people care about you, and we're not going to let anything terrible happen."

"Please don't make me cry, not now—"

"Absolutely, *no crying*. Not until he's gone, anyway, then we'll bawl. Oh, Caddie, you are so much stronger than you think you are."

"I don't feel strong. I feel like my life's been leading up to this, one big—monstrously stupid thing—"

"Now, stop. You know how many girls this happens to?"

"Girls."

"And grown women, too. Don't be silly."

"I know, I'm just trying not to think about the real—the real *problem* here. Thea," she whispered frantically, "it's a *baby*."

They held on to each other for a long minute and didn't talk.

"Should I tell him? *I don't know what to do.*" She was back to that. "I know he has a right to know, but honestly—I don't think he'll care."

"You don't have to decide right now. Just because he's here. You've only just found out, you need some time. It's—"

"Caddie?" Christopher's voice, calling from the bottom of the steps. "Look, uh, I'm in kind of a hurry!"

"Bastard," Thea said with venom.

Caddie stood up. "I'm just going. I don't know what I'm doing." Panic flickered along her skin, made her hands perspire.

"Do whatever you like." Thea got up more slowly. "Tell him or not, it's *your* perfectly good decision."

The high, righteous arch of Thea's eyebrows gave her a swell of courage. "My decision." She squared her shoulders. "God, I'm glad you're here." Books, she'd forgotten the books. She found them on top of the radiator. "I never read them," she confessed, blowing the dust off the top one. Thea's laugh carried her out of the room and down the stairs on another little wave of bravery.

Three heads swiveled when she walked into the living room.

Somebody, probably Magill, had put a Lucinda Williams record on the stereo. He stood far across the room from Christopher, glaring at him and flexing his jaw muscles. Cornel looked belligerent, too. Only Christopher seemed relaxed and unconcerned. And Finney, who lay at his feet, gazing up at him adoringly.

"Well," Christopher said, "really nice meeting you folks."

Was she imagining a sarcastic edge to his voice? What in the world had the men been saying to each other? He crossed in front of her, heading for the door, and she followed. She had to put her foot across Finney's chest to keep him in the house. "Stay," she ordered, and slipped through the screen after Christopher.

It was hazy and hot outside, moths zipping and pinging off the porch light, fireflies flickering in the honeysuckle hedges. All at once the music inside the house went low—someone had turned down the volume. Christopher turned to face her at the top of the steps. When he looked at her, did he see the same old Caddie? He looked strange and familiar to her, as if he were wearing a disguise or a costume. Over his shoulder, *Crone*, one of Nana's scrap-metal constructions, swayed in the soft breeze, porch light dancing on her bicycle-chain hair and coffee-can breasts.

"Thank you for the loan," Caddie said, passing the stack of books over.

"Sure thing. Think they helped?"

"Oh, definitely, he's much more obedient. How's King?" she asked, stalling.

"He's got an ear infection. Nothing serious, but he hates the drops."

"I bet. Poor thing." It wasn't his fault he loved his dog more than her. He was still a good man. And she had to tell him. She twisted her hands, struggling for a way to start.

"Oh, hey, I got the news this week that we're moving."

"CAT's moving?"

"Well, no, I mean I am."

"You're moving? A new office?"

"Moving to D.C. I'll be doing national PR and some political work. If everything works out and I do a good job, they want me for their full-time lobbyist."

He was willing her to smile back at him with his smile, urging her to join with him in his gladness and pride, but she took two steps back and came up hard against the sharp edge of the living room window. "You're leaving?"

"Not right away. The timing's still iffy, but definitely by the end of the summer."

"Well, that's . . . I know you were hoping . . . so you're taking it? It's for sure?"

"Yeah, definitely. It's what I've been wanting."

She wrapped her arms around her waist. "Listen. We've never really talked about what happened. And—I have to tell you, I never understood. I thought . . . I was *completely* wrong, but I thought it was good, I thought you liked—us. What—what—"

"Caddie, let's not start this."

"I know, but what went wrong? What happened? It's important," she explained past the tightness in her throat.

"Nothing happened." He put his hand on his forehead and looked up at the porch ceiling. "I told you, it was one of those things. It didn't work out, that's all."

"Maybe we can fix it. If we talk, if we have a conversation."

"Hey, I'm sorry, really sorry, but there's no sense in going into it again."

"Nothing in common, you said."

"That's—yeah, basically, I mean—" Amusement flickered for a split second in his sad, sympathetic face. He made half a gesture: he lifted his arm and swept it back, but stopped just before it could indicate the yard. The sculptures. "We're different people, that's all. We want different things."

"How do you know what I want?" She held her hands out to him. "*I* don't know what I want."

He smiled in sad agreement. "And, see, that's just not much of a turn-on for me. I'm sorry, Caddie. That's all I can say." He started to turn away.

"Wait. Christopher, wait."

He looked so pained and patient, and yet—there was something in his eyes that gave her a sick feeling. He was only pretending to hate this. "What?"

"Do you think we'll ever see each other again?" The spasm of disbelief that flashed in his face was just another layer of humiliation. But she plowed on, because that was her job now, all she had left to do. "What I mean is, there aren't any circumstances—under which—you can ever see us getting back together. Right?"

He hesitated, as if he suspected a trick. "I said we can still be friends. If that's what you want."

"No, that's not what I'm asking." She sucked her lips in to wet them. "You don't have any feelings for me anymore. Real feelings. And there's nothing—you can't think of anything that would change your mind, can you? It's over, it's completely over. No matter what."

"No matter what?" He started to laugh, but it caught in his throat. She'd said too much; the horror in his fixed, staring eyes told her he'd guessed.

She said quickly, "No, I'm just asking—"

"Jesus, oh, God—"

"No, no—if I had a fatal disease! If I won the lottery, if I won—a genius award!" She flung a hand out, tamping down a bubble of hysteria. "It wouldn't matter to you, it wouldn't *change* anything, isn't that right? Just answer. You wouldn't suddenly fall in love with me. Nothing could change your mind. Christopher, just answer, that's all you have to do."

It felt like forever, but it was only a couple of seconds before he spoke. His smile was ghastly when he tried to say lightheartedly, pretending he had believed her, "Okay, no. I guess I wouldn't fall in love with you. Nothing would change."

She sagged a little. "Okay, then. I just wondered, that's all. I just wanted to make sure." She didn't feel much of anything, not relief, not disappointment. Sore, that was all.

The screen door squeaked open. Magill stepped out on the porch, barefooted, holding Finney in his arms. "Oh, hi, kids. *Que pasa?* Thought I'd get some air."

"Me, too." Cornel shuffled out after him. "That the moon?"

"*Hey*," Christopher said.

"Caddie?" Thea cleared her throat in the open doorway. "Everything all right?"

Christopher's disbelieving laugh made her wince, it sounded so artificial. "What's this, the cavalry?"

"Why?" Magill said interestedly, coming up close. Finney strained in his thin arms, but he held on tight. "Caddie need a cavalry?"

Christopher snorted. Caddie regretted everything she had ever told him about Magill, and she thanked God she hadn't known about his accident, the awful details, until tonight. Otherwise she would surely have told Christopher, and he didn't deserve to know.

But she didn't trust the sparkly, reckless look in Magill's eyes. "Nobody needs anything," she said quickly. "Christopher has to go, he was just leaving."

"Right." Christopher pulled his lips into a patient smirk. What a relief for him that this scene was ending with other people behaving badly. "Nice meeting all you folks. Caddie, you take care." He went down the steps.

Magill either couldn't hold on to Finney any longer or he let him go on purpose. Either way, as soon as the dog hit the porch floor he flew down the stairs and latched onto Christopher's foot, snarling and growling with mock ferocity, eager to play his favorite game.

"No," Christopher commanded in that calm, godlike voice that never failed.

Finney let go long enough to bark, then clamped back onto Christopher's loafer, wagging his tail with delight.

It could have been funny, and someone who wasn't feeling very kind could've had a small laugh at Christopher's expense. But he said "*No*" again, and Finney backed up, confused. Christopher pushed his hand down like a stop sign. "*Sit.*"

Finney sat, smacking his lips, tilting his head like the RCA Victor dog.

"*Stay.*" He and the dog locked eyes. Christopher turned on his heel and sauntered off down the walk between the sculptures, and Finney stayed.

"Damn," Magill swore softly.

Nobody spoke on the drive back to Wake House. Her friends thought they were being tactful, and besides, what was there to say? But Caddie could hardly stand the silence. Even when they pulled up to the curb and the men got out of the car, nobody said anything. And the jig was up—Magill and Cornel knew all about her situation, because she'd told them—but they still weren't talking.

She got out, too, because Cornel wanted to hug her. Then Magill, and that was when she came closest to breaking down; something about the frailty of his body, the breakable feel of his bones as he squeezed her in his arms. After he let go, he rubbed the back of his neck and stared at the ground for a while. But the perfect comforting remark never came to him—she'd have had to give him some sort of a prize if it had. "Okay if I call you later?" he ended up asking.

"Oh, gosh. I'm so tired."

"Sure. Caddie?"

"Hmm?"

"You know how lucky you are he's gone."

She wasn't feeling very lucky. "Night," she said, spreading her lips to smile, and got back in the car.

Calvert Street was quiet for a Saturday night. Wake House looked fat and mysterious, bottom-heavy in spite of the dark bulge of the tower and the chimneys against the lighter black of the sky. All the upstairs lights were out except for one on the second floor, Mrs. Brill's room. She had insomnia.

"It's a pretty house, isn't it?" Caddie said.

Thea pressed her thumb on the window button. "Does this—"

"No, that's as far down as it goes." It wouldn't go up, either. She needed a new car.

"Well, I wouldn't say it's a pretty house. But I've always liked it."

"That's what I mean. Actually, it's kind of ugly. Thea . . . did you ever fall in love with somebody who turned out . . . not to be good?" When Thea only smiled, Caddie said, "Of course not. You're too smart."

"Ho ho. My first marriage was a disaster."

"How come?"

"I was looking for what I'd lost. A father, I guess. I should've been looking for what I needed."

"All right, but you weren't a complete—*fool*, you didn't go out and—"

"You're thirty-two years old, Caddie, old enough to know this disaster with Christopher doesn't say anything terrible about you. That *you're* not a good person."

"But I loved him. I thought. Maybe I just wanted to be in love with him, but that's even worse."

"Maybe you would've loved him in time. If he'd deserved it. You were just starting."

"Yes, just starting." She put her head back, tilted it to look out her window at the moon coming up behind the roofs across the way. "But I wanted it to go fast," she said to the street, a car hissing by. "I wanted to have what everybody else has. I wanted to be normal. I feel so ashamed."

"Well, he is handsome. He has a beautiful voice, like somebody announcing the news on the radio. And nice hair."

"I loved his hair." She looked at Thea shyly. "He was good in bed. Very . . . sensitive. I called him 'Cristofori,' for a joke—that's who invented the pianoforte, Bartolomeo Cristofori. 'Pianoforte' means soft-loud, it was the first touch-sensitive keyboard . . ." She trailed off, pink-faced. Thea's smile said there wasn't any need to go on. "Anyway, he was really nice. I thought."

"He looks perfect. Anyone would be fooled."

"No, I should've realized. He's good with dogs." She gave in and started to cry. "Finney loves him" came out muffled through her fingers.

Thea scooted over and put an arm around her shoulders. "You do know your dog is a complete moron." She found a tissue in her pocketbook and handed it over, and after that they sat quietly for a time, watching the light at the corner turn from red to green, yellow to red.

"Did you like getting stoned?" Caddie asked.

"Yes and no. I'm glad I did it, but once is enough."

"Probably so." She was thinking how grateful she was to Thea for not bringing it up, the main thing, the elephant in the room, when all of a sudden she blurted out herself, "I can't have a baby! I can't!"

"Well, then, if you can't, you can't."

She blinked at Thea, stymied, feeling as if she'd walked into a wall she wasn't expecting.

"What?" Thea said. "You expect me to talk you out of getting rid of it? I wouldn't. I'd go with you when you did it."

Caddie put her head in her hands.

"And it would be the saddest day. The saddest day. I hope you won't do that."

"But I might. I think I might have to."

"Well, then." Thea reached over to smooth the hair back from Caddie's cheek. "Let's talk about it tomorrow. Believe it or not, everything's going to look better in the morning. The trick is not to look at the *whole* of it, just one piece at a time."

"Right. Okay."

"Also, you'll feel better as soon as you get *mad*."

"I will?"

"I promise you will." Thea kissed her, then slid out of the car. She leaned over to look in through the half-open window. "Don't forget how many people love you."

The damn tears started again.

"It's true. Count 'em up, Caddie. You can start with me." She blew another kiss and went up the steps to the walk slowly, holding on to the rail. She looked tired in the raw, blue-white glow of the streetlamp. *Don't get old*, Caddie thought. *Please don't get old, I've just found you.*

At home, she turned off the porch light and sat in the dark on the bottom step while Finney snuffled around in the yard. She ought to put him on a lead, but it was late, the chances of anybody walking by were slim. He had a habit of lunging at pedestrians, scaring the daylights out of them. Nana's fault; she used to secretly encourage him. "*Get 'em*," Caddie had heard her whisper to the dog as some poor guy passed by on the sidewalk. "*Go get 'em.*" "Nana!" Caddie would say after the ruckus died down. "Why did you *do* that?" She would look tickled and chastened at the same time and not answer. Although one time she'd said, "Keeps 'em on their toes."

Christopher had an all-American family. He liked to tell about the time, a few Christmases ago, when they'd all gathered around the festive dining room table to wait for Mom, a woman Caddie always pictured in a bib apron over a shirtwaist dress, to bring in the Christmas bird. Time passed, and finally one of the sisters had gone to find out what was causing the delay. She'd come back red-faced, convulsed. "Shhh, I swore I wouldn't tell—she dropped the turkey on the floor!" When Mrs. Fox came out, nobody said a word, everyone behaved perfectly, until the straight-faced jokes started. "The turkey's really different this year, Mom," one said. "It has kind of an *earthy* flavor," and another one asked, "What kind of stuffing is this? It's got a real *crunch*."

"We didn't tell her till the end of the meal," Christopher related. "She was so mad! And every Christmas since then when my dad says grace, he always adds in this deadpan voice, 'Most of all, Lord, we thank you for letting the turkey make it to the table this year,' and Mom pretends to bop him over the head with the serving fork. It's a hoot."

Last Christmas, Nana put cheap ladies' wigs on the statues in the outdoor creche at a Catholic church on Pine Street, to protest sexism in religion. She said her Nativity scene depicted the Blessed Virgin, her life partner, Josephine, the Three Wise Women, and Baby Christina.

Caddie got up and went in the house. Nana used to keep her outdoor art tools on the front porch, but Caddie had stored them in the basement the day after she went to Wake House. She found them where she'd left them, between the furnace and the hot-water heater. She wasn't interested in the trowels or the rake. She got the shovel and the spade and started for the steps, then turned around and went back for the pickax.

The moon didn't cast much light, but it rode high and the sky was clear and full of stars. She carried her tools over to *Fecund Goddess,* her personal least favorite, and took aim at its earthen, grass-sprouting center with the flat of the shovel.

Whack!

Her teeth clashed; the whole right side of her body went numb. When sensation returned, she saw that she hadn't gotten anywhere because she'd aimed too low. The sculptures were so solid and they'd been here so long, attacking from the bottom was useless, like trying to topple a hill. She threw down the spade and got the pick.

Whap!

Much better. Whittle them down from the top a little at a time. Finney darted over to the porch in fright, rushed back to run around in circles under her feet. She demolished *Fecund Goddess,* reduced it to giant clumps of dirt and turf, and started on *Passionate Ones United.*

It came down easier but made more noise. Mrs. Tourneau's bedroom light blinked on. What was left of *George Bush in Love* proved tricky, because Nana had used construction adhesive to glue the cowboy boots together; the best Caddie could do was knock it down so at least its suggestive shape lay flat on the ground, not pointing up in the air. Next: *Oppression.*

It took an hour and a half to destroy all Nana's sculptures. Halfway through, she went inside and got a cold beer from the kitchen and brought it outside to drink on the porch. Mrs. Tourneau's light was out now, but her blinds were open; she was still peering through them in her dark bedroom, Caddie was sure. Nothing this good had happened since Nana hung the mayor in effigy. She lifted the bottle in a toast to Mrs. Tourneau and went back to work.

Finney tired himself out and watched the rest from an anxious crouch on the grass, whining occasionally. But he went nuts again when the coffee cans she knocked off *Crone* went flying, ricocheting off more metal litter in the yard. After everything was down, she went from mound of rubble to mound of rubble, smacking at protrusions with her spade to lower the level of destruction. Like finishing off the wounded after a battle.

She flopped on the ground and slung her arms across her knees, sweating and exhausted, too tired to climb the porch steps and go in the house. Her wrists were trembling; everything ached, especially her hands; she had blisters on her palms under every finger. *But I killed them*, she thought, surveying the carnage, waiting for triumph or elation, at least satisfaction. Finney sidled over. He put his chin on her knee and looked up at her with worried eyes.

Whatever had made her do it, that cold rage like an icicle running down the middle of her, had melted about a half hour ago. She'd done the rest out of duty, or neatness, just to finish what she'd started. She didn't feel better. It wasn't as if she'd symbolically renounced one thing in order to embrace another thing. She hadn't turned over a metaphorical new leaf or become a new, better person. She was still Caddie Winger, and Frances Winger was still her grandmother. She still taught piano and violin in her house, and she still had nothing in common with a man like Christopher Fox, and she never would. And she was still pregnant.

16

Everything hurt. She could hardly get out of bed, out of her nightgown. If only it were rainy and cold, she thought, if only it were winter and she had the flu. How pleasant to huddle under the covers in her hot, dim room, drifting up from a spacey doze to read a few pages of a novel or sip a little tea, then pass back out. But it was a perfect summer Sunday, the morning after, and she had no good excuse not to drag herself out of bed and face it.

She kept getting stuck, though, deciding what to wear, making a cup of coffee, putting away last night's dishes. She'd wake up and catch herself staring at nothing with an empty head, or almost empty: vague dread like a milky, low-lying fog lay at the bottom of every trivial thought. Being pregnant must be like living with a terminal illness. You tried to go on with what was left of your life, but you could never really *forget*. The dire nature of your condition lay on top of everything like a heavy, wet tarp.

One way not to get depressed was just to *say* you weren't going to get depressed, then obey yourself. Proactive self-therapy. She'd go outside and weed the garden. Fresh air and exercise, that was the ticket.

But she should've picked something more brain-involving, like the Sunday crossword or a Mozart violin sonata, because digging in the clay soil around her tomato plants in the backyard was just a come-on to more dark, festering thoughts. Not only that, the smell of the tomato leaves made her feel nauseated. Oh, great. Was she going to be one of those pregnant women who threw up all the time?

She'd have to tell Nana. Probably. Or maybe not. What good would it do? She'd just worry. She might even be angry. *Another Winger bastard on the way*, she might say. *Thanks for carrying on the family tradition.*

I need a mother, Caddie thought, pulling crinkled yellow leaves off the plum tomatoes.

Think how many people love you.

A few weeks ago, she'd gone around the house singing. And speaking right up to strangers, laughing at nothing, feeling *alive*, a different person from the worrywart sleepwalker she'd been before Christopher. Now she wasn't even back where she'd started, she was much further back. She had never really longed or yearned for a child the way she assumed most women did—but if Christopher had loved her, if she'd told him about the baby and he'd said, "Oh, darling, oh, my dearest," like the man on Nana's soap opera, she believed she would feel joyful. *A baby*. Oh, imagine it, a little person they'd made together—

No no no no, she wasn't going to think of it that way. Not until she decided what to do. She had about five and a half more weeks to make up her mind. If she thought of it as a baby, she'd be eliminating the easiest option of all. It was a fetus. Better yet, a problem. And she wasn't a mother, she was a temporary host.

What was that game—try not to think of a spotted giraffe, something like that, and then of course it was *all* you could think of. She picked out the clover and chickweed under a cucumber plant and imagined having a child, raising it. A little girl. She'd name her Frances, after Nana, and call her Frankie. She'd bring her up right here, in this house, on Early Street. Live frugally. Hand to mouth, and hope for no emergencies, ever.

How criminally irresponsible. She didn't even *want* a child—she felt like a child herself. Not only that, Winger women didn't make the world's best mothers. She'd have to start seeing Dr. Kardashian again when all kinds of things came up, a whole *bog* full of *issues*, her mother's "abandonment behavior" on top, and she couldn't face that again. Some things you weren't meant to get over, it would be unseemly to get over them. No, no, no, from every angle she cared to look at it from, this baby was a mistake.

Tiny slugs were infesting the lettuce. She picked them off and tossed them in the yard. That reminded her of Cornel, telling everybody in that silly game that she was the kind of person who caught bugs and let them go outside. Well, so what, sue her, it wasn't a character flaw. A minute later, a red ant bit her on the ankle. "Ow!" She whacked it with her trowel over and over until it lay still, a crumpled corpse.

Get mad, Thea advised. Dr. Kardashian had, too; that had practically been his mantra. But she'd gotten mad last night, she'd gone on a veritable rampage, and look what she had to show for it: sore muscles and a lot of explaining to do. Anger was overrated. She always felt worse, not better, afterward.

The phone rang; she heard it through the open kitchen window. Bother. Let the machine pick up. No—it might be a student. She made a dash for the back door and got to the phone while her grandmother was in mid-message. "Hi," she interrupted, breathless, "it's me, I'm here."

"You're there?"

"I'm here. This is me. How are you?"

"Do I have to start all over?"

"Well, or I can listen to the tape, but—"

"I'm having a terrible day. I thought you'd be here by now. When are you coming over?"

"I'm sorry, Nan, I should've called. I don't think I'm going to make it today. I'm not feeling too well."

"Hung over."

"Ha. No."

"Because you had such a good time last night with your *friends*."

She sank into a chair. Not inviting Nana to the fictitious "music recital" had hurt her feelings. But she disapproved of drugs, so Caddie could hardly have said, "It's not a real recital, Nan, it's just Thea wanting to get stoned."

It went further than hurt feelings, though. As silly as it sounded, she had an idea Nana might be jealous of Thea. Jealous because Caddie liked her.

"We didn't have all that good a time," she said truthfully. "You didn't miss much."

"You don't sound good. Do you have a cold?"

"Why are you having a terrible day?"

"Oh, everything. The sun won't behave. I'm doing a painting and the light's wrong, I kept moving the easel and moving it, moving it, *bang*. Over it went, I hit it with my walker, but do you think anybody came to help when I pressed the thing, the button? No, ma'am. What if I had a heart attack? What if I fell in the tub?"

"Nobody came?"

"*Finally* Brenda came, but by then I could've been dead. Are you coming tomorrow?"

"Yes. Definitely tomorrow."

"Bring me my acid dyes. All I need is the greens, but you might as well bring them all."

"Your acid what?"

"Acid dyes, they're in little tiny jars, powder in jars, you can't miss 'em."

"Where are they?"

"In a box, like a shoebox. In the storeroom."

"Oh, *Nan*." The storeroom was a horrible pit of no return, it was so crammed with stuff that nothing new could fit, they went in it only for emergencies.

"It's an emergency. I have to have my dyes, they're for my new project."

"Couldn't we just buy new ones?"

"No, these are special. Hard to find, you'd have to go on the whatchacallit. Internet."

"Do you have *any* idea where they are? What half of the room?"

"They might be on the desk. Or *in* the desk, maybe. No. But maybe. Or in the shelf thing by the window. Or, hmm, one of those boxes in the closet? One of those boxes on the floor in the closet. Or else on top with those shirts I was going to tie-dye. Or, and I don't think so, but it's possible they're in the basement."

Caddie leaned over and rested her cheek on the table. She held the phone with one hand and let the other go limp in her lap.

"Or the closet in my room. No, why would they be there? I really think they're in the storeroom. Somewhere."

Monday morning, she slouched, listless and exhausted, in the doorway of her mother's old room, now the dreaded "storeroom." "Why couldn't you be a bloodhound?" she asked Finney, who was sniffing everything he could get to on his level. "You could save me a lot of time."

When she was little, she'd liked to come in this room and lie on the bed, try to get Mommy's view of things when *she* was a girl. There were enormous dark posters on every wall, close-ups of a scary man's face (Bob Dylan, she found out later), a beautiful but stern black-haired angel (Joan Baez), and other shaggy, grim-looking people holding guitars. Fascinating things crowded the shelves under the window— bongo drums, harmonicas, a dusty Silvertone guitar with strings missing. Her mother had a picture of a kind-faced man (John F. Kennedy) on her bedside table, and when she was very little Caddie used to imagine he was her father. But when she'd asked Nana, she'd said, "No, honey, that man's gone to heaven. Your daddy's just gone."

Sometimes she'd go in her mother's room just to remind herself, convince herself she *had* a mother. And she must be coming back, because so many of her things were still there, clothes in the bureau drawers and the closet, ceramic horses, stuffed animals, her record albums, books and notebooks, even her high school yearbooks. And sometimes she did come back, but only to visit, and never for long.

Caddie learned the signs early, always knew when her mother was about to go away again. First she and Nana would stop speaking. Then Nana would start talking in a strange, tight voice, high and mean but also full of tears. After that Mommy would cry, and there would be yelling and slamming doors. It would be just a matter of hours then, or at most one more night, before her mother would pull her into a hard hug and tell her to be good and do everything Nana said. Then she would drive away in her little gray Volkswagen.

Caddie sighed, already tired. "Well," she said—she talked to herself constantly these days—"here goes nothing."

She started with the closet, which was stuffed not only with her mother's old clothes but also cardboard boxes of Nana's with labels on them: "Electric," "Fur," "Ideas." But when she looked inside, the labels didn't match the contents: "Fur" contained stuffed toys, "Ideas" was a collection of plastic eggs, and the only thing electrical in "Electric" was an extension cord.

The closet was a bust, so she cleared a path to the desk, moving boxes and photographic equipment and cast-off furniture. She paused at the sight of a rolled-up rug. Boy, did that bring back memories. And there were the floor ashtray and matching lamp that went with *Woman as Man*, a "living tableau" for which Nana had sat in an easy chair with her feet up, sipping a beer and reading *Sports*

Illustrated while she blew smoke rings from a smelly cigar. The only problem was, she'd built it in the basement, so nobody saw it except a few friends and Caddie. Art wasn't art without an audience, Nana said. Not long after that, she got the idea for her outdoor sculptures.

The desktop was a hopeless clutter of hardened paintbrushes and used sketchbooks, stamps and inkpads, calligraphy tools, printmaking stuff. "Acid dyes, acid dyes," Caddie repeated, to keep herself on track. Drawers first. She found a shoebox in the first one and said "Aha!" to Finney, who was chewing on a stuffed teddy bear he'd rooted out of somewhere. "No, can't be, that was too easy." She took off the lid, and there was Chelsea. Her doll.

She sat down on the floor. Finney darted over and tried to take it from her hand, but she shooed him away. She hadn't forgotten her Chelsea doll, but she hadn't thought about it in a long time, and it had been years since she'd seen it. She fingered the miniature fringe on the rust-colored suede jacket Nana had made for it; particles, like a sprinkle of paprika, came away in her fingers. The curly yellow hair was still greasy from the time Caddie had put on Vaseline to try to straighten it. So it would look more like Mommy's hair.

Her mother had sent the doll to her when Caddie was about five, and immediately it had displaced all her other toys. She'd named it Chelsea because that was Mommy's stage name. She'd taken it to bed every night, cradling it, whispering to it, pretending she was its daughter, or sometimes its mother. She'd imagined every kind of expression on its bland face, had a thousand conversations with it. Her favorite game was talking on the phone with Chelsea, who would be calling her from some exotic place like Virginia Beach or Wheeling. "You should come and stay with me," the doll would say. "I really miss you. Tell Nana to pack a suitcase and put you on the train right away." Caddie would hold her hand to her cheek, pretending it was the phone, and say, "Yes, I can come. I'll come right now. Can I still visit Nana sometimes?" and the doll would say, "Oh, yes, you can see her anytime you like. You'll live with me instead of her, is all, and we'll all have a wonderful time."

Then she'd imagine it, helping Nana pack a little bag with just her favorite things, kissing her goodbye in the doorway of a steaming train, and riding away in a window seat, waving and blowing kisses. And then the best part, hardly imagined at all because there weren't many details to focus on: being with Mommy. She had the haziest notion of what a hotel room was, and that's where she put the two of them, lying beside each other. On a bed with high posts and a white spread. Taking a nap together in the afternoon. It was a time-out, a break between two exciting events, shows or something where people clapped and clapped because Mommy was wonderful. But in between the exciting events, they went in the vague hotel room and lay together on the bed, rested together quietly, their skin brushing lightly when they turned.

At the bottom of the shoebox was a packet of papers bound by a dry rubber band that snapped as soon as Caddie touched it. Inside were news clippings, ads, and flyers announcing appearances of Red Sky in bars and clubs in distant cities, and later a band called Lightning Twice. Her mother must have sent them to Nana; they weren't from the local papers. And postcards to Nana, sparse messages in her mother's handwriting: "En route to Cincinnati—Eddie says better pay. Hug my girl. J." A handmade birthday card, red construction paper and a glued-on doily: "To Mommie From Caddie I Love you."

Letters to her mother from Nana. They were mostly about Caddie, how she was liking kindergarten, how her permanent teeth were coming in, a first-grade report card. ("Catherine's shyness inhibits socialization, but she is a sweet, tractable child. Needs to build inner confidence.")

An envelope addressed to her mother with an Eastern Shore return address, someplace in Delaware called Clover. An eight-cent stamp.

The letter inside, scrawled on a sheet of lined notebook paper, was dated 3-16-72.

> Dear Jane, Writings not my strong suite, that's why I never wrote you before. Guess I was hoping I'd never have to. Wanted to try again to say what didn't come out right last time. That I'm OK and you don't have to worry about me. It hurts but I'm the one who wrote about changes so I get it. Don't feel bad, anyway I got that covered for us both. I miss the guys, and you know I miss you, but its easier this way. You were right, a clean break. Well that's it. Take care of yourself. Get famous & dedicate a song to me. I'll know because I'll always be listening. Love, Bobby.

March 16, 1972.
Caddie's mother would've been about two months pregnant.

She drove to Wake House that afternoon, in the hour-and-a-half interval she had between piano lessons. She found Nana slumped in her wheelchair, staring out the window with a slack, lifeless expression. She didn't hear Caddie until she shut the door—then her long, pale face lit up, all the features lifting. Caddie felt her own spirits rise, and the hug they gave each other lasted longer than usual.

"*Finally*," Nana said, with a laugh to lighten the fervor. "Feels like an *age* since I saw you."

"Sorry, I know, yesterday was just—" She made a face and a flapping motion with her hand. "But here I am, and I brought your dyes. They were in the *basement*, I'd like you to know."

"My what?"

"Your acid dyes. For your project. Don't you remember?"

"Course I remember." She pushed her lips out and blew a puff of air. "Hey, want to go downstairs? It's Charlie Lorton's hundred and twenty-fifth birthday, we can get some cake."

"Ninety-eighth. Sure, but wait, I wanted to ask you—I found something this morning, a letter in Mommy's old desk." She pulled the desk chair out and set it across from her grandmother's wheelchair so that they could be eye to eye. "It's to her from somebody named Bobby. Do you know who it is?"

"Bobby?" Nana squinted her eyes and wrinkled her nose. "There was a Bobby, but I can't just call to mind . . ."

"I was thinking he must be the boy who played in their old band, Red Sky."

"Red Sky."

"You said you went one time to hear them, remember?"

"I did?"

Caddie lifted her shoulders and let them fall. "It was a letter about breaking up. She'd broken up with him, and he was sad, and—Nana, according to the date, she'd've been pregnant with me. Do you remember him at all? There was a Bobby Haywood in the band, I saw his name with the others on a flyer, one of their ads." Nana kept shaking her head. "Bobby Haywood. Are you sure? Because I was thinking." She leaned forward and whispered it. "He could be my father. Did you ever ask my mother—anything?"

"Nope. No, I didn't." Nana reared back, arranging the folds of her skirt over her knees just so.

"Why not? Nothing? Why not, Nana?"

"Because. Wouldn't have done any good. I'm the last person she'd have told that kind of thing to."

Caddie's hopes for some startling revelation collapsed, but she told herself she was no worse off than before. "I know you and Mommy used to fight a lot," she said.

"Oh, Lord. We were like two cats in a bag. Your mother had no use for me whatsoever in those years."

But she gave me to you, Caddie thought. Her oldest wound. And it was odd that she'd lived in a state of half-mourning for her mother most of her life, but she'd always taken fatherlessness for granted.

"Course, back then it seemed like the whole world was turning inside out. What year was it? This letter? Nineteen . . ."

"Seventy-two."

"But me, I was still back in the fifties, still being Mrs. *Buchanan*." She shut her eyes. "God oughta try harder to save us from the good deeds we do for each other."

"You'd tell me if you knew, wouldn't you?"

"Knew what?"

"Who my father was."

She opened her eyes. "Oh, honey. That was a door your mama just never was going to open for me. Plus I don't even know if *she* knew. That sounds bad, and she wasn't, she just . . . what was that band that had the girl who turned around in circles? She wore those filmy clothes, and they named it after the one who played the drums. You know that band."

"No."

"Yes, you do. She married one of them and the other girl married the other one."

"Fleetwood Mac."

"Fleetwood Mac. Well, that's how it was with Jane and all her bands. They weren't bad, they just didn't know how to behave. It was the sexual revelation, free love, all that. Which I was against. *Then*."

"Revolution." Caddie had to smile. "But now you're for it?"

"Oh, I just wish I had the time back. I wouldn't fuss and carry on, I wouldn't be so *mean*."

"You weren't mean."

She didn't hear. "I went around scared all the time, that was my trouble. Scared of getting found out, and now it all seems so ridiculous.

What a waste of time. You know what I hate? People who say they have no regrets."

They watched the windows of the building across the street turn blinding-gold in the late afternoon sun, while Caddie thought, *I go around scared all the time, too.* She didn't have her grandmother's excuse, though; she wasn't trying to protect a reputation or a child. At least Nana had finally gotten free. Boy, had she gotten free.

Which reminded Caddie of the other thing she'd come to tell her.

"Nan?"

"Hmm."

"I've done something wrong. I don't even know why I did it. Exactly."

"What did you do?" She was smiling, ready to brush it away.

"I took down the sculptures in the yard."

The smile faded.

"I'm so sorry. I apologize to you. Are you upset?"

"My sculptures?"

She nodded.

Nana's face drained white. "What do you mean, 'took them down'?"

"I don't know, they . . . it . . . I just . . . I wanted to see how the yard would look without them. They've been there so long, and you haven't made any new ones in quite a while, over a year except for the cowboy boots, and the neighbors—I didn't do it because of the neighbors," she raised her voice to say over Nana's outraged snort. "I just . . . I thought . . . when you come home you can start all over, a clean slate, a—clear field. All new."

Nana's hands gripped and released the sides of her chair. "When did you do this?"

"Saturday."

"Saturday. Before your *friends* came over. Because you didn't want them to see."

"No."

"Because you were ashamed!"

"No, I did it *after*. Saturday night, late. I *wasn't* ashamed."

"Then why'd you do it? Were you drunk? How *could* you, Caddie? That was my *work*, you had no *right*!"

They both started to cry.

"I'm so sorry, you're right, I had no right. I shouldn't have done it."

"Go away, I don't want to see you right now." She jerked the wheel of her chair, trying to turn it toward the window.

"I wish I could undo it. Please don't be mad."

"I am mad! You can't fix anything, so leave me alone. I mean it, go away, I don't want to talk to you anymore. I'm grieving."

"Nan—"

"What I should do is sue you. Maybe I will, too. Out of my sight while I think about it. Out!"

Caddie slunk out.

Next, she had a fight with Angie.

"*God*, why don't you get an air-conditioner in here? It's the middle of July, for cripe's sake." Angie set her violin case on the piano bench with so much force, the instrument vibrated inside it.

"Good afternoon to you, too," Caddie said.

"I mean, *God*." She stripped off her filmy, see-through shirt as if it were a fur coat and put her hands on her hips; she looked beautiful and indignant in her cutoffs and a pink tank top. "*Everybody's* got central air, Caddie, and you've got a *fan*."

"It's hot, I know." She aimed the big square fan on the floor directly at Angie. "But my grandmother hates air-conditioning, so what can I do?" She shrugged, smiled.

Angie not only didn't smile back, she rolled her eyes in disgust. It was the first clue Caddie failed to pick up on that she'd come to start a fight.

"Why don't you warm up while I go get us some cold drinks?" Caddie retreated to the kitchen.

Teenagers were great fun to teach, but also unpredictable. Flexibility was the key, because you never knew what mood they were going to show up in. Well, one of the keys; the other was, *Don't take it personally.* Caddie reminded herself of that while she poured soda over ice in glasses and brought them back to the living room.

"You look pretty today." She set the drinks on coasters on top of the piano. "I like your hair that way." She could usually jolly Angie out of a bad mood by giving her a compliment. She wasn't any vainer than a seventeen-year-old girl with shiny brown hair and big dark eyes, perfect roses-and-cream skin, and a great figure ought to be, in Caddie's opinion. Angie made her wish she'd appreciated her own youth more. Not that she'd ever been that lovely and poised, or ever would be, but she wished she'd relaxed and had a better time. Not been so unhappy with herself.

"My uncle says I sorta look like Natalie Wood, whoever that is, and I should cut my hair to look more like her. But I like it long."

"Oh, me, too." How Angie was going to wear her hair in the Miss Michaelstown pageant was a topic of endless discussion and indecision in the Noonenberg family.

"Actually, I was thinking of dying it blonde."

"*No,*" Caddie said, aghast.

"But then I decided not to. It was Mom's idea, just for the pageant, but I don't think so."

"Oh. Whew." She patted her heart in a show of relief.

Angie stopped doing her scales. "Actually, I don't even know if I want to be in the stupid pageant."

Once that would've shocked Caddie—since she'd known her, winning beauty and talent contests had been Angie's life goal—but lately she'd been saying things like that at almost every lesson, hints of dissatisfaction, veiled threats of quitting. Caddie made a point of underreacting, since Angie's moods changed on the hour. "Well," she said, "why don't we talk about it after your lesson, so we don't waste time."

Angie scowled.

"I thought we'd do something different today, anyway," Caddie improvised. "Instead of playing your piece, I thought we could listen to the recording we made last week and critique it."

"We already did that."

"We listened, but we didn't study it, which is why we taped it to begin with. I think it would help to listen carefully and pick out the sections that need more work—"

"Oh, yay, pick it apart, in other words. That sounds like fun." She slumped down on the bench, stretched her long, tanned legs out, and stared stonily at her painted toenails.

Caddie kept quiet and put a tape in the player.

Angie thought *she* was sick of "Meditation." Caddie had to keep reminding herself why it was still a good piece for the pageant. It was familiar, and therefore a crowd-pleaser, and yes, it was corny, but only because of overuse. If you hadn't heard it a hundred times, it was lovely, genuinely moving.

They listened to it in silence the first time. It was from an opera about a monk and a prostitute. Lots of angst. "Now, right here," Caddie said on the second run-through, "right there, hear it? You have to hold that note even longer, because it's almost like a lullaby, you can't play it too slowly."

"Lullaby for a dead person."

"And that measure—do you hear how you're almost a quarter note ahead of the harp?" Caddie was simulating the simple harp

234

accompaniment on the piano, not just to fill out the music but to help slow Angie down. "Hey, you know what I should do? Record myself, and you could use that to practice with at home. What do you think?"

"Look, Caddie, I don't want to do this."

"Okay, but it's either that or the metronome, and you know how much you love *that*."

"No, I mean the whole thing. I don't want to do it anymore. I didn't practice all weekend."

"Ah."

"Oh, I knew you'd look like that!"

"Like what?"

"That face! I knew you'd do that sad, disappointed look and make me feel all bummed!"

"Well, sorry—"

"Can you turn that off?"

She turned off the tape player.

The deep, nervous breath Angie took revealed her belly button under her top. "Here's the thing. I don't think I want to study music anymore. Not even in college." She looked out the window to finish—Caddie must be making that face again. "Because it's not fun anymore, it's just pressure and duty. Music should be for fun, not studying. I really feel that."

"That's just shortsighted. You can't have one without the other. Angie, that's—shortsighted and immature."

"I'm *not* mature! *You've* got enough maturity for six people! I've thought about it—when I graduate, I'm taking a year off and joining a band."

"You're what?"

"A bluegrass band."

Caddie had to sit down.

Angie started walking around the room. "That's what I want to do most, play fiddle in a band. But a progressive one, not just like all Bill Monroe or whatever. There's this guy at school—"

"Oh, *ho*."

"No! There's this guy, he plays three different instruments and he's really good, and he thinks *I'm* good—"

"You are good, but—"

"Never mind him, anyway, I can see what you're thinking and you're wrong. There are these great girl fiddle players you probably never even heard of, like Deanie Richardson and Martie Maguire, Sara Watkins, not to mention Allison Krause—"

"I've heard of her."

"Caddie, this is what I want to do. I've decided, I've made up my mind."

A band. A bluegrass band. All the things Caddie wanted to say sounded unkind or insulting—she should never have said "shortsighted and immature." "I—I just feel this is a mistake. I'm so afraid you'll regret it. You know I just want what's best for you, and I can't help thinking this is—frivolous. I'm sorry, but I don't see how you could've considered all the—"

"I have, too!" She relaxed the fists she'd made out of her hands and brought her voice down to a calm, grown-up level. "I have. Considered all the consequences, ramifications. Whatever."

"But it's too dangerous, it's too—I honestly think you'll be sorry if you do this."

"What do you mean, too dangerous? What does that mean?"

Caddie had no idea what it meant.

"Just because *you're* afraid to play in public—" She turned away, pressing her lips together. "Anyway, that's what I'm doing."

"Doesn't it matter, don't you care that you're throwing away your wonderful talent? That you've wasted the last four years of your time and hard work? And mine? And your parents' money? What does your mother think about this?"

"I can't believe you'd say that to me." She threw open her violin case. "You're the one who said I should have *passion*. I'm not coming here anymore."

"I guess I don't have anything to teach you anymore."

She left the room rather than watch Angie pack away her instrument. Was this really happening?

Angie came out to the hall, red-eyed. "Well," she said, with a wavery smile, and Caddie melted.

"We don't have to fight. Oh, Angie, this is silly. After all these years."

"It is silly. I know."

Relief flooded her. "Go home, I think you should, but I'll see you on Thursday and we can talk more. I didn't say *anything* right today."

Angie flushed bright pink. "Um, I think it's better not. I feel like we need a break. I appreciate all you've done, I really do. You're a fantastic teacher, I've learned so much. Well, everything. But maybe it's time to, you know . . ."

It was like Christopher all over again. "No, you're right, you can get stale with the same teacher. It's good sometimes to shake things up, get a new, a fresh—"

"My mom says she'll send this week's check for both lessons, even though . . . sort of like giving notice."

Caddie nodded and smiled, but that was a stake to the heart. Angie had known before she came that this was going to be her last lesson.

"Well, Caddie—we'll stay in touch."

"Sure. Of course we will."

They faced each other, awkward and miserable. Caddie was the first to reach out. They shared a stiff embrace, bumping cheeks. "Okay, bye."

"Bye."

And that was that. In disbelief, Caddie went back in the living room and listened to the whir of the ugly, inadequate fan. The piano looked inert to her, a black, hulking thing, incapable of anything consoling or beautiful, least of all music. In fact, the whole room looked like the enemy. How quickly things could change. She looked at her watch to confirm it. Yes: in twenty-five minutes, Angie had come and gone. Her favorite student, her sweet, funny friend. Caddie hadn't even had a chance to compromise. Or capitulate! She'd have given in if she'd had time, told Angie she could become a rap artist if she wanted. It made her sick, literally nauseated, to think that wouldn't have done any good. Angie's mind had been made up before she came.

A bluegrass band. "Revolting," she said out loud, holding her stomach. *Too dangerous*, she'd told Angie. What *did* that mean? Perilous; more than just risky. Something bad.

She was so tired, she had to lie down on the couch. Everything was falling apart, everthing all at once. What else could go wrong? She leaned over the edge of the sofa and rapped her knuckles on the wooden leg. *Never* ask what else could go wrong—Nana had taught her that. Anyway, she could be having quintuplets, Nana could break her other leg—just stay far, far away from rhetorical questions. Superstitious, yes, but in bad times, why tempt fate? She closed her eyes, trying to clear her mind of dangerous thoughts.

The phone ringing woke her up from a dream, something about Finney having a litter of puppies in the piano, they started crawling out on the keys like worms during Mrs. Patterson's lesson—it took a few seconds to register what Brenda was saying to her. Nana had put something in the washing machine—it smelled like vinegar—and now everybody's clothes were coming out green.

"Should I come over?" Caddie asked fearfully. This day couldn't end fast enough. If she went outside, left home and went back into the real world, who knew what might happen next?

"Well, there's nothing you can do about it now." Brenda,

normally the soul of patience, sounded exasperated. "I'm running empty loads with just soap and bleach, so it's bound to clear up eventually."

"I'm really sorry. I don't know what she was thinking. If anybody's lost anything valuable, I'll be happy to pay for it."

Brenda made a sound like a suppressed sigh. "You know what kind of house this is, Caddie," she said, lowering her voice to that sympathetic tone Caddie had always dreaded. "We're not quite a nursing home, not quite assisted living."

"Elder care," Caddie said, while pinpricks of premonition made the hair on her arms stand up.

"What we don't have the facilities for, unfortunately, or the expertise, or the *credentials*, is caring for people with Alzheimer's disease or dementia."

"Oh, but—"

"I'm not saying Frances has either of those conditions—anyway, I'm not a doctor, I'm just the landlady."

"I know she can be forgetful at times, but don't you think—"

"It goes a little bit beyond forgetfulness. There've been other things."

"Oh, God."

"Nothing really serious, I don't mean to alarm you."

"What did she do?"

"Well, there was an incident on the porch last week. With a slingshot. Don't ask me how Frances got hold of a slingshot, and no one actually saw her *shoot* it, but apparently she made a gesture at some passersby—"

"Kids, little boys . . . she never did it, she *never* did, but she used to say she was going to bing somebody if she caught them defacing her art . . . she had . . . sculptures out in the yard, but they're gone now. I really think she must've been teasing, Nana's not violent, never—"

"Caddie—"

"But see, that's the point, this is nothing new, she's *always* been like this. She's an *artist*, she's . . . peculiar. It's not dementia, it's not."

Brenda's sigh was audible this time. "Well, I don't know, I just don't know."

"She loves it there so much. And anyway, it's *temporary*. Till her leg heals." That sounded unconvincing even to Caddie: Nana got around fine on a walker these days.

"I have to go, sorry," Brenda said quickly; she had an old-fashioned phone, and Caddie could hear the other line ringing. "We'll talk about this again. Bye. Wait! I forgot—Cornel says he'll give you fifteen minutes, so have your questions ready."

"What? For what?"

"His interview. For the memory book."

"Oh. Okay."

"And he can only fit you in between now and dinner."

"*Today?*"

"Today." Brenda hung up.

INTERVIEW WITH CORNEL MONTGOMERY

Q: What is your name?

A: Cornel Windermere Montgomery.

Q: When and where were you born?

A: August 3, 1925, Michaelstown, Maryland.

Q: How did you get the name "Windermere"?

A: Is that on your list of prepared questions?

Q: No.

A: Move on, then.

Q: I can't add questions?

A: No.

Q: What were your parents like?

A: Nice folks.

Q: Could you be more specific?

A: Is that on your list?

Q: Cornel!

A: If you have to know, my father came over from Scotland in the 1890s and worked all his life for the railroads. He was strict. Presbyterian. The only person who could make him laugh was my mother. Whose name was Alice Windermere, to answer your other snoopy question, and she came from Mount Airy.

Q: Did you have a happy childhood?

A: That on the list?

Q: Yes.

A: It was happy, it was fine. For a while.

Q: And you had a brother? Frank? Who died?

A: If you know everything, why bother asking? I had a brother. Two years younger than me.

Q: You don't have to say anything else if you don't want to.

A: Hell, I know that. It's a short story. We used to go swimming in a creek down back of where we lived. Course it's all built up now, creek's not even there anymore. We'd swing on these long vines across it, playing Tarzan. I'd gone home, I wasn't there when it happened. A vine busted and he fell on the rocks, split his head open. One of the kids ran and got somebody's father and they carried Frank to the house, our house. Too late to do anything for him. So that's that, go on to your next question. Go on. Is that it?

Q: What was your best subject in school?

A: Arithmetic and geography. I liked memorizing poems, too. They quit making kids do that, another mistake. "Into the valley of Death rode the six hundred." I still know that by heart. Want to hear it?

Q: Sure.

A: [Recites "The Charge of the Light Brigade"]

Q: What sports did you enjoy?

A: Baseball. Oh, man, I loved baseball. But it's all money now, I don't bother to watch, not since Ripken's gone. It's just a show, they ruined it.

Q: Tell me about your first date. Or your first girlfriend, either one. These are both on the list.

A: My first date and my first girlfriend were both Erma McDormond. You want more?

Q: Much more.

A: Well, there isn't much more, unfortunately. She had long blonde hair and brown eyes. Her little brother was born deaf, I remember. She went to my church but not my school, so I only saw her on Sundays. One day I got up the nerve to ask her if she'd go to the church bazaar with me.

Q: How old were you?

A: Thirteen, fourteen. We went on a Saturday afternoon. I had two dollars and sixty cents, a fortune, and blew it all on the dart game trying to win her a stuffed bear. Never did win a damn thing. She paid for a couple of lemonades, and that was our first date.

Q: How many more were there?

A: Not many.

Q: Did you ever kiss her?

A: None of your business. No.

Q: Who was the first girl you kissed?

A: What is this, the *Playboy* questionnaire?

Q: You won't tell?

A: No.

Q: Okay, what did you do after you got out of high school?

A: Joined the air force. I wanted to join up after Pearl Harbor, but my folks wouldn't let me.

Q: Did you fight in the war?

A: Long story, but I ended up a gunnery sergeant in the 306th Bombardment Group. I flew B-17s as turret gunner on nine bombing missions.

Q: Wow. But you never talk about it.

A: Nobody wants to hear old war stories.

Q: Did you win medals?

A: Some.

Q: What? Say what they were, Cornel, this is your *history*.

A: Air Medal with Oak Leaf Cluster, Bronze Star, Theater Medal with Combat Star. Next question.

Q: Then what?

A: College on the GI bill. Engineering degree. Surveying job. Started a little locksmith business on the side. Got married. Locksmith business got bigger, I quit the surveying job—

Q: Wait! Back up!

A: This is going to take forever. I'm an old man, my time is precious.

Q: You got married. To whom?

A: Peggy Craddock.

Q: How old were you? How did you meet? Why did you fall in love?

A: What makes you so nosy?

Q: It's interesting. It's your life!

A: We met on a double date.

Q: A blind date?

A: No, a double date. We liked each other better than our dates, so we switched.

Q: That *night*?

A: No, not that night, the next date. She was twenty-four, I was twenty-eight. She worked for the phone company.

Smart as a whip. We just hit it off. She was easy to talk to, and pretty, lots of fun. We courted for about eight months, then tied the knot.

Q: How long were you married?

A: Thirty-five years. I lost her in 1989.

Q: And you had a son.

A: We named him Frank after my brother. Called him Junior till he was grown. They didn't look alike, Junior was a big, strapping boy with blue eyes and curly hair like his mother, but they had a lot in common. The way they laughed, the things they thought were funny. Mischief they got up to. When Peg and I had Junior, it was the closest thing to getting Frank back. But of course it never lasts long because that's not how life works. For everything you get, you have to give up something else. First Peggy, then Frank six years later. He stopped to help a woman change a flat tire. Good Samaritan. A truck hit him, he was killed instantly. Thirty-eight, with a two-year-old son and a wife. So you want to know my philosophy? Keep your helmet on and your head down. It won't do you any good, but neither will anything else, and meanwhile you got something to occupy your mind.

Q: What about your grandson? Zack?

A: What about him?

Q: Don't you miss seeing him?

A: You're not listening. Anyway, I'm done with all that, I'm too old.

Q: Too old for what?

A: You got any more questions? I can't waste the whole day on this.

Q: You were one of the earliest residents of Wake House. Do you remember your first impression?

A: Yes: "Christ almighty, these women all look like my mother."

Q: What is your proudest accomplishment and your biggest regret?

A: My son.

Q: What are you thankful for?

A: My health. If you don't count thyroid, my arthritis, cataracts, and hiatal hernia. I'm thankful Bernie's using those nose strips at night; he only sounds like a freight train now instead of a B-52. I never knew anybody who could make so much noise just turning the pages of a newspaper. Or sucking on his false teeth. He makes this loud sighing sound when he sits down, like he's doing something important and satisfying. Cuts his nose hairs with a little pair of scissors and leaves 'em in the sink. Thinks nothing of letting go a long fart in bed at night—although he controls himself during the day in public, which is more than you can say for some of 'em.

Q: Anything else you're thankful for?

A: I'm thankful this is almost over.

Q: Were you ever a cheerful, optimistic person?

A: Not as I recall.

Q: When you look back on it, do you feel as though your life mattered?

A: Oh, hell, no.

Q: What is your biggest fear?

A: That I'll live forever.

Q: Thanks, Cornel. I guess that's it.

A: Say, what's the matter with you?

Q: Nothing, I'm just a little depressed.

17

Punky, scary stylists and European dance music, that's what Thea wanted when she dyed her hair red. "I'm striking an item off my life list, I want it to be an *event*." Too bad there wasn't a place like that in Michaelstown, or if there was, Caddie didn't know about it. She took Thea to the Curly Wave, because that's where she always got her hair cut.

"Hey," said Wanzie, the operator Caddie had been coming to for, off and on, about fifteen years. "How're you doing, honey? This your friend?" Caddie had made appointments for herself and Thea last week. Middle-aged and heavyset, Wanzie had a tired but game face and unsurprisable eyes that said she'd seen and heard just about everything. Caddie always felt bad because she didn't have any good gossip for her. Till now. What would Wanzie say if she told her she was pregnant?

"Thea should go first, because she'll take longer," Caddie said, and Wanzie said okeydoke, sat Thea down, and unfurled a brown cover-up over her. "What can I do for you today, honey?"

Thea's eyes glittered with excitement; her usually calm face had spots of color on each cheek. She pushed her fingers into her hair and pulled it out from her head in handfuls. "Everything!"

Wanzie laughed and did her own inspection of Thea's hair, running her hands through it, examining the roots, the ends. "So you want red, huh?" Caddie had warned her ahead of time. "How red?"

"Well." Thea folded her hands and made her face look judicial. "I'm turning seventy this year. Not fire-engine."

Wanzie kept playing with her hair, turning Thea's head to different angles. After a minute, a look replaced her usual pleasantly bored expression. In fifteen years, Caddie had never seen it before. Creative enthusiasm. "Hold on, I'll be right back."

She returned with four swatches of hair, like little rug samples. Caddie never knew there was such a thing. Hair colors, like paint chips. "Like any of these?"

The three women hovered over the snippets of colored hair. They ranged from light blondish-red to dark blondish-red. Thea pointed to the first one.

"That's what I thought, too. Nice with your coloring." Wanzie held the swatch to Thea's cheek. "What about highlights?"

"Highlights," Thea breathed, thrilled.

"It'll make the red look more natural, for one thing, but it'll also be pretty. Light up your face. Talking subtle, now, nothing loud, and mostly around the front."

"Oooh, let's do it. Don't you think?"

"Very daring," Caddie said. Somebody had to be the cautious one.

"I know," Thea said, vindicated. "Very daring. It's unanimous!"

"If you want to do it gradually, I can start you off with a rinse. Live with that a while, see what you think."

"Live with it a while? At my age?" Thea laughed out loud. "Dye it!"

Caddie sat in the empty operator's chair next to Thea's while Wanzie went to work with foil strips and a bowl of whitish goo. Leafing through a magazine, she came across a feature on how many sex partners people had had. "Look," she said, showing it to Thea and Wanzie, and they laughed at the photographs of ordinary women, not celebrities, holding up signs with numbers, fourteen, two, eight. One woman had combed all her hair over her face because her number was forty-two. *Forty-two*, they exclaimed in astonishment. Caddie waited, half hoping Thea or Wanzie would mention something personal about their own love lives, maybe even offer a number. But they didn't, so of course she didn't either. If she had, her number would've been four.

"Pregnancy doesn't have to trump fashion!" read the headline for an article on maternity clothes. She held the magazine close, studying the models' serene faces. Were they really pregnant? No, she decided; they were just wearing pillows on their stomachs. She closed the magazine, not interested anymore. She watched pregnant women on television or on the street or in the grocery store like a spy, searching for clues, a secret. She recognized her motive: it was the same way she used to scrutinize other girls in school when she was a teenager, looking for a sign of the thing they knew and she didn't. She had the same fascination and envy now when she watched pregnant women. Longing. A kind of hunger.

She'd been reading up, so she knew it wasn't possible to feel the baby yet, but she did. Sometimes it was like a soft, deep humming, other times a scratchy sensation. She was of two minds about everything, so it was impossible to *enjoy* the scratchy sensation. She went back and forth between silly personal pride in the fact that her body had *worked*—*I did this, I functioned perfectly, my ovaries, my follicles, my fallopian tubes all ran like clockwork*—and a sick, panicky dread because the thing growing inside her felt at least as much like a cancerous tumor as a baby. *What was she going to do? What was she going to do?* This wasn't like a toothache, or a mysterious lump, some personal affliction she could suffer with if she chose to. Procrastination was never going to make this go away.

While Thea sat under the dryer with her head covered in foil strips, Caddie stared at her reflection in the mirror at Wanzie's station and mulled her question, "And what can I do for *you* today,

Caddie?" When she didn't answer right away, Wanzie said in a more resigned tone, "The usual, just a trim?"

"I guess. Or—maybe *short* this time," she said boldly. "Oh, I don't know." She thought of something Magill had said. They were out on the front porch and it was a blustery day, the wind blowing her hair in her eyes, in her mouth. "I'm cutting it all off," she'd said in exasperation—not seriously, just out of annoyance—and he'd said, "No, don't do that, your hair's the only thing you haven't tamed." What did that mean? She stared in the mirror at her same old longish face, her straight-across lips and straight-across eyebrows. Did he think her hair was too wild? She tried to keep it combed and neat. Since she was a girl, she'd parted it on the left and let it go, shoulder length. Once in a while she pulled it back with two barrettes.

"How about some bangs?" Wanzie said. "For a change." She was still infected with Thea's daring.

"Bangs? I've never had bangs . . ."

"If you don't like 'em, they'll always grow out."

"Bangs. I don't know. I think . . . I'll just have the usual."

Wanzie shrugged. Not surprised.

An hour later, Caddie looked the same and Thea was a new woman.

"Oh, I love it, I love it," Thea cried, turning her head this way and that in the mirror. "It's a pixie—I look like Shirley MacLaine!"

"Almost a pixie." Wanzie stood back proudly. "A little longer on top than a pixie, but you've got good hair for it, lots of body."

"It's so *natural*," Caddie marveled. "You look so *young*."

"The magic word," Thea exclaimed, and jumped out of the chair to hug a delighted Wanzie. "It's fabulous—*you're* fabulous."

At the reception desk, Caddie felt let down. "I should've done something dramatic, too. Why didn't I? My hair's just mousy."

"No, it isn't," Thea said, signing for her cut and color with a credit card. "You have lovely hair."

"Then it's me. *I'm* mousy." She picked up a bottle of shampoo on a shelf of hair products and set it down. Conditioner, gloss, gel, brightener, straightener. "Remind me never to buy any mousse," she cracked, "then I'd be even mousier." She pretended to elbow Thea in the ribs.

Thea gave her hair a playful yank. "Pretty. And you're *not* mousy. You just think you are."

"What'll we do now?" Caddie asked in the parking lot. It was a hot afternoon, but not muggy for once; the air smelled fresh, and there wasn't a cloud in the sky.

"What I'd like to do is go for a ride in your car with the top down."

"Sorry, it won't go down. Anyway, you'd mess up your hair." She gasped when Thea stuck both hands in her brand-new hairdo and scrambled it with her fingers.

"That's what it's for!" She laughed at Caddie's shocked expression. "Let's go for a ride with the top *up*, then. Come on, I'll show you where I used to live."

The Pontiac needed a new muffler; it sounded like a hot rod when Caddie fired it up and glided out onto Main Street. "Have things changed a lot since you were a girl?" she asked, passing city square, the heart of downtown, with its old stone banks on three corners.

"It's bigger, naturally, more spread out. Right here, this is where it's changed the least. I remember all these bank buildings. That tae kwon do place," she said, pointing, "that was a candy store, it was called Emmy Lou's. And the Triple A was a shoe store, I forget the name."

"Where am I going?" Caddie stopped at the light at Main and Antietam, the last cross street before downtown ran out and turned into suburbia.

"My old school's gone," Thea said, gazing wistfully at the Best Western.

"Your school? You didn't go to that one-room place of Cornel's, did you?"

"Oh, my *dear*. I went to Miss Adams's Academy for Young Ladies. I can't believe it's gone. Turn, Caddie, I'll show you my aunt and uncle's old house."

They drove along the in-town part of Antietam, a boring street, nothing but parking lots and anonymous brick buildings. You only used Antietam to go the four blocks from Main to Maryland Street, which went one way the other way. Caddie noticed a sign and did a double take. "Thea, look!" The car behind her honked, and she pulled over to the curb. "Look—it's Magill's company."

"Where?"

"There. I recognize the name, Kinesthetics, Inc." The sign stood in front of a long, low, two-story brick-and-stone building next to a parking lot. A black glass door marked the modest entrance, and all the windows were covered with open Venetian blinds. "That's where he makes feet." It looked like a cross between a house and a factory.

"It looks empty," Thea noted.

"I guess not, though. Cars in the parking lot." But only two. Thea was right, the place looked abandoned.

"We should get Henry to take us on a tour, a field trip."

Caddie laughed, uncertain, but Thea looked serious. "Are they on an assembly line, do you think?" She pictured the scissorlike contraptions he'd showed her, walking out in line on a long conveyor belt. "He calls me sometimes."

Thea turned to look at her. "Henry?"

"To cheer me up."

"Huh. And does he?"

"Yes," she decided after a second. "He makes jokes about Christopher. I can't help it—I laugh."

"Excellent."

They looked for a while longer at Magill's sad, dusty, unkempt foot factory. Nobody was watering the dry shrubbery or the browning plantings. The place might still be limping along, ha-ha, without Magill, but it needed its heart back. And he needed it. It was so *clear* to her sometimes, what other people needed.

Thea's aunt and uncle's house was a flat-fronted brick colonial on a tree-lined street in the oldest part of town. "How *little* it looks," Thea exclaimed, leaning back in the seat so that Caddie could see across her. "Oh, the willow tree's gone. It had a long, low branch, I used to lie on it and read. That was my room," she said, pointing at the second-floor corner. "I wonder who lives here now. No toys in the yard."

It didn't look that little to Caddie. And Thea's neighborhood had aged a lot better than hers had. Early Street was run-down; Thea's street was just old. "Do you want to knock on the door? Tell the people you used to live here?"

"Oh . . . I don't think so. I wasn't that attached to the house. My uncle got a job in Washington when I was twelve, and we moved."

"So this isn't really where you grew up?"

"It's where I moved after my mother died."

"When you were nine," Caddie said leadingly. She wanted to hear the story.

"When I was nine."

"Was it sudden? Was she sick?" She thought of Bea and Edgie's mother, how she'd invited the two little girls into her big bed to say goodbye. Labelle was her name. "What was your mother's name?"

"Grace. No, she wasn't sick. She died in childbirth."

"Oh, no. Was she at home?"

Thea looked at her curiously. Was she being too nosy? But she wanted to know, wanted a *picture* of how Thea had lost her mother, so she could . . . hold it next to a picture of how she'd lost hers?

"Well, it started at home—people had their babies in their own beds in those days, or at least they did in my family. With plenty of doctors and nurses around, mind you." She put her head back on the seat. "It was a big family, plenty of aunts and uncles, and my grandparents, lots of cousins, but I was an only child. When my mother told me she was pregnant, I wasn't jealous, Caddie, not even for a second. Because she was so happy. I remember a party in the summer on our front porch—I don't think it was a shower for the baby, just a party, and my mother in a white dress with her stomach out to here. Laughing. We had a swing, and I remember her pushing my father in it because he wouldn't let her swing."

She stared out the window with cloudy eyes. "When I think about my childhood, that's what I see. The party that summer. My mother in her white dress, and my tall, handsome father. Outside on the lawn with all the others, everybody talking and eating, laughing and drinking. The men smoking cigars. A hot summer, like this—my grandfather taking off his jacket, so then all the other men could take off theirs."

Caddie waited for the bad part.

"She died in September, so I expect she was about seven months pregnant for that party. At first everything was fine. My grandfather had hired a nurse, and she came, then the doctor. I wasn't allowed in; they told me to go to sleep and when I woke up, who knew, I might have a little brother or sister." She looked down at her hands. "It was like Christmas Eve. I thought I'd never fall asleep, but I did. I didn't hear the ambulance come and take her to the hospital. That's where she died. I never got to see her."

"And your father?"

"Oh, my father. He went away. He went west—that's what people said, 'Your father's gone west.' I used to think of it as desert and buttes and—chaparral, like a Western with John Wayne. My father was out riding the range on an old cayuse. I stayed with my grandparents at first, and then I went to live with Aunt Dot and Uncle Nate in this house, and they were very, very sweet to me. They had two kids, both boys, so it was almost like having two brothers. I wasn't miserable at all. But I missed my father. I longed for him." She turned in the seat to face Caddie, resting her reddish-blonde head in one hand. "He died when I was seventeen. In Chicago. I guess that's as far west as he ever got.

"So naturally I went and married a man just like him—tall, black-haired, and elegant. And remote. You know what I was thinking?"

"What?"

"You and I did different things for the same reason."

"How do you mean?"

"You fell in love with Christopher because he was the opposite of your grandmother, and I fell in love with poor old Carl because he was the same as my father."

"No. My grandmother—she's not like your father. I *had* my grandmother. You didn't have your father, you *longed* for him, you said."

"Well, either way, I think we both found men we thought could fix us, don't you? Oh, I wish I were your age again," Thea said, sighing. "Just to learn that one lesson while there's still time to do something about it."

"But—what *is* the lesson?"

Thea laughed, not unkindly. "I'm not sure, but I think it's to make the break between the past and the present *now*, not drag it around with us all our lives."

Was that the lesson? Caddie traced her finger through the coating of dust and yellow pollen at the bottom of the steering wheel. The clock on the dashboard was permanently stuck at ten-twenty. The radio played only AM stations and the air-conditioning came and went, same as the heat. "I need a new car," she said.

Thea flicked her broken window button up and down. "I think you do."

"I never got to say goodbye to my mother, either. She died in a spectacular car crash out in California. That's what Nana called it, 'spectacular.' I don't know where she got that word—it doesn't sound like what they'd put in a police report, does it? She was working for a radio station, selling ads. I guess that was a disappointment for her, a sort of come-down."

"You told me she was a musician."

"Actually, I *did* say goodbye to her, now that I think of it. That's—" She laughed, so this wouldn't sound pathetic. "That's the picture I see when I think of *my* childhood—me saying goodbye to my mother. In the doorway of Nana's house, both of us waving to her. Her name was Jane. She was always leaving. She had a suede jacket with fringe, and she carried her guitar in a black case. She had long blonde hair, like Joni Mitchell."

"And when she was gone," Thea said, "you longed for her."

Caddie nodded. "I had so many theories for why she didn't want me. You know, scenarios."

"I pretended my father had become a Pinkerton man and was working undercover. Out west."

"I pretended my mother was a big star, she had so many shows and concerts she couldn't come home. People were depending on her."

"Caddie."

"Hm?"

"Let's go shopping. Before we slit our wrists. Start the car and let's go shopping."

"Okay. For what?"

"Girly things, earrings and funky greeting cards and candles, things we don't need. Potpourri."

"Funky." She turned the car around in somebody's driveway. "I don't know anybody who says that but you."

"I know. That's your problem," Thea said with a motherly smile, and turned on the AM radio.

They wandered in and out of the book and antique stores on Federal Street, and the gift shops and small clothing boutiques Caddie rarely shopped in because they weren't in her price range. Then, too, who really needed a pair of high button-up boots or a scarlet burnt-velvet cloak? In the end they didn't buy much of anything, but it was fun to look. And afterward Caddie felt better, knowing she didn't really want much from the stores she couldn't afford to shop in.

"I used to like *things* more than I do now," Thea said wistfully, fingering a printed silk scarf in a store called Ampersand. "Every time you move, when you're my age, you leave more behind. If I live long enough, I'll be down to my handbag and a toothbrush." Caddie laughed. "I mean it, it's like being a horse. The older you get, the less you feel like carrying."

In a bath shop, they had an argument over some soaps they both liked the scent of. "Get them," said Thea. "No, you get them." "I don't *need* them." "Well, I don't, *either*."

Thea bought them and stuck them in Caddie's handbag when she wasn't looking.

"After that, I need a drink. Where's a bar around here?" Thea gazed up and down Federal Street. "I don't know a thing about the bars in this town, I was too young when I left."

"There's a café up there—it's sort of ladylike, but I'm sure they have booze."

"Lead on." She took Caddie's arm.

"Is your toe bothering you?"

"Oh, my curse. They can put a man on the moon but they can't cure arthritis in my toe. I should have it amputated, that's what, and Henry could make me a new one." They chortled.

The pretty young waitress at the Amaryllis Café started to seat them at one of the tiny round tables with hard, spindly iron chairs, but Thea asked, with a smile and just the right amount of charm, if they might have a nice comfy booth instead. Sure they could, the waitress, whose name tag read "Ginger," said agreeably, and Caddie thought, *Why can't I ever do that?* She always went where she was told to go, sat where she was told to sit. She had a horror of appearing bossy or aggressive—slight as that chance was. Maybe you had to be old before you could get your way, but she didn't think so.

"Ahh," Thea sighed, settling herself on the cushiony seat, spreading her things out. "I'm taking off my shoes." She looked at herself in the mirrored wall beside them. "I love my hair, I love it, I love it. Don't you love it?"

"I do," Caddie assured her, and Ginger said she did, too.

"What can I get you ladies this afternoon?"

Salads, they decided, but wine first. Caddie ordered without thinking, and the waitress brought two large, beautiful glasses of Chardonnay. "To vanity," Thea toasted. "To looking fabulous for as long as we can." They clinked glasses and drank.

"Oh, it's delicious," Caddie said. "I haven't had a real drink since . . ."

"Since you found out." Thea waited for her to explain why she was having one now.

"I still don't know what I'm doing. Except I know I can't keep it."

"Last time we talked, you said you couldn't 'have' it."

"Well, that's progress."

Thea didn't return her wan laugh.

"I did have thoughts of keeping it. For a little while, about an hour, before Christopher—said what he said." She moved her wineglass around to the four corners of her place mat. "I could see this picture, you know, us and a baby. A little family." She'd seen the picture from behind, two hands reaching down on either side, holding the tiny hands of a toddler. Perfect symmetry. "But then, afterward, when I knew he didn't want either one of us, it was as if he'd obliterated the baby. As if I'd miscarried, or there never was any such thing. Here." She sighed, pushing her glass across the table. "I can't drink this. I'm not thinking straight. I'll have the baby, because otherwise it's . . ." Like erasing herself, her own life. She'd rather tear out an organ.

Thea reached across and touched her hand. "It's going to be hard."

"I've been to an agency, and I think it'll be okay. Thea, these people—they show you pictures of them, and they all want a child so *badly*. All I have to do is pick the couple I like best."

The couples, "Jackie and Todd," "Maria and Bernard," wrote descriptions of themselves under their photos. Of course they all claimed they were loving and stable, devoted to each other but still lots of fun, and the only thing they needed to complete their happiness together was a baby. Whom they swore to love and care for and cherish as if it were their very own. Caddie had only to choose who she liked the looks and the sound of best, and the counselor would arrange a meeting. Or not; if she preferred, she could pick a couple without meeting them at all. It was up to her.

"The birth mother has all the rights; the parents don't have any. It's like a dating service designed just for me."

"I don't know if that's better or worse," Thea said, smiling.

"I know. Sometimes I think it was better in the olden days." When you had to have faith in the system to find the perfect family, to whom you handed over your newborn child through tactful intermediaries without anybody meeting anybody. Like modern warfare; no muss, no fuss.

"All the couples sound wonderful—it's impossible to pick. They're all so much better than me. As parents, you know, so— that's making it easier. A little."

The only ones she didn't trust were the ones who went out of their way to compliment her, the unknown mother, on her "courage." As soon as they started on about the "selflessness" of her decision and how much strength and "heroism" it must take, she crossed them off. They were just sucking up. She didn't understand her own motives, so how could they?

Thea started to say, "Caddie, are you—" but she stopped.

"What?"

"Nothing." She shook her head. "How are you feeling—how's your health?"

"Perfect, no problems. Except for being tired a lot. And I have the most powerful sense of smell, like a dog."

"Any cravings yet?"

"No, but I have aversions, things that cannot pass my lips. Like mayonnaise. And melted cheese."

"Have you told Frances yet?"

"I was going to, but she's mad at me."

Thea sat back. "Frances is mad at you?"

"Furious."

"*Why?*"

As hard as it had been telling Nana what she'd done to her sculptures, it was even harder telling Thea.

"You didn't. Oh, Caddie." Her eyes had gone white around the rims with amazement.

"I know. It was awful. It was mean."

"It's *wonderful*. Oh, I wish I'd been there to see it. That night? With a pick and shovel? Caddie Winger—you're an ax murderer!"

"I am!"

"Did it feel good?"

"Yes! Well, not afterward. *While*, yes, it was great, like I was on a mission. But afterward, it was awful. I had no right, Thea, no right, and I hurt her feelings. I don't even know why I did it!"

259

Thea smiled, arching an eyebrow. "You don't?" When Caddie didn't respond, she said, "I've been meaning to ask you—*why* did Frances put green dye in the washing machine? I didn't mind, my underwear was getting a little dingy, but what was she trying to do?"

"I think she was dyeing things green to stand for newness. As a contrast. To the *old* things in her project—you know she's doing a project on oldness."

"What color are *old* things?"

"You'd have to ask her. She's gotten very secretive about it, though. The whole thing embarrassed her."

"What did Brenda say?"

Caddie had been trying not to think about that. "She said it's 'suggestive.' Nana doesn't want to go home, she *loves* it at Wake House, but Brenda says she might have to. She can't keep her if she gets—really wacky."

"Well, I don't understand that. What sort of elder-care place is she running if she can't keep someone like Frances?"

Their salads came. While they ate, Caddie told Thea about the letter she'd found in her mother's old room. "It's signed 'Bobby,' and there was a Bobby Haywood in the band she was playing with then. There's no return address, but it's postmarked from a town called Clover in Delaware. I looked it up on a map," she admitted. "It's tiny, only about four hundred people."

Thea looked puzzled. "Who is it?"

"Well." She inhaled. "It might be my father."

"Oh, Caddie." She brought her folded hands to her mouth. "Oh, honey."

"I know."

"Did you try to call him?"

"Not yet."

"You didn't call? Why not?"

She pretended to think. "Mousiness? I *will*. Sometime. But you know, Thea, he's probably not there anymore, that was over thirty years ago. If he even *ever* lived there—he could've just been passing through, he could've been driving by a mailbox. He could live *anywhere*."

Thea looked patient.

"I will! One of these days. I think about it all the time. But—this isn't something you just *do*."

The waitress came over to ask if they wanted another drink. "No, thanks. It's no fun if I'm the only one," said Thea, who'd finished hers and about a third of Caddie's. "Besides, I might get even *wiser*."

Caddie paid the check while Thea was in the ladies' room. "So," said Ginger, making conversation, "you and your mom having a nice day out?"

Caddie smiled up at her. "We went shopping, got our hair done."

"Nice."

"Yeah. We've had a wonderful day."

Thea confirmed it on the ride home. "I had the best time. Thank you for lunch—you sneak, I'll get you for that."

"I did, too, the *best* time." She found a place in front of Wake House and parallel parked.

"I know what I'm going to do," Thea said, yawning. "Take a little nap. Wine in the day puts me right to sleep."

"I'll go in with you, I guess, say hi to Nana. See if she'll speak to me yet." She took Thea's arm as they crossed the street. This time of day, people were usually out on the front porch, watching the sun start to set while the afternoon cooled off. But the porch was vacant. The house was empty inside, too, nobody but Cornel and Bernie sitting on the sofa in the Red Room, hunched over, hands between their knees. They looked lost.

"Where is everybody?" Caddie asked from the hall.

"In their rooms." Cornel stood up.

"My grandmother, too?"

He nodded.

"What's happened?" Thea asked, going over and taking him by the arm.

He patted her hand, blinking into her face, his turtle lips spread in a pained smile. "Edgie's gone and had a stroke."

"Edgie! Oh, no."

Bernie lumbered up, too. "It happened right after you left."

"Edgie?" Caddie quavered. She'd been here, she and Bea, sitting on the couch. Both sisters had waved goodbye and told her and Thea to come back from the beauty shop looking "glamorous!"

"She was reading the *Reader's Digest* out loud to Bea," Cornel related. "Bea said she started slurring her words and saying how she couldn't see too well all of a sudden. Bea knew what it was right away and ran to get Brenda, who called the ambulance. Meanwhile, Edgie's on the couch—Bea told her not to move, but she gets up and *bam*, her leg gave out. She didn't know, just thought it had fallen asleep. She's got a bruise on her face, but otherwise not too much. From the fall." He looked down mournfully.

"Is she in the hospital?"

"The medics came," Bernie said, "and took her on a stretcher in the ambulance. Brenda took Bea and Magill in her car, and Mrs. Brill went in the ambulance with Edgie."

"Mrs. Brill?"

"Calm as a cucumber. Very efficient. Good in a crisis, turns out."

"Should we go, too?" Caddie asked Thea. Shouldn't they do *something*?

"Not yet, we'd just be in the way." Thea moved between the two men and lowered herself to the sofa with a muted grunt. "There's nothing for us to do, and Bea's got Brenda and Henry. And Mrs. Brill."

"Poor Edgie," said Caddie, looking from face-to-face. "What will happen?"

Bernie cleared his throat. "Depends on how bad a stroke it is. Sometimes it's the end of everything and they're never the same, sometimes they get right over it. Just depends."

"On what part of the brain it hits," Cornel explained.

Thea nodded slowly.

They knew all about strokes, these three, Caddie thought. Getting old made you an expert in all sorts of things you never wanted to know about.

"Magill's s'pose to call as soon as there's anything to report," Cornel said, taking the seat beside Thea, lowering his backside creakily.

Bernie dragged a chair close and collapsed on it.

"I'd like to wait with you," Caddie said. Thea started to move over, make room for her on the sofa. "But I think I should go up and wait with Nana. Because she'll be . . ." She didn't know what Nana would be. But maybe frightened and upset, and if so, Caddie should be with her. "Let me know if you hear anything?" she asked, and Cornel said sure, of course they would.

"Thank you," Thea called softly. "Thank you, Caddie."

She turned back in the doorway. "For what?"

"For the *loveliest* day."

"It was great—we'll do it again soon."

Thea covered a sad smile by blowing her a kiss. "I hope so!"

18

Bea was the only one allowed to see Edgie for the first couple of days. The first time Caddie went, Edgie was asleep, and the second time she was out having physical therapy. Finally, a whole week after the stroke, Caddie found her in her room and wide awake.

They'd given her a triple, but nobody was in either of the other two beds right now. She didn't see Caddie at first—Bea, perched on the edge of her bed, blocked her view—but Magill did. He'd been slouching on the heater-air-conditioner unit under the windowsill; he stood up carefully, holding the sill with one hand and sleeking his hair back with the other. "Hey." He greeted her with his shy-sly smile. "Look who's here, Edgie."

Bea stood up, too. "Why, it's Caddie—look, Edgie, Caddie's come to see you."

Bea looked exhausted; in one week, she'd aged ten years. Caddie set her jelly jar of petunias down on the cluttered bedside table and hugged her. Bea was as tall as she was, and strong for her age; despite all her infirmities, she'd always seemed powerful, like a farm woman, a pioneer, somebody who took care of business with her tough, capable hands. But her sister's stroke had cut her down and changed everything. She looked ready to surrender.

Edgie made a sound like "Ehhmm" from the bed. She was listing a little to the side, one arm tucked under the sheet, but she lifted the other and held it out in welcome. "*You*," she said. "*Fine-ly.*"

264

"I know." Caddie kissed her cool cheek and took her one strong hand, and got a good squeeze in return. "You look wonderful," she said in relief, and it was nearly true. Edgie looked pale and tired, but the old impish twinkle in her eye was the same, and the same glad smile when she saw Caddie lit up her face.

"I fixed her hair." Bea sat down on the other side of the bed from Caddie. "The nurses were doing it all wrong."

"Oh, it's pretty." Like soft yellow cotton. "I hear you're coming home soon."

Edgie's smile was off-center, but pure joy. "I hear."

"Boy, we've missed you. It's not the same with you gone."

She said something Caddie couldn't make out.

"Says she can't wait," Bea said.

"This place," Edgie said clearly, then made a face, including sticking out her pink tongue.

Caddie had to remind herself not to speak too slowly or loudly; Edgie wasn't deaf and there was nothing wrong with her mind. "Well, it won't be long now, you'll be out on the front porch in your green rocker." The green rocker was Edgie's, the blue one next to it Bea's. Unofficially.

Edgie put her right hand to her lips, as if praying.

"Talk," Bea urged, "don't pantomime. She gets so tired, but she's got to talk."

Her sister sighed, grunted. "I talk," she said with effort.

"And to think I used to *wish* she'd shut up once in a while." Bea laughed with watering eyes, and Edgie gave her hip a push with her good hand.

"She's doing great," Magill spoke up from the foot of the bed. "She's the queen of rehab. You should've seen her on the parallel bars today, Caddie. Sheena of the jungle."

Edgie snickered. "'Cuz of her," she said, patting her sister's knee. Then something garbled. She scowled, frustrated, and tried again. Caddie still didn't catch it; it sounded like *timer rain*.

"Time is brain," Bea explained. "That's what Dr. Cao says, the neurologist. They got her to the hospital fast and gave her clot busters. The faster the better."

"It could've been much worse," Magill said. "If you hadn't called 911 as quick as you did."

Caddie already knew that, everybody at Wake House knew it, but it was good of him to say it again in front of Bea. It was the only thing that consoled her, the only bright spot in this whole disaster: that she had done right, acted properly.

Caddie had been warned to keep her visit short. They talked for a little longer, then she stood and said she'd better go.

"I'll walk out with you," Bea said quickly.

Caddie leaned over and put her cheek next to Edgie's. "I'll come see you again."

"You better," she said clearly.

"You get strong, you hear, and come home soon. Because we really miss you."

"Miss you." She draped her arm around Caddie's neck and hugged her hard. "Take care o'*her*."

"I will. I will." They kissed again, and Caddie straightened up quickly—how awful it would be to cry in front of Edgie. "Bye, see you. Need a ride?" she asked Magill. "I was going over to see my grandmother now."

"Guess I'll stick around a little longer," he said, taking her place on the edge of the bed. "Thanks anyway."

Bea was already out in the hall. "Let's go in here," she said, guiding Caddie into a tiny, too-bright waiting room. Full of people; there were only two empty seats left together, and they were underneath a blaring TV set. "No, let's—" She pivoted, and they went back out in the hall. "There's a place down here." A bench under a bulletin board at the other end of the corridor. "Can you sit for a minute, Caddie, do you have time?"

It was Sunday, she had all the time in the world. They sat on a vinyl-covered bench with a water fountain on one side and the red-lighted emergency exit door on the other. No real privacy, but the dead-end hall was relatively secluded. Good thing, Caddie thought, when Bea put her hands over her eyes and burst into tears.

She'd brought her handbag, a square black carryall with a silver clasp. When she opened it, Caddie caught the mint-and-cellophane scent of Nana's purse and wondered if all old ladies' pocketbooks smelled the same. "I'm a wreck," Bea mumbled into her wrinkled handkerchief. "Can't keep this up."

"You're not getting enough rest. Edgie's in better shape than you are." She'd never seen Bea cry before. She could hardly stand it.

Wiry strands of pewter-gray hair had come down from her careful coronets; she swiped at them with the back of her hand. "I'm not holding up well at all. I feel ashamed to be this frightened."

"But Edgie's going to recover, I'm sure of it. And mostly because of you, Bea. And once she gets home, she'll *feel* a lot better."

"She's not coming home." Bea raised her wet face from the sodden handkerchief; fresh tears trickled down the deep furrows in her cheeks. "She can't come home, Brenda can't take her."

"What? *Why?*"

"She thinks she is and I can't tell her otherwise. I'm afraid it'd kill her."

"Why can't she come home?"

Bea dug the hard heels of her hands into her eye sockets, as if she could push the tears back in. "She needs special therapy right now or it won't do any good, speech therapy, physical, occupational . . . Medicaid won't pay for home care, and every bit of our savings is already going to Wake House. I'm not even sure the insurance can pay for therapy here, not all of it. Brenda wants to take her back, but there's some rule against it if she's bedridden. I don't know what to do. We've never been separated before, and I don't know what to do. Why couldn't it have been me? That's what I keep praying to God to tell me. It was always supposed to be me, not Edgie."

Caddie put her arms around her. "Well, I don't agree," she said in a voice as steady as she could make it. "If it had to be either one of you, it's better that it's Edgie."

"No."

"I think so. Poor thing, she couldn't handle this happening to *you*, Bea. She'd feel overwhelmed, because she's never been the older one. That's *your* job."

"I can't do it. Oh, Lordy."

"You have a lot of friends to help you."

She inhaled a deep sniff and sat up straight. "That's the one good thing about being the oldest woman on earth. Everybody else is younger." After she blew her nose, she mashed it back and forth with her handkerchief. "It's not true that we've never been separated. When Daddy first found out his heart was bad, they sent him for tests over at Johns Hopkins. I drove him, and we stayed two nights in a motel and Edgie stayed home to keep things going. The first night she went wild—had a glass of sherry all by herself in the parlor and turned on a dance program on the radio. *Loud*—she told me that so proud, Caddie, you'd've thought she shot heroin in her arm. She stayed up till eleven-thirty and didn't even listen to the news. Racy! Next night, all the fun was out of her, though. She called up on the phone and wailed about how lonesome she was, would we please hurry and come home." She laughed, smearing one last tear out of her eye.

"I don't know how healthy it's been, us two being so close. You don't see it in sisters so much nowadays, everybody's so independent. Girls with jobs, and keeping their names when they get married. Well, it can't be helped, we are what we are by now, and if she goes before me, I swear——" She put her head back against the wall and shut her eyes tight. "It'll be like cutting off my leg. Both legs."

Caddie didn't know what to say. Except, "I think she's going to get better. And Brenda will work something out, I'm positive."

Bea made a try at a smile. "I hate to say it, but I think sometimes things really are as bad as they seem. Sometimes there's not going to be a happy ending. And if that's the kind of wisdom old age gets you, I can do without it."

Magill found them a few minutes later, leaning against each other, holding hands. "Um," he said, and they straightened up, sending him shaky, reassuring smiles. "Edgie fell asleep, so I . . ."

"Well, that's good," Bea said in her hearty voice, getting to her feet with a grunt, "now you can go on home with Caddie. You've been here since morning, you look terrible."

"You've got that backwards, Miss Bea, except for the looking terrible part, of course." He had a funny, courtly way of talking to the old ladies at Wake House that they loved. "You go with Caddie now, and I'll stay just a little longer."

"Nope. Brenda's coming over to pick me up, we've got it all arranged. Go on, get." She gave him a push. "Anyway, I've got a plan: I'm gonna sit down, put my feet up on Edgie's bed, and take a snooze."

Hugging Bea goodbye, Caddie whispered in her ear, "I *know* everything's going to be all right." But she wasn't sure she believed it.

Out on the pavement, the heavy August heat smacked into them like a wet towel. Caddie took Magill's arm when he wobbled, and he took hers, she guessed because she was pregnant, and they tacked across the wavy parking lot toward her broiling car.

"Hey, look at you, you've bulked up," she noticed, squeezing his bare biceps under his short-sleeved shirt, and of course then he had to flex the muscle for her and she had to exclaim over it with even more enthusiasm. "Bulked up" was an exaggeration, but he did have a stronger, tougher feel to him. "Yeah, been working out," he said in a deep-throated, mock-manly voice. She told him she'd been taking long walks in the mornings, for health and to work off some of Finney's manic energy, but she really ought to do more. Teaching piano and violin all day didn't exactly keep you in shape. Magill said she looked okay to him.

"Actually, I'm not teaching all day," she confessed, trying to steer out of the lot without burning her hands on the wheel. She opened all the windows but Magill's, which was stuck, but the car still felt like a sauna. "This time of year, I lose a lot of students because of vacations and what have you. My schedule's about half what it should be."

"No students, no income," Magill realized. "That must make it rough."

"Well, you know it's coming, so you try to plan ahead in the good times." It seemed worse this summer, though, or else she was just worrying more. Nana's pension had been enough to get her through the first two months at Wake House, but with the higher rates coming, they were going to have to dip into savings. Nana's cast was off and she'd graduated from the wheelchair to the walker—she could come home if she wanted to. But she didn't want to.

"It's just the nature of my job," Caddie said, "it's seasonal. I'd planned to work part-time at the music store, I've done that before, but then, I don't know, I just sort of punked out." No, what happened was, she'd started going out with Christopher, and that had been so thrilling and unexpected, the idea of working in a store at night when she could be with him had come to seem wasteful and ridiculous. Another wrong choice in a summer of wrong choices.

270

"Oh, no, what is this? Oh, brother, a traffic jam. On *Sunday*. It must be an accident. Or else that construction on Lee Street . . ." Cars were inching along in her lane and not moving at all in the one beside her. "Good thing we're not in a hurry," she said, trying to be positive. But if the Pontiac idled too long on a hot day, the radiator boiled over. She looked over at Magill, who didn't appear to be listening. He was drumming his fingers on the knees of his jeans, frowning at the dashboard. He turned toward her suddenly and cleared his throat. But then he didn't say anything.

"It's the traffic light, I think," she said, squinting into the distance. "I can see a cop. Oh, boy, now we're in trouble."

"I, um." He cleared his throat again. "I was going to wait for a better time, but I don't know when that would be."

"What?" She gave him her full attention. He looked as if he had a present for her, something chancy he wasn't a hundred percent sure she'd like. The sun through the window struck his face on one side, illuminating his beard stubble. Some men only shaved every few days for fashion; Magill did because for him shaving was a dangerous adventure.

"I was thinking about the situation, your situation, and I was thinking . . ." He grinned without looking at her, gazing past her out at the car stopped next to theirs. "What you said before about the second generation of Winger bastards, and it made me—"

"The what?"

"The second generation of bastard daughters. You said that, remember, or else Frances did, that time we—"

"Oh. Right."

"Yeah, and so I thought maybe, possibly, I might be able to help you out. Since you're sort of a . . . of a conservative person. Wouldn't you say?"

She peered at him. The car in front moved a few feet; she put the Pontiac in gear and crept up behind it.

"In a good way, nothing wrong with being conservative, especially for a woman. These days. That's not the right word, anyway; I mean . . . cautious, maybe, not . . . not . . . well, anyway." He gave up trying to think of the right word. "I was wondering if it wouldn't solve everything if you—and I"—he spread his arms in a sort of all-embracing way—"got married."

She giggled. He was so funny, he—

"I'm serious." He stopped smiling hopefully; his face went stiff.

Dear God, he was. She burst out laughing.

"Oh. Okay, well." He folded his arms and slid down in the seat.

"I'm sorry!" Was he offended? But it was so *funny*. She was amazed and delighted with the sweetness of it. "I'm just surprised— you took me by surprise—"

"Forget it, I know it sounds crazy. I agree. But in a way, it's a stroke of genius."

"It is?"

"Yes." He hauled himself up, rewarming to it. "It makes a lot of sense when you think about it. You're in kind of a bind—I'm free. I'm no prize, we agree on that, but that's the *beauty* of it. Here I am, nothing if not available. Magill. It's a good, solid name. We came from Cork, I think, I'm not positive, my father used to say that but he wasn't exactly a genealogist."

He put his hands together, growing earnest. "I'm not doing this very well. You've been worried about the baby, so I just wanted you to know. I could help you solve the problem, that's all. Think of it as—" His face lit up: an inspiration. "Think of it as elements in an alloy. You're titanium, you're strong, but you're much stronger if we add aluminum."

"You're aluminum?"

"Yeah. And niobium, I'm aluminum and niobium, Ti-6Al-7Nb— okay, that's not the best analogy because it's three elements, not two, but you get the point."

"I get the point." The car behind her blew its horn. It was so hot, she could feel sweat on the backs of her knees. Magill's face shone with it. And his blue eyes were liquid with sincerity, gazing into hers. "Why," she said eventually. "Why would you do that?"

"Because I can. Here I am—I've got no other plans." He grinned winsomely. "Use me."

"Don't you have a future in mind for yourself?"

"Not that I can see. Not currently."

"So it doesn't matter what you want?"

"No."

"Because you're finished. You don't deserve any happiness."

Awareness dawned in his face, followed by alarm.

"You think your friend is dead because of you. So you'll keep hurting and punishing yourself forever, by marrying *me*, for instance, since that's only what you deserve."

"Hey, wait. Let's backtrack."

"It's like starving yourself."

"No."

"I appreciate the offer—I'm sure you meant it kindly."

"I did. No, not *kindly*."

"I'm no prize either," she said, laughing. "Obviously."

"I didn't say it right."

"You did, and I understand, truly. I'm not trying to give you a hard time. Thanks. Really. Thanks."

She kept a frozen smile for as long as she could. She'd been feeling teary and blue off and on all day—hormones. A big, blubbery puddle of emotion was ready to overflow; the only thing keeping her steady was a weak little spark of anger. Umbrage. How pitiful did he think she was? She'd never known anybody as full of self-hate as Magill, and here he was asking her to be part of his penance. A charity case to help him carry on his tradition of suffering. Caddie the hair shirt. She shouldn't be mad, but she was.

"It's moving. Thank God." The hated brake lights of the car in front went off; traffic began to inch forward. She shifted into second, and finally a breeze began to circulate. Good: they needed a change of air in this car.

They drove the rest of the way in pained silence. By the time they got to Wake House, she wasn't angry anymore, just anxious to get away. She parked in her usual spot but left the motor running. "Well, I guess we're not getting married, but thanks again for the offer." She said it in a final way so that he would get out of the car.

He looked miserable, which was a small consolation. "Aren't you coming in?" he asked. "I thought you wanted to see Frances."

"I'll come back later. It's so hot, I think I'll go home." That made no sense, Wake House had air-conditioning and her house didn't, but Magill didn't argue. She didn't even think he heard.

"Okay, you were right. It was a stupid idea. Sorry. I don't know"—he made a twitchy motion around his head with both hands—"what I was thinking."

"It's okay. It's sort of funny."

They tried smiling at each other.

"I thought of a better analogy than titanium and aluminum. I guess you don't want to hear it, though."

"You know . . . I really . . ."

"Never mind." He leaned over and started picking at the edges of an old peace decal on the dash. "But it's not like you're an illegal alien and marrying me would get you a green card. We already know each other. You've seen me at my worst, and you, you don't even have a worst. I'd definitely be getting the sweet end of the deal."

That made her smile. "Christopher called me," she said for some reason. "He wanted to give me his address and tell me about his new job. Brag about it, actually."

Magill mumbled something vulgar.

"I told him the baby wasn't his."

He sat up and stared at her.

She hadn't been going to tell anybody this, not even Thea. "And he *believed* me—that's the amazing thing. I told him I got mixed up counting the days. Don't you think that's funny?"

"I thought—I thought he didn't even *know*."

"He knew. We just pretended he didn't."

Magill frowned, absorbing that. "Why tell him *anything*, then?"

"Well, in case he ever found out. I wanted to make sure—I just wanted him out of the picture. So all the decisions are mine." If she could ever make them.

Magill looked at her in a funny, pleased way, as if he knew something she didn't know.

"Oh, no—no, don't think it's because I want the baby for myself. That's not it."

"Sure?"

"Absolutely. No. I'm giving it up for adoption."

He recoiled. "You're not."

"Why not?" His dismay made her defensive. "I am. I've been working with an agency, all I have to do is fill out some more papers. I just have to sign. Well, what did you think? I can't *keep* it."

"Why not?"

"Why not? I'd be an unfit mother! For one thing. I'm poor, single, I don't *want* a child—and anyway, Nana's my child."

"See, if you married me, you wouldn't be poor or single, you'd—well, poor, okay, but not forever, not—"

"Magill, could we *please* drop this? I'm not marrying you," she said with an angry laugh.

"Right." He stuck his thumb in a hole in the knee of his jeans and pulled, *rip*. "Right."

After a minute she added more gently, "But thanks anyway for, you know. Trying to save me."

A wasp flew in and began to throw itself against the windshield with furious rasps. Magill froze. Caddie used her cupped palm and calmly guided it out the window.

He kept sitting there, baffled or something. This conversation was awful. She tried to telegraph a message into his left temple: *Open the door.* The car engine gave a sick, timely wheeze, and finally he reached for the handle.

Outside, he leaned down, storklike, to look at her through the frozen-open window. "Where I went wrong, Caddie, I was thinking of myself the way I used to be. You'd've entertained the possibility of me then."

"What?"

"Yeah, I know, but you'll have to take my word for it. I used to be the kind of guy you'd've considered."

"Magill, wait."

He gave her a sheepish salute. "Sorry I screwed up," he said, and started down the sidewalk, stiff-arming the stone wall beside him to keep in a straight line. She called to him again, but he passed the steps to Wake House and kept going. The farther he went, a narrow blade of a man in flapping clothes, the less sure Caddie felt about which one of them had screwed up.

19

Caddie apologized to her grandmother five times on four different occasions before Nana finally gave in and forgave her for wrecking her lawn sculptures. The last time, Caddie said this was it, she'd run out of ways to say she was sorry, if Nana couldn't excuse her for what she'd done they'd just have to live estranged for the rest of their lives. Since they weren't even estranged *now*, that was a pretty idle threat. It was just that Nana couldn't bring herself to say "I forgive you" in words.

Caddie's ultimatum, or more likely her exasperation, finally worked. "Oh, hell. Give it up already," Nana begrudged one evening after dinner. "You're forgiven."

"Well, *thank* you. About time."

"But you were wrong, just so we're clear on that. Terribly wrong."

"Oh, boy, are we clear on that. But you forgave me, I heard you. No taking it back."

Nana had already put on her nightgown. She was tucked in bed with her sketchbook on her knees and a handful of pastels, making a chalky mess on the bedspread. "Caddie, what's the essence of oldness?"

"Pardon?"

"Oh, never mind, how would you know. What's up with you these days, anyway? You look funny."

She gave a nervous laugh. "I do?" She wasn't showing yet, her clothes fit fine, but she was nine weeks pregnant and she still hadn't told Nana. Here was a perfect opening—she could tell her right now.

"You look wired or something. You getting enough sleep?"

How *shrewd*. She was wired and tired at the same time, but imagine Nana noticing. Caddie cleared her throat, but the two words that would have explained everything didn't come out. "I'm fine. What's that you're working on, something new?"

"Nope, something old." She cackled. She looked witchy with her grizzled gray hair loose on the pillow. "Old as the hills, old as time. You coming to my program?"

"I wouldn't miss it."

"You can bring that dog man."

"No, I told you. I don't see him anymore."

"Damn, I forgot." She squinted up, forehead furrowing with sympathy. She reached for her glasses on the bedside table.

Caddie didn't want to be seen better. "Gotta go." She leaned over and gave her grandmother a quick kiss. "Night, sleep well. I'll call you tomorrow."

Nana wasn't the only one turning in early. Soft snores came to Caddie clearly as she passed Mrs. Brill's door. Doré was singing in the shower, and Maxine was watching television. The canned laughter sounded harsh and personally derisive, but Caddie told herself she was just in a mood. She was always in a mood lately, and not always a bad one. Sometimes she felt euphoric, for no reason at all. Hormones, she'd read in a book. Her face was breaking out, too; this morning she'd woken up with a pimple on her chin. Lovely.

A corridor off the main second-floor hall led to a private staircase, one of two entrances to Thea's tower room; the other was on the third floor. Seventy years ago her room was the Wakes' master bedroom suite, the finest in the house. Thea always rode the elevator, but Caddie took the private stairs. Heat lightning through the window on the landing lit the way, illuminating the ancient striped wallpaper in flashes. The door at the top of the stairs stood half open, probably for a breeze—it was a stifling hot night, and by the time the air-conditioning got to the third floor it wasn't what you'd call robust.

The sitting room was empty, but a light shone from the bedroom. Caddie knocked on the wall. "Thea?" she called, soft-voiced. "It's me."

"Come in!"

Thea sat under a tasseled floor lamp in her big Morris chair with a book in her lap, her legs stretched out on a leather ottoman. She'd banished Wake House's sturdy but plain furnishings to the basement and decorated the tower suite with all her own things, a comfortable couch covered in rich scarlet velvet, an old rocking chair, enormous pillows scattered on the floor, everything soft and warm and always smelling of flowers. Caddie loved Thea's rooms. They were like the fantasy dorm digs of the coolest, most sophisticated coed you'd ever known.

"Aren't you hot?" She plopped down on the edge of the great four-poster bed. "This room is boiling. Oh, you've got your window open, no wonder." And Thea was still fully dressed in gauzy pants and an orchid silk shirt, the tails tied in a knot around her waist. She didn't look hot, though.

She wriggled her bare feet on the ottoman. "Don't move, that's the secret. And I'm getting the sweetest little breeze. Much better than air-conditioning."

"What are you reading?"

"I was hoping you wouldn't ask."

"Oooh. Something racy?"

"Definitely not." She brushed at rust-colored specks on her lap. "This book's so old, the cover's disintegrating."

"What is it?"

"*Freckles*, by Gene Stratton Porter. Who was a woman, not a man. I read this book first when I was about ten." She made a face. "So it's finally happened, I've regressed to childhood."

"Nana only likes Jane Austen these days, she won't read anyone else."

"See? The slow infantilization of the mind. Very sad. But I don't care, I'm re-reading all the old books I used to love, and it's making me happy."

"Nana says she likes knowing how they end."

"Well, there's that. Freckles finds out he's not a penniless orphan after all, he's the son of a nobleman, and everyone lives happily ever after. Oh, it's a lovely book." She marked her place with a nail file and put the book down. "How are you? You look a little fagged out."

"I guess I am."

"Anything wrong?"

"No. I don't know. I'm just all . . . I don't know."

Thea waited, but when Caddie couldn't do any better than that, she pulled her feet off the ottoman and stood. "If you feel like talking, I know a terrific place. But it's a secret, you can't tell anybody about it."

"Is it cool?"

"Cool*er*."

"Lead on."

Down the hall past the men's bedrooms, past Bea and Edgie's room, past the staircase and around the corner, along a dark, unused corridor to a door Caddie had never seen before. It wasn't locked and it led to two short, narrow flights of stairs covered in black rubber or linoleum, lit by one dusty bulb Thea flicked on at the bottom. "Are these servants' stairs?" Caddie asked, whispering for some reason.

Thea paused, holding on to the railing to catch her breath. "No, just attic steps. That's where we're going."

"Oh." She followed after dutifully, thinking, *How could it be cooler in the attic?*

At the top of the stairs, they stopped again. "Whew," Thea said, patting her chest. "I need more exercise. Look at this place, Caddie. Wouldn't it be fun to explore? You could get an American history lesson right here in the attic."

"Or an allergy," Caddie said nasally, right before she sneezed twice. She could only make out shapes under the rafters in the semi-dark, trunks and wardrobes, cast-off furniture, things covered up under sheets. Everything smelled of dry wood. "Wow, it's huge. Is this where we're, um . . ."

"No, silly." She laughed and took Caddie's hand, leading her confidently along a twisty path through piles and clumps of this and that. Pale light shone around the edges of an enormous old cabinet or armoire against the raw, slanted, uninsulated wall. Not flush against it: Thea dropped Caddie's hand and slipped around the back of the heavy piece of furniture. A click; a shrill creak. More light. Caddie peered around the corner and saw a long, open casement window. "What in the world?" She squeezed through behind Thea, and a moment later she was looking out over a low stone balustrade at a sky of rushing clouds and a cityscape of roofs, black treetops, and winking lights. "Where are we?" she cried, delighted. "I didn't even know this was *here*."

"Isn't it fabulous?"

"There's the alley, so we're on the north side, but where?"

"We're between two sloping roofs, all but hidden. That's really the only place you can see us from." She pointed to a faraway house in the next block. "I told you it was a secret."

"How did you ever find it?"

"Exploring."

"This window wasn't even locked? There could be others—"

"There's one directly opposite, I'll show you when we go back, but it won't open. *Why* you'd build two invisible little balconies off the attic, I can't imagine, but I'm grateful. Sit, Caddie, these stones are nice and cool at night."

There was room for them to sit on opposite sides of the tiny porch with their backs against facing walls and their legs stretched out side by side, but not for much else. "Are we sure this is safe?" Caddie knocked on one of the balusters, half joking, half not.

"Oh, this house will be here a long time after we're gone. Me, anyway."

"Nana says she knew the Wakes. Knew *of* them, she means. I guess they were the big deals around here. Did you know them?"

"I was pretty young when the bubble burst and they wandered away. The Wake diaspora."

How sad to lose everything, even your home. Sad for anybody, but worse if you were famous and the whole town got to watch. Caddie heaved a deep sigh.

"What's going on with you? You look heavy. Hearted," Thea clarified when Caddie looked down at her flat stomach, "heavy-hearted. What have you been thinking about lately?"

"Nothing, really, my head's empty. But I'm kind of on this ride, this emotional . . . up and down. I've just about settled on a couple. The Benedicts. They're perfect," she said gloomily. "The wife is a veterinarian and the husband's a social worker. There's *nothing* wrong with them."

Lightning flickered, closer, revealing the surprise outline of clouds. Electricity prickled in the air, and the dull rumble of thunder was almost constant. Storm coming.

"Oh God, oh God. I don't know. Maybe I should've had an abortion."

"Why do you say that?"

"Because. Eventually she's going to find out I gave her up."

"She?"

"He, she. I think it's a girl—that's what we always have."

"So . . ." Thea spoke slowly, as if feeling her way, "it would be better for this baby not to be born than to find out she was adopted."

"No, not find out she's adopted, find out I gave her away. I'm not saying this makes sense."

"Oh, good." Thea leaned her head back against the wall. "When exactly is she due?"

"Late March."

"Right before spring."

"Yeah." A drop of rain fell on her wrist. "It'll be nice weather, she can go outside and lie on a blanket in the shade." Caddie folded her arms over her eyes. "I'm trying not to think about it, the details. If I make her a real person, if I put *myself* in the picture—but sometimes I can't help it. Which do you think is worse," she asked, lowering her arms, "losing your mother because she died—or because she left, she didn't, you know, want you, didn't care very much about you. Which is worse, do you think?"

"Which one of us had it harder, you're asking?"

"*No.* Okay, yes. Your mother, at least you always knew she loved you. But Thea, which felt worse to you, her dying or your father— going out west?"

"That's an excellent question, but what difference does it make? It was a lifetime ago."

"I know, but how did you get over it?"

"I never did. But I stopped letting it follow me around like a lost dog."

"How?"

She shrugged. "By facing the alternative. And also by looking around and seeing how *short* life is, Caddie," she said intensely.

"Facing the alternative. You mean turning into somebody like me."

Thea smiled in the dark. "Plenty worse things than turning into someone like you."

"But that's what you meant."

"No, what I meant was, being afraid takes too much energy and it's hardly ever worth it. I'll take pain over fear of pain any day. My worst mistake, and I've made more than you think, was marrying Carl, and I did it to try to correct the past. Which you cannot do. What a waste of time, two people's short, precious *time*."

Caddie said, "I thought I fell in love with Christopher because he was so normal, and he could make *me* normal. And invisible—that's always been a goal of mine. But . . . maybe the real reason I fell in love with him is because I knew I couldn't have him. Maybe what I really want—*wanted*," she corrected hopefully, "was nobody. Peace and quiet. Just me and Nana, because then I'd be safe. Nobody could ever leave me. Thea . . ."

"Hm?"

"How did you get to be so brave?"

She laughed, dropping her head to ruffle her hair with her hands. "One of the things I love about you, Caddie, is your . . . what would you call it . . . cluelessness."

"Oh, thank—"

"Over how nice you are. And how much stronger you are than you think."

"You say that, but I don't feel strong."

"You just haven't had enough practice. You need to start asking for what you want. And sometimes *not* asking."

"But there *are* things about ourselves we *can't* change," she argued, "don't you feel that? Sometimes, yes, I want to keep the baby, but I know I shouldn't. It's like—I'm a child and there's something I want very badly, but I know my parents can't afford it, but I want it anyway. So then I'm ashamed."

"Because you'd like to keep your own baby? *Ashamed?*"

It was so hard to explain. "Listen. Once, I was inside my mother, the same way this baby is inside me."

"Yes?"

"I *tell* myself that, but I can't make it real. On any level. If my mother could leave me, if my father could leave me—" She held out her hands. "Who are we, Thea, if we're not the people who made us?"

Thea took hold of Caddie's shoe. "Well, now, you do whatever you have to do, for whatever convoluted reasons you've got for doing it, but listen to me. First of all, being 'normal' is a false goal, a child's goal. So is being 'invisible.' "

"I know." She hid her face against her bent knees. It was starting to rain; she felt the heavy drops thud on her back like little slaps.

"You know. Good." Thea gave the shoe a shake. "Do you also know you're not your mother? You're the opposite of her, from what I can gather. You've *made* yourself her opposite—that's your accomplishment. My dear Caddie, you would be such a good, loving mother to this baby."

Sudden stinging tears burned behind her eyes. Her chest ached, as if her heart had a crack in it. "I would?" was all she could say. Otherwise a dam would burst.

"Oh my, yes. Lucky, lucky baby. Too bad for Mr. and Mrs. Benedict, but if they're that perfect, they'll find another one soon."

"But it's so scary. It's so scary. For a million reasons."

"You won't hear me deny that life's scary. But so is avoiding it. You can set yourself free any time you like. Everything you're looking for, everything you need, it's already inside you. If your life were ending instead of beginning—if you were as old as I am, or *older*, if you can imagine such a thing—if you had a terminal disease—and let's face it, we all have a terminal disease—what would matter most, what would make it all worthwhile? Do you think it's that you managed to stay invisible?"

"No, I know."

"I know you know, I'm not saying anything *wise*. No, this is wise—you don't love yourself enough, Caddie, and that's a little bit of a sin, I think. That's a little bit petty of you. It's that shame business again. What do you call it when two words always go together?"

"You mean like—"

"Like *hardy mums*; you never see *mums* for sale, they're always *hardy* mums. Well, *senseless shame*, that's another pair in my book. Shame is almost always senseless. Being a better little girl would not have made your mother stay. Or my father. It wasn't our fault." She leaned close and looked into Caddie's eyes. The message wasn't as intense as it could have been, though, because at that moment the rain turned into a downpour.

They scrambled up. Caddie stood back to let Thea go ahead of her through the latticed casement, but instead Thea flung her arms up and put her head back. She stuck out her tongue. "Mmm, tastes like nothing. Pure. God, don't you *love* a storm? Will built us a dock on the creek and we used to lie down on it in thunderstorms. Flat—so we wouldn't get electrocuted."

"Weren't you scared?" Caddie didn't care much for the nearness of the jittery lightning stabs over their heads or the powerful claps of thunder coming one after the other.

"Yes! And thrilled—we'd get soaking wet, like this—"

"Thea, that blouse is going to be ruined."

She looked down, as if she couldn't remember what blouse she had on. "Right you are." She untied the tails, unbuttoned her silk shirt, stripped it off, and pitched it through the window. "Much better." She laughed at Caddie's face. "Much!" She lifted her arms again, cupping her hands to catch the rain. She wasn't daring Caddie, she wasn't even looking at her, she had her eyes closed and she was catching raindrops on her tongue again—but all at once Caddie reached down and zipped off her own T-shirt. For a second she thought of flipping it over the balustrade onto the roof below, but that was a little beyond her. She threw it in the attic after Thea's blouse.

Thea laughed. She looked glad but not *astounded*—Caddie loved that. They stood in the cool, hard rain, twisting, pirouetting in their cramped space, two women in white brassieres that flashed lavender-blue in the lightning, their laughter audible only in the watery roar between tremendous cracks of thunder.

"We're beautiful!" Thea crowed.

"We are!" Water pelted her face and streamed in her eyes.

"I used to be a dancer! I gave it up to marry Carl." Suddenly she seized Caddie's slippery shoulders and gave her a long, fierce shake. "Don't you dare stop playing your music. *Your* music."

"I won't!" Caddie promised.

Later, drying off in Thea's room, Caddie would've liked to keep her friend's high opinion of her daring and joie de vivre a little longer, but she also needed to tell her the truth. "I still don't know what I'm going to do. For sure, about the baby. It's a big decision."

"Of course it is." Thea was bent over in half, fluffing her hair with a towel. "Whatever you decide, I'm for it." She straightened. "I mean it, whatever you decide. I only want you to make the decision from the right side of your heart, that's all that lecturing was about."

"You weren't lecturing."

"You're sweet." She went in the bathroom and came out presently in a short, sassy robe of lime satin. "New. On sale. Like it?"

"You could be the godmother," Caddie realized.

"Put this on," Thea said, tossing over a dry T-shirt. "It'll fit, we're both small up top. Pants, I don't know."

"Thea, you could be her godmother. If I kept her." Thea didn't say anything, so Caddie turned around modestly, took off her wet bra, and pulled the T-shirt over her head. She turned back. "What do you think?"

"What about Frances?" Thea went to her dresser and rummaged around in the bottom drawer.

"She's the great-grandmother, I'd still need a godmother. If I kept her."

Thea stood up, empty-handed. "No pants."

"What do you think?"

She put her hands on her hips. "Are we making a deal? Some kind of a bargain?"

"No."

"What, then?"

"I'm saying—*if*, that's all. Never mind, it's silly, I was just thinking out loud." She felt embarrassment and the beginnings of hurt. Which was ridiculous. Still, new as the idea was, it came as a shock that Thea might not *want* to be her baby's godmother.

"Sweetheart." Thea crossed to her, holding her hands out. "All I'm saying is I don't want to make a deal. Or a promise, even if it makes it easier for you." She smoothed a long, wet lock of hair behind Caddie's ear and cupped her cheek with her palm, holding gently. "Don't think about me or anybody else when you make up your mind. Look inside, nowhere else."

"Okay." She felt comforted and rebuffed at the same time. Was the true, adult goal to be strong all by yourself, never to ask for help from the ones you loved? Presumably Thea knew best, but maybe Caddie didn't value autonomy as much as she did. The important thing, though, was not to feel rejected. Because that would really be stupid.

"Why don't you stay here instead of going home this late by yourself? You could sleep on the couch in the sitting room, it's very comfortable. I've taken enough naps to—"

"I can't, I have to get home to Finney."

"I forgot about him."

"Thanks for showing me the secret porch." Caddie found her

288

purse and put the strap over her shoulder. "That was great." Did she sound stiff? After they'd just danced together half naked in the rain? Thea was looking at her out of narrow, concerned eyes. "Really great," Caddie repeated, and hugged her. When she'd have let go, Thea held on.

"I don't even care what you decide, except for *you*," she said into the air over Caddie's shoulder. "I want you to feel proud of yourself, with no regrets. You deserve to be happy." She squeezed tight. Caddie didn't understand the glaze of tears in Thea's eyes, but she was glad for them.

Firing up the Pontiac, watching the wipers smear the windshield with rain and blown honeysuckle blossoms, she reflected on what an interesting person she was these days. How varied and complex her reactions. Thea didn't care to be her baby's godmother, and she was okay with that. She was mellow with that. Fairly. Magill, on the other hand, had invited her to *marry* him just so the baby could have a name, and she'd *snapped* at him. She'd all but ended their friendship! She patted her chin, fingering the tender place where the pimple was. Must be hormones.

20

The Gray Gurus scheduled a program for the third Friday of every month, at eight P.M. in the Blue Room. Doré Harris, the self-appointed coordinator, said twelve programs a year was a serendipitous number, since Wake House at capacity housed twelve residents. Some people were on their second and third presentations, while others, like Cornel, who called them the Gray Geezers and considered them irrelevant by definition, had never given one. Audience size varied. For Nana's program, "Spots on the Turtle, Rings on the Tree: Musings on Oldness in Words and One Big Picture," the Blue Room was packed. Standing room only.

There wasn't a lectern; presenters stood or sat behind a card table in front of the fireplace, the audience gathered around on folding chairs. At eight-ten, Doré, sitting next to Caddie in the second row, stood and went to the card table.

"While we're waiting for our speaker, who I'm sure will be here any second, let me take this opportunity to tell you all about our delightful schedule for the next few months." Doré always dressed up for the presentations; tonight, presumably because the subject was artistic, she wore a long, fuzzy, umber-colored tunic dress with a necklace of heavy, clanking wooden stars and quarter-moons. "In September, we have a returning favorite—Bernie's going to show slides and tell us about his cruise to the Panama Canal."

290

Cornel groaned, sliding lower in his front-row seat. "Cripes, not again."

"I know we'll enjoy this *new* program, which shouldn't be confused with Bernie's trip to Puerto Rico, which was fascinating and which we heard about last *March*. And then in October, it's going to be *my* turn again. Doesn't time just fly?"

"Not fast enough," Maxine Harris, seated on Caddie's other side, said in a low but carrying voice. "Just so she doesn't do another 'Scenes from Excalibur.' I'd need my nausea pills to get through that."

Magill, lounging against the door post, had a coughing fit.

Doré's thin nostrils flared. Her mouth turned down before she straightened it with a freezing smile. "Then in November, we'll hear from Maxine, who's doing something about insurance, I wasn't quite clear on the—"

" 'The Wisdom of Term Life,' " her arch-enemy spoke up loudly. "My son, Stewart Ray *Junior*, is one of the top-selling life insurance agents in the eastern region. They give him bonus trips to the Caribbean every time he turns around."

"Well, *idn't* that nice. I'm sure we all can't *wait* to hear that." In case this sarcasm was lost on Maxine, Doré slowed down her southern accent to a sticky-sweet crawl to add, "There's nothin' I personally love *mo-uh* than somebody's secondhand report on a teeny-tiny part of their son's boring career specialty." The freezing smile flashed again before she went back to her chair and sat down.

Caddie stared at her fingernails and tried to ignore the sensation of heat rolling in on her from either side. From the corner of her eye she saw Maxine uncross her legs and plant both Dr. Scholl's sandals on the carpet. "It's better than feet."

Better than feet? She caught Thea's eye by accident and had to look away quickly. This was no laughing matter.

"It's better than doctoring people's feet all day," Maxine clarified. "Pays better, too, I'm sure."

Oh, now she remembered—Doré's daughter was a podiatrist. In the front row, Susan Cohen and Mrs. Brill looked at each other and rolled their eyes. Brenda cleared her throat in a soft, tolerant, voice-of-reason way.

Doré tinkled a laugh. Caddie quailed when she turned to her, reaching out to give her a confidential pat on the hand. "Idn't it sad," she murmured, "when people have to hold up the accomplishments of they-uh children because they-uh *own* are so sparse and pitiful?"

"Idn't it *sad*," Maxine mimicked, "when people's children move clear across the country to get away from them?"

Doré gasped.

"Idn't it *sad*, Caddie, when people think 'Dodo' is an *endearment?*"

Doré's wooden necklace made hollow, knocking clacks when she drew herself up tall. "What's sad—"

"Idn't it *sad*"—Maxine's voice shook with suppressed rage—"when people who've broken up three marriages in a row tell you straight to your face, Caddie, that they've never cared about material possessions? Don't you find that *sad?*"

"I'll tell you what's sad, it's women who can't hold on to a man and have to blame everybody else—"

"Not everybody else, just the Jezebel responsible for breaking up her happy home!"

"Happy home! Ha!"

"Happy home! Till somebody wrecked it. Somebody who calls that *romantic*—only she's not like Romeo and Juliet, she's like Lady Macbeth!"

Doré was gathering herself for a counterattack when Bea Copes burst out from the back of the room, "Stop it! Shame on both of you, *shame!*"

Caddie turned around with everybody else to see Bea hauling

herself to her feet with the help of Mr. Lorton's chair in front of her. Visiting her sister every day had made her haggard and sunken-eyed, and thinner than Caddie had ever seen her. But she was so angry, her braided hair looked like sparks were shooting out of it. She shook her fist!

"You *idiotic* women. How much time have you wasted, how much of *my life* have you wasted with your sniping? What kind of fools are you?"

Doré said, "Well now, just a—"

"How could you not know what you've got? I'd like to bop your two heads together!" Caddie was pretty sure she would have if they'd been sitting next to each other. "Do you like being alone and lonely? That's what you are, but you don't have to be, and it purely *burns me up*. If you could see two inches past your own nose—" She swatted at her cheek, angry at the tears. "You could save each other if you had any sense, let go of some of that poison. Lord, if you only knew." She flapped her hand at them and let her shoulders sink. "Oh, hell." She collapsed in her chair and started rooting in her pocket, her sleeve; people turned away so that she could compose herself in private.

Magill detached himself from the wall and went toward her with something white in his hand: a clean tissue. She put her cheek on his shoulder when he knelt beside her chair. Then Caddie looked away, too.

On either side of her, Maxine and Doré stared straight ahead with their hands in their laps, so quiet they didn't seem to be breathing. Their silence sounded shocked and regretful, or at least that's how Caddie interpreted it; but the silence in the room sounded vindicated, like a courtroom after the jury comes back with a popular verdict.

Eventually Brenda said, "Well! Why don't I just go see what's keeping our—oh! Here she is."

Nana loved making an entrance; Caddie probably should've warned people she wasn't going to be on time for her program. She looked a bit frazzled as she limped into the parlor with a cane instead of her walker, clutching a bundle of loose papers in her other hand. What was she wearing? It looked like a sheet. It was, a white sheet, wrapped around her tall, droopy frame like a toga and tied around the waist with a white cord. She had on white tennis shoes, too, and her white enamel earrings that said "Truth" on one and "Beauty" on the other. Were the smudges of white paint on her hands an accident or part of the costume?

She'd been working on something all afternoon, an artwork that was to be the finale of her program, but it was very mysterious, she wouldn't talk about it except to say it would be "simple." Good, Caddie had thought, and what a change from her usual, all-encompassing artistic visions. Whatever it was, she planned to unveil it at the end of her formal remarks, which were to be merely introductory; the big project was upstairs in her room.

She poked her way to the card table/lectern and peered around nearsightedly. "Well? Who's introducing me?"

There was a moment of uncertainty while Doré, Brenda, and Caddie all hesitated, then started to rise, like mystery guests on that old quiz show—but before anybody could get up Nana said, "Oh, never mind, I'll just start in." Her glasses were hanging from a chain around her neck; she lifted them from the bosom of her toga and stuck them on her nose. She rearranged the order of her papers. Cleared her throat.

Caddie broke the death grip she had on her own hands and took a deep breath. In, out, from the diaphragm. Only one thing made her more nervous than performing in public, and it was watching her grandmother perform in public. The old sinking feeling descended, same as always, the compulsion to run away, disappear, anything but sit through another writhing, palm-sweating embarrassment brought on by Nana's need to make a spectacle of herself. Why did Caddie care so much? She was thirty-two years old, when was she going to grow up? Never. It was too much a part of her, like her molecular structure, her fingerprint. Nana was periodically going to make her cringe with shame until one of them died.

"Oldness. What is oldness? Let's say it's purity. Old age, a purification process. The sloughing-off of all things unnecessary, getting down to the bone. Mummies. Indian burial ceremonies." Nana thinned her lips and turned a few pages, rejecting what was written on them.

"Cycles. Closer to wisdom, rising in spirals higher and higher. Where does it end? Some say in eternal contemplation of the face of God, a mystical experience I myself have had, and I'm sure I'm not alone here. I can tell you it's not boring. It sounds boring, yes, but it's not, it's like sleeping with Montgomery Clift, or Leon Russell, it's like very good sex all the time. It's perfect."

Apart from some shifting of position, the uncrossing or recrossing of legs, there wasn't a sound in the room.

"Hard to believe, I know, because youth owns everything. They always have, but nowadays it's completely out of hand. We're like Israelites crying in the desert. We're ghosts. People look right through us like we're Saran Wrap. But where youth goes wrong is, they think death is the end—so that's why we depress them so much. Even the religious ones think that, deep down. You have to get old to see the light, or maybe it's that the light only shines on the old. Who believes in God?"

It took a minute for people to realize this wasn't rhetorical. All hands went up except Cornel's and, to Caddie's surprise, Brenda's.

"See, we all do, it's unanimous," said Nana, who could always see what she wanted to see. "So what's there to be scared of?"

Caddie wondered if she was going to start preaching. This was a new side of Nana. She'd always dabbled in religions, the further from the mainstream the better, but her spiritual searches had seemed more for entertainment than enlightenment. Then again, she was a pragmatist, and everything served her art; if God helped justify whatever her new creation was, she'd use him as readily as a number-ten paintbrush.

"Put up or shut up, either God saves or he doesn't. Either we go to heaven or we rot in the ground, but either way, like the T-shirt says, no fear. No fear." She smiled and turned her head from side to side, as if conferring a benediction. It made her lose her place.

"Oldness. What is the essence of oldness? Is it decrepitude? Is it decay? Yes and no. Take a worm. Please. A worm eats to live, same as we do, but we call a worm corrupt. That thing from Milton—I was going to look that up, but I forgot. But a worm's the same as a bird or a butterfly. Underground, above ground, God made the ground. Creatures above or below, what's the difference? Corrupt *this*, that's what I say.

"Anyway, the essence of oldness is purity, that's the key. A thing is born, it exists, it ceases to be. It's a dead parrot. What's so bad about that? Why make everything so *personal*? Oh, poor me," she said in a weepy, mock-pitiful voice, "it's so sad, I'm going to die, we're all going to die, my best, sweetest friends, all the people I love so dearly, oh, it's so sad, so sad.

"It's *bigger* than us," she resumed in a brisk tone, "so suck it up and be strong. Buddha said—something something—anyway, look beyond this vale of tears, people. It's not about you, you're a flea, a fleck. It's all going to be all right. One way or the other. We worry too much is the problem. Well, me, anyway. You Baptists, you don't worry enough."

Mrs. Brill bridled.

"The whole point of oldness isn't despair, it's victory. We won! Aren't we here? Aren't they in the ground? The thing is, now they're catching up because you get old faster in the ground. I mean *a lot* faster. Me, I want to be cremated, then there's no contest. Talk about your purification, am I right? Think of your skin melting right off the bone. Think *simplicity*. Think ready to meet God, whoever she may be. Your soul is now a gigantic eyeball. Are you with me?"

Magill was the first to realize it was over and to start clapping. Pretty soon the others joined in, and to Caddie's surprise and intense relief the applause sounded genuine, not polite or just relieved because Nana's speech was finished. They'd *enjoyed* it.

Sorry, she couldn't take questions, her work would have to speak for itself, she said when Mrs. Brill raised her hand to ask what she'd meant about the Baptists. It was time for the unveiling of her "installation." She'd wanted to serve white wine in plastic glasses in her room, like an art opening, but Brenda had vetoed the idea on the grounds that it wasn't a house-sanctioned holiday. "Wait for me in the hall, don't anybody go in without me!" Nana instructed as the group broke up and people headed for the stairs or the elevator. "Very interesting," Mr. Lorton waylaid her to say. "Who's Leon Russell?" And Brenda said she'd made some "very unusual points." Nana basked. Caddie was dying to know what Magill had made of it, but when she looked around for him he was gone. He was avoiding her.

She and Nana rode up in the elevator with Susan Cohen, who wanted to tell them about the Jewish burial rite. Nana tried to look attentive, but she wasn't listening. Too excited. She hadn't been nervous for the talking part of her presentation, but whatever was waiting in her room was making her mash and massage the handle of her cane like biscuit dough. That was funny, because now Caddie *wasn't* nervous.

The odor of paint had been faint but definite in the elevator, but when the door opened on the second floor it became a stench. Maxine was grumbling, "I won't sleep a wink with this godawful smell," in the group milling outside Nana's door. Nana hurried down the hall toward them, thump-thumping with her cane, her toga-sheet billowing like laundry on a line. "Caddie," she threw back, "you stay there and turn out that light when I say." The crowd parted; she waded through it and stood with her back to her bedroom door, legs braced, holding her cane in both hands like a nightstick.

"This is a visual experience. We can talk and talk about the essence of oldness, which is the essence of *us*, but a picture's always worth more. That's my creed and that's my philosophy. And now— here's my vision. I'm not saying anything else.

"Except don't come in till I tell you." She reached behind her for the doorknob. "Caddie, turn that hall light out now."

Caddie hesitated, worried about plunging all these old folks into darkness, people tripping and bumping into things, falling. Magill could lose his balance and hurt himself.

"Caddie!"

She turned out the light.

Sounds of self-conscious laughter. Nana's door opening. Her saying, "All right, come on in but be careful. Just come in, there's nothing you can trip over. The light goes on when we're all in." Movement, shuffling feet.

Caddie hesitated again. Was she supposed to stay here? Did Nana mean *this* light? They should've had a dress rehearsal.

"Come on, everybody in," Nana was saying. "Okay, are we all here?"

Caddie started to call out, "I'm not," but her sense of the theatrical, dim as it was, warned her that might hamper the start of the show. Using the wall to feel her way, she crept down the blackish corridor, and in the next second the light in Nana's room clicked on, throwing a slash of yellow onto the hall carpet, the opposite wall. Inside: gasps.

With a spot of light to aim for, Caddie trotted the rest of the way. She wheeled into Nana's room. White! Her eyes hurt—she squinted in the sudden dazzle. White!

"Oh, my heavens."

"Dear Lord."

"What on earth?"

In the center of it all, Nana squeezed her cane and kept trying to smile, smile, but uncertainty started her lips quivering.

She'd painted everything in the room white. Everything. The wallpapered walls, the bureau and everything on top of it, her bedside table, her desk, her clock, the ottoman, both chairs. The bed! The picture frames on the white walls, the lamp and the lamp cord, the bookshelf and the spines of all the books in it—the windows! Her clay statue of David! Everything. Everything was white. The floor—no, thank God, thank God, she'd put white sheets down on the beautiful old wood floor.

In the stunned silence, Caddie made a mistake. She said, "Oh, Nana. What have you done?"

Her grandmother's face collapsed. In an instant she went from apprehensive to devastated, and it was all Caddie's doing. She reached out to her in a reflex, but Nana yanked away before she could touch her.

"Out, then! Get out, all you Philistines. It's for purity, but you wouldn't know. Everybody out of my room. Get out, get out, get out, get out, get out."

They were going as fast as they could. Brushing against the door frame, Doré let out a squeak—the shoulder of her umber tunic came away with paint on it. "I think it's latex," Caddie called, "I'll wash it!" Brenda was walking out with the others— Caddie stopped her by grabbing her hand. "I'm sorry, I'm so *sorry*, I'll fix this, I'll get it all cleaned up. Anything that's ruined, I'll pay for."

Brenda, the soul of calmness, could hardly make her mouth work. "We'll talk."

Thea was the last to go. She didn't want to leave; she asked Caddie what she could do to help. "No, you, too," Nana snapped, and began moving toward her in a menacing way, herding her out with the shelf of her bosom. As soon as Thea was out, she slammed the door behind her.

That was the last straw. "Nana!"

"What?" She limped in circles around the room, striking the white bureau with her cane on every other pass, muttering. "It's for *purity*, how could they *be* so stupid, how could they be so *stupid*? I don't know why I'm surprised. I don't know why I thought *they'd* get it when it only came to *me* this morning."

"What?"

"I couldn't figure it out for the longest time. I even asked people, what's the bottom line on oldness? What's a symbol for longevity, for lasting and surviving, for elderliness. Cornel said a coffin, but that's death. What is the essential form of *age*?" She waved her arm around the room. "And here it is, purity and light, the return of innocence. This is it."

"But—"

"But *what*?"

"But, Nana, for the Lord's sake, couldn't you have painted a *canvas* white?"

"You don't get it. Of course not, how else would you get the *feel*?" She held her hands out, then clutched them to her heart. "I don't understand, I swear I just don't understand. How people could be—"

"You really don't? You truly can't understand why people, *most* people, would think this is completely nuts?"

"Ohhhh, *Caddie*." She tuned her voice to a low, deep, guttural accusation, the very sound of betrayal. It would've destroyed

Caddie, but it was the same tone Nana used to use before Finney was housebroken when she'd come upon one of his accidents.

"Nana, I'm sorry, but we're in trouble. I don't even know if Brenda will let you stay here after this."

"Don't be silly. It's my room, isn't it?"

"No!"

"Well, I'd like to know what we're paying an arm and a leg for every month if it's not. All right, all right, all right. All right!" She cupped her ears with her hands. "Stop talking. Stop reasoning with me. You're just like them—you get out, too. To think I raised you. You're even worse, because you're a fraidy-cat *and* a Philistine. Fraidy-cat, fraidy-cat! Scared of your own shadow!

"No, don't leave! I don't know what I'm even saying." Her shoulders slumped. She took her hands from her ears and put them over her eyes. "Oh, God, look what I've done."

"It doesn't matter." Caddie went to her and led her over to the bed.

"No, don't, it's still wet!"

"Who cares, Nan. It's only paint." She plopped down on the sticky cotton quilt, ignoring the squishy sound.

Nana hesitated. "Oh, hell," she said, and collapsed beside her.

Foot-wide tracks from the roller had left white diagonals on the quilt, obliterating the gaily colored squares. Nana should've put on two coats; red and blue were starting to bleed through in patches. "Well, here we are," she said, "and I'm losing my mind."

"No, you're not."

"It's why I wanted to come here in the first place. So you wouldn't see."

"You mean you came here because of me?"

"Sometimes I know, sometimes I don't. Caddie, don't hate me."

"Never."

"Don't remember me like this."

"But you're all right. You're the same as always."

She shook her head, chuckling and sniffling at the same time. She'd been leaning back on her hands. She brought them into her lap, holding the white palms up, as if to say, *Look, here's proof.* She touched Caddie's face with her fingers and looked into her eyes, straight on, showing herself.

"You are," Caddie insisted. "A little eccentric, that's what you are."

She gave Caddie's knee a squeeze, leaving a palm print. "I didn't mean what I said. Whatever it was. I can't even remember."

"Never mind."

"But that's what I'm *talking* about," she declared, anxious again. "Don't let them kick me out, don't let them send me home, because I don't want you taking care of me. Listen to me. Listen."

"I'm listening."

"Do not, do not take me back home. Shoot me first. It's not funny! Are you listening?"

"I'm listening."

"I will not be a figure of fun. I'm an *artist*."

"I know you are."

She pushed her away. "No, you don't, you think I'm crazy, you've always been ashamed of me. Ever since you were a little girl, you've been my shadow, my little black cloud. Oh, I don't *mean* that—I'm so tired, I've been working so hard to get ready—"

"I know. It's all right."

"How am I going to sleep in here? You see?"

"I'll ask Brenda—"

"I didn't think about it once, the aftermath. You see? You're right, everybody's right, I'm losing my brain." She fell forward, rocking herself over her knees.

Caddie put her arms around her and rocked with her. "You're all right, Nan, don't worry, everything's all right, it's all right." The stink of paint was making a spot in her head ache. Nana had painted three bobby pins on top of her bedside table white, as well as the cover of a paperback book, an emery board, and her reading glasses. Under the bed, the heels of her furry slippers poked out, white. The closet door was shut; no telling if she'd painted her clothes. "It's really . . . it's really amazing, Nan. So this is old age."

"A symbol." She sat up. "It's a flop if I have to explain it."

"No, I get it, I think. Purity, just as you said. Getting rid of all the things you don't need."

"Till you're nothing but light." She frowned. "Maybe I should've used a lightbulb. A *roomful* of lightbulbs—you walk in and *bam*. Or the whole house! Or, I know, *fire* instead of light . . ."

"Nan."

"If I could've set the *house* on fire, *then*—"

"Nana—"

"You don't even know when I'm kidding."

"Oh." She let her grandmother poke her in the shoulder and cackle at her. They leaned against each other.

"Don't let me forget any of this," Nana said presently, her voice wistful. "Remind me. Because I might forget."

What a blessing that would be, Caddie couldn't help thinking. Maybe the worst of this was ending for Nana just as it was beginning for her. It felt like quicksand, the thought of losing Nana, like sitting in a sinking boat. This wasn't how it was supposed to be, it was backward. *Don't leave me, Nan, I'm not ready.* She'd been planning to tell her about the baby tonight. She'd been looking forward to the relief of that, the naturalness of sharing the news of her baby with the woman who might as well be her mother. Now she couldn't, she wasn't sure why but she couldn't, not now, and maybe it was the beginning of not telling Nana things.

"This shouldn't be how it works." Nana sighed, and Caddie

smiled because she'd read her mind. "It should get brighter at the end."

"It will. It'll get brighter."

"When?"

"Soon."

Wet white paint made a squishy sound when they clasped hands. Nana held on so hard, it hurt.

21

August gave out and September took over without much energy. Fall wasn't "in the air" yet, as Mrs. Tourneau had claimed this morning when she and Caddie had come outside for their newspapers at the same moment. "Isn't it?" Caddie called back in a cheery and-that's-final voice, not because she agreed but because that way Mrs. Tourneau couldn't capture her.

Something was changing, but it wasn't the weather, which dragged on hot and humid day after day, blurring outlines in haze and sapping initiative. Everything looked tired, from the strawlike lawns to the blackish-green leaves on the maple trees overhanging Early Street, tired and too heavy to hold themselves up. Dreary limbo time, when summer was dying but autumn was still gestating, or perhaps hadn't even been conceived yet. Dregs of days. Burntout fag ends of days. Days like hunks of barely smoldering charcoal—

Jason Newbinder shrieked a note on his A string so far out of tune, Finney whimpered under the piano. "Let's try that one again," Caddie advised, speaking so gently she amazed herself. Because what she really wanted to do was throw Jason's violin out the window into the bare front yard, bare of sculptures, bare of everything but weeds, and then throw Jason out after it.

"I don't get why I have to play these stupid scales anyway." He was seven years old, an azure-eyed, towheaded angel sent to torment her.

Too young for violin lessons, but his mother had insisted. And Caddie needed the money.

"I don't see why, either."

He looked at her narrowly, suspecting a trick, but she was serious. If he packed up his instrument and went home right now, she wouldn't lift a finger to stop him. She'd hold the door for him.

She got a grip on herself and turned in his music book to "Frère Jacques." "Let's try this, then. Let's see how much better you can play it this week than last."

"Okay," he said, brightening. He began to saw away, and something in the way he pressed his tender cheek against the chin rest, gripping the bow in his stubby fingers and sticking his tongue out between his sucked-in lips, punctured a hole in Caddie's exasperation. She felt it leak away until nothing was left but a peculiar achy wistfulness, like waking from a sweet dream you can't quite remember.

Jason's lessons were only for half an hour, but even that was too long for a seven-year-old. When he started playing more clunkers than right notes and her effusive praise stopped cheering him up, she suggested they finish up with lemonade and a duet on the front porch. That cheered him up *too* much; she didn't yell, "Don't run!" in time, and he banged his instrument on the edge of the screen door on his way out. "Uh-oh," he said worriedly, showing her the scratch beside the tailpiece. "Don't tell my mom, okay?" Caddie promised.

"What's that?" he asked while he slurped his lemonade, pointing to a pile of paint supplies under the porch swing.

"That's paint. And brushes and stuff that I haven't had time to clean yet."

It had taken all weekend, with some help from Brenda and Claudette, to put Nana's room to rights. Before Nana had painted them white, the walls had been papered with a dark floral print no one liked anyway, so Caddie had repainted them a pretty shade of peach. She'd put a second coat of white on the furniture, used paint remover on objects with hard, nonporous surfaces, and thrown out the rest, including the bedclothes and the curtains. Result: a fresh, airy-looking room, much brighter than before. Really, a tremendous improvement. She kept saying that to Brenda in hopeful tones, but the older woman's face had remained circumspect. "We'll talk later," she'd replied every time Caddie apologized, which was frequently.

Even out on the porch, Jason's attempt to play double stops was painful. Not many students, maybe three in all Caddie's years of teaching, had ever tempted her to wear earplugs, and he was one. She didn't like Mrs. Newbinder, who was pushy and insensitive and wouldn't *listen*—but it was a relief when she pulled up in her tan station wagon and beeped the horn, leaning down low to wave through the window and holler, "Jaaaa-son."

"You were *great* today," Caddie fibbed, helping him snap his bow back in the case. "I saw *so* much improvement. Didn't you? Did you have fun?"

He grunted; he wasn't much of a talker.

"Next week, I know—if you practice your new piece really well, we'll save five minutes at the end and make root beer floats. If your mom says it's okay. How's that?"

He was so young, so little, yet already he'd mastered the art of the put-down. "Yeah, maybe," he said out of the side of his sweet angel's mouth. She watched him rumble down the walk with his miniature tough-guy slouch and thought again how unsuited he was to the violin. Mrs. Newbinder should make him take guitar lessons. Heavy metal.

At least he was her last student for the day. Standing at the kitchen sink, cleaning the paintbrushes she'd been too tired to deal with till now, Caddie thought about the meeting she'd finally had with Brenda last Sunday night. They'd had it in Brenda's office. She'd dragged her chair out from behind her desk and put it next to

Caddie's—not a good sign. Caddie could never guess Brenda's age; she might be a haggard forty-five, a spry sixty, or anywhere in between. She was a widow with a married daughter out west someplace, but much more than that Caddie didn't know.

Caddie had started by apologizing again, saying how sorry she was for Nana's "brainstorm," as she'd taken to calling it, and how she hoped it wouldn't lead to any *drastic measures*—by which she meant Brenda kicking Nana out of Wake House.

The older woman had listened patiently, leaning forward with her large hands folded around her knees, dark eyes sympathetic, until Caddie ran down. "The thing is," she began, "nothing's changed since the last time you and I talked about this. Wake House is still struggling along, underfunded, overtasked, and we're still not equipped or even *safe* for taking on residents with dementia."

"But aren't there degrees? You don't get rid of somebody for forgetting to come to lunch, there must be *levels*. The white room was bad, I know, but now it's fixed, and—it's not like Nana's taking her clothes off and running around naked, she hasn't set fire to anything, she hasn't threatened anyone. I promise I'll never sue. Would that help? If she hurts herself or gets lost, I promise not to hold you responsible. Nana doesn't really *bother* anybody, most people *like* her—"

"*I* like her, I'm very fond of Frances, I think she's a stitch. And yes, there certainly are degrees. She doesn't have to go *tomorrow*, I'm just—" She blew her bangs out of her eyes tiredly. "I'm alerting you to the probabilities, Caddie. For the future. It wouldn't hurt to start looking around for another place for your grandmother."

"A nursing home."

"There are some nice ones."

"Not like Wake House," she'd argued childishly. She imagined telling Nana she had to leave, had to move to a real home. "I don't know if she'd even go."

"It'll be hard," Brenda had agreed. "I'll help all I can." She'd pressed her middle fingers against the sides of her nose, as if she had a headache. "You can't imagine how frustrating it is. I'm trying to get Edgie back into the house, we're working on an arrangement, but there are so many obstacles, legal, logistical, you just don't know. I want this place to be a *home*, not an institution, but the insurance goes up and the repairs never stop, and then I have to raise rates again. It feels like a losing battle."

She'd stared at Caddie bleakly. "I'm trying to keep people, not throw them out when they need help the most. But the more you do the more you're regulated, and the more you're regulated the more it costs. My late husband used to say I was too idealistic. I don't know. But I love old people. Most people don't. I like trying to make life nice or even *decent* for them after they've had to give up just about everything they have. Their lives shrink down so. They live in these little rooms, Caddie, sleep in single beds, they eat when I say they can eat. They had homes of their own, families, people used to need *their* help. Now the best I can do is let them live with me in my house. And I don't know how much longer I can do that."

Caddie had gone home that night feeling more burdened down than before. She had one person to worry and fret about, Brenda had twelve. Life was too hard. She'd had to get up and play the piano for an hour that night before she could fall asleep.

The phone rang. She answered it with dripping, paint-stained hands.

"Caddie! Are you in the middle of something?"

"Hi, Thea—no, my last student just left. Great timing."

"Good, because we need you. Mrs. Brill's granddaughter's here, or maybe it's her great-granddaughter, yeah, I guess it's a great, the *sweetest* little thing, and her parents gave her a violin for her birthday yesterday and nobody even knows how to *tune* it. So here the poor thing is, visiting Granny and just dying to play something for her on her new toy, and nobody has the least idea how the thing even works. So we need you to rescue her. Her name is—well, I forget, how embarrassing. A senior moment. Her name's . . ."

"Marcy?" Mrs. Brill had a great-granddaughter named Marcy. She was about two; she lived in Cleveland.

"Marcy, that's it. Can you come? I know it's an imposition—"

"I can come."

"Wonderful! Right away?"

"Um . . ."

"Well, after you get cleaned up and everything, of course. You probably want to change clothes, and that's fine, no *great* rush, but soon, because they're leaving, you know—eventually."

Caddie had a fiendish urge to make things hard on Thea, ask her penetrating questions or suddenly remember a previous engagement. But that would be mean. Fun, though. "Okay, I'll change and get over there as soon as I can."

"Super! See you."

"Wow, that was pretty lame," she told Finney while she riffled through her closet for something to wear. "I was expecting a cleverer ruse." They'd had over a week to plan it, or even longer for all she knew. But last week was when Nana had accidentally blurted out the news to Caddie that she was getting a surprise party. She was thirty-three years old today.

It wasn't hard to act surprised. She walked across the mysteriously empty porch and entered the strangely silent front hall, and from around the four corners of both parlors people in party hats jumped out and yelled "*Surprise!*" blowing paper horns in her face. She clapped her hands to her mouth and exaggerated a shocked shriek, but not by much, and afterward, whenever someone asked if she was *really* surprised, she said "Absolutely!" and it almost felt like the truth.

"You sneak," she told Thea, who was beside herself with glee. "You told me such a *whopper*."

"I know! I thought it up on the spur of the moment. Caddie, were you *really* surprised?"

"Flabbergasted. This was your idea, wasn't it?"

"No way," Thea denied, but Caddie thought everything looked exactly like Thea's handiwork, from the flowers and favors in the dining room, to the table set with paper plates and matching cloth, to the punch bowl and little sandwiches in the Blue Room, to the pin-the-tail-on-the-donkey game tacked to the wall. And crepe paper garlands strung everywhere. "Oh, happy birthday, Caddie," she said, giving her a long, strong hug. "I hope this is the start of your *best year ever*. Oh, I *hope* it is."

Caddie didn't see how it could be, but Thea's intensity woke her up. She shook off her blues and looked around for Magill. Could he still be avoiding her? Even today? That hurt her feelings. Naturally things had been strained between them, and she'd sort of been avoiding *him*, but how could he not come to her party? Maybe he was sick.

"Where's Magill?" she asked Brenda, then Cornel, but they didn't know.

They made her sit on the sofa in front of a small pile of gifts on the coffee table—most people had just given her cards, she was relieved to see—and open presents. "Who's this from?" She read all the cards out loud. "You guys. You are too much. I haven't had a surprise party since—gosh, I don't even know. Oh, Mrs. Brill. Did you *make* these?"

"With my own two hands."

Crocheted slippers with grosgrain ribbons around the ankles. Caddie held them up so everyone could see.

"Do you like them?" Mrs. Brill looked at her over her intimidating nose. "I hope they fit. Frances said you have size-nine feet."

"Huge feet," Nana corroborated. "Gigantic."

"Oh, but they're so thin and aristocratic," Thea exclaimed. "Long, thin feet. Not like mine—I'm a peasant." She stuck out her perfectly nice sandaled foot, using Cornel's shoulder for balance. People started talking about their feet, what size they were now, what size they'd been forty years ago, foot doctors they had known, including Doré's daughter out in Seattle.

"You've got good feet," Cornel told Thea, "good solid feet. Healthy feet. I've always admired them." He coughed violently, and Thea laughed, which made his ears turn red.

More cards, more sweet little gifts, a cactus plant from Maxine, a commemorative bicentennial silver-dollar plaque from Mr. Lorton. Bea and Edgie's card was funny, a joke about old age, but Edgie's quivery, illegible signature gave Caddie a pang.

She guessed what was coming next when Thea made everyone get up and go into the Red Room, where the piano was. "My last surprise of the day," she announced, sitting down at the bench with a flourish. Caddie went to stand at her right, as she had so many times for their lessons. They smiled tremulously at each other.

"This is my present to Caddie, but it's really hers to me. Apologies in advance for all the mistakes, which are entirely the fault of the student, not the teacher!" She put her fingers on the keys. "Also, apologies to everybody who's heard me massacre this six hundred times already. Your patience has been saintly." She took a deep breath. Caddie realized how nervous she was, and immediately her own pulse rate shot up. Thea banged the two introductory bass notes with authority and plunged into "Maple Leaf Rag."

She only stumbled in the seventh measure, that fast, barrel-rolling, left-hand-over-right booby trap, but when it came around again she played it perfectly. Never play ragtime fast: Scott Joplin himself had said that, and Thea was an obedient student. Her pace was more stately than sprightly, but so *steady*, it wasn't long before feet started tapping and heads nodded in time. Thea was right, this song made people happy. Bea had been sad and worried for so long; how wonderful to see her relax and pat out the beat on her hips with her hands. Old Mr. Lorton was practically dancing a jig on his short bowlegs.

When she finished the song, Thea laughed and clapped along with everybody else, giddy from pleasure and relief. Caddie kissed her warm cheek, exclaiming, "Beautiful, perfect, thank you, oh, wonderful—play it again!" and she did.

She saw Magill slide in—literally, bracing his back on the wall and stepping into the room sideways, crablike. He must be having a bad balance day. She waved to him over all the bobbing heads, and he sent back a wink and a rakish salute. Just what she wanted, the old Magill, quirky and teasing, not serious. Thea's gift to her was this song, and Magill's was his funny smile that said—she thought it said—they were friends again.

Thea grabbed Caddie's hand and made her take bows with her to applause, like the soloist and the conductor. "Is that it?" Brenda said. "No more presents? Okay, then—who's for some cake and ice cream?"

Caddie wasn't surprised when, in the middle of the shuffling exodus to the dining room, Nana poked her on the shoulder and drew her over to an empty corner of the foyer. "Hold on a minute. You didn't think I'd forget your birthday, did you?" She had a funny look in her eye. She'd dressed up for the party in her favorite sundress, even put a bow at the end of the long braid she'd wound her wiry gray hair into. But there was something going on behind the glitter in her smile. Something up her sleeve.

"No, Nan, of course not. You never forget."

313

"Here." She took Caddie's hand and slipped something smallish into it. "Careful, it's fragile. No wrapping paper, but that's not my fault. I'm living like a monk here."

Caddie gently pulled away the tissue paper from around the object. "Oh, it's a . . . a . . ." A clay figure. Of a woman. She had an instrument in one hand, a violin, so Caddie recognized herself, but that wasn't the only giveaway. With her other hand, the nude, smiling, flat-chested, long-haired female was holding up a great, sloping, pregnant belly.

"Like it?"

Caddie felt her cheeks getting hot. She kept staring at the figure, not looking up. "How did you know?" she finally managed.

"I'm psychic."

"No—really."

"A grandmother senses these things."

"Who told you?"

"Maxine."

She looked up. "Maxine!"

"Who heard it from Bernie, who got it from Cornel. Everybody knows, Caddie Ann. The question is, when were you going to tell *me?*"

"Today," she blurted. "Today, Nan—it was going to be my birthday present to you."

"Hey, you two," Brenda called from the dining room, "the ice cream's melting!"

"Well, well. That's all I can say," Nana said, folding her arms. "Well, well, well."

"Are you mad?" Caddie asked. She felt like a child.

"Course I'm not mad. What do you take me for?" Her stern face gentled. She reached out and patted Caddie's stomach with the soft cup of her palm. "Chip off the old block," she said in a tender voice. "Whose is it, the dog man?"

Caddie nodded.

"Hmph. Well, don't you worry, we'll get through this."

"I know we will."

"Like we always have." She linked arms with Caddie and they began to move toward the dining room. "You know I always said men stink."

"You never said men stink."

"Well, I should have. The point is, you're much better off without that guy."

"You think?"

"Oh, sure. This way's purer. You, me, and the baby—who's a girl, it goes without saying. Winger power. The way it's always been, right?"

Caddie's brave smile wavered only at the corners.

Maxine and Doré had made a three-layer chocolate birthday cake. Not together—Maxine made the cake and Doré iced and decorated it—but still. Pretty amazing. Bea's outburst had accomplished something, even if it was subtle, a change in the atmosphere if not in the women themselves. After the singing and candle-blowing, there was a champagne toast—Caddie's birthday qualified as a house celebration, so there could be booze—and with her own eyes she saw Doré and Maxine lean across the table and clink glasses. Wow. What a shame Bea wasn't there to see it, but she'd left early, gone back to the rehab place to be with Edgie. She went every morning and stayed till the nurses made her go home.

They'd put Caddie at the head of the table, Magill on her right. His voice was a true, full-hearted tenor, she discovered during "Happy Birthday." But he looked ridiculous in his cone-shaped party hat, which he wore low on his temple like a horn. "How come you never mind looking silly?" she asked.

"I look *silly*?" He made a stricken face.

She giggled—that quarter glass of champagne. "Most people, men especially, they, I don't know . . ."

"Care about their dignity."

"Yeah. No."

"Hey, I've got dignity up the ying-yang." With his teaspoon, he carefully cut out the fat yellow rosette of frosting on his piece of cake and dropped it on her plate. She'd have demurred, but she craved the oily sugar blob, had to have it—how had he known that? He said, "You don't think clowns have dignity?"

"You're not a clown." Even with his goofy hat, even with the loopy smile he turned on her. They were the same age, but because of his thinness, his hollow cheeks and knobby wrists, the way his Adam's apple bobbed in his throat, the way his clothes swam on him, she used to think of him as a boy. But not in a long time. He'd merged, boy and man, and now she thought she knew him. The real Magill.

"Promise me something," he said.

"What?"

"Promise."

The humor in his eyes reassured her. "Okay, I promise. What?"

"You'll sing a song with me this afternoon."

"Out loud? You mean in front of people?"

He laughed.

"Wait, I don't—"

"Too late, you promised." He stood up. "Time for Caddie's big present," he announced, and everybody quieted down. The anticipation on their faces, especially Thea's, twisted Caddie's nerves. "You'll need some help," Cornel said, and started to get up, but Magill said no, he wouldn't, he had it right here. He walked over to the window, the floor-length drapery at the side. "Caddie, close your eyes."

"Why?"

316

"Close your eyes!" everybody yelled.

"Because I didn't wrap it," Magill said, "that's why." She heard scraping, something heavy being shoved across the floor in her direction. "I got it, I got it," Magill said when Cornel tried again to help him. What on earth? Something big and bulky, something heavy. She had no idea.

"Okay. Ready?"

"No."

"Wait—my camera," Thea said.

"Okay. Open your eyes."

A machine. A big, silver machine with a million dials, buttons, and knobs. A tape player? No, too big, and it had microphones on the sides and two enormous speakers at the bottom, a place for CDs. A boom box? Then she knew.

"It's a karaoke machine."

"Yes!" Clapping and exclamations of delight, laughter. "Isn't it great?" "It was Magill's idea." "Don't you love it?"

"Ohhh" was the best she could do. She leaned over it and clasped her hands together, as if overcome. She was overcome. They all thought this was so *funny*. "How funny," she said enthusiastically. "What a riot."

"You hook it up to the TV and it shows the words," Bernie was telling her, "then you sing in the microphone and drown out the real singer's voice."

"We tried it last night," Thea said.

"We didn't think you'd mind," Maxine said. "We wanted to iron out all the kinks first."

"But there weren't any," Magill said. "There's nothing to it, you just turn it on and put in a CD."

"You don't have one already, do you?" Mrs. Brill asked anxiously.

"No," Caddie said. "No, I sure don't."

"Plug it in, let's play it," Cornel said, and people started getting up. Bernie picked up one side of the machine, Cornel took the other, and they carried it out of the room.

"Oh," Caddie said, "now? Right now? Here?" Nobody even heard, they were too busy making a beeline for the Blue Room.

"So," Magill said, taking her arm. "How are you on 'I Believe I Can Fly'?"

She *wanted* to be a good sport, heaven knew. Why wouldn't she? How much easier to go along with what everybody wanted her to do—*sing!*—than draw even more attention to herself by begging to be excused. What *was* this? She thought something had changed, she thought for sure she'd gotten over this stupid, sickening stage fright the night she'd played and sung for Thea and Cornel and Magill, but here it all was back in a big, hot, soupy wave, no better than before. Worse.

"Caddie, come on, everybody's doing it," "It's your present, you *have* to, if you don't you'll hurt our feelings," "But you're so *good*, and there's nothing to it, come on, Caddie . . ."

Luckily for her, there were so many surprise hams at Wake House—Mrs. Brill! Maxine Harris!—that her reticence was passed over as temporary, cute, not antisocial, not a negative comment on the gift itself. Certainly not evidence of any humiliating personal pathology.

The worst moment came when Magill crouched on the floor in front of her—she'd taken a seat in the "audience," as far away from the "stage" as possible, the stage being a cleared space before the television set and the hated karaoke machine—and tried to jolly her into a duet. He made it sound like such innocent, cheesy, uncool fun, it was painful to turn him down. "I got 'It's Only Rock 'n Roll,' so we can be Mick Jagger and Tina Turner. Come on, Caddie, let's do it."

She shook her head, helpless.

"No? Okay, did you ever hear Dr. John and Etta James—"

"No, honestly, I can't do this. I know I promised, but you tricked me."

"Sure you can. Okay, watch for a while, we'll do one later. How about the Carpenters? I'll be Karen."

And it wasn't as if whatever song she might've decided to "sing" with the machine, with or without Magill, would've been that much worse or more foolish or any sillier than anybody else's impromptu performance. Then again, maybe not so impromptu: Brenda, Maxine, and Nana performed "Stop! In the Name of Love" with so many coordinated hand moves, they had to have practiced last night. And Bernie wasn't bad at all on "New York, New York," even though he mangled the words because he couldn't find his glasses. The best singer was Mrs. Brill—she sang "Amazing Grace" and brought down the house—and the worst was Doré Harris, who was tone-deaf. She chose "Somewhere over the Rainbow," and she sang it cocktail lounge-style, very dramatic; she even used a scarf. But nobody laughed or snickered; they smiled, but they didn't *laugh*— and if that wasn't a good reason to just get up and join the party, Caddie didn't know what was.

"Oh, quit asking her," Nana finally advised all the coaxers, "she'll never do it, not in a million years. She's a scaredy-cat."

No, the worst was when Magill tried one last time. He knelt in front of her again, and this time he even took her hands. His persuasive grin was nothing but hopeful and sweet, and she thought vaguely, *Good, you still don't know about me. What a flop I am.* "What's the problem here?" he asked, giving her hands a gentle shake. "You're not really scared. You sang for Thea and Cornel and me, before, and you were . . ." He looked past her, as if he were picturing that night. "Incredible. You blew my head off, Caddie. So what's the trouble?"

He made her blush. "I don't know. It's me, I'm just like this. I thought I was better, but—turns out I'm not. It's a wonderful present, really, you were so nice to think of it. I hope it didn't cost too much."

He looked up at her through his black lashes, his eyes all tolerant and accepting. "It's safe here, you know. Nothing to be afraid of. Act out a little," he said softly. "It's not going to turn you into your mother."

"Oh." She pulled her hands away and folded her arms across her chest. "Hey. It's not really that big a deal, is it? I'm not doing that." She gestured toward her grandmother, who was trying to sing "Mack the Knife." "That's all, I'm not doing it."

"Okay."

"And I'd appreciate it if you wouldn't try to second-guess my motives. You told me not to psychoanalyze *you*, so I'd—appreciate—"

"Okay." He wobbled slightly when he got up. "You're right, it's no big deal. Sorry I nagged you." He made a bow—she hated it; he probably meant it kindly, but to her it looked ironic and horribly final—and left her by herself.

She must've looked pitiful. Thea came over and sat down on the arm of her chair. "Happy birthday," she said, and pulled her in for a kiss on top of the head. Wouldn't it be nice to lay her head on Thea's lap just for a minute, Caddie thought. It wouldn't cure her of anything, but it would make her feel better. "Sorry I'm such a jerk," she mumbled.

"Oh, hush."

"I am, though. I can't do anything. Can't sing a song, I can't even decide on a family for this baby. I can't pick up the phone and call . . . some man." Who might turn out to be her father.

"Everything in good time."

She let out a heavy sigh. "What does that mean?"

"Mmm." Thea patted her lips, thinking. "I guess it means you and I are on different schedules." She looked tired and dreamy, as if Caddie's troubles weren't particularly important to her at this moment. "I'm going to have to learn a new song, aren't I? What should it be? Chopin? You could simplify one of the Preludes for me." Caddie couldn't tell if she was kidding or not. Probably not. Thea smoothed her skirt over her knee with a pink-nailed hand. She had small hands, veiny with age; the pretty wedding ring Will had made for her was too big for them. "I'm sorry I'm having a better time at your party than you are."

"Me, too." Thea's light laugh made Caddie smile. "You always cheer me up."

"That's funny," Thea said, "you always cheer *me* up." She stood. "I'm going outside and watch the sun go down."

"Okay. Magill's mad at me."

Thea rolled her eyes.

"Okay, disillusioned, not mad."

"So?"

"So. I hate that."

"Fix it, then." She started away.

"Fix it, then," Caddie mimicked.

Thea heard, but she only laughed and kept going.

People stopped asking her to sing. She should've felt relieved, but instead she felt finished, as if there were no more hope for her and finally they all knew it. It was bad enough to be a flop in private, but much worse to be a public one, in front of so many people you'd learned to care for.

Magill, who had disappeared for a while, was back. He'd put on one clip-on earring, a gold hoop—it looked like Doré's—and twisted a blue-and-white handkerchief into a headband around his forehead. Shoeless, wearing the same holey jeans and loud Hawaiian shirt he'd had on all afternoon, he commandeered the karaoke machine and broke into a very realistic cover of "Lively Up Yourself." He managed to keep his balance while he did deep knee bobs to the reggae beat, really nailing the Jamaican accent. Caddie had to laugh along with the others, filled with the same fondness and affection for him. And something else, too, a pang of pain or pleasure, she couldn't quite tell which.

Do you know why Henry took up skydiving? Thea had asked her once. *Because he was afraid of heights.*

Magill had gone on to "I Shot the Sheriff," but Caddie felt his eyes on her when she crossed in front of him and began to pick over the karaoke CD collection. The artists weren't really the artists, they were soundalikes, she'd figured out earlier, but as Maxine Harris said, "They're close enough for us!" A CD called *Pop Duets by Your Favorites* was exactly what Caddie was looking for. The Bob Marley song ended; she exchanged it for her CD.

"How does this work?" she asked Magill. "How do you make it play number seven?"

He frowned at her suspiciously. "Like this." He pressed two buttons on the remote control.

Sonny and Cher began to sing "Baby Don't Go."

Caddie put out her hand.

Magill grinned, looking tickled but not *astounded*—and it struck her that Thea had reacted just that way the night Caddie had whipped off her T-shirt and they'd gotten soaked together on the roof: glad but not *incredulous*. So. Her friends had more confidence in her derring-do than she had.

Magill handed her the second microphone. "Baby, don't gooooo," they crooned in nasal, effortless harmony, mimicking the originals as if they'd been practicing all day. They held hands and stared into each other's eyes, Magill arching his black eyebrows soulfully,

Caddie trying to resemble Cher by keeping her face a perfect blank. It wasn't easy, because what she was dying to do was burst out laughing.

They were a huge hit. "More!" people called out. "Encore!" Tune number eight from *Pop Duets by Your Favorites* came on: "Don't Go Breakin' My Heart."

"Wait, it's too high," Caddie said, breaking off before the chorus. "This one's no good for me."

"That's okay. Switch."

"Switch?"

"You be Elton John." Magill began to sing the Kiki Dee part in a wonderful, ridiculous falsetto. They brought down the house, but Caddie ruined the end by getting the giggles. She laughed so hard her stomach hurt. She flung her arms around Magill's thin waist and swayed with him for a long, sweet, satisfying hug while their good-natured audience clapped and cheered. *Oh, maybe we should just get married*, she thought, drunk on success. *He'd make us laugh all the time. The baby and me.*

He was raking through the karaoke CDs, searching for something. There were so many; he must've paid a fortune for them, and she couldn't imagine him taking up a Wake House collection. No, he'd bought them himself. For her.

She recognized the song he put on after the first bar: "I'll Be Seeing You," very close to the old Jo Stafford recording. She had it; she liked to sing along with it at home.

Magill handed her Doré's scarf. "You know this one, Caddie, I saw it. Sing," he commanded.

"By myself? I didn't promise that!" Butterflies she hoped had flown away for good fluttered in her diaphragm.

Magill sat down in a chair next to Mr. Lorton and folded his arms, smiling up at her sweetly, expectantly. Everybody was smiling. Ready to like the music, ready to like her. Mr. Lorton thunked his cane on the floor in sudden recognition. "This was our song," he said wonderingly, "Sarah and me. She dearly loved this song. Oh, my goodness."

Caddie began to sing.

She and Jo Stafford didn't sing in the same key, but Magill had done something to the machine, turned the whole thing down so it played lower and slower. But still such a beautiful song, full of loss and longing and fine romantic yearning. She did her best by it. Halfway through, it came to her that she wasn't nervous. That was such a shock, it almost made her nervous. But the deliberate, melancholy phrasing carried her through, and in the end she wasn't thinking about anything except the music.

After that it was the Caddie Winger show. She sang "What'll I Do?" like Rosemary Clooney, "Night and Day" like Keely Smith. She sang "Ain't Misbehavin'" and "I'll Get By," and she sang "You've Got to See Mamma Ev'ry Night (Or You Can't See Mamma at All)." She stuck with the standards until Magill put on "Any Old Time," and she sang that one like Maria Muldaur. Mrs. Brill couldn't contain herself; she got up and danced a dreamy jitterbug, bad hip and all, by herself until Bernie trotted over and joined her.

"No more," Caddie told Magill after "Georgia on My Mind," Anita O'Day–style, and everybody said "*Awwww.*" But it was time to quit. She was exhausted, for one thing, still high on the thrill of success but emotionally wrung out, and for another, a smart performer always left her audience wanting a little more. She told her students that before recitals, so it must be true.

Nana brought her a blown pink rose from the dining room table centerpiece. "Caddie, honey," she said, putting it in her hand, squeezing her fingers around the thornless stem. "Caddie, honey, I don't even know what to say." Her faded eyes were wet. "I'm sorry about that crack. 'Scaredy-cat' crack. You know what, I think there's a little bit of me in you after all. Not that that's the world's biggest compliment."

"Yes, it is," Caddie said, and kissed her on both cheeks.

Across the room, Magill caught Caddie's eye. He looked worn out, too, sagging in the doorway, waiting for her to see him. When she did, he straightened up and waved, and she blew him a goodbye kiss with both hands. She'd thank him later, try to explain what this day had meant to her. He probably knew, though. Maybe she'd call him tonight. Maybe she'd propose to him.

"Where's Thea?" Cornel asked her. He was looking very spiffy these days, no more ancient golf shirts with saggy seersucker trousers. He'd put on a bow tie for the party, and new khaki pants, and slicked his shock of platinum hair back with oil. He took a lot of ribbing for these improvements, especially from Bernie, but it didn't bother him. "Some people take pride in their appearance," he'd say, "and some people let themselves go. To the dogs."

"She was listening through the window, I think," Caddie told him. "She went outside to watch the sun go down. I'll go with you," she decided when he turned around and shuffled toward the door. In spite of the new attention to his dress, he still wore running shoes for every occasion. Bunions.

A breeze had come up among the tired trees, making a dry, scratchy background for the drone of cicadas. Thea might've missed Caddie's concert, but she had the right idea; it was much cooler out here than in the house, and now that the sun was down, layers of scarlet and pink flamed in the sky through the tree leaves. Lightning bugs winked and swooped; crickets chirped.

Thea had stretched out on the glider and fallen asleep, one arm across her waist, the other flung out. "Oh," Caddie said, indecisive, softening her footsteps. "Should we wake her—" She collided with Cornel's back, stepped on the heel of his shoe when he stopped short. "Oops. Sorry—"

He put his arms out. He made a sound, indescribable.

Caddie gasped. She looked over his shoulder. Thea was fine!

325

She'd expected to see something hurting her, a snake, an animal—but she was fine! She'd pulled a cushion from the back of the glider and tilted it up against the metal arm to pillow her head. She'd taken her shoes off; they peeked out from the bottom of the glider, neat, the toes together. She . . . she looked girlish in her white blouse, her hip a soft curve under her skirt. "What is it?" Caddie whispered, fearful.

"Get Brenda."

"Thea?"

"Tell her to call the ambulance."

"Why?"

Cornel grabbed her arm and shook it. "Go."

She ran in the house. Brenda wasn't in either parlor. People took one look at Caddie and alarm replaced whatever had been in their faces. She raced down the hall to the back of the house, burst into Brenda's office.

She was on the phone, smiling, saying, "I *know*," but when she saw Caddie, she took the receiver from her ear and stood up.

"Something's wrong with Thea. She won't wake up. Cornel says call an ambulance."

"Oh, God." She threw the phone down and bolted around the desk, around Caddie. She ran out the door.

"Wait!" Caddie picked up the receiver on the desk. Somebody said "Hello?" "Hang up," Caddie said, but the person on the other end of the line, a man, was confused; he kept saying, "Brenda? Hello?" She punched the button for the second line, and when a dial tone came on she pressed 911.

A lady wouldn't wake up, she told the dispatcher. She was out on the porch, she was at Wake House on Calvert Street—"I can't remember the number! It's on the corner of Calvert and Ross, and it's got a sign in front, Wake House." That's fine, an ambulance would be on its way very shortly. Was the lady conscious? Was she breathing? Caddie didn't know, she didn't know anything. "That's okay, ma'am, you just stay calm, we have a team out that way right now."

"I'm hanging up," she warned, "I can't do anything in here!" and the dispatcher said all right, okay, just try to stay—

She hung up.

People had gathered around the divan in a tight half circle, but at a distance, and the women had their heads turned away. Doré Harris was crying into her hands. Caddie pushed between the lumpen bodies of Mr. Lorton and Mrs. Brill. "I called the ambulance, it's on the way. What are you doing? What are you doing?" Brenda—she was putting Doré's scarf over Thea's face. "Don't!" Caddie went down on her knees and snatched the scarf away.

"Honey," Brenda said, "she's gone."

"*No*. We have to do CPR till they come. Who can do it?" She looked around, frantic. "Who knows it? Brenda, *help*. Is it a heart attack?" Thea's face was slack but warm, not cold—whatever had happened to her had *just happened*. "You have one of those machines, those defibrillators, I've seen it—"

"She signed a DNR."

"DNR—"

"Do not resuscitate."

"No. *Why?*"

"Because she had a bad heart."

"No, she doesn't, she has a bad *toe*."

Brenda just shook her head.

"She'd have *told* me."

"She didn't tell anyone. But she knew it wouldn't be long."

"No." Thea gone? Nobody looked surprised. Except for Cornel, hunched in the porch swing with his head in his hands, they looked resigned but not shocked. Nobody argued or tried to stay when Brenda asked if they would please go inside. How could

327

they *go* like that, like sheep, how could they give up without even trying?

Thea lay on her side as if she were about to get up, her face turned toward the floor; she was looking down through half-closed eyelids at her shoes. It was too soon, she was still recoverable, she couldn't be lost. "Thea," Caddie murmured, bending low to see into her blind eyes. She could wake her up—that wouldn't be artificial means or heroic measures, just Caddie's voice calling to her, calling her back. "Thea?" She touched her cheek with light, respectful fingers. "Thea?"

A hand touched her on the shoulder. She reached for it automatically. Tough, gnarled, knuckly old hand—not Brenda's. Nana's.

"I'm so sorry, honey. At least you can see she didn't suffer one bit."

Caddie nodded. A siren wailed. An ambulance stopped in front of the house. Lights kept flashing, but the siren went off in a dramatic last whoop. Brenda walked down the steps to meet the hurrying paramedics.

Caddie took hold of Thea's outflung hand. Time was running out, they'd be here in a second. But she couldn't form "goodbye" in her mind, and Nana was saying something to her. "What?"

"I'll try to do better. I can't be her, I know."

Caddie looked up, her grandmother a blur through her tears. Nana put out her hand, and Caddie took it in her other one. Now she was in the middle, the child between her two mothers, but neither of them could comfort her.

Footsteps on the porch stairs. She pressed Thea's fingers to her cheek. They felt cool and light, already disembodied. *Did you finish everything on your list? I love you.*

She rose and drew Nana over to the porch swing. "Cornel? Do you want to see her or—"

"No."

"Let's go over here, then. Let's sit on the side porch, Cornel. Come on." She had to help him straighten up when he got to his feet. She led him around the corner, Nana in their wake. No one ever sat here, it was airless and there was no view, only dusty, gangly hydrangea bushes and rhododendrons hanging over the porch rail, staining the floor with their rotting leaves. Cornel sat down in a wooden rocker, Nana in one next to it.

Caddie tried to close her ears to the sounds and low voices coming from around the corner. This is what happens, she thought. She'd mistaken Wake House for a glad place, a pleasant substitute for home, a funky old boarding-house for interesting old people. How naive. Look at Nana and Cornel, she thought. Look at their frail, blue-veined, hollowed-out hands, that useless dent between the thumb and index finger, like a purple pit. Their croaky voices. Why did old people lose their *voices*? They lost everything, one ability after another, and then the muscle and flesh melted off their bones. Look at Cornel's thighs, just horizontal sticks holding up his pants, look at the heavy, indistinct bag between his legs that used to be his testicles. His life force. *I don't love these people*, Caddie thought. *I hate them*.

That passed, the passionate revulsion passed, dissolved as fast as it had formed. Cornel's and her grandmother's bodies became themselves again. She loved them again. Her old world righted itself, and all she had to do was learn to live in it without her friend.

22

Dearest Caddie,

If you're reading this now, it must mean events have overtaken me. Oh, my, what a euphemism! It means things have happened a bit faster than the doctor suggested they would. Doctors never *say* this sort of thing directly, you know, they only *suggest*. Mine *suggests* I can "go at any time," but it's most likely in nine to twelve months from now.

(Should I have told you this before? I ponder that question from time to time, and the answer is always no, absolutely not. It would only churn up a great deal of mud and smoke and clouds, and I prefer things clean and clear. Anyway, what difference does it make? We're all suffering from a terminal disease—I said that to you tonight during that flurry of unsolicited advice on the roof—so what does it matter that mine is a little more advanced than most people's?)

It does seem as if I've done an inordinate amount of lecturing and advice-giving to poor you. You say no, but I think it's true. I'm not sure why I love you so dearly, Caddie, I mean beyond the obvious fact that you're lovable. You don't remind me of myself when I was your age or anything of that sort. That first day when your moronic dog bit me, I liked you so much. You were so very sweet, so appalled and solicitous. Here is a gentle spirit, I thought, here is a very good person I would love to know.

330

Luckily for me—not you—you were lonely and felt the same. I didn't know what to expect when I came to Wake House. I'll just go home, I thought—not much beyond that. I can truly say I never expected to make a friend of a woman a good deal less than half my age. We aren't quite mother and daughter, are we? But not just friends, either. Something in between, I think. Whatever we are, you've made this twilight time of mine much brighter than I ever imagined it could be. You'll be sad that I've gone, but cheer yourself up knowing how much unexpected joy and pleasure you've brought me. You pluck on every maternal heartstring I've ever had. And I can play "Maple Leaf Rag"! If you'd given me nothing else, I'd be grateful, but of course you have. You've made this childless old lady content. I thank you.

I'm moved to write this letter now because tonight you asked me to be your baby's godmother. I tried to hide what that meant, but I don't think I did a very good job. Everything, Caddie. It meant the world. If only I could've said yes! But under the circumstances . . . well, you know. I'm not allowed to make promises anymore. But I want you to know I would be the *best* godmother, I would love that little girl to distraction, and she would love me back, she wouldn't be able to resist. I still have the little tea service my grandmother gave to me when I was five—I'll give that to you anyway, one way or the other, but how I wish I could give it to her myself. Well, who knows, maybe a miracle will happen. You know me, I never rule miracles out.

Now it's time to reveal my other secret. This one's not important at all. Ancient history. Why do I keep it a secret, then? Oh, I guess I'm afraid the truth will muddy those waters again, and you know I'm all for clarity. And this secret is *truly* irrelevant, a mere detail, an accident of birth—but I'm afraid people will make something of it, and in this case, this *one* case, I'm in agreement with you on the advantages of invisibility.

I know—I'll write down my life story (briefly! don't worry), and you'll be kind enough to adapt it for me for the memory book. You're so good at it, Caddie, truly, you have a real knack, and it's part of what makes you you. I'll trust you to take out the personal stuff, make it suitable for public viewing. But now don't get your hopes up, my life story is not all that interesting, I don't mean to build it up, it's not as if I've accomplished a great deal or changed the world or anything. I've loved and been loved, which seems to be what it all comes down to. If I have regrets, they're of the "Why didn't I do that sooner?" variety. That's why I have so much tiresome advice for you—I don't want you to make the same old mistakes I did.

I was born Dorothea Elizabeth Alexandra Wake, in this house on November 2, 1934. Not this room—this was my grandparents' tower suite—but in the large corner bedroom on the second floor, the one currently occupied by Maxine Harris. My father was Alexander Pankhurst Wake Jr.; he worked for his father, my grandfather, in the Bank of Michaelstown, and he was a tall, dramatically handsome man who used to put me on his shoulders and run along Calvert Street while I pretended he was my horse. My mother, the former Julia Grace McGregor of Philadelphia, loved parties and dancing and flirting and playing tennis before I was born, and after I was born she loved me. She was beautiful and gay, with white-gold hair and a laugh like music, and I adored her. I had a childhood I can only call *blissful*, filled with loving parents, aunts and uncles, cousins, grandparents, dozens of friends, and it often seemed they were all in this house at the same time. I was an only child, but never lonely, never. I was spoiled rotten, I'm sure, but it didn't feel that way to me. It felt like love.

And then in 1943, after a numberless succession of miscarriages, my mother died in childbirth. She was thirty years old. A light went out of my life, and out of my father's, too, who left me with his sister's family and went away. One year later, my grandfather lost everything from bad investments. To cover some of his debts he sold the bank and this house, and he and my grandmother spent the rest of their years (only two more for him, four for her) in a small house on what's now called Clarendon Street on the west side.

Over the years the Wakes scattered, and since the early fifties (as far as I know) none of them have lived in Michaelstown. Until now. I've come home, so there's one.

When I was twelve, I moved to Washington, D.C., with my aunt and uncle, Sarah and Geoffrey Townsend, and their three sons, my cousins Geoff, Teddy, and Blake. We started over, living more modestly than we had in Michaelstown, but still quite comfortably and happily. My uncle, who was an attorney, eventually started the firm Townsend and Magaffin, and it still has offices on K Street. I graduated from high school in 1951— and am ashamed to say that was the last of my schooling. No college, and to this day I regret it. My passion was ballet, I was *wild* for it, I wanted desperately to go to New York and study to be a ballerina.

But my cousin Teddy brought his roommate home from Princeton for spring break, and that was the end of that dream. Carlton Spencer and I married eleven months later, and instead of a ballerina I became the wife of a junior investment banker.

We were together for seventeen years, separated for two, reunited briefly, and divorced once and for all in 1976. If we could have had children, if we'd had anything meaningful in common, if I'd had the courage to take my life into my own hands and make something of it, maybe we'd have worked it out. I blame Carl for nothing; we simply didn't suit. He married again and lives today in splendid retirement in Taos, New Mexico. Good for him.

So there I was, forty-two years old, and not exactly a gay divorcée. I thought I was over the hill, I thought my life was over! Oh, if we could come back again, knowing what we know in our old age. I spent the rest of the seventies doing good deeds, Caddie, volunteering for causes and charities, committees and foundations, maintaining the social style of life to which my husband's money and my grandfather's name had accustomed me.

The only thing I did for myself was start dancing again—it was as if I'd started living again! Why, why did I abandon the thing that had always given me the most pleasure? For security, I'm afraid. I saw Carl as a chance to regain something I'd lost, and I was too besotted with that prospect to notice what I'd have to give up in exchange. But when I began to dance again, I felt true to myself for the first time in years and years.

Eventually I left Washington and moved to the house on Heron Creek Carl had kindly left me in the settlement. It had always been a summer place, it wasn't even insulated, so I had my hands full making it habitable year-round. As soon as I did, I started my little dance school for children, a very modest enterprise from which I derived an enormous and wholly disproportionate amount of satisfaction. I suppose that's when I found myself—*before* I met Will, I'm glad to say, which means I didn't need a man to make me whole or happy. I just needed to find my work.

The rest is happily ever after, and that's never the interesting part of the story. I met Will, and all the places left in me that were still sleeping finally woke up. I think that's what love does, nudges us out of the light doze we go through our lives in. Will and I were sorry we hadn't met sooner, that we'd spent so long looking for each other, but other than that we made it a rule to keep regrets out of the house. He truly lived in the moment, and I did the best I could to copy him. I must've succeeded a little, because even though we only had nine years together, it feels much longer to me. It feels like a life.

I love what Charlie Lorton wrote (or *you* wrote, rather) at the end of his life story—"Here's the part where I'm supposed to say something wise." I'm sorry to say I'm as wisdom-challenged as Charlie. Wrap this up in some elegant, dignified way for me, Caddie. I've had the *nicest* life. I wish it could've lasted longer, that's all. And everybody else's, too. Do you believe in God? If he exists, I've got to say he's arranged things very peculiarly. Why did he make it so hard at the end? I can't even bear to say goodbye at the end of an evening! So I won't say it now. I don't want to. I'll go back to *thank you*.

Thank you, and please, please be happy. It's the least you can do for an infirm old lady. Who loves you very much. My last request: for the love of God, don't name that poor, innocent child Dorothea.

I love you,
Thea

23

Some early start. Parked in front of Wake House, Caddie drummed her nails on the steering wheel, taking note that her watch and the Pontiac's broken clock happened to say the same thing: twenty after ten. Finney stopped crossing from one window to the other in the backseat and jumped into the front. Her window was open; he climbed into her lap and stuck his head out to sniff the air.

The angle of the sun picked out every white or shiny black or doe-brown hair on his lithe body. She watched idly as his face changed with each sensation he took in. His nostrils flared, his almond eyes blinked and stared, his whiskers twitched. A car honked, and he twisted his head, cocking one brown ear. She loved to pet him, stroke his rough fur, scratch under his collar until he fell over on his side in ecstasy. She even liked his smell, a sort of doggy-manly, devil-may-care musk.

Finney could take her out of herself for a few minutes, the perfection of his body, his thoughtless affection. So could a certain piece of music or the wild sound of wind at night, somebody's unexpected smile. This is what we get, she would think, these hedges against the knowledge of our fast-approaching ends. With nothing else to occupy them, her thoughts started down a familiar track. What was the best way to get through this? She needed a philosophy, a better religion. How should we live? Aging and dying: what a strange combination of commonplace and extraordinary. Everybody got old and died, it was as simple as—peeing, and yet still the biggest mystery, top secret, dreadful and alien, more wrenching than birth. And so sad, so sad, it broke your heart. *Goodbye.* Never again. The stinging pain of *you are gone and I am left.* How could you reconcile with that and still find peace?

She was glad when she saw Cornel, finally, lugging an old Samsonite suitcase, scuffed white and hard as a coffin, down the porch steps. She got out to open the trunk and move her small bag and Finney's fleece bed and his cardboard box of supplies out of the way, but she knew better than to ask Cornel if he needed any help. "I thought this was a two-day trip," she had to say, though, as he flung his giant suitcase into the trunk with a grunt.

"It's not full," he said, which she thought missed the point. "You're not bringing that dog, are you?"

"I have to. Nana won't let me leave him in a kennel. He'll be all right, he loves to ride in the car. He'll probably just sleep. You look very nice, Cornel."

He had on the same dark brown suit he'd worn to Thea's funeral, but with an old green army sweater instead of a shirt and tie. "It's going to get windy on that ferry," he warned, "you better have a coat. I got this *plus* a coat."

"So are we about ready?"

"*I'm* ready. Except I can't find my damn glasses, I gotta go back in."

"They're on your head."

He looked startled, then disgusted. "These are my reading glasses, I need my long-distance glasses. What do you think, I'm crazy?"

Watching him trudge back up the steps, she started to get back in the car, then changed her mind. "I'll be right back," she said to Finney through the window. "Stay put and *no barking.*" She'd already told everybody goodbye, including Nana, but she was restless out here with nothing to do but contemplate the meaning of life.

"Back already?" Bea joked from her blue rocker on the porch. She had her fringed plaid shawl tucked to the chin against the morning chill, and Edgie, in the green rocker, was wrapped in a trench coat and a pink scarf. Caddie had fussed at them half an hour ago for coming out too early, they could take cold in this wind, but Edgie said she was so sick of being cooped up she'd risk it.

"You two sure are a sight for sore eyes," Caddie said impulsively. "I'm so happy you're back." She meant Edgie, who'd moved out of rehab and back to Wake House a week ago, but in a way she meant Bea, too. "This porch was lopsided without you."

"Isn't that the truth?" said Bea. She reached over to adjust the pillow on the arm of Edgie's chair; Edgie had to keep her elbow on it or she had a hard time staying upright, not slumping over sideways. "We're like two old bookends, take one away and the whole shelf collapses."

"How come you're still here?" Edgie's speech was much clearer than before, but for some reason she'd lost an octave; she spoke in a breathy, gravelly rasp everybody told her was sexy. She loved that.

"Oh, you know. Men. And Cornel forgot his glasses."

Bea said, "Well, I think it's mighty nice of you to drop everything you've got to do and drive all the way out to Cape May for that man."

"I'm not really dropping that much." Tomorrow was Sunday, no lessons; she'd only had to cancel today's. "And it's not just for Cornel, it's for me, too."

Cornel wanted to go to Cape May in October, bird migration time, because of Thea. It had been the last thing on her life's to-do list, he said, and since she couldn't go, he was doing it for her. Going in her place. "Really, it's no sacrifice," Caddie told the sisters. "If it doesn't rain it'll be beautiful, and it's only for one night."

"Don't forget what I said," Edgie grated.

"I won't."

She wanted Caddie to say a prayer for Thea when they got to Cape May. "I mean it. I don't expect I'd be here right now if it wasn't for her."

That was the rumor. Caddie didn't know if it was true, but people were saying Thea had left money in her will to Wake House. How much, nobody knew, but Edgie wasn't the only one who thought Brenda's turnaround about taking her back had something to do with a sudden windfall.

"You all be careful driving," Bea told Caddie again. "And make sure to rest whenever you feel like it." A delicate reference to her condition. "Too bad neither one of those men can help you with the driving if you get tired."

"Oh, I'll be fine." Her back hurt, though. Just enough to be annoying.

Inside, she cruised the two parlors and the dining room, even asked in the kitchen, but nobody had seen Cornel's glasses. She said hi to Bernie and Mr. Lorton, who were reading the papers in the Red Room. Susan Cohen had moved out, gone to live with her boyfriend. Nobody had taken Thea's tower suite yet, but last week a woman called Mrs. Shallcroft had moved into Susan's old room. She seemed nice enough.

Caddie stopped in the foyer, drawn to the framed photographs on the wall. She'd always liked looking at them, but now that Thea's secret was out, they had a stronger fascination; she couldn't walk through the hall anymore without stopping to look. The grand old man, the white-haired, potbellied paterfamilias standing on the front steps or under a thick-trunked, long-gone oak tree in the front yard, surrounded by wife, siblings, sons and daughters, grandsons and granddaughters—old man Wake, town father and founder of the venerable Bank of Michaelstown, amasser and loser of the vast Wake fortune, was Thea's grandfather.

And she was the little girl in the white dress at the family lawn party. The date at the bottom said July 15, 1939. The picture was crowded with Wakes of all ages, but that was Thea, could only be Thea, not just because she'd have been five in 1939, but because that lovely, pale-gowned, pregnant lady holding her hand couldn't be anyone but her mother. And the man sitting on his heels beside her, dark-haired, roguishly handsome in striped shirtsleeves and suspenders, must be her father.

Little Thea had ringlets, shiny as gold—maybe they were the same reddish-blonde she'd dyed her hair last summer—and a pixie face with a shy smile. She looked well loved and contented; she looked as if she knew she was lucky. "Blissful," she'd called her childhood. It wouldn't last long enough—a few years after this picture was taken her mother would die and her father would "move west"—but she'd had a fine start. Nine years to learn lessons for life about trust and optimism, and faith that the world was a safe place. In the end, they'd make her who she'd turned out to be.

When she'd read Thea's letter, Caddie hadn't known at first what to think or feel. *Why didn't you tell me?* her first reaction, had given way very quickly to acceptance, even an intimation that in some oblique corner of her mind she'd already known. Thea had never lied to her, only sidestepped. "So this isn't really where you grew up?" Caddie had asked, that day in front of the aunt and uncle's house. "It's where I moved after my mother died," she'd answered. Eager to hear that story, Caddie hadn't noticed the blurring of details. Eventually she'd come to see that Thea's reasons for not telling who she was were so inseparable from her reason for coming home—which was, simply, to die (although she'd have put that another way; *to live to the end*, or something else positive)—that she couldn't have revealed one without the other. Not even to Caddie.

"Are you still here?" Brenda bustled down the corridor from her office. "I thought you'd be gone by now."

"I did, *too*," Caddie said, wide-eyed with surprise. Half an hour ago she'd told Brenda she couldn't stop in her office and talk about Nana because she didn't have time, oh no, she was on her way out the door. An exaggeration, obviously, and now Brenda had caught her. "And they say *women* are always late," Caddie joked for a diversion. She wasn't ready for a showdown over Nana this morning.

"Well, we'll talk when you get back, because it's definitely—oh, here's Cornel."

"I can't find 'em," he grumped before the elevator doors were all the way open. "Somebody took 'em, and it wouldn't be the first time."

"What?"

"My goddamn glasses." He stalked over to Brenda like an irritable goose. "What we need is a lost and found, I keep telling you."

"We have a lost and found."

"Yeah, but nothing of mine's ever in it."

Watching them bicker reminded Caddie of Nana's first day at Wake House. They'd argued about the hot-water supply right here, under this chandelier. And then a barefooted Magill had come around the corner, bumped into the wall, and broken the glass in one of the picture frames.

Here he came—around the corner.

Not barefooted. He had on hiking boots and corduroy trousers, a denim jacket over a T-shirt, and a bulging backpack on his shoulder.

"Is that it?" Cornel demanded. "That's all you're taking?"

"Sure. It's just for one night, isn't it? Hi," he said, smiling at Caddie. "Sorry I'm late, I got a phone call at the last second. Hey, look at your hair. What did you do?"

Thank goodness *somebody* noticed. "Highlights," she said, patting her head, shy. "Subtle, right? Supposed to look like the sun did it."

"It's *great*."

"Thanks." She was so glad to see him. Among other things, the thought of two days on the road with nobody but Cornel and Finney had started to take time off her life. "I was afraid you were sick, or you'd changed your mind or something."

"No way, I'm feeling terrific. Will you miss me?" he asked Brenda, surprising her with a smacking kiss on her cheek.

She laughed; she might've blushed. "Somebody's feeling his oats. Watch yourself with this one, Caddie. Where's your cane?" she asked him.

"Don't need it."

"Sure?"

"Abso—" He lurched forward, stopping just short of head-butting her.

"Funny," Brenda said. "Cornel, have you got your blood pressure pills?"

At eleven o'clock, they finally got on the road.

Magill had to sit in front by the open window or he might get carsick. In the back, Cornel commandeered the map and announced he was the navigator. He took the job seriously, so Caddie kept it to herself that she already knew the way. Finney couldn't decide which man's lap he wanted to sit in, so he jumped back and forth, annoying both of them, front seat, backseat, front seat, backseat. Caddie explained all the things on her car that didn't work. "Isn't it a beautiful day?" In spite of the somber purpose of their trip, she was in almost as good a mood as Magill. It felt fine to be flying down the interstate at seventy miles an hour with her two good friends and her dog. They had no particular schedule, just an easy half-day's drive to Delaware, where they'd catch the ferry in Lewes to Cape May. They didn't even know where they'd stay when they got there. She caught Magill's eye; the wind mussed his hair and put pink color in his cheeks. They grinned at each other. This was going to be fun.

They talked about inconsequential things, not the reason for the trip, until the Baltimore beltway, when Cornel mumbled something from the backseat.

"What?"

"Said, I wrote something down. It's a poem."

"A poem?"

"For Thea."

"Oh, Cornel." Caddie looked at him in the rearview mirror. "That's wonderful. She'd've loved that."

"It's not finished." He fished a piece of notebook paper out of his jacket pocket.

"Can we hear it?"

"Heck, no, it's personal."

"Oh, come on."

"Read it," said Magill.

"Out loud? Naw."

"Let's hear it. I bet it's good."

"Nah, I don't wanna read it."

"Let me, then."

"Huh?"

"I'll read it." Magill held out his hand.

"You can't read."

"Come on, Cornel." Like Magill, Caddie could tell he wanted them to hear his poem, he just didn't want to admit it.

More coaxing and cajoling. Finally, "Oh, all right, read it if it means that much to you," and he handed the paper up to Magill. "But it's not finished, I'm telling you. It's a rough draft."

Crabbed handwriting covered both sides of the paper, Caddie saw from the corner of her eye. A long poem. She hoped reading it in the moving car wouldn't make Magill sick.

He squinted his eyes, holding the paper close.

There once was a hard and a crooked old man,
With stones in his pockets and sticks in his hand.
He didn't like folks and they didn't like him.
His heart was like flint, that crooked old man.

He lived in a house full of good folks and cheer,
But he had on a blindfold, just saw darkness and drear.
He cursed his long life, wished it'd be over soon,
Couldn't see any purpose, just boredom and gloom.

Then one day a lady, like a rare beam of light,
Shone a lamp in the dark and he recovered his sight.
She came unexpected, for the old man had thought
All his races were run and all his battles were fought.

It's a pretty rare thing that a man like that fellow,
All ready to end it, gets a glimpse of tomorrow.
"Gift of the goddess," that's what her name meant.
Dorothea, Dorothea, to him heaven-sent.

Well, it's hard now and dark, life's gone back to before.
It'd be easy to quit, say goodbye and close the door.
But she wouldn't approve, that wasn't her style,
So he'll try to be patient and he'll bide here a while.

And meanwhile there's memories to warm him at night
When loneliness pains him and no friend's in sight.
He'll never forget her, never could, never can.
Without her he'd still be that crooked old man.

Caddie couldn't think of anything to say. Magill either; he kept his head down, as if re-reading parts of the poem to himself. She didn't want to gush, it would embarrass Cornel to death, but she was moved. He'd sat stony and silent through the funeral and Thea's interment in the Wake family plot in Michaelstown, not shedding a tear. Caddie had thought this trip to Cape May was as far as he could go, that he was capable of honoring Thea with *action* but nothing else.

And it turned out she was completely wrong.

"Well, I *told* you it was just a draft," he said in a shaky, defiant voice, and somehow that freed her to tell him what she thought: that she loved his poem, Thea would've been so touched and so glad, it was a lovely poem—how did he know how to write poetry?

Magill said the best thing, though. "I never thought you were all that crooked, myself. I know it's not the same, but any time you feel like you need straightening out, you can come to me. You know that, right?"

"Why," said Cornel, taking his poem back, "because it takes one to know one?" He said it with a smirk, trying to be cool now, probably half sorry he'd revealed so much of himself.

"Yes," Magill answered, looking into his eyes.

Cornel's turtle lips curved into a genuine smile before he ducked his head and mumbled, "Okay, deal. Likewise."

A pleasantly self-conscious silence settled over them.

"She used to say I oughta write my own biography," Cornel broke it to say. "Make it turn out any way I wanted."

"She told me that, too," Magill said.

"Me, too," Caddie said.

They looked at one another, then away, smiling. They crested a hill, and all the colors of autumn unfolded like a carpet rolling away to the horizon. Red horses grazed by a stream in a leafy, faraway meadow, and the clouds rolled high in the sky, casting shadows like moving mountains on the highway.

"But," Cornel said, "I get mad at her sometimes. I feel like telling her off."

"What for?"

"Lying."

Caddie didn't like that word applied to Thea. "Don't say that."

"What else do you call it? Why couldn't she at least tell us who she was? Why keep it a secret?"

"Why not keep it a secret?" Magill said. "What good would telling it have done?"

"At least she coulda told *me* she was sick. We talked about things like that. I told *her* things." He sounded cheated.

"What would you have done if she had told you?" Magill asked.

"I would've . . ."

"Not loved her?"

"Maybe I would've held back some. If you go to the pet store and they sell you a sick dog, you . . ."

Magill turned around in his seat.

"You feel like suing 'em," Cornel finished weakly. "You got cheated. Hip dysplasia. Don't look at me like that."

"I know how you feel," Caddie admitted. "I've felt the same way, angry with her for not telling, not trusting. But Cornel, we can't hold back. We don't want to get our hearts broken, but we can't just—love the healthy dogs."

"Hell, I know that."

"I know you do."

Magill looked like he wasn't so sure.

What a relief to be able to talk about Thea this way. At Wake House some kind of niceness or reticence had come over people, they could only say the most conventional things about her and about their sorrow over losing her. Maybe that's how it always was when they lost one of their own—maybe it came too close, they could say only the kinds of things they'd want said, when the time came, about themselves. But today, the three of them in this car, the ones who had loved Thea the best, could tell one another the truth, and it didn't have to sound pretty or dignified, it could be as confused as they felt. They could admit what they didn't understand

346

about her and not worry about anybody mistaking it for disloyalty or bad faith.

"Hey, guys?" Caddie said. "I've made up my mind about something." Was this the right time to tell them? It felt right. "Thea helped me decide. Not directly, because we didn't talk about it all that much, not really, and she was pretty careful not to give me advice, as in do this, don't do that." She glanced around. She had their attention, although Cornel was starting to look impatient.

"I've decided to keep the baby."

She knew they'd be glad. Cornel leaned over and smacked her hard on both shoulders, crying, "Good! Good!" Magill laughed out loud. "That's . . ." He shook his head. "Great. It's great, Caddie. Finally, some good news."

"I know—that's what I thought, too, finally some good news. And I know it's a selfish decision—"

"No, it's not," they said in unison.

"No, but you should see these people who register at the agency, they're *perfect*. They'd be much better parents than me, they have money, they have each other—they have everything."

"*Eh*," said Magill. "Who wants perfect parents."

"Anyway," said Cornel, "there's no such thing."

"Well, that's kind of what I thought." She laughed and let it go. The biggest decision of her life had been a little more complicated than that, but it wasn't the right time to explain.

"What are you now, four months? When is it due?" Magill asked.

"Three and a half. She's due in late March, which is perfect. Because then it's spring, and then summer. So she can go outside."

"She?"

"No question. That's what we have."

"You Winger women."

She told them about her doctor, who looked like Patty Duke.

"She says I can gain thirty or forty *pounds* if I want to, because of my height. Can you *imagine?*"

Magill looked at her as if he were trying to imagine it.

"I'll have to get another car, something newer and safer. But I'll be able to keep working the whole time, and I can start back right away, too." She kept on, aware that she was babbling. Poor men, they were the first, after Nana, to hear about her decision, and she had a lot stored up. She wasn't nauseated anymore, she told them, but she couldn't even be in the same room with cooking meat. Being pregnant took a lot of mopey, empty-headed energy, so she was tired a lot. It made time slow down, too; she did a lot of staring into space and thinking about nothing, because nothing seemed to matter very much. Except gestating.

She didn't tell them how ashamed she felt for once thinking she could give her baby away. *I apologize*, she told it all the time. *I'll never tell you. I hope you don't know anyway, through blood or enzymes or something.* She didn't tell them how primitive her love was. She'd been like a kite with a snapped string, floating loose high in the air, and now there was somebody to keep the line taut, to pull back when she tugged. Now that she knew she could keep her, she was letting herself love this baby so *hard.*

"I'm hungry," Cornel said. "When do we eat?"

They hadn't even gotten to the Bay Bridge yet. Fast food wouldn't do; he had to have a sit-down restaurant with waiters and silverware and water glasses. "Okay, okay," Magill agreed, and Caddie joined in quickly, "Fine, no problem." They were in league, humoring Cornel so that he couldn't work up a head of steam. Fast-food restaurants would set him off, and from there it would be litter, concrete, cars, graffiti, moral decay—then immigrants and people on welfare, smog, lines, rap, and MTV. And then how comparatively wonderful everything had been in his day. It was easier to just find a sit-down restaurant.

He brought his map with him into a place on Route 50 called the Pig and Hen. "I got some scenic routes in mind." He spread the map on the table, covering up the menus, knocking over the salt shaker.

"Scenic routes?" Caddie looked at her watch.

"Look here." He put his horny forefinger on Talbot County. "Sure you can go 404 if all you want to do is get there. But why not take some of these byways, see the real country, your vanishing America."

"It's the Delmarva," Magill said. "It's flat farmland."

"I don't mind," Caddie said, "as long as we catch the ferry early so we can find a place to stay in Cape May while it's still light." They should've made reservations, she *knew* it.

"No problem," Cornel said breezily. "Look, we just go along here instead of here, and we see more. It's more civilized."

"You can't see anything without your glasses," Magill pointed out, "so what do you care?"

That set them off on one of their eternal, needling arguments. Caddie glanced idly at the map, and a name jumped out at her. *Clover.* It was on one of Cornel's byways.

She ordered a tuna fish sandwich and a vanilla milkshake and withdrew from the conversation. Let the men decide on the route. She agreed with everything. *It's out of my hands.* Then Cornel said this way it was more like a pilgrimage, seeing more of the countryside where Thea used to live (which wasn't even true; she and Will had lived in Maryland, down by Berlin, nowhere near Clover, Delaware), and after that Caddie had no grounds at all to protest the scenic route. Who could be against a pilgrimage?

So it was fate.

And anyway, all they were going to do was drive through.

24

Magill was right, Talbot County was mostly flat farmland. So was Caroline County. But it was ripe, golden autumn, and the wide fields of brown, foot-high cornstalks stretched far away to forests of changing oaks and sycamores and scruffy pine trees. Geese honked overhead in formation or strutted in gray-and-white hordes on the low-lying grasses. Pumpkins lolled for acres, and the air was dusty and mellow. The fields, the infrequent houses, even the changing trees had a drowsy, bedraggled look, as if they were pleasantly tired and passively waiting for winter.

"Turn here," Cornel said.

"Wait, now." Signs on the road they'd turned off of a while ago had designated it a "Scenic Byway"; this new detour would be a scenic byway times three.

"Turn."

She turned. "Why? What's up here?"

"Nothing that I know of."

Magill chuckled, but Caddie wasn't amused. What about fate? What about driving through Clover? If Cornel was going to alter the scenic route whenever the spirit moved him, they'd miss it. That wasn't fate, that was—childish. "This road doesn't even have a number," she complained. "Cornel, there's scenic and then there's just . . ."

"Nothing." Magill had Finney on his sharp thighs, holding him steady when the car shot around curves. The dog stared straight ahead with wide eyes and cocked ears, stiff as a hood ornament.

Farmer John's Market, white wooden benches under an open tent canopy, was closed for the season. A house on cinder blocks had a satellite dish on the roof and a lone black goat in the garden. Farmland, farmland. Plastic-covered greenhouses, chicken coops, a tiny graveyard in the middle of nowhere.

"You never know what you might find," Cornel explained. "That's the point. When I was a kid I used to take my bike and a penny or a nickel, and every corner I came to I'd flip the coin. Right, heads, left, tails. It's an adventure."

"So you could never go straight," Magill noticed.

"No, sometimes I'd say head, straight, tails—what have you. The point is—"

"But that would be cheating."

"The point— No, it wouldn't."

"How far ahead of time would you decide heads was straight?"

"How the hell do I know? A block."

"So you'd see what was coming and change the rules if you knew you wanted to go one way instead of the other."

"I did *not*. Anyway, I still only had a fifty-fifty chance, I wasn't changing any *rules*. Would you shut up? I was ten years old, for— Why are we stopping?"

Caddie wanted to know the same thing. The accelerator didn't work. One minute they were sailing along fine, and the next the car didn't have any power. "Look—nothing." She showed them by beating the pedal with her foot. "It won't go!"

"Turn the wheel, get off the road," Magill said. "Hurry."

Too late. With alarming speed the car rolled to a stop, leaving the back end stuck out four feet over the faded white side line.

"Put it in neutral and steer. Do the lights work? Put on the blinkers. Come on," he said to Cornel, opening the door, "let's push."

Luckily no cars were coming. Luckily they weren't on a hill. They pushed and she steered, over the verge onto the strip of grass between the road and a ditch. Beyond the ditch lay a broad, dusty cornfield and nothing else. Same thing on the other side.

"Stay," she told the excited dog, and got out of the car. "Well, this is great. Can you believe it?"

"I don't know why you're surprised," Cornel groused, "your car's a pile of junk."

"I just had it inspected. You know, if we'd stayed on 404 and then gotten on 18——"

"This wouldn't have happened?"

"There'd be cars going by to help us."

"Now, ladies." Magill fiddled with the latch and popped the hood, raised it over his head and stood staring into the black, hissing engine. "Yep," he said eventually, securing the hood with the rod. "It's your scraffinator."

"The——" Oh. Ha-ha.

"Did the generator light come on?"

"Um, I don't know," Caddie said, "I didn't have time to notice."

"Check and see."

She looked in the car window. "Yes! It's on!"

"Could be your generator," Cornel said, pursing his lips and rubbing his chin.

"No, it would run off the battery for a while. It wouldn't stop dead." Magill wriggled hoses and poked at fastenings as if he knew what he was doing. "Could be the fuel pump." He disconnected a hose going into the big round thing she thought was the carburetor. "Caddie, turn the key."

"In the car?"

He looked over and smiled at her.

"Right." She got in the car and turned the key.

"Okay."

"What happened?" She had to hold Finney by the collar to get out of the car without him.

"Fuel pump's okay." Magill was wiping gasoline off his hands with a red handkerchief.

"Something electrical?" Cornel guessed.

"Well, except it would still run off the battery for a while. Then again, if a coil broke . . . but that's not likely. My guess is it's the timing belt."

"Huh," Cornel said, nodding wisely. "Timing belt."

"What is it?" Caddie asked. "Can we fix it?"

"It's in here." He touched a metal cover behind the ticking radiator. "The belt runs off the crankshaft and operates the valves, see, two valves per piston. It connects to the camshaft and turns—"

"Can you fix it?"

"No. Well, if I had tools. But to get to it you have to take out the radiator and the fan belt, some of the electrical wiring, maybe some pumps. What we need is a mechanic."

They looked at each other. They looked around at the buff-colored, spreading expanse of nothing. In the field on the other side of the road, a flock of starlings suddenly shot up in the air like a raggedy black net.

"Do you have a cell phone?" Magill asked.

"No." She stuck her hand through the passenger-side door and petted Finney to calm him down. "Sorry. I don't. A car!"

A pickup truck, coming toward them in the far lane. It slowed as it approached—she could hear the engine change notes—but the occupants, a whiskery, red-faced man and a white-haired woman, craned their necks, bug-eyed, and never stopped.

"How could you not have a cell phone?" Cornel wanted to know. "Everybody in the world's got a cell phone."

"Except any of us," Magill said, sweeping them with a rueful glance. *Misfits*, he was thinking. Caddie knew, because she was thinking it, too.

"And I suppose nobody belongs to an auto club," Cornel guessed. "Christ almighty. What a bunch."

Another car passed by without stopping, even when all three of them waved at it.

"I don't get it. Do we look like the Barrow gang or something? If nobody's stopping, I might as well let the dog out. He hasn't been for a walk in a whole *hour*," Caddie added grumpily.

"Lift your skirt next time," Cornel suggested. "Ever see that movie? Claudette Colbert lifts her skirt—"

"I've seen it. I'm not lifting my skirt." Her back was killing her. This wasn't supposed to happen. They should've been in Lewes by now, waiting in line for the ferry. Not only that, the sky, which had been bright blue thirty minutes ago, was filling up with mean-looking gray clouds. Oh, terrific, a storm, that's just what they needed.

"I'll take him." Magill gently took Finney's leash from her hand.

Immediately the dog pulled him over the ditch and up the other side into the stubbly cornfield. "Don't fall—!" But she had to laugh, they looked so funny, long-legged man running after short-legged dog, the man's jacket flying out behind him and his pants flapping around his calves. Finney was on the scent of something, probably a field mouse, and when that happened nothing could stop him.

"He's getting better, isn't he?" Cornel said, resting his backside on the taillight.

"Finney? Not really, he's—"

"Magill."

"Oh." She squinted against the glare of sky at his dark silhouette, thin legs churning, one long arm stretched out toward the dog. He made her think of Ichabod Crane. "I hope so. Do you think he is?"

Cornel glared at her in a searching, peevish way. "Why don't you pay more attention to him?"

"What?"

"Don't you know how he feels?"

"Um, about . . ."

"*You.*"

She looked away sharply. She laughed. She sidled away, moved out into the empty lane. "No. Are you kidding? No. Don't be silly."

Cornel clucked his tongue and shook his head, but he didn't say anything else.

"Silly," she repeated, to encourage him. She had the queerest flush, she could feel the heat of it crawling up her neck. "You're crazy, we're not like that."

Cornel wasn't even looking at her, he was peering over her shoulder. "Car coming. Lift your skirt."

She wanted to muse on what Cornel had said, she wanted to ponder and ruminate and figure out what she thought about it. But an old station wagon, older than her car, and rustier, slowed and then stopped right beside her. A thick-shouldered man rolled down his window and put his elbow on the ledge. He had grizzled white hair and a lined, dignified face the color of muddy coffee, and he wore the strangest pair of round, cobalt-blue spectacles. As if he were blind.

"Hi," said Caddie, and "Howdy," said Cornel when the man didn't speak first. "We've had some trouble with our car."

He gave a slow nod of agreement. Just then Finney saw his car and began to bark madly and drag Magill across the field toward it.

"My dog," Caddie said quickly, "he's terrible, he barks at *everybody*." That was true; Finney was an equal-opportunity nuisance.

No reply; the old man sat resigned, stoic, as if some white people's yappy little dog was the least of his worries. He looked like a country preacher, Caddie thought, except that he didn't have much to say.

Magill snatched Finney up in his arms and somehow made it over to the car without falling. Muttering curses, he dumped him in the front seat, leash and all, and slammed the door. "Hi," he called cheerfully. He started to tilt over backward and grabbed for the side mirror. Using the car for handholds, he made it around to where Caddie and Cornel were standing. "How's it going? Thanks for stopping."

"Is there a gas station around here?" Caddie asked. "Or a garage? With a mechanic? Anybody with a tow truck?"

The old man pushed his lips out, thinking. When he stared straight ahead, she could see from the side of his blue glasses that he had bleary, light gray eyes. "There's Ernest Holly's," he finally answered in a smooth, surprisingly youthful voice.

"Is he a mechanic? Can he fix cars?"

He gave the long, thoughtful nod again.

Pause.

"Would you happen to have a cell phone?" Magill asked politely.

Finney was hurling himself from one side of the car to the other; the frantic, muffled bangs sounded like a mental patient trying to get out of his cell.

The old man shook his head.

Long pause.

"I guess I could carry you up to Ernest's."

"Oh, that would be great! How far is it?" Caddie asked.

"About half a mile."

They decided Magill should go with Mr. Clark, as he turned out to be, while Caddie and Cornel stayed with the car and the dog. Magill was back in practically no time, in a red-and-white pickup truck beside a skinny, hatchet-faced young man in denim coveralls and a leather cap. Ernest Holly.

Ernest diagnosed the problem quickly. "Gotta be your timing belt. Ever had a new one? What's this, an '83, '84? Belts can go twenty years, but then you're pushing it."

"Can you fix it?"

"Oh, yeah."

Ah. "Today?"

Ernest had a gold eyetooth. Caddie saw it when he grinned at her as if he appreciated her sense of humor. "Not today."

"Why not?"

"Gotta call over to Denton or Bridgeville for the part. It's Saturday, I'm backed up till late. But I can get to it first thing in the morning, you're on your way by eleven. That's if I don't run into anything funny."

"Funny?"

Ernest reached up under his cap in back and scratched his head. He smelled like burnt oil. "Car this age, you never know. Might find anything."

She looked at Magill. *Is this guy okay? Can we trust him?* Not that they had any choice.

Cornel had his map spread out on the trunk of the car. "Okay, so where's to stay around here? They got a motel in Denton?"

"In Denton?" Ernest flashed his gold tooth again.

"How about Bridgeville?"

"Not that I ever heard of." He put a grease-blackened finger on the map. Fate again: Caddie half expected him to say there was a motel in Clover. "Place here, maybe eight or nine miles north of where we are, which is here. It's sort of a motel, like."

Hmm.

"Use to be for goose hunters, just cabins, no electricity or what you might call luxuries."

"Well, you know—"

"But it got sold, then it got sold again, and these new folks fixed it up. I *hear*; can't promise you nothing." He looked at their faces with a certain satisfaction. "Bad place to break down. You're in kind of a pickle, aren't you?"

"How would we get there? Could you drive us?" Caddie asked.

"Nope. You saw all them cars I got stacked up," he said to Magill, who had to confirm that by nodding. "Everybody waits till the end o' the month to get inspected, nobody plans ahead. Tell you what." He narrowed his eyes on each of them in turn. They must look pretty harmless, because he decided, "I'll add twenty-five bucks to the bill and loan you my wife's car."

"Twenty-five dollars!" Cornel exploded.

"Deal," said Magill.

"You might have to buy gas. She never remembers to fill it up."

"You know, from here they don't look so bad."

Caddie poured more coffee for everybody and added a splash of cream to hers. She never used to take cream, but these days coffee without it gave her heartburn.

"They *aren't* that bad," Magill said, pushing away his plate with half a ham sandwich still on it.

"No, but the outside is nicer than the inside, you have to admit," she said. "Were you not going to finish that?"

Goose Creek Guest Cottages, formerly Hunter's Haven Cabins, were spread out on one side of the flat, two-lane highway, and the building with the owner's office, the registration desk, and this coffee shop sat on the other side, behind a gas station consisting of an island with one pump. Texaco. Luckily it was a sleepy highway, so all the traipsing back and forth you had to do to stay here wasn't dangerous. There used to be six cabins, all duplexes (so really, twelve), but the new owners had knocked down the center walls to make the rooms bigger. They'd been tiny before; now they were just small. And turquoise, with orange trim. Magill said they looked like Howard Johnson's babies.

They'd rented two side-by-side cottages for the night ($49.99 each, including continental breakfast in the coffee shop), to the delight of the owners, Mr. and Mrs. Willis, Peg and Ethel—Peg was the husband. They might not be so delighted if they knew Finney was taking a nap right now in the farthest cottage, the one you couldn't see from here because a billboard was in the way. Then again, maybe they allowed dogs, who knew? But during a hasty conference before registering, Caddie, Magill, and Cornel had agreed that in this case it was better to be secretive than sorry.

Cornel had his map out again. By now every time Caddie so much as glanced at it, the word "Clover" leaped out at her like flickering neon. The men were arguing about Maryland and Delaware, which state was better for taxes or something—Caddie silenced them by standing up. "I have to make a phone call."

They looked at her as if she'd announced she was hitchhiking to Dover. "Who to?" Cornel wanted to know.

She'd tell them if it worked out. Although what *working out* meant in this situation, she didn't know. "I, um, have a friend in the area. Maybe; have to check. Be right back."

Peg manned the motel office and the gas station while his wife handled the coffee shop. "Is there a pay phone in here?" Caddie asked Ethel, a hefty woman in her forties with a net over her wavy brown hair. She reminded Caddie a little bit of Brenda.

"Around the corner, right next to the men's room."

"Does it have a phone book?"

"Sure does."

Why were restroom corridors always paneled in the same dark, depressing wood? They always had the same carpet, too, thin dark blue speckled with stains and ground-in chewing gum. The telephone book swiveled out from under a metal platform under the phone. It covered four counties in two states, but it was only about an inch thick. For Kent County, there was one Haywood listed in Clover. Mrs. C. R. Haywood. A woman?

As soon as she got her money out, her hands began to perspire. The quarters stuck to her palm. She had to put her weight on one leg because her other knee was trembling. She dialed wrong twice in a row, and on the third try somebody answered so fast, she wasn't sure what they said, or even if it was a man or a woman, or a child. "Hello?" she said. "Hello?"

"Hello?" It was a woman. Old; quavery-voiced.

"Hello—my name is Caddie Winger and I'm trying to locate a Mr. Bobby Haywood."

"Bobby? Who is this?"

"Caddie Winger. I'm—"

"Caddie? Who is this? Where's Bobby?"

"No, I'm . . ." She heard a scrabbling sound, a woman's voice saying, "Mother, I'll take it," and then—

"Hello? Who's calling?" in a strong Eastern Shore accent.

"Um, hi." She started over. "My name is Caddie Winger, I'm in a phone booth in the neighborhood and I was looking—at the book, and wondering if by any chance this is the residence of Bobby Haywood."

"Bobby?" Not rude, but sharper. "I'm sorry, who'd you say this is?"

She repeated her name. "I think he knew my mother, if I have the right number. Years ago." Thirty-three years ago. If she had the right number. "Who's this?" she asked politely.

"Well, my name's Dinah Krauss, but . . ." She hesitated. "My brother was Bobby Haywood. Robert Charles Haywood."

Caddie's skin prickled; she felt as if she were getting a mild electrical shock. "Is he—" She had to clear her throat. "Is he there?"

"Oh, honey." The voice softened. "Bobby died a long, long time ago."

She didn't feel anything. Then she did, a wave of disappointment so swift and heavy her legs went weak. She'd have sat down on the floor where she was, but the phone cord wouldn't reach.

She got over it fast, because it was silly: how could you grieve for someone you'd never known and never even expected to meet?

The lady gave a little cough of concern into the silence.

"Um," Caddie said. "He was a musician, wasn't he?"

"Why, he sure was. Who did you say is your mother?"

"Jane Buchanan."

"Jane . . ."

"But she used the name Chelsea."

"Oh, lordy, you're Chelsea's girl."

"Yes. Did you know her?"

"I never met her, but I sure heard all about her from Bobby. How's she doing?"

"She died, too. In a car accident out in California, a long time ago."

"Oh, no. Did she? Well, I am real sorry to hear that."

"Thank you." There was so much sympathy in the lady's voice, Caddie got a stupid lump in her throat. "The reason I knew to call— I found a letter from Bobby to my mother, and it seemed like . . . they knew each other real well." *Real well.* She was falling into Dinah's idiom for some reason. She guessed because she wanted her to trust her.

"Well, Bobby was deep in love with her," Dinah allowed after a funny pause. "That I know. Like I say, I never met her myself." She said that carefully, as if trying to be fair.

"Dinah?" Might as well jump in. That's what Thea would do. "The reason I called is because I think, I'm pretty positive from the letter and the dates and everything, that your brother, um"—she almost lost her nerve—"might've been my father."

"Whoa." A thump, as if Dinah had sat down. "Oh, my goodness gracious. Caddie?"

"Yes?"

"Your name is Caddie?"

"Catherine Ann Winger. My mother was Buchanan, well, actually Buckman, but—oh, that's a long story, but Winger is my name."

"Where're you calling from?"

She told.

"Why, that's hardly any piece at all!"

"I know. Would you like to meet?"

"Why, heck, yes, wouldn't you?"

They laughed together.

"Well, you could come here if it's—"

"No, come over here," Dinah interrupted, "Earl's working and I can't leave Mother. Besides, you'll want to see the house. Bobby grew up here."

Caddie hunched her tense shoulders with excitement. "I'm traveling with some friends, two people, I really *was* in the neighborhood—"

"Well, just bring them, too."

"Really? I'd like to if it's all right. There's not much to do here, and I hate to just leave them—"

"Bring 'em with you. I'll give you directions, but it's easy as pie. Earl, my husband, he'll be up after a while, and you can meet Mother, too. Lord, Caddie, just think. She's probably your grandmother."

25

Even downtown, the streets of Clover, Delaware, were only a lane and a half wide, with rutted dirt shoulders for passing. *Downtown*—ha. Two churches, one gas station, the post office, and a place to buy lottery tickets, that was about it. The rest was Victorian and gingerbready houses, old and not restored, with flat, grassy-green yards only half a step down from the front porches. The big shabby-stately houses gave way within a block or so to smaller ones, also old and mostly frame, painted white, blue, and pale yellow. "Sleepy" was too dynamic a word for Clover, but Caddie liked it. *My dad grew up here*, she practiced. *My father. He grew up in this town.*

"Thank you again, you guys, for coming with me. I really appreciate it."

"Don't mention it. What else did we have to do?"

"Don't be nervous," Magill said. "This'll be a cinch."

"I don't know why I am—she sounded perfectly nice. I know they're not going to *eat* me."

"Just be yourself, they'll be crazy about you."

She smiled gratefully. "I hope." When she'd first told him and Cornel about the phone call, Magill had said, "Caddie Winger, you are full of surprises," and he'd looked at her with the nicest mix of admiration and sympathy. Cornel had said, "I can't take too many more of these goddamn *revelations*."

"Turn here," he instructed. Even now he had to navigate, from the slip of paper she'd written Dinah's directions on.

"Here?" Away from town? She steered onto a frontage road paralleling the highway, surrounded by stalky, dry, sawed-off cornfields and far-off houses dwarfed in clusters of tall trees. Mrs. Ernest Holly's car was an SUV. Caddie wasn't used to her new, superior relationship to the ground, or to the stick shift, which she kept grinding between first and second. Her nerves were jumping. After talking to Dinah she'd gone back to her room to fix herself up, and the sight in the mirror of her plain old self—except for the highlights, which Magill liked, so thank God for them—had been disheartening. She'd never wanted to look attractive, smart, and full of character more than she did right now, and all she looked like was her usual old self.

"Should be the next house. I can't see numbers that far," Cornel said.

"Krauss," Magill read on a black mailbox in the distance. "There it is."

Things were happening too fast. She couldn't take in her surroundings; she couldn't prepare. Here was a gravel driveway leading up to a one-story frame house, yellow with brown trim, and then beyond it to a green aluminum outbuilding and a parked school bus. The house had a weathervane on top and a Pennsylvania Dutch ornament over the door. Somebody had decorated a leafless dogwood tree in the front yard with plastic pumpkins. Where should she park? Down by the school bus? Here? What if she blocked somebody in?

Magill started to say, "This is good, right here," when the front door opened and a woman came down the two steps to the concrete walk. She waited, smiling, her arms down but her palms out, shifting her weight from foot to foot. Rather than grind the gears in front of her, Caddie left the car in third and turned off the ignition. "Well!" she said brightly, for courage. Magill winked at her. She took a deep breath and got out.

She was only halfway up the walk when the woman, tall and solid-looking, big-boned, with frizzy hair the color of the rusty geraniums in a box by the front door, held out her arms and said, "Oh, Lord, I see Bobby all over you. Come here, darlin', I'm your aunt Dinah." She had tears in her hazel eyes. Caddie blinked her own eyes clear and went into her arms, unprepared for the ferocity of her embrace. Dinah pushed her away to look at her—"Aren't you *sweet?*"—and then grabbed her back, mashing her against her bosom. She had on a long, scratchy sweater vest with a blouse underneath, green stretch pants, and white sandals.

"I don't know," Caddie said in a tremulous voice. Her hands felt small and childlike in Dinah's strong grip. "I think I might look like you." Not the eyes or the fleshy features, but something in Dinah's smile, happy and sad at the same time.

Caddie introduced Magill and Cornel, who were hanging back self-consciously, missing nothing but trying not to stare. "Well, hey," Dinah said, and she hugged them, too. "Come on in, every-body come in, gracious, you all look so *hungry.*"

Small, formal living room cluttered with pictures and knick-knacks and a suite of matching furniture. "The room nobody ever sits in," Dinah explained, leading them through it to a smaller room, a den, with a wide-screen TV on one paneled wall and a cluster of lounge chairs and ottomans around it. The TV's sound was off, captions running along at the bottom. Caddie didn't see the woman stretched out on one of the recliners until Dinah said loudly, "Mother? Mother, look who's here. Oh, Lord," she said in a softer voice, "I don't think I'll try to explain it all to her now. *Mother*—this is *Caddie* and these are her friends, Mr. Montgomery and Mr.— Magill. They're visiting. *Visiting.*"

She looked like a wizened doll, tiny in the enormous padded chair with her hands folded, feet together in furry white slippers under a knitted afghan. Caddie bent close and put a soft kiss on her cheek.

Her hair was white as cotton. She smelled like baby powder. She blinked rheumy blue eyes and smiled a sweet, trusting smile. "Hello," Caddie said. "I'm so pleased to meet you."

"Mother doesn't talk much anymore," Dinah said softly, "not for a while now." She smoothed the old lady's forehead with her hand. "She's fine—you all come in the kitchen, won't you, I just baked four pies, I hope you like pumpkin. Sit, sit. Who wants a cup of coffee? It's just made. Caddie, I wish you could've met Mother a year and a half ago, she was sharp as a tack. She lived here by herself, drove her car, went to church, you name it."

"How old is she?" Caddie sat down on a stool at a long Formica island opposite the sink in the cheerful yellow kitchen. Magill and Cornel took seats on either side of her. For the rest of her life, she would associate the smells of cinnamon and warm, baking pastry with her aunt Dinah.

Dinah turned a knob, dimming the lights in a chandelier shaped like a wagon wheel over their heads, and leaned back easily against the sink as if that were her spot, her station. "Eighty-four in January, she'll be eighty-five next year. The doctor said it was little strokes one after another, taking bits of her mind each time. Earl and I moved in a year and three months ago."

"Oh, this isn't where you live, usually?"

"Well, it's the house I grew up in. We're down in Salisbury, but we came up here when Mother couldn't do for herself anymore. Long story, but this was easier. She looks little and harmless, but she would *not move*—but you don't want to hear about all that. Anybody want ice cream on top?"

She was cutting huge wedges of pumpkin pie and pushing plates across the counter. "Anyway, here we are for who knows how long, and I got to thinking after you and I hung up, Caddie, it's a good thing Earl never got around to changing the phone. He's got his business phone out back, but so far we've just left Mother's name in the book even though she never talks on it anymore—her answering today was most unusual—and if we hadn't, if we'd had them put Earl and Dinah Krauss, you'd never've found us!"

Mighty good pie, Cornel told Dinah, smacking his lips in appreciation. Even Magill, who usually had to force himself to eat, was making pretty good headway on his piece. Dinah asked how they all knew each other, and Caddie let the men explain it while she and Dinah stole looks at each other, flashing quick, thrilled smiles.

"I wish I'd brought the letter your brother wrote," Caddie said when there was a pause. "I could send it to you if you like. It was very sweet. And sad. It sounded like he loved her a lot."

"Oh, he did, I know that for sure. Bobby was four years younger than me, so he told me things. We were real close, although I didn't see him as much after he got so taken up with his bands. Music meant the world to him, he was off from the time he was about twenty, off traveling and playing, trying to hit it big. You know, that big break that was coming any second, just around the corner. And once Chelsea joined up as the singer in Red Sky, why, that was it, *nothing* was going to stop them."

"Did you ever hear them play?"

"Not in person, not after your mother joined. After that they were moving around so much, it seemed like they were always too far to go, and then of course I had just had my first baby, Sherry, she's a little older than you, Caddie, but not much. She'd be your cousin. She lives in Dover, has two kids of her own already, she will *love* to know you."

Caddie shivered with excitement.

"Barbara, our other girl, she's over in Germany with her husband, you'll have to wait to meet her. But so, no, I never did hear Bobby and Chelsea play in person, but I've got a tape you can listen to, a demonstration he had made for them to try and get a record contract. That never panned out, but your mother sings on it, and Bobby, too."

"Oh, my. A recording of them together?"

Magill squeezed her knee, and when she looked at him, she thought her eyes must be shining the same way his were.

"What finally broke it up as far as I know is that Chelsea—Jane—wanted to go solo and more into rock and roll, with Red Sky just a backup band. Bobby loved their country sound and thought it should stay Red Sky with a girl lead singer. I think your mother wanted to go off and be Janis Joplin or something, and Bobby wanted a band like, oh, the Flying Burrito Brothers. You won't remember them, but sort of weird country rock, it sounded like to me.

"So they split up, and Bobby came back home to regroup. He took a job in construction to make some money while he tried to get another group going. He wrote a lot of songs during that winter, real sad love songs—but he'd always put some humor in, they weren't corny, you know, they'd make fun of the person who was crying in their beer or whatever. Too bad he didn't write any of 'em down, I'd give them to you, but he couldn't read music, he played everything by ear. He could play more instruments than anybody I ever knew, all the different kinds of guitar, and banjo, the mandolin, fiddle, you name it. Harmonica. He was a one-man band. Oh, honey, what did I say?"

"Nothing." She'd let a tear fall out of her eye. "I'm a music teacher, that's all. That's what I do."

"You are?" They shook their heads at each other in sad-happy wonder. "Come on, I'll show you some of Bobby's things. You-all want more coffee, would you please just help yourselves. To anything, you know where the refrigerator is. Or watch TV if you want, Mother won't care what channel."

In a narrow hallway, she opened a closet door, stood on tiptoes, and pulled down a white cardboard box. "Let's go in my room."

Caddie followed her into a bedroom. "Pardon the mess, Earl's got a project going." No mess, really, but birdhouses everywhere, on every surface, made of wood or twigs, and some were the kind that was edible—the whole thing was seeds and nuts, and the birds ate the entire house.

"He'll be up soon," Dinah said, moving four birdhouses from the bed to the floor. "Sit." They sat on the bed. "Mother's got more stuff in the attic, but this'll start you off. And of course there's pictures of Bobby all over the place." She opened the cardboard box.

It looked like a jumble at first, papers and letters, loose photos, a baseball, newspaper clippings, ribbons and medals, a birth certificate. Caddie's hand fell on one of the snapshots, and she gave an involuntary cry. "Is that him?"

"High school graduation."

Long blond hair and wire-rimmed glasses, straight-across eyebrows, broad shoulders under a royal blue academic gown. Her father had his mortarboard pushed to the side of his head and the tassel in his teeth, grinning hugely, probably laughing.

"He was always cutting up, you won't find a serious picture in here. Look—he's about two in this."

"Is that you?"

"Yes."

They were in a sandbox together, Bobby sitting in the V of his sister's legs, holding a plastic shovel in one hand and a rubber snake in the other. "He's so *blond*."

"White. And it never turned brown, it was still light-colored when he died. Much lighter than yours, but it waved the same way. You look like him, I swear you do."

She still couldn't see it. She looked at pictures of Bobby on a baseball team, his yearbook pictures, snapshots of him with his friends, his family—"Oh, look at your mother," Caddie exclaimed, "she was so pretty."

"She was."

"Are there any of your father?"

"Not here, but I can find you some. He died before Bobby was born. I barely remember him myself." She was rummaging through the box. "Here it is, here's the one you want to see."

"Oh, Dinah."

"Red Sky. The whole band."

"Oh, God. They're all hippies."

"I know."

"My mother. Oh, my God."

"You can have it."

She'd been hanging on to her composure, but that snapped it. Dinah put her arms around her, and she wept on the scratchy wool flowers of her sweater vest until the tide passed. When she pulled away, it was a relief to see Dinah wasn't exactly dry-eyed, either.

"How did he die?" Caddie asked, blowing her nose on a tissue Dinah yanked out of a box on the night table.

"An aneurysm. We thought it was a stroke at first, but they said he probably had it for years and it could've happened anytime. It was very fast, that was the blessing."

"Do you think he knew about me?"

"No, I do not. If he did, he'd have told me, for one thing. He never kept a secret, Bobby was open as the sun."

"I want to think he didn't know." She picked up a small, browning piece of newsprint. His death notice. He had died on January 8, 1973. So they'd been alive together for four months.

"He'd've wanted his own child, ambition or no. Your mother didn't tell him, I'm sure of it, although I cannot imagine why. Especially if she meant to keep you, because Bobby was steady— maybe too steady for her. He'd tell me some things. Not that she was bad in any way, not at all, but just so young. And not careful. Thoughtless and full of big dreams about herself."

"Yes."

"So your grandmother raised you, and you still live in Michaels-town? What do you do besides teach music? Come in the kitchen, I want to hear about *you*."

"Did you say you have a tape?"

"I forgot, it's in the other room. I used to listen to it every once in a while, but it's been a long time. Just a sec."

She came back with a cassette and a dusty boom box, which she plugged, grunting, into a crowded outlet behind the night table. Caddie watched her, bent over and graceless, her rear end stretching the fabric of her green pants, and she thought, *I love you already. I really do.*

"Okay, you listen, and then take as long as you want in here. Come on in when you're ready, we'll probably still be eating pie. That one, the young one, my Lord, he looks like a starving crow." She swooped down for another fierce hug, and then she was gone.

There were two songs on the demo. Caddie put the tape in the player, then sat still with her finger on the play button, not thinking about anything, just listening to the quiet of her own breathing. Drawing out the moment. She admired the shape of her hand, how long and thin the fingers were, just the right sort of hand for playing a violin. She couldn't remember her mother's hands very well. Maybe she had her father's. As soon as she pressed play, she would hear their voices. His for the first time in her life. What a day.

She pressed the button.

Electric guitars ripped out a fast, twangy, upbeat intro to the verse—her mother singing about wishing she was home, she'd had enough of the bright city lights. *Ha,* thought Caddie with real amusement, no cynicism, waiting for the chorus. Here it came—but it was the whole band, and she'd been wanting her father's voice by itself. Verse again. *Oh, Mommy,* she thought. She hadn't heard Jane's voice in a long time; it was softer and higher than she remembered. And pretty, but not hard or bluesy, not really a rock-and-roll voice at all. Had she wanted to be Linda Ronstadt or someone like that? Her soprano was too breathy and feminine even for this driving song about being on the road too long, missing her sweet someone.

Serves you right, Caddie caught herself thinking, and in the next instant, *Poor Mommy*. She felt both sentiments about equally. She must still be angry—odd, she hadn't known that about herself.

The second song was a love song. Jane's voice was just right for this—yes, because, *oh God*, here came Bobby's voice, winding the harmony around it. Caddie went blind, lost every sense but one. If she could have, she'd have climbed inside the tape machine. But in spite of her intense concentration, when the song ended she couldn't remember it. She ran the tape back and played it again. This time her head was clearer, the path between her ears and her brain not as cluttered. She could hear. Well, it wasn't really a love song. Against the sweetness of the melody, the subversive lyrics made her laugh.

> *Honey I haven't felt this blue*
> *Since the day before I walked out on you.*
> *So if you could find it in your heart,*
> *Let's do it again,*
> *Let's part.*

She wanted more of his voice; she wished she could turn everything else off, like reverse karaoke. She played the song again with her eyes closed.

He was a tenor. Warm but not trained, a little gruff around the edges. He sounded like a grown man, but he looked like a boy to her in his photos. Well, no wonder: she was older now than he'd been when he died. Sweet hippie boy. In the picture of Red Sky, shot in front of a rusty old barn, he wore faded, low-slung jeans and a collarless Mexican shirt, a belt with a turquoise buckle, saggy suede boots, and a black hat studded with silver stars. It made her laugh, but she pressed it to her heart.

Her mother wore jeans, too—everybody in this picture wore jeans—and a cardinal-red poncho down to her knees. No shoes, and feathers in her hair. She and Bobby stood together, close but not touching, with the other band members behind or off to the side. Think if they had stayed together—and lived, saved each other somehow. Think if they'd never stopped being in love.

Would Dinah lend her this tape? She couldn't get enough of it. She wanted to play it until it was a part of her, till the music entered her bloodstream and beat in her arteries and veins. How else could she get her parents back? She listened to them sing together over and over, and dreamed.

When she went back in the kitchen, Dinah was setting the dinette table for six. Magill and Cornel were still at the counter. They turned when they heard her and looked at her with interest, the way you look at someone who's come back from a long journey or an illness. To see how they've changed. A burly, thick-necked bald man, *completely* bald, who was sitting between them, also turned around and lumbered off the stool to his feet.

"Caddie, this is Earl," Dinah said with a wide smile, holding a stack of plates to her stomach.

"Caddie." He put his enormous hands on her shoulders and gave her a gentle, ardent shake. "Welcome to the family."

"Thank you."

He had a long, olive-skinned, bullet-shaped head and a pug nose, thick lips, and crinkly, penetrating blue eyes. His belly sloped over the top of his pants, but the rest of him was built like a furniture mover. "I knew Bobby since he was born," he said, keeping hold of her shoulders, "same as I knew Dinah. He was like my little brother, too, almost. I wish I'd known he had a kid when he died. He was so young, and it just broke everybody's heart." Suddenly his eyes welled with tears that spilled over and ran down his smooth cheeks. He finished in a high voice, "If we'd've known about you, I just believe it would've made it a little bit easier."

"Earl, now, don't go getting everybody all blubbery. You should hear him say grace when the whole family's over. We tell him he ought to've been a preacher." She made a face at Earl, as if to warn him not to embarrass Caddie.

He paid no attention. He grabbed her again and hugged her against his flannel shirt, which smelled of chemicals or mothballs, and she didn't mind at all.

They were staying for dinner, Dinah announced, there was no point in arguing. Could everybody eat pork chops? Caddie mashed the potatoes and wondered why the odor of frying meat didn't send her running for the bathroom—maybe pregnancy was a state of mind—while she filled Dinah and Earl in on her unadventurous life, where she lived, how she'd grown up, what she was doing these days. "My, my," and "Mmm, mmm," they said after every revelation, as if they were proud of her. As if she belonged to them already.

Have I found it? she thought. The family she'd always wanted, with La-Z-Boy recliners in the den and a quiz show on television, and a "Home Sweet Home" sampler in the kitchen shaped like a rooster? A family the neighbors could rely on, who went to church but didn't make a big deal of it, who had normal troubles and ate in the kitchen and went to the movies and the library and high school football games? Had she found them?

"Earl, what do you do for a living?" she felt comfortable enough to ask over dinner, a feast of juicy pork, mashed potatoes and gravy, corn, fresh kale, a Jell-O salad with pineapple chunks and Redi-Whip. Dinah sat beside Mother Haywood, cutting her meal into tiny bites, and the old lady picked at it in contented silence.

"Well, now." Earl stopped eating and put his elbows on the table, knife in one hand, fork in the other. The question pleased him, she could tell. "I'm in business for myself these days. I used to work for the chicken plant and do some taxidermy on the side, but now I'm pretty busy full-time with my own little company."

"Not so little anymore," Dinah put in.

"What do you do?"

"Well, I freeze-dry people's pets."

Caddie stalled, a forkful of potatoes halfway to her mouth. "Really." If she were at home, she'd have put her head down on the table. So much for her dream.

She made the mistake of looking at Magill, whose eyes were dancing. He'd read her mind. She felt a rush of tenderness wash over her like a wave, so strong it made her dizzy. She liked it that he was laughing at her. God help her, she liked it that his job was making feet.

Cornel was thrilled, he wanted to know everything about freeze-drying pets. Was there a special machine? Did the animals still have their innards? How much money could a fellow make in that line of work? He peppered Earl with a million questions, all except the one Caddie wanted to ask, which was, Why would anyone want to freeze-dry their pet?

"The thing most people don't get," Earl wanted them to know, "is how much of an art there is to it. Sure, your customer sends pictures and writes a letter about how their cat used to sit, how she cocked her head or what-not, but posing an animal you never knew in life is not something just anybody can do. You've got to have a *feel* for it. Now, most taxidermists won't touch a pet, it's too personal. A hawk, marlin, deer head, turkey head, no problem, but Fluffy the cat? They can't take it."

A turkey head?

"Now here, I just finished up a golden retriever, the prettiest dog you ever saw, and I did a darn good job."

"Oh, is she out?" Dinah asked. "Does she look good?"

"Come down and see." He looked around at all of them. "I mean if you want," he added, suddenly delicate. "Some people don't, and that's fine. But now these folks'll get Honey back, see, and they'll set her by the front door, and every time they go by they'll pat her on the head and say, 'Hey, Honey girl,' and they'll feel good."

"Can they just keep on patting her on the head," Cornel asked, "or eventually does her hair start to fall out?"

"Nope, nope, just give her a fluff and a little spritz of cedar residue to keep her shiny, she's good to go for eternity. Or as near as any of *us*'ll ever get to it." He winked.

Dinah shook her head with fond tolerance, as if that were a line and a wink she'd heard and seen a million times, but the guy they were coming from was still a winner in her book, a sweetheart, so she wouldn't complain.

Across from Caddie, Magill had his elbows on the table and his chin in his hands, gazing at her steadily, looking drowsy but fascinated. He had the longest eyelashes she'd ever seen on a man. More like a little boy's eyelashes. She felt so tired, so wonderfully tired. It looked to her as if all her people were tired and all the Krausses were wide awake.

But she roused herself to help Dinah do the dishes, and Magill and Cornel found the energy to go down and take a look at Earl's workshop with him, check out Honey, as well as a freshly freeze-dried bird, a cockatiel named Floyd.

"I hate to go, but we have to," Caddie said when the men returned.

"I wish you'd stay *here*," Dinah protested, "there's room if Cornel and Magill don't mind sharing."

No, Caddie explained, they'd left Finney back at the cottage, he'd been cooped up for—she looked at her watch—four and a half hours, and that was about his limit.

She kissed her new grandmother goodbye. The old lady was back in her recliner. She reached up and patted Caddie's cheek, smiling familiarly. "Bye," Caddie said, and Mother pressed her lips together twice, as if she might be saying *bye-bye*. "I'll come back," Caddie promised, and Mother nodded as if she knew that.

Outside in the yard, Dinah put her strong arm around Caddie's waist. "I feel like I've got another child."

The men were already by the car; Earl was explaining how the freeze-drying process preserved the animal's size and shape but eliminated eighty percent of its body weight.

"I'm pregnant." She'd wanted to tell Dinah that, Caddie realized, almost from the moment they'd met.

"You are? Well, *child*. Is it his?"

"Whose? *No*." Dinah was looking at Magill. "No, somebody else, and he's not in the picture now."

"Well," Dinah said, shaking her head in sympathy. "Well, bless your heart. Anything I can do, you let me know, hear?"

"I'm all right—I just wanted to tell you." She put her arms around her aunt's solid body and held on.

Earl held the car door for her. She rolled down her window as soon as she was in. "Thank you. For everything. It's been . . ." She couldn't think of a big enough word.

"Come back soon," Dinah said, shiny-eyed, holding on to Earl's arm. "Now that you know where we are."

"I'll call you," Caddie said.

"We can e-mail," Dinah realized. "I *love* e-mail."

They kissed. Caddie backed out of the driveway, waving, savoring the smell of cinnamon.

26

Finney found the perfect tuft of grass and peed on it long and blissfully in the field behind Goose Creek Guest Cottages.

Magill, on the other end of the leash, said, "Good work," in a proud voice, man-to-man. Ignoring him, Finney pulled him over to a different tuft and went again.

The moon was full but hiding in a crowd of fast, serious-looking clouds, and the wind felt cool and damp, as if rain were on the way. If this was Goose Creek, this smallish body of water the moon picked out at coy, irregular intervals, it was really more of a pond because the murky silver water didn't appear to be flowing anywhere. Finney wanted to explore it more fully by jumping in, but Magill held steady on the leash and dissuaded him.

"I like it better where we live." Caddie's voice silenced a cricket somewhere nearby in the meadowy underbrush. What was it doing here so late in the year? "It's beautiful, but I like hills and mountains."

Magill nodded. "Impediments. I want to feel there's more to what I'm looking at than I can see."

"Obstacles in the way."

"Like life."

"Not necessarily mountains, but there *have* to be hills," she said.

"Otherwise, your inner and outer geography don't reflect each other."

They nodded wisely.

"It's getting colder," Magill said.

"It is getting chilly," she agreed.

He put his arm around her shoulders.

"Well," he said after a nice, quiet pause. "Looks like you've got a new family."

"Looks like."

"Aunt Dinah and Uncle Earl."

"And two cousins and a grandmother."

"How does it feel?"

She shook her head. Indescribable.

"I've got cousins," he said thoughtfully. "I ought to go see them."

"Or your mother. You could go see her."

He looked up at the sky. "Does it feel like things are changing? It feels like a big wheel is turning, just enough to make everything different."

"I'm ready for that," she said.

"Me, too."

Finney stopped prowling and sat down in front of them, sniffing the air, drinking in the night.

"Once my grandmother, I mean Nana"—how funny to have to distinguish between grandmothers—"organized something called the Frame Project. Well, *she* called it that, and 'organized'—I think she got one other woman to do it with her. The idea was to go around framing anything they saw that struck them as art. So, you know, people would see it with new eyes, whatever it was, a fire hydrant, the bus stop bench, a sleeping dog, a child's toy. And realize that art is everywhere."

"A sleeping dog," Magill said appreciatively. "What did they make the frames out of?"

"Anything, wood, PVC pipe, whatever was around."

"*Big* frames."

"Some were. I remember they tried to frame the garbage man. He wouldn't stand still, I think he felt patronized. But anyway—you asked me how it feels. The Frame Project didn't last long, but it's always stayed with me. I still do it in my head sometimes, frame things. Tonight—I put a frame around a hundred things."

The moon came out long enough to glitter, delta-shaped, on the surface of the pond. Then it disappeared, and the stars caught in the intervals between the racing clouds seemed to wink more brightly to compensate. An owl hooted somewhere across the water, *hoo hoo-hoo hoo*. The wind picked up, smelling of rain and earth. It blew a lock of Caddie's hair in her face; she swept it away, and in the same smooth move she slipped her arm around Magill's waist.

"I told Dinah about the baby," she said.

"I heard."

"You did?" He'd been so far away.

"I'm glad you're keeping it, Caddie. I mean *her*. You'll make a great mom."

"I don't know about that."

"Oh, yeah. But I was wondering."

"What?"

"Does this mean we're getting married after all?"

She laughed a little too loudly. Magill watched her from the corner of his eye. She thought of what Cornel had said—it seemed much longer ago than just this afternoon. A lifetime. "I think what I was thinking, before, is that abandonment is something you catch, like a bacteria. Or a gene you pass down, mother to daughter, father to son. But it's not, it can stop wherever you want it to. I've figured out that the only person I have to worry about as far as this baby is concerned is me, and I won't be leaving. It stops with me. I'm steady."

"You're steady."

"I am."

They agreed. A puff of breeze blew her hair in her eyes again, and this time Magill stroked it away with his fingers. "Getting late."

"We should go in, I guess."

They dropped their arms and stepped away from each other.

"Come on, Fin." The dog wouldn't budge. Typical; he probably wanted to go in, but now that he knew *they* did, he was against it. "Rotten dog," Magill said amiably. "You are *this* close to being freeze-dried."

"Well," Caddie said in front of her cottage door. Magill handed her Finney's leash. "Would you like to come in?"

He said yes and followed her and Finney into the room. Things could be so easy sometimes.

Back when it was a cabin, it was probably rustic, but in making it a cottage they'd covered the log walls with drywall and painted them green. So now it was just a regular motel room with too much furniture—two double beds, a bureau, desk and chair, TV set, closet, miniature bathroom. Finney, ignoring his dog bed, had staked out the double bed nearer the bathroom. You could tell, because he'd scratched one of the pillows out of the way and burrowed under the spread, making a jumble of the covers. Caddie and Magill sat on the other bed.

"Are you tired?"

"Yes." She was exhausted.

"Me, too."

"But don't go yet."

"All right."

They smiled at each other. She traced her finger around the faded shape of a flower on the quilted bedspread. "Does Cornel snore?"

He cupped his ear. "Can't you hear him?"

She laughed, standing up. "Move." She pulled the spread back, folding it into thirds at the bottom. She took off her shoes. "We could turn on the TV."

He sat down and untied his hiking boots. They got in bed,

bunching the pillows behind their heads. "Uh-oh. The remote's over there."

"Rats."

They looked at it, sitting on top of the TV, but neither one moved. Caddie could see herself in the section of mirror over the bureau the television set wasn't blocking. Her back hurt. She had to pee. She looked happy, though. "'Scuse me," she said, got up, and went to the bathroom.

When she came back, Finney was on their bed, making himself comfortable between Magill's long legs. *"Hey."* She did have *some* rules. Finney even knew this one. He dropped off that bed and jumped back on his, careful not to look at her. Pretending it was his idea.

"It seems a lot longer than just this *morning* when we were home, doesn't it?" she said, continuing her train of thought from the bathroom. "So much has happened. Do you miss Thea?"

"Yes."

"I thought of her so many times tonight, how much she'd have loved this. Dinah and Earl, Mother. Everything."

"She'd have loved Earl's job."

Caddie watched herself smiling in the mirror.

Magill said, "Thea told me I can never be forgiven. She said I can only forgive myself."

Was that what she'd whispered to him, that night at Caddie's house? "That's true, I guess. Except *I* forgive you," she said softly. "For what that's worth."

"She did say I'd need a little help from my friends."

She rested her head on his shoulder. She couldn't see her face in the mirror anymore, just the white of her bent neck. "You need to eat more. Your shoulder's bony."

"Holly's parents can't see me."

"What do you mean?"

382

"They can't look at me. They say it wasn't my fault, but they can't be around me. I don't hold it against them."

"Oh, I do." She put her hand on his chest. "I wish I could heal you," she said on a sigh. If she could just change his heart with the palm of her hand. If she could just fix him. "Henry." She said it just to hear how it would sound. "I saw your factory, where you make feet. Thea and I drove by." Their faces were very close; she could see specks of her own reflection in the blue of his eyes. "You should go back. You can't be a scarecrow man forever."

His lashes came down; her image disappeared. Without opening his eyes, he leaned toward her and put his lips right where hers were. A soft, light press. She was surprised and not surprised. She moved her hand in a circle on his shirt and kissed him back, made it a real kiss.

They pulled away to look at each other. Had he just wanted her to stop talking? If so, it worked. She smiled, worried about his serious, searching face. He had a big nose, it was his most prominent feature. But a nice nose. Like the prow of a ship, very sharp and determined. Nice whiskers, too, not too spiky, coming out of his smooth skin, shiny-brown and distinct.

Sliding down in bed, he lay flat with his head on his pillow. He took her hand and pulled her down with him. "If you'd said yes, you'd marry me, you know what I was thinking?"

"What?" She reached over and turned out the light.

"There's something about me you don't know." Yellow parking-lot light gradually brightened along the thin vertical line where the curtains didn't meet. Pretty soon it wasn't dark in the room at all. "I can play the saxophone." He turned on his side; when he drew up his knees, they bumped her leg. "I pictured us in your grandmother's living room in the evenings, noodling away."

"Family musicales, I'd love that. Which grandmother?"

"You like jazz, right? We could play jazz so progressive, nobody would know if we were hitting the right notes."

"I can see it," Caddie said.

"Me, too," Magill said. "It's very vivid to me."

She wasn't sure which one drifted to sleep first. It felt like a dreamy, tender, mutual abandonment. Something woke her— Magill sitting up, struggling to take off his jean jacket. She was warm, too; she stripped off her sweater and dropped it on the floor. "Cornel won't worry, will he?" she asked as they stretched out again under the covers. Magill said no, and they fell back to sleep as easily as before.

When she woke again, the parking-lot light wasn't a line anymore, it was a bright rectangle glaring in her eyes. She blinked, disoriented, and glanced over her shoulder. Magill lay with his head propped on his hand, eyes wide open.

"I opened the curtain," he whispered. "Sorry."

"Why?"

"So I could see you."

She turned over. His face was all cutting, angular shadows. Usually his eyes were the warmest blue, but the harsh light made them glitter like chips of stone. She touched his raspy cheek, to warm it. She wanted him to smile. She kissed him.

They slid into each other's arms, pressing together to kiss, pulling away to see each other's eyes. She wasn't dreaming, and yet everything was happening so slowly and smoothly, as if they knew what they were doing because they were duplicating something they'd done before. She sighed against his lips, his nice warm lips, but he wouldn't go any further, do anything more, until she said, "Let's," on the softest of breaths, not even a whisper, he could hear it or not. It was out of her hands.

He heard.

Being with him was strange at first, like lying with a long, rangy rack of bones with hot skin and a lot of sharp joints. She'd honestly thought his body might be something she'd have to *get over* to enjoy, and that made her feel tenderer toward him. It made her hide less of herself than she usually did in bed with a man. She felt generous and flowing, womanly, as if her relatively abundant flesh was her gift to him, more freely given than ever before.

After a while, though, none of that mattered, wasn't even true. Nobody was giving anybody a gift, it was more fundamental than that. More romantic. Layers of herself peeled away, she felt as if she was diving down through levels of soft veiling, swimming down toward what true nakedness, not just of the body, felt like. Christopher, her old touchstone for physical passion, surfaced in her mind from time to time, but always he was bested or unmasked or overwhelmed in some way by the more raw, factual, incredibly sweet honesty of Magill.

"Henry," she called him, and every time she did it sort of woke him up, made him smile and frown and focus on her eyes. He didn't know if he liked it or not, her calling him Henry, she could tell. But she liked it.

She liked slicking her hands down over each protruding knuckle of skin on his bumpy backbone. She liked his weight on top of her, just right, and she liked cupping his shoulder blades and pressing his hard plaque of a chest to her breasts, and curling her legs around his sharp, stuck-out knees.

"Don't let me do anything to hurt you," he said, just on the brink, the cusp, and she didn't understand for a second what he was talking about. Then she remembered: the baby.

"I forgot," she said, and went into a very odd, bubbly gale of solo laughter. Nervous euphoria, she assumed. She indicated to him in some fashion, not words, that all was well, and would they please return to whatever they were doing before, she couldn't remember exactly what it was, maybe it wasn't a particular thing, but if he could get them back to that place, that moment—

He did, or she did, one of them did. Afterward she lay very still beside him, debating whether he would be glad or frightened to hear that what had just happened to her had never happened before. Not even with Christopher. Or sad, maybe he would be sad. It made her sad, a little, so she didn't tell him.

The jig was up. Caddie could tell by the way Cornel glowered at his newspaper and wouldn't talk throughout the entire free continental breakfast in the coffee shop. Magill had given her a goodbye kiss and sneaked back to his room even before the sun came up, but Cornel wasn't born yesterday. This wasn't even his predatory-bird scowl, it was worse, it was his wrath-of-God scowl, the face God probably put on when he found out what bounders Adam and Eve were.

Except for her back, which was worse, and some mild cramps, which were new, Caddie was in a mood to find Cornel's attitude cute. She got up to get more serve-yourself coffee, and when she came back, something about the back of his head, the still-boyish shape of it or maybe the vulnerable-looking tendons in the back of his skinny neck, made her put her cup down and wind her arms around his shoulders from behind for a sneak-attack of a hug. She put her lips on his piney-smelling, just-shaved cheek and kissed him.

He sputtered, he flushed, he wiped his cheek with his paper napkin. "Cut it out. What the hell's that for?"

She grinned at Magill, who was snickering into his orange juice. "It's to show I'm an equal-opportunity kisser." If that wasn't laying all her cards on the table, she didn't know what was. Cornel rattled his newspaper and harrumphed.

Magill put his chin on his hand and smiled at her. He'd just gotten out of the shower, she could tell by his slicked-back hair, shiny and straight, the neatest it would be all day. She imagined him in the shower. His lanky body. He had bruises on his shins and his elbows from getting dizzy and bumping into things. Last night she'd made a game of it, finding the bruises and making them all better.

After breakfast she called Ernest Holly, who said her car was ready. It didn't take long to pack up and throw their suitcases into Mrs. Holly's SUV. Caddie walked Finney one last time. He was a little off his feed, hadn't eaten much of the dry kibble she'd brought along for him. She'd buy him a hamburger when they stopped for lunch.

It was a blustery, gray day, rain spitting sideways with enough force to hurt your skin. Bad luck; now they'd have to sit inside on the ferry, not stand out on deck and look at the bay, and strolling around Cape May would be a trial instead of fun. It was hard to care much, though. Hurrying back from the motel office after settling her bill, she spied Magill, hurrying toward her to settle his. He was watching his step and didn't see her yet. When he did, his face went from preoccupation to gladness, and she skipped a heartbeat. He covered one eye with his hand, for better perspective. The wind tore at his jacket and slapped his pants around his legs like corduroy flags. They converged in the middle of the road and stood there, smiling stupidly until they heard a truck coming. Getting close. They brushed hands and parted, and as Caddie went on her way she felt lifted up and flung down at the same time by a luscious wave of lust.

She'd loved sleeping with him, maybe more than the sex. No. No, but *sleeping* with him, lying beside or across all those nooks and crooks and pointy corners of him, it should've been *un*comfortable, like sleeping with a fork or a pair of dice—but instead she'd felt like a lucky little boat, safe and snug in a calm, peaceful harbor. Home port. She'd woken often, to stretch her arms and legs into the four corners of the bed, *ahh*, and also to increase the surface area of her skin on his, and always she'd fallen back into sleep like a pebble slipping down, down into deep, clear water.

*   *   *

"No more scenic routes." In the rearview mirror, she caught a glimpse of Cornel unfurling his map over a dozing Finney on his lap. "We just go straight, Cornel, due east, no diversions, and when we—"

"We could go see Thea's house."

"Thea's *house?*"

"You got to have that window open?" he complained to Magill. "Me and the dog are getting wet."

"It won't go up," Caddie explained for the fifth or sixth time. "I'll turn the heat on. Scootch over more to the left."

Instead he sat forward, shoving the map over the seat. It crackled annoyingly in her ear, and she couldn't look anyway, she was driving. "She used to live right here," he showed Magill, tapping his finger on the spot. "How far is that from here?"

"I don't know," Caddie answered before Magill could, "but we're already behind schedule by a whole day." And she wasn't feeling well. Were these cramps normal?

"So what? What have we got to do?"

"Well, *I*—"

"When are we ever getting back this way again? I'll be dead before I ever do."

"We'll come back, Cornel, I promise."

"The weather stinks. I don't want to be on a ferry in this, anyway."

She stopped herself from snapping back that she didn't feel much like driving in it, either.

"We could go to Thea's house *instead* of Cape May," Cornel argued. "More personal. I could read my poem from the dock on that creek."

He was being disagreeable on purpose, because she and Magill had changed the balance last night. He felt excluded, and her light-hearted attempt to bring him back into the circle this morning hadn't worked. Oh, her back hurt and she was sick of arguing.

"From here," Magill said mildly, "it looks like about forty miles there, forty miles back. Eighty miles. What do you say we take the ferry today, and see how we feel about seeing Thea's house tomorrow? On the way back."

"Fine," said Cornel.

"Fine," said Caddie. She smiled at Magill. The diplomat.

Cornel saw the smile. When she looked at him in the mirror, he was back to glaring. Now he thought they were conspiring against him.

Phooey. She had other things to worry about. "Pit stop. Sorry, guys." She pulled the car into a gas station next to a pottery outlet. "I'll be quick." She trotted through the rain to the ladies' room—locked; ran back around, got the key on a dirty wooden paddle from the attendant, ran back outside.

Grungy ladies' room. No tampon machine, and she was spotting, she could tell. What next? She pulled down her slacks and checked her underpants.

Blood.

She screamed. She slapped her hand over her mouth and made a sound in her throat, *urrrr*. Real blood, it was blood, like a period. She turned ice-cold. *A little spotting is normal*, the doctor said; *don't even call me*. But this wasn't spotting.

Or maybe it was. Spotting all at once instead of gradually. What about the cramps? Now that she knew about the blood, they were worse. This wasn't right. She pulled off handfuls of the cheap toilet paper and made a pad.

Maybe it was the sex. Maybe this was what happened when you stirred things up by having intercourse. Then it *was* normal, because married people had sex when the wife was pregnant all the time. *Oh, please be normal.*

She had her doctor's telephone number. "Do you have a phone?"

she asked the man in the gas station office, who was reading a car magazine. He pointed out the window, "Over there."

On the side of the road. She waved to Magill and Cornel as she ran past the car, making a silly face, like *Look what I forgot to do*, or something. The glass door of the phone booth wouldn't close; rain beat on the roof and blew inside. Did she have enough change? She put in money and dialed.

The answering service picked up. Of course: it was Sunday. The lady said she would give Dr. Anders Caddie's message; did the doctor know her number? No, because she didn't have one! "I'll have to call back—I'm traveling. Can she give you a message, and then I'll call you?" Well, no, because she probably wouldn't get the same operator again. But she could try. It was all very complicated, and then the other operator came on to say she needed to deposit more money, and she didn't have any. "I'll call back," Caddie yelled to the answering service lady before the line went dead.

"Who'd you call?" Cornel had to know as soon as she got back in the car.

She couldn't say "my doctor." Once she said it, she'd have to deal with it. It would be real.

"Brenda. I wanted to check on Nana. Who's fine."

They believed her.

"Where are we, Cornel, how much farther? When do we get to where we're going?"

Ostentatious map-crackling. You'd think he'd have it memorized by now. "Well, we're coming up on Georgetown in about five miles, and then it's one, two, four, six, nine . . . fifteen miles to Lewes. Give or take."

Twenty miles. She could do that.

More flat, dun-colored farm country, some of it under water as rain pooled in vast puddles, submerging the low trunks of trees in the copses. They drove by a house with a sign in the yard,

PALM READER–ASTROLOGIST. In the middle of a stubby field, a white cow huddled in the rain all by itself. A million black dots in the next field turned out to be starlings pecking at the wet ground. PUMPKINS 4 SALE. She had to slow down for a dump truck going forty-five.

"Mmm." It came out involuntarily.

Magill looked at her. "What?"

"Funny feeling." Immediately she felt a little better. Half of what ails us, Nana used to say, comes from keeping it a secret.

"Funny how?"

"Like a cramp. Like . . . grinding."

"Have you had it before?"

She shook her head. "A little bleeding, too. It's nothing. I'm sure it's nothing." She could feel him staring at her, but she didn't look over. But she was glad he knew.

"You know what I remembered last night?" Cornel spoke up.

"What?"

"Lying all alone in my lonely bed?"

Magill folded an arm over the back of the seat and rested his chin on it. "What did you remember last night, Cornel, lying alone in your lonely bed?"

"I remembered the time I saw Thea when she was a little girl."

Caddie forgot her cramps and turned around to look at him.

"It had to be '38, because that's the year my daddy got my brother and me jobs toting bags part-time at the train station. We weren't real redcaps, it was just Saturdays and after school, helping out the colored fellows who were the real redcaps; we had to give them half our tips, and plus they always got the good customers, we only got the leftovers."

"You saw Thea?" Caddie reminded him. "How old was she?"

"Little. Five, six, four. It had to be her because it was the rest of the whole Wake family on their way to upstate New York, Chautauqua, I guess, for a vacation. Here they all come on a

Saturday morning, dressed like pictures you'd see of that girl who married the king of England, forget her name—"

"I know who you mean," Caddie said.

"Wallis Simpson," Magill said.

"Right, her, fashionable and fast-walking, the whole kit and caboodle, old-man Wake leading the parade. Thick-chested fellow with a gold watch chain. Had on a white suit, I remember. A white suit. I never saw anything like that before. Aunts, cousins, servants, there's so many of them, even I get to haul some of their bags. I'm sure this little girl was Thea because she'd've been the right age for 1938. I was twelve."

His voice trailed off. In the rearview mirror, Caddie saw him stroke Finney's head softly, absently. "I wished I'da remembered that before. I could've told her, we could've talked about it. Can't you see how she'd've looked, how it'd've made her laugh?"

"Yes," Caddie said. "I can, Cornel. She'd have loved that story."

A fresh cramp seized her. They were coming into a town. "Is this Georgetown? Where do I go? Cornel, where do I go?" She slowed through a green light; the car behind honked. "Right or straight? Why aren't there any *signs*?"

"Right," Magill said when Cornel went mute.

"But it doesn't say!"

"Go ahead, I think this is it."

Finally a sign, Route 9 Bypass. "Is this right? What happened to the ferry signs?" Were they lost? They were driving through the middle of the town, this was no bypass.

"There," Magill said, pointing. " 'Lewes Ferry.' We're okay."

Whew. More flat, straight highway. "How much farther, do you think?"

"Not far, about twelve miles."

But she was bleeding, she could feel it. And the pains were worse.

"Pull over," Magill said.

"No, I have to get somewhere. This isn't right."

"What's wrong?" Cornel asked, sticking his head between them.

"Caddie's not feeling well."

"I don't feel too good myself. That coffee gave me indigestion."

"Pull over, Caddie. You shouldn't be driving."

"You need someone to drive? I can drive," Cornel said. "I just can't see."

The pain passed. "No, I'm okay to drive, but I need to stop somewhere. I'm afraid I need a doctor."

Cornel finally got it. "Keep going. There's a big blue *H* on Lewes—" he showed Magill the map—"just keep going straight, there's a hospital right in the town."

But she couldn't keep going. The pain wasn't excruciating, but the fear was, because it was impossible now for her to believe this was normal. "Look, I just have to—" She slowed the car and jerked it to the shoulder, stopping half on, half off the grass verge. "And once again, we are in the middle of nowhere," she tried in a light tone. She put the brake on, the car in park, and let it idle. She put her head on the steering wheel.

Magill's hand felt cool on the back of her neck. "You're pale as a ghost."

"I'm in trouble. Oh, God. This is wrong."

"I'll flag a car down," Cornel said.

Magill was getting out on his side. Instead of flagging down a car, he pulled open Caddie's door. "Come on," he said, and started to help her out. She put her feet on the ground. They saw the blood at the same time, a blotch of bright red like a wound, staining her groin and the inner thighs of her tan slacks. She started to cry.

Magill picked her up. He kicked the back door. "Open it, get the dog, get out." Cornel came out of a dumb, staring trance and scrambled to obey.

"I can walk," Caddie protested. But all she wanted to do was curl up in a ball.

"No, you don't move." Magill laid her on the backseat and covered her with his jacket. "Cornel, give me your coat and get in front with Finney. *Hold* him." He bent close, tucking Cornel's coat around her, too. He put his hand in her hair. "All you have to do is lie still, Caddie. You're going to be okay."

"I'm afraid I'm losing the baby."

"No, I don't think so. We'll be at the hospital in about ten minutes. They'll take care of you."

"I don't want to lose it."

"You won't."

"I want us to have—musical evenings, us three, with your saxophone."

"We will."

"Who's driving?"

"I am."

He made the tires shriek on the wet pavement when he started off. On purpose? She shut her eyes and didn't think about it. The car seat smelled like dog and motor oil and wet wool, but she pressed her cheek to the cold vinyl hard, wanting any sensation but pain. Oh, this would be so cruel. If she lost her baby, it would be a punishment for not wanting it in the beginning. Could it really be happening? But it was so *mean*.

She sat up to see where they were. Magill wasn't covering one eye, he was just driving. He was flying—the number on the speedometer terrified her. He had both hands on the wheel tight as clamps, his scarecrow shoulders rigid. "How are you doing?" he asked, eyeing her in the mirror. She just nodded. "Lie back down, Caddie, we're almost there."

Cornel looked grim. Finney kept trying to squirm out of his lap and jump over the seat, he had to hold him by the collar. "Good dog," she crooned, reaching down to stroke him. "Good boy, you're all right."

"Lie down," Magill said, and flicked on the turn signal. Oh, Lord, he was going to pass the car in front of them. She lay back down on the seat.

Rain, trees, telephone wires, red and yellow leaves blowing in the gusts of wind like confetti. Along with the cramps, she felt nauseated. Where would she throw up if she had to? *Oh, baby.* It could suck its thumb now, she'd read in a book. It had very thin skin, its tiny blood vessels were visible right through it. She'd never felt it move—but that was normal, that wasn't even supposed to happen for two or three more weeks. She rubbed her stomach gently. *It's okay, I won't let go of you.* What God should she pray to? Hers was so vague; Nana was the one with vivid gods. But she was as angry as she was scared. *No fair* sang in the back of her mind, in time to the slap of the tires. *No fair, no fair.*

"There it is right there, the hospital, right on the road. Emergency entrance," Cornel directed, "go in there."

Rain-stained yellow brick and glass doors, wings, extensions, parking levels. The car stopped with a lurch; Magill jumped out and disappeared.

"Cornel, don't let Finney go or he'll run away," Caddie instructed, sitting up to put on Magill's jacket.

"I won't, I've got his leash on. How do you feel? Don't worry about the dog." His grumpy old face was screwed up with distress. "Is it bad?"

"No, not too bad now. I'm just scared."

He worked his lips, trying to think of something to say, something comforting. When it wouldn't come to him, he put his hand back and gave her shoulder a soft pat.

A man in blue scrubs yanked her door open. "Hey, how you doing?" he said in a sympathetic voice, and helped her out of the car.

Magill hovered behind him. "I can walk," she told them, but the man, the orderly or whatever he was, opened a collapsible wheel-chair and made her sit down.

"I'll be there in a second," Magill called as she rolled away through hissing automatic doors. "Gotta park the car!"

Hurry, she thought, and moved her fingers in a frightened wave.

The triage nurse had a tiny office in the ER waiting room, nothing in it but a desk and two chairs, a sink and a scale. Caddie liked her attitude, concerned but businesslike, and tried to answer her questions in the same style. But when the interview was over and the nurse told her she had to sign in with her insurance information at the emergency department registration booth next, she blurted out, "But am I losing the baby? Shouldn't they do something *now*? Do you think it's a miscarriage?"

"It could be, but I can't say. The OB on call will see you as soon as he gets here, and he'll definitely want a sonogram. But I'm sorry, they won't know anything before that." She got up from behind her desk. "Are your friends out here? Let's get you registered, then I'll buzz you into the ER, you can wait there for the doctor. Do you need a pad?"

Cornel couldn't believe it. "You have to register? Now? You're in pain, you're—and they want to see your *insurance card*? This is what's wrong with this country—"

Caddie tuned him out. "What did the nurse say?" Magill asked, and she told him. He wheeled her over to a woman behind a counter next to the triage office. More questions. Magill had her purse; he found her wallet and read the information on her card to the registration lady. Caddie couldn't think anymore, only worry, so when the lady, writing on her form, said, "Oh, you're from out of state?" a complete, fully formed nightmare unfurled in her mind: They couldn't take her here, people from out of state weren't allowed, and Magill would have to drive her back to Maryland. Cornel would get them lost, they'd never find another hospital, and in the smelly, moldy backseat of her own car, she would lose her precious baby.

"Okay, you can wait over there and somebody will come and get you in a few minutes." The registration lady stapled papers together and handed them over.

"Where?"

"Right over there. They'll buzz you in in a sec."

"Can I go with her?" Magill asked.

She shook her head with an apologetic smile. "But the nurse will keep you informed."

He pushed the wheelchair over to an empty space in front of the double doors. Cornel came over from wherever he'd been. "This is an outrage," he started—but Magill shooed him away. He wrapped his arms around her shoulders from behind and brushed her cheek with his lips. Whispered encouraging words she wanted more than anything to believe.

"I wish you could come in with me."

"We'll be right here. We're not going anywhere."

"Don't forget Finney."

"I'll make Cornel walk him."

She put her hand on his face and pressed it to hers. "You went eighty miles an hour. I saw." She rested her chin on his forearm. "What does it mean?"

"One crisis at a time." He stayed like that, bent over her, holding her around the chest, for a long time. Then he kissed her on the temple and straightened up. As soon as he did, the doors swung open and the same man who had wheeled her into the hospital came striding through. "Hey, there. You ready?" The badge on a chain around his neck said his name was Albert Johnson.

"She's ready," Cornel said irritably from behind her. She hadn't known he was there.

"See you," Magill said. "See you soon, Caddie. We're right here."

He was so thin, almost insubstantial, standing with his hands flexing at his sides, trying to smile with confidence. She still had his jacket, she realized, but it was too late to give it back. "Bye" was all she had time to say to him—and Cornel—before Albert Johnson stepped behind her, blocking the view, and rolled her across the black rubber mat into the emergency room.

The technician wouldn't tell her what the sonogram showed. She only asked once, "Is everything okay?" but the tech, a sharp-featured, pale-haired girl who looked too young for her job, only hummed something unintelligible. She kept her eyes on the screen while she moved the greasy scope around on Caddie's abdomen, occasionally clicking a pedal with her foot. When she finished, she stood up too quickly, Caddie thought, and scooped up a paper. "Okay, you relax now, I'll be back in a minute."

"Are you going to show it to the doctor?"

"That's right. You just relax." She disappeared through the curtain.

Usually Caddie liked ultrasounds. The darkened little room was always warm and humid, almost like a womb itself, and the tech always chatted with her, pointing out this and that on the screen: "That's your uterus, that's your bowel," and especially, "That's your baby." Men must come, too, to get things looked at, but she'd never seen one; for that matter, she'd never seen a male technician. It was a woman's place, and, since she'd made the decision to keep her baby, a place to hear good news.

This room oppressed her. She couldn't lie comfortably in any position on the narrow cot. Snatches of casual, soft-voiced conversation beyond the curtains sounded threatening; she listened like an animal, but not one clear word surfaced from the low, ominous undertone. What did the machine say? She craned her neck to see the screen behind her, but the usual grainy-gray fan shape was all it showed.

Footsteps. A man's voice she recognized—the doctor who had examined her before the sonogram. She put her hands over her face.

"Caddie?"

"She's dead, I knew it. Oh, God." She heard the wheels on the technician's chair squeak, heard the doctor sit down. His name was Dr. Bhutra. Finally she had to look at his face.

It told her everything. "I'm sorry. Your body's aborting your pregnancy, just as we thought."

"Is she dead?"

"You're terminating your pregnancy," he said, his voice kind but clipped. "It's common to have some bleeding afterward, like a period, but in your case we feel the bleeding is a little heavy for this stage."

He kept talking about hemorrhaging and tissue, something about her uterine wall, the need for a D&C, but the words ran together and she concentrated on the half-moon-shaped bags under the doctor's eyes and the pouches of flesh at the sides of his lips. The space between his nose and his top lip was very long, with vertical wrinkles all the way across. What was that space called? It had a name.

A new nurse appeared behind him. "Let's get another H and H," he said to her, or something that sounded like that. More words; she heard "OR" and "incomplete AB." The chair squeaked when he stood up.

"Why?"

He halted with his hand on the curtain. "Why did it happen?" He came closer. "There's probably no reason. Sometimes it just happens, a spontaneous abortion. It doesn't mean you can't have another pregnancy."

"But why did it happen?"

He shook his head. "Hormone levels, chromosome defects, the

shape of the uterus, a thyroid disorder, a weak cervix. Think of it as nature's way of protecting what was too weak to survive or thrive. It just happened. No reason. And nothing you could've done to change it. I'm sorry," he said, and patted her knee.

They left her alone for a while in the dim, warm room. She lay with her hands on her belly, cupping the tiny bulge. The emptiness was only starting. She couldn't imagine that, how it could be any worse, but it would be. "Here," someone said, and she opened her eyes. The pale-haired technician put something in her hand. A wad of tissues. She looked at them for a while before remembering what they were for. She wiped her face.

"I can get that man in if you want to see him."

"What?"

"The fellow outside. Your friend you came with, I can let him come in and visit for a minute even though he's not family. You want to see him?"

"No."

"Okay. You can come back to the exam room now."

Caddie looked at her blankly.

"Where you were before. You can wait there for the anesthetist to come down. He'll ask you a lot of questions about allergies and so forth."

"What?"

She said it all over again.

"I don't know. I don't know what to do."

The technician handed her the box of tissues. She was rolling something, it smelled like a mint, back and forth in her mouth. She pulled the chair out and sat down.

Caddie said, "Did you say I have to move?"

"Just back to the exam room." That cold, bright cube where she'd taken off her bloodstained clothes and lain on a paper-covered table. "Are you sure you don't want to see your friend?"

She didn't even know who she meant for a second. She was unconnected; she had no friend, no attachment. "Oh." Magill, that's who she meant. "No, thank you. I'd rather just wait by myself."

27

Dr. Anders, Caddie's ob-gyn, told her she might benefit from some counseling and gave her the name of a therapist. She joined a group. She didn't have much to say in it. She couldn't get over how articulate some of the women, who had had miscarriages or stillbirths or otherwise lost their babies, were about their feelings. They could describe them precisely; they had a lot of words for their emotions. They told her she was blocking or holding back, but that wasn't it. She just didn't have any words.

Talking was too hard. When students came to the house for lessons, she'd be fine at first, but gradually she would drift away. The music they played would sound muted, as if it were coming from behind glass; a sensation would come that she was alone in a darkened theater watching a play. She didn't have to react; she was in the audience. She wasn't really there.

Magill called every day. She listened, but she couldn't hold up her end of the conversation. He'd done so much for her, he and Cornel, including the endless drive home from the hospital while she slumped in the backseat, blind to the view from the streaky window, blind to everything. And he'd stayed in the house with her for two nights, sleeping on her couch, walking the dog, bringing her soup and toasted cheese sandwiches while she lay in bed with her face to the wall, waiting for the bleeding to stop and the pain to go away. When they did, she'd asked him to please go away. He kept trying to *talk* to her. "No, just go," she'd begged, and at last he'd kissed her goodbye, saying he would call.

She hated the sound of the phone. Hated it that Magill seemed to think, although he didn't say it, that she should be ready now to resume what they'd started, whatever that was. She could hardly remember it. "Would you like me to come over?" he would ask. "Let me take you out. Or come to Wake House, Caddie, your grandmother misses you."

Once he asked her if she blamed him. "Why should I?" she'd asked, wary, staring out the window at Nana's ruined yard. A cold rain was turning the ground to mud. She'd planned to rake it up and plant grass seed after the Cape May trip. October was the best time to plant grass, people said.

"Because we made love." His voice on the phone sounded too intimate, as if he knew her. She resented it. "The night before," he added, in case she wasn't sure which night he was talking about.

"I asked the doctor. She said that had nothing to do with it."

"Thank God, Caddie."

She didn't like his relief, either. How nice for him that he was off the hook. "But I'm in a mood to blame everybody. You, me, God."

He said something in a consoling voice, but she didn't catch it. Her thoughts drifted. ". . . come over," she heard distinctly.

"What?"

"Let me come and see you. We could go for a drive. Or a movie or something."

"No." She couldn't stop him from calling, she was too passive, and anyway what difference did it make. But seeing him, seeing anybody she didn't have to, that was different. "I can't. Sorry." She hung up.

Why would he want to see her, anyway? She only had two moods, two personas, ghost and crybaby. She'd made an awful mistake in the recovery room: She'd asked Dr. Bhutra what the baby's sex was. A boy. He'd said it gruffly, as if he disapproved of the question and knew the answer would be bad for her. He was right. The most harrowing storms of grief came when she imagined what her baby, her little boy, would've been like if he'd lived. She saw him so clearly. She knew him so well. The anguish had been a little easier to bear before, when he was only a genderless "fetus."

"You have to grieve," the counselor advised. "Your hormones are having a party inside. Don't expect anybody else to understand, and don't let anybody hurry you. You've lost a child. No one can understand the pain of that but you."

She never thought of Christopher anymore, but one sleepless night she had an idea of calling him. "I have some good news and some bad news," she would say. "Good for you, bad for me." But she didn't pick up the phone, although she knew the number. She didn't want to hear the sound of Christopher's voice. It felt like a hundred years had passed since she'd thought she loved him.

It rained almost every day in November. Magill kept calling. She couldn't make him stop. She thought of the old music video, the man trying to dance with the dead woman, hauling her limp body around, her head flopping on his shoulder. "I'm moving out of Wake House," he told her one night. He always called late, often when she was already in bed. It didn't matter; she was hardly ever sleeping. "I've got a little apartment on Tyler Street. Know where that is?"

"Yes, mm-hmm." Near his foot factory. He used to have a house, but after the accident he'd sold it. "Will you go back to work?" she asked.

"Try to. Things are sort of falling apart. It's nobody's fault. Well, mine, it's my fault for not being there. I've got great people, the ones who have stuck, but they couldn't run the place on their own indefinitely. Leadership vacuum, I believe they call it. Caddie? You still there?"

"I'm here. Well, it'll be hard," she acknowledged. "I'm sure it'll work out, though." She watched the numbers change on her digital clock. Finney slept with her every night now, a bad habit she didn't have the heart to break. He liked to press up against her hip, under the covers. She liked the company.

"I miss you, Caddie. I'm starting to think I imagined you."

She sympathized. Sometimes she thought she'd imagined herself.

"I've read all the things I'm not supposed to say."

"What?"

"A list at a grief site on the Internet. Things not to say to someone who's lost a child. I can say I'm sorry, but that's about it. And I can offer to be with you. Would that be okay? We could just sit. Anywhere. When we get tired of that, we could get up and walk the dog."

"Magill . . ." It was easier to be receptive or noncommittal—or like smoke, not give him anything to grab onto, nothing he could use to force the issue. But that's what she'd been doing for weeks. She kept thinking he would give up. Since he wouldn't, she had to dredge up the will from someplace and finish it herself. She had a little bit of kindness left inside her.

"I'm sorry, but I can't. I don't have anything. I'm out."

"Why don't you let me try to help you? Give me a chance, Caddie. I don't want you to hurt like this."

"There's nothing you can do. I wish you would believe me. I'm sorry." She hated disappointing people. "I'm not who I was before."

"I'd like to wait till you are."

"No, don't, that would be—and anyway, it's not—a *disease*," she said, some strange bitterness rising in her throat, "I'm not going to get *better*. Please stop, just don't call, it's better if you don't call anymore. I'm glad you're all well, it's great, you can get on with your life now. I'm so happy for you, truly I am. But when you call me, it—I know it shouldn't, but it makes it worse."

There was the most awful silence. She took the phone away from her ear and cried through most of it.

"Okay, Caddie. I think I've got it."

"I'm so sorry."

"Yeah, you said that."

"Are you angry?"

"Am I *angry*?" He made a sound, a sigh or a laugh. "I don't want to make it worse for you, but you broke my heart. And I'm only telling you that so you'll know how far I am from being *angry*. Here's my new number in case you ever need it."

He recited it, but she had nothing to write on. "Thanks." If she said "I'm sorry" again, it would be the fourth time.

"Take care of yourself, Caddie."

After that, he stopped calling.

Nana moved back home on a cold, ugly Sunday, in a biting wind that blew through clothes and skin straight to the bone. She'd never bothered unpacking most of her art supplies, so the move out went faster than the move in had six months ago. Caddie avoided farewells by telling people she'd be back, she had lots more stuff to haul, they'd probably *never* see the end of her. It was true, there were a few more boxes of junk in the basement she didn't have the heart to deal with right now. But mostly what she didn't have the heart for was last words, even with the addition of "But I'll come back and visit all the time!" Maybe she would, maybe she wouldn't, but the emotional strength to say goodbye even provisionally just wasn't in her. Saying it to Magill had depleted her storehouse.

For Nana's first night back, Caddie made a special dinner with all her favorite foods, but neither of them felt like eating. It was no use trying to pretend they were celebrating. Nana hadn't wanted to come home, for reasons Caddie still wasn't a hundred percent clear on, but Brenda said the time had come. Her patience ran out when Nana used the private office phone to charge over three hundred dollars' worth of 900-number calls to a TV psychic. When Brenda confronted her with the bill, Nana denied everything, excused herself, and ran down in the basement to hide. It took half a day to find her. Thanks to Thea's generosity, Wake House was improving, upgrading, even expanding, but its *purpose* hadn't changed. Elder care and convalescence were still its mission, and the elderly it cared for still had to be compos mentis. It was so unfair.

In some ways it was good to have her grandmother back, someone to talk to and look after, someone who needed her. They watched TV after dinner, and it was pleasant to look over and laugh with Nana at the silly jokes on the program and make cracks about the products in the commercials. Nana had Finney on her lap, Caddie had some mending on hers. An idea of what the two of them looked like, what a third person would make of them, would chill her if she thought about it for long, so she didn't think about it. Was it so bad that they were back where they'd started last spring, before Nana broke her leg?

But they weren't, of course. Caddie felt as if she'd lived a lifetime since then. And yet if that was true, why wasn't she a stronger, better, wiser, braver person? Six months ago she wasn't sure she wanted Nana to go away: now she wasn't sure she wanted her to come home. Time changed most people, but even her *ambivalence* was the same. A sense of missed opportunities plagued her; time squandered; something precious she'd let slip through fingers too weak or indecisive to close together and make a cup.

"Time for bed?" she suggested at a little after ten. "It's been a long day for you."

Nana was watching the news. She got off the sofa and looked around. "Which room is mine? Do I sleep here?"

"No, your old room, Nan, you know. Upstairs, where you always sleep."

She had to help her get undressed, remind her to brush her teeth, take her hair down for her. Had Brenda or one of the aides been doing this? Oh, surely not—it must be the newness of home. After Nana got into a routine, she'd be back to normal.

Caddie tucked her in. "It's so great to have you home," she said, smoothing her hair back from her forehead. She looked anxious and wide awake. "Do you need anything? Glass of water?"

"No."

"Well, holler if you do, I'm just down the hall." Why did she feel she needed to remind her? She lingered, straightening things on the bedside table, unwilling to turn out the light and go. Then Finney jumped up, licked Nana's cheek, and burrowed under her arm. Nana smiled and closed her eyes with a tired sigh. *I knew he was good for something*, Caddie thought, and kissed them both good night.

The next day she got a long, newsy letter from Dinah. "Aunt D," she signed herself. Caddie had written first, just a note to tell her about the baby, and Dinah had instantly called to commiserate. This was her first letter. Everybody was fine, she wrote, except Mother had a cold that wouldn't quit and at her age a thing like that could go into pneumonia before you knew it. Earl was hard at work on his biggest project ever, somebody's pet pig. Not a Vietnamese one, either, a regular pig, big as a sofa. He sent his love. (Earl.) First of the year, they might get Sherry to come stay with Mother while they drove up to Atlantic City for a night or two; they hadn't been off somewhere together, just them, in over a year, and that wasn't any way to keep the spark lit, if Caddie knew what she meant.

"How is Cornel? How's Magill? Send them my regards. Most important, how are you? I hope you are feeling better, honey, than when we last talked. My only advice is that time heals all wounds. Not that that ever made anybody feel better. I still miss my sweet Bobby, so there's a wound that didn't heal. I guess they scar over, though. That's the best we can hope for, some thick skin to form between our pain and our tender hearts. Caddie, call me *any time* you want to talk, and know that I'm thinking about you. It's still a miracle to me that we found you, or rather you found us. Lucky day! Hugs and kisses and much, much love, Aunt D."

Nana kept mixing up the Miss Michaelstown pageant with one of Caddie's community orchestra concerts because they were in the same building. "Shouldn't you be up *there?*" she asked several times as they took seats in the back of the civic center. They were late, and the hall was already full. They'd missed the swimsuit competition, but the talent portion was just beginning. A girl in a long gown played the "Appassionata," and Caddie wrung her hands. *Oh, Angie,* she thought, *see what you're up against!* But the next contestant was a juggler, so maybe not. Then a girl who sang "The Wind Beneath My Wings." A lovely, graceful ballet dancer. A girl who told jokes.

When Angie's turn came, the announcer called her "Miss Angie Noonenberg," not Angela Ann or Angela May. She looked beautiful. She'd cut her long hair after all, and it was very punk and stylish, chopped-off chunks shooting out in all directions. Caddie could swear she'd gotten taller. She had on a short skirt and boots, and a sleeveless top with sparkly beads across the chest. Caddie's heart was pounding like a machine. She had to grab Nana's hand when Angie lifted her violin to her shoulder.

She didn't play "Man of Constant Sorrow," she played a stark, raw ballad about the death of a coal miner in Harlan County, Kentucky. A hidden guitarist played acoustic accompaniment while she sang the lyrics in her natural voice, not the flat, nasal twang she'd affected for the other song. It was better this way; it was more honest. She played the haunting, minor-key melody with her eyes half closed, her body straight and tall and very much alone on the stage. Caddie had tears in her eyes before it was over and looked around to see if anyone else was as moved as she. Hard to tell, but the auditorium had gone very quiet; no one coughed or shuffled their feet. And when the applause came, it sounded serious, no whistling or calling out. That had to be a good sign.

It was—Angie won! The talent part, not the pageant—the girl who juggled won Miss Michaelstown. "What did you expect?" Nana said when the emcee announced it and Caddie groaned under her breath. "I knew she'd win, she had the biggest tits."

When the house lights came up, all the contestants and their families and friends converged in front of the stage. "Nana, sit right here and don't move, okay? I'm going to see if I can find Angie."

"Why can't I come with you? I want to see her, too."

"Oh, okay, come with me. I didn't think you'd want to."

"Why wouldn't I?"

"I don't know." Because she hadn't wanted to come to the pageant in the first place. Because on the way over she couldn't quite remember who Angie was. Caddie took her arm and they went off in search of Angie.

They saw her in the middle of a milling crowd of pageant beauties and well-wishers in front of the first row. Trying to get close wasn't easy. Nana nudged one of the unsuccessful contestants, a red-haired girl who'd played the clarinet and told the crowd her wish for the world was peace and rapture through Jesus Christ. "You were very good," Nana told her. "You just need bigger—"

"You were," Caddie cut in, "you were great—come on, Nan."

Over the heads of her admirers, Angie saw Caddie and let out a whoop. "Hey!" she cried, waving, jumping up on her high heels. "Hey, Caddie!" A moment ago she'd been a sophisticated young woman in a sleek white evening gown, but now she was a teenage girl again, the old Angie. She jostled people out of the way, Caddie did the same, and they threw their arms around each other. "You came!"

"*You*—you were fabulous!"

"Oh, I'm so happy you're here."

"Did you think I wouldn't come? Angie, you *won*, you *won*—"

"I know! Did you like my song?"

"You should've won *everything*, you were robbed."

"I don't care about that, I just wanted to win the talent. And I did!"

"How's your mother?" She could see her in the Noonenberg crowd, smiling and chatting, not a hair out of place.

"She'll get over it. I'm done with pageants—I only did this one for her. So did you really like my song?"

"Oh, Angie, you were right and I was wrong. People weren't even *breathing*. Because we knew it was real, it was *you*. From the heart!"

Angie got tears in her eyes, so of course Caddie did, too. "Then I guess you're not mad at me anymore?"

"I never was—I thought you were mad at *me*."

They laughed, giddy.

"I know I'm totally not going in the direction you wanted, Caddie, but I love what the band's doing—it's called Bitter Root, you have to come hear us—and if it weren't for you I wouldn't have had the guts to even *try*."

"That's not true."

"It *is*. Be excited by your music, that's what you always told me. Remember? *Be passionate.* You said it a million times. Nothing matters but what you love to do."

"I said that?"

"So really, this is all your fault. When I'm rich and famous, I'm dedicating an album to you!"

It felt as if no time had passed since last summer; they could've been drinking Cokes in the kitchen after a lesson. Caddie hadn't let herself know how much she'd missed Angie.

A woman with Mrs. Noonenberg's haughty eyebrows turned Angie around by the shoulders. "Aunt Chrissie!" Angie exclaimed, and the woman kissed her on both cheeks. Caddie smiled a goodbye and began to back away.

"See you, Caddie—don't forget to come and hear Bitter Root!"

She blew Angie a kiss and turned around.

Nana was gone.

She found her outside, standing under a buzzing fluorescent light pole on a hillock of dead grass in the parking lot. A feathery snow had started to fall, had already dusted her black beret and the shoulders of her unbuttoned coat. She looked lost.

"Nana!"

"There you are," she said in an airy voice, but relief was all over her face. "What took you so long?"

"What are you doing? Why are you out here?"

"I was—I can be out here, don't talk to me in that tone. I wanted to wait in the car, is that a crime?"

"The car's way over there—!"

"Well, *I* know that. I certainly know where the car is. You worry too much, that's your problem." She let Caddie take her arm.

"Don't go *off* like that, you scared me half to death." She was still trembly from panic. In the five or six minutes Nana was missing, she'd imagined a hundred horrible things.

Nana laughed and deftly changed the subject. "Let's get ice cream on the way home; we haven't done that in a long time. Let's stop at Griffin's and get sundaes."

Caddie chafed her grandmother's freezing hands as they walked through the crowded parking lot; Nana's gloves were still in her coat pockets. "Okay, that sounds good." Except Griffin's had gone out of business about six years ago.

At home, Caddie ran a hot bath for her in case she was chilled, and afterward Nana put her nightgown on inside out. Caddie found her in front of the bathroom mirror, cursing the goddamn buttons, turning red-faced from frustration. "Well, no wonder," Caddie said, and zipped the flannel gown over her head, put it back on, and buttoned it. "There you go, that's better."

Nana brushed her teeth in a resentful silence, and later she grabbed the brush out of Caddie's hand and dragged it through her wispy gray hair herself. "I can do it. I can do *something*."

From her own room, Caddie heard her get in bed and went in to say good night. She could tell Nana wasn't listening to her small talk about Angie and how the evening had gone, her music lesson schedule this week, what they needed at the store. Nana sat up and cut her off in the middle of a sentence.

"This is *exactly* what I didn't want to happen. You and me in this old house, waiting for me to croak."

"What?"

"Crack, I mean, not croak, crack. Go bonkers. Croak, too, but crack first. I put my goddamn nightgown on backwards."

"Oh, Nana." She dropped down on the bed.

"You're laughing? You think it's funny? It runs in the family—you won't be laughing when it happens to you."

"I'm not laughing."

"Both my uncles on my father's side. Winger blood. You could be next."

She was right. It wasn't funny.

"I hate this. I didn't want to be *here* when it happened," Nana mumbled, plucking at lint on the blanket. "You can feel it coming on, that's why I wanted out."

"I don't understand. Even if it's true, why is it better not to be in your own house?"

She turned her face away.

"Don't you like it here? It's true, we don't have an elevator or motorized wheelchairs. And Mr. Lorton's not around to be the oldest, so I'm afraid that'll have to be you."

She wouldn't smile.

Caddie clasped her thin, wrinkled old hand. "When spring comes, we'll start a new sculpture garden in the front yard. We'll start all over. I'll do the muscle work, you just have brilliant ideas. You're the creator, you just point to things and say, 'A little to the left.' " A fat teardrop landed on the hand Caddie was holding. "Why are you sad, Nan? Why?"

She whispered something.

"What?" Caddie leaned closer.

"I don't want . . ." Her lips moved, but no more words came out.

Caddie whispered, too. "What don't you want?"

"I don't want you to leave me."

Caddie's chest felt constricted, as if a cord were tightening around it. She couldn't get a deep breath. "Nana." She watched their entwined fingers gently clench and unclench on top of the blanket. "I will *never* leave you."

"Shh," Nana said, while silent tears slipped down her cheeks. "Bad luck."

"No, I won't. I promise. Do you know why? Because you never left me. Everybody else did, but not you. My crazy grandmother."

Nana snorted and dashed at her eyes.

Caddie handed her a tissue. "I've never even thanked you."

"Pete's sake. For what?"

"For keeping me. After Mommy left me with you. Dumped me on you."

"Oh, honey." She honked her nose into the Kleenex.

"You were in your fifties, it must've been kind of a shock. But I always knew you wanted me. Oh, I was *so lucky*."

Nana wiped her face and smiled, watery-eyed. "Course I wanted you. You were my baby." Her face crumpled again. "But dammit to hell, I never wanted to be *yours*."

Caddie hummed in sympathy, then ruined it by laughing. They slipped their arms around each other and held on, smearing the tears together on their faces.

"I love you."

"I love you, Nan."

"I've decided I don't want you to shoot me anymore."

"Oh. Good."

"Which is funny, since I've never needed shooting more. But the whatchacallit's always the last to know."

"The shootee." She kissed her. "Are you sleepy? Should we read for a while?"

Nana slid down in the bed and got comfortable, closing her eyes and folding her hands over her stomach. She used to love to read, but she said the words wouldn't stay put anymore. "Where'd we leave off?" she asked, yawning. "I can't remember."

"I can't, either. Shall we just start over?"

"Good idea."

Caddie opened the book to chapter one. " 'It is a truth universally acknowledged,' " she began, " 'that a single man in possession of a good fortune must be in want of a wife.' " It was where they started their story every night.

28

Caddie called her aunt on Christmas Eve.

"Your present just came!" Dinah exclaimed in a hoarse voice—she had a cold. "Who told you I had a sore butt from that school bus?"

"You did," Caddie said, laughing. Dinah drove the elementary-school bus in the mornings while Earl stayed with Mother. Caddie had bought her a special foam-filled, shape-retaining, shock-absorbing seat pillow she'd seen on television. "Be sure and tell me if it works."

"How could it *not* work? Did you get mine yet?"

"Yes, but I didn't open it. *I've* got willpower."

"Well, call me when you do, I want to hear what you think."

"Will I like it?"

"Could be, could be. I just wish you could be *here* when you open it. Sherry and Phil and the grandkids are coming for dinner—I feel like I've been cooking since last month. And Earl's gone overboard on the house again, I told him it looks like Chernobyl. I just wish you could *be* here."

"I do, too," Caddie said. "I wish I could, too."

Dinah's gift was a photograph album full of copies of all the pictures of Bobby she could find. Caddie sat with it on her lap on Christmas morning, looking and looking, feasting her eyes, wishing she'd opened her present sooner. Nana only cared about the pictures of Bobby with Jane, and there weren't very many of them. But when she heard there was a tape—Dinah had also sent a copy of the Red Sky demo—she insisted Caddie play it immediately. "Are you sure?" Caddie worried. "It won't make you sad?" Nana made a face and said "Pshaw," and Caddie played the tape.

Her grandmother listened as if she were hypnotized. "Play the second one again, Caddie, I love that high, sweet part. Oh, what a pretty voice she had. Play it again."

Caddie played the song for her over and over.

It started to snow in the afternoon, big flakes sifting past the kitchen window, but before long Caddie could only see them under the streetlights. It got dark so early these days. Smells of the turkey she was cooking for dinner filled the house. It would be too much food for two people. Too much of everything, tree, stockings, the wreath on the door, candles in the windows, Christmas music on the radio, all for two lone women. It was stifling. Nana felt it, too; she claimed she was tired and went up to bed for the afternoon, leaving the whole overheated, overdecorated downstairs to Caddie.

She missed Thea. She had all day; she'd woken up missing her. She thought of calling Cornel, just for someone to talk about her to. He hadn't gotten to read his poem for her in Cape May, and they'd probably never go back now. *Oh, Thea.* If she were here, she could help take this ache away, this pointless loneliness. Last night Caddie dreamed she was walking in a dangerous part of town and someone shot her in the back. It was a low-key dream; she wasn't frightened or surprised. She could see herself from behind, a perfect, gaping hole in the middle of her, like a cartoon character shot with a cannonball. She could see right through herself.

She could call Magill. It was the only way she'd ever be able speak to him again; he wasn't going to call her, that was for sure. And yet, all day she'd thought he might. Both times the phone rang, she thought it was him. But the first time it was Dinah and the second time it was Morris, her stand partner in the orchestra, inviting her to come to a party tomorrow night. Last-minute. She told him she couldn't leave Nana and it was too late to get someone to stay with her.

So Christmas passed. Only a handful of students wanted to bother with lessons during Christmas week, so the short, gray days yawned dull and empty. She tried to fill them with trips to the mall with Nana for the after-Christmas sales, violin practice on a new piece she was learning, reorganizing her lesson schedule for the new year. But the stretches of time when she only sat with Nana in the living room and stared at the TV or played sad songs on the piano came too often and brought her down. Even Finney, curled under the piano with his chin on his paws, looked depressed. Just the thought of New Year's Eve made her want to run away from home. Then, in midweek, Brenda called.

"We're having a party, can you and Frances come? It's for New Year's, but it's also a farewell party for Cornel."

"Cornel! Where's he going?"

"His daughter-in-law talked him into moving down there with her and her son."

"Oh, that's *great*," Caddie rejoiced, even though it felt like one more friend abandoning her. "Yes, absolutely, we can come."

"Good. Eight-thirty, and don't bring anything unless you want champagne. We're only serving punch."

"Is Magill coming?" she asked casually.

"I haven't called him yet, but I hope so. It's short notice, Cornel didn't decide till yesterday."

After they hung up, Caddie ran upstairs, thinking what a pity case she was, thrilled because she'd been invited to an old folks' home for New Year's. But even knowing she was hopeless couldn't keep her from making a beeline for her closet to check out the possibilities.

"I'm not going," Nana said. "I don't feel like it. New Year's Eve, I'm not going anywhere. Those days are gone." Caddie argued, but she wouldn't budge. What was the real reason? Every time Caddie suggested a trip to Wake House, Nana found an excuse. It was as if she'd shut a door on that life and nothing could make her walk back through it. "Okay, then. If you're not going, I'm not, either," Caddie threatened, but Nana said, "Good. We can watch Guy Lombardo."

Caddie called Rayanne Schmidt, the teenage neighbor she'd been trading piano lessons for Nana-sitting with. She was free on New Year's Eve. "You, Rayanne? You don't have a party to go to?" Secretly she was delighted, but mystified, too—Rayanne was cute, bright, full of personality. Nana loved her. "I did," Rayanne said, "but I got grounded." For? "Smoking. Mom walked in and caught me, she didn't even knock. *She's* the one who should be grounded." Caddie didn't ask, so she could only hope Rayanne was talking about tobacco.

The tasteful white lights across the front porch roof and the candles in all the windows of Wake House made Caddie think of Dinah and Earl and their little rambler in Clover, lit up "like Chernobyl." She'd always wondered what kind of people did that to their houses at Christmas, and now she knew. People like Earl. She wished Dinah would send a picture.

She could hear music before she even got to the porch steps. And singing; Doré's voice, that unmistakable atonal soprano. Could it be—the karaoke machine was out already? She saw Cornel in the foyer, talking to Claudette, but he abandoned her and darted under the chandelier—and the mistletoe—as soon as he heard the front door open. "Happy New Year," he said perfunctorily, and kissed Caddie on the lips. Bull's-eye; lipstick smears on his cheeks said his aim had been less deadly with others.

"Happy New Year. You're leaving!"

"She wore me down, I got tired of saying no."

"I think it's *wonderful*. Richmond, that's not so far, I'll come and see you all the time."

"Richmond." He sniffed. He had on his brown suit with a festive red tie. "They wave the Confederate flag down there at the drop of a hat, y'know. Just what I—"

"Now, don't you start. You're going to like it, Cornel, you'll be with your own family, your very own *grandson*."

"Kid'll probably ignore me, probably be ashamed of his old—"

She grabbed his shoulders and shook. "Quit it."

"What?"

"Being an old grump."

"I *am* an old grump."

His turtle-lipped smile melted her. "Oh, gosh, you are." She put her arms around him and squeezed. "I'm going to miss you so much."

"You really going to come see me?"

"I promise I will. Magill, too, I bet." She looked around. Milling people in both parlors, and blazing Christmas trees, fires in both fireplaces. "Is he here?"

"Said he'd be late."

He started talking about packing, what a pain that would be, and how he could've accumulated so much stuff when he was down to living in half a room. A sight distracted her; she lost track of the conversation. "Edgie? Oh, my goodness—look at you!"

She was walking. Slowly, and tilted to the side, using a three-pronged cane for balance, but she was walking. "Speed demon, thass me," she said with a crooked grin. "Lookit *you*. So pretty."

Caddie rushed over to kiss her. "Oh, you're gorgeous." She had a new perm; it framed her face like soft yellow cotton balls. "What a treat to see you up and around!"

"Where's Frances? You all by yourself?"

"She didn't quite feel up to it. Where's Bea?"

"In there." She shrugged toward the Blue Room. "With the *new man*."

"The *new man*. How exciting."

"Take off your coat and stay a while. Bea!" She didn't call out with much force, but over the music and the chitchat her sister heard. Her face lit up. She turned back to the new man for a second—Caddie had a glimpse of white hair and broad shoulders—then left him and came toward her with open arms.

"You! Months since we've seen you, months!"

"One month," Caddie countered, letting herself get swallowed up in a bear hug. She'd forgotten how strong Bea was. She looked like a new woman—or rather her old self, tough and handsome and no-nonsense.

"No, it's more than a month. You said you'd come see us all the time, and here—well, never mind, we forgive you."

"In the spirit of Christmas," Edgie said.

"How've you been?" Bea's voice went low with sympathy. "Has it been rough on you, hon? Bet the holidays weren't much fun."

Caddie was afraid of sympathy. "Oh, not too bad." She shrugged off her coat and hung it on a hook behind the staircase. "So tell me about the new man! And who's the lady over there in the hat?"

"*Well.*" Bea rubbed her hands together.

"Tom Kowallis," Edgie said before she could speak. "Bea's boyfriend."

"Oh, he is *not*."

"Everybody's boyfriend, then."

"That's more like it," Bea said ruefully.

Caddie moved to get a better view of Tom Kowallis, who was talking to Doré. "Handsome." He looked like somebody, she couldn't put her finger on who. Gregory Peck? He was tall and erect, with thick, shaggy white hair and black eyebrows, a wide chest, an imposing belly, and no rear end at all. "What's he like?"

421

"Thinks he's died and gone to heaven. Look at Doré. See that handkerchief in his pocket? She made it for him."

"Doré made a handkerchief?"

"She had to—Sara made him slippers."

"Sara. Who's Sara?"

"Mrs. Sha . . . Shar . . ." Edgie's tongue got tied up.

"Shallcroft," Bea said. "I thought you met her already, she came after Susan left. Over there." She nodded toward a slender, attractive woman in a long black dress, wearing her silver hair in an elaborate chignon.

"Oh, Mrs. Shallcroft, I remember. She just lost her husband."

"And don't we get to hear about *that* every day."

"Edgie," Bea said, tittering.

"Thinks she's the world's firs' widow. Hasn't been outta black since she got here."

"She's a *tragic figure*," Bea said, eyes twinkling. "Meanwhile, *Mr.* Shallcroft's been gone for at least three years."

"And—" Edgie leaned over on her cane and spoke in a stage whisper. "Maxine and Doré *speak*. Tell her, Bea."

"I don't believe it. To each other?"

"It's true," Bea confirmed. "Not a lot, they're not *girlfriends*, but they talk."

"'Cause they're in league against Sara," Edgie said. "For the love of Tom. It's a regular Peyton Place around here."

"I can see. Who's the new lady?" A tiny, birdlike woman in a pillbox hat with a veil, sitting on the sofa in the Red Room beside a portly, pink-faced bald man.

"Mrs. Spinetti. Very nice. She's ninety."

"Bea likes her 'cause she's older than she is."

"That's her son with her, the bald one, visiting from New Jersey. He's sixty-two and still a bachelor."

They gossiped in the hall until Bea said, "Well, we can keep this

up all night, except you probably came to see somebody besides us."
But Caddie thought the real reason she made them disperse was
because she knew Edgie was getting tired and needed to sit down.
"Mingle," the sisters told her, and moved off into the Red Room.

Wake House looked beautiful, and not just because of the Christmas
decorations. The wood floors shone with fresh polish, every mirror
gleamed, the chandelier sparkled, even the walls looked brighter, less
dingy or something. Caddie had never seen a fire in either parlor's fireplace before, much less in both of them. Mr. Lorton was fast asleep in
front of the one in the Blue Room. Caddie kissed him on top of his bald
head, and he smiled up at her fondly and without surprise, as if he saw
her every day.

She found Brenda, festive in a green sweater with a sequined Santa
Claus on the chest, and complimented her on how pretty everything
looked.

"Well, we could afford to do a little more this year. Thea's estate
isn't settled, won't be for a while, but I'll tell you she made a very
generous bequest to Wake House."

"That's wonderful news."

"Caddie, you just don't know." She shook her head as if at a near
miss. "Last summer, I wasn't sure we could last out the year. And
now—isn't it grand? This is how it *should* look. I've got a new cleaning service that actually does what I tell them. This is just the tip of
the iceberg, what you can see. We've got plans for a new elevator
and a new roof, storm windows on the third floor, heavy-duty wash-
ers and dryers—"

"But, um, if the money is still tied up . . ."

"Oh, I know! If it doesn't go through, we're in trouble!" She
didn't look worried, though. She threw her head back and blared
out her great, booming laugh, and everybody within hearing distance smiled in sympathy. "Where's Frances? Didn't she come with
you?"

"She wasn't feeling up to it. Sends everybody her love."

Brenda sobered. "How is it, having her home? Not wearing you out, I hope."

"No, we're fine. She's—there are a couple of things I didn't really realize we'd be dealing with, but so far—"

"Like?"

"Well, the forgetfulness, I didn't know how bad that was getting. We've been to the doctor and he put her on some pills, but it's hard to say how well they're working. Especially with Nana—I mean, with her it's hard to say anyway, what's just her normal, you know, and what's . . ."

"Oh, honey." Brenda put an arm around her shoulders. "It's an awful thing, isn't it?"

"Thank you for keeping her for so long," Caddie said past a lump in her throat. "She really—she loved it here."

"We miss her."

"The worst is that she knows."

Brenda gave her shoulders a sad, buck-up squeeze. "Yes, but in time she won't. I'm so sorry, dear. That's the good news and the bad."

Caddie saw Magill before he saw her. He had on a tuxedo, an orange bow tie, and high-top sneakers. Everybody was hugging him, thrilled to see him, even the grieving Mrs. Shallcroft. Caddie could see why. They were glad to see her, too, of course, but she was still one of them. Not Magill. He didn't belong here any longer. He'd healed and moved on, back to the world of the healthy and young.

Everything about him looked vivid to her, from the blueness of his eyes to the shine of his hair. His cheeks weren't gaunt or sunken any longer, so he looked older—he looked his age. Even his voice came to her sounding stronger. No wonder everybody wanted to touch him, try to catch some of his spirit. She did, too.

She nodded to him and smiled a welcome, but she was in the middle of a conversation with Dolores, Mrs. Brill's daughter, and she couldn't break away. "Mama sent her life story in her Christmas card to all the children, Caddie, all my aunts and uncles, and they *loved* it. And guess what—Aunt Belinda *called* her. Those two haven't spoken in ages, and now my aunt wants to come visit next summer so her littlest child can get to know his grandma."

"Oh, wonderful."

"Mama would thank you, I know she feels grateful, but you know how funny she is about 'family business.' "

"But I didn't do anything," Caddie protested. "I just wrote it down." She could feel Magill's eyes on her from all the way across the room.

"Well, then *I'll* say thank you. It's really meant a lot. Do you think you'll keep on doing it now that your grandma's not here?"

"I guess I haven't thought about it."

"Seems like it'd be a shame to quit. Mr. Kowallis over there, he was just telling Mama *he'd* be interested. Said he used to be a newspaper reporter, so I bet he's got some interesting stories. Caddie, who are you looking at?"

She started. "Oh—I was looking at Henry. Magill."

Dolores did a double take. "That's Magill? The guy with the *football helmet*?"

"Dolores—excuse me a sec, I have to go say hi."

He had a glass of punch in one hand, a piece of cake on a paper plate in the other. He held out his arms and made a helpless face, as if he'd embrace her if he could. Caddie stepped in and touched cheeks, kissing the air by his ear.

"Happy New Year."

"Happy New Year."

"You look great. A *tuxedo*, wow. Does your bow tie light up?"

"Thanks, you look pretty spiffy yourself."

"Oh, this old thing." That was a joke, but she was too nervous to explain it—that she'd bought the dress she was wearing this afternoon. She felt warm and pleasantly uncomfortable under the intensity of his stare. Nobody had looked at her like that in a long time. "So you're back at work and everything?" she asked. "How is it?"

"Like running a marathon the day after they let you out of the hospital."

"But you love it," she guessed.

"Yeah." He smiled, sharing the secret. "Good thing, because I practically live there now. Long hours, trying to get back the accounts we let slip while I was gone. So it's more marketing than engineering right now, but that's temporary. I hope. How have you been doing?"

They wandered over to the fireplace. "Oh, I've been all right. Well, you know. Sad. It's been a pretty quiet time."

They talked about Cornel leaving. About how much they missed Thea. It was like old times.

"I heard Frances is back home," he said.

"Yes, so that's been, you know—we're all right, though. An adjustment. It's getting better. Did you have a nice Christmas?"

"I flew out to Phoenix to see my mother and stepfather."

"Oh! How was that?"

"Hot." He popped the square of cake in his mouth all at once, the way men but not women were allowed to do in public, and licked yellow icing off his lip. She'd never seen him enjoy food like that before. "Heard anything from Dinah?" he asked.

"We talked on Christmas Eve. And we write. She's fine; Earl, too. And Mother. Dinah asks about you sometimes."

"What do you say?"

"I say—I haven't seen you in a while." She stopped fiddling with a piece of candle wax on the mantel and looked into his eyes. She wasn't sure what she wanted to give him, or what she expected to get back, but it was time to make contact. "I've missed you."

"Hey," he said softly. "You want to get out of here?"

"What?"

He touched the side of her hand with his. "I know a much better party." He smiled hopefully. "Come with me."

"Oh." He was going too fast. Too fast. She was still so tender. Anyway, he didn't mean a party—he was making a double entendre, a suggestion. At least she thought he was. "I don't think so, no." He'd become *his* old self, so he thought she must have, too. Her fault; she'd been sending dishonest signals. It was this *dress.* "But thank you for asking me."

"Come on, Caddie, let's go. You'd have fun."

She shook her head. "Actually, this party feels like my speed. I think I'm where I'm supposed to be. I'm s—"

"No. Please don't say you're sorry." Last time, he'd said he wasn't angry with her, but this time he was. But trying not to show it. "Never mind, bad idea." He put his cup on the mantel and left her without saying any more.

She stared at the gay fire in the fireplace, transfixed. A log exploded behind the screen, shooting blue sparks. When she backed up, she saw her reflection in a round gold ball on the Christmas tree. She looked like a pear, squat and tiny-headed. Freakish.

Be passionate. Angie claimed that was *Caddie's* advice. It didn't sound like her; she must've been speaking in the abstract. *Do what I say, not what I do*—that's what she should've told Angie.

She went through the motions of having a nice time, talking and laughing, eating and drinking. Susan Cohen arrived late with Stan, her boyfriend, and they announced they were getting married. Caddie congratulated them long and heartily, but inside she felt like a fraud. What did she know about romance? Why pretend to be happy for Susan and Stan when she didn't even get the *point*? But that wasn't true, she did get the point, and it wasn't fair that Magill was through with her. She was still in mourning, and all around her people were saying "Happy New Year!" Why couldn't life stop for her, or slow down? She needed to rest and think things through, get her bearings, she was a very deliberate person, but nobody would *wait* for her.

"Announcement!" Brenda called from the hall on her way to the dining room. "People? Could everybody please come into the Blue Room? Just for a minute. I have a special announcement, people! Lord, it's like herding cats."

Caddie wandered toward the foyer. As she crossed the hall, she stopped short at the sight of Magill coming toward her in his overcoat. "I have to go," he said, jingling keys or change in his pocket. "Good to see you. Happy New Year."

"You're leaving? It's not even midnight."

"Yeah, I've got this thing, I told you."

He really had a party? "Oh, don't go yet. It's so early. And— Brenda has an announcement."

"So long, Caddie."

"Wait. Let's do karaoke. Do you know 'Indian Love Call'?"

He frowned at her while he wound his scarf around his neck. He thought she was drunk.

"Nelson Eddy and Jeanette McDonald. You know that song."

His face was a complete mystery, all locked up. She couldn't even read his eyes; he was keeping them blank so she couldn't get inside. "I've got some people expecting me. Night, Caddie," he said, and went out.

"Come on, everybody! Caddie," Brenda called, "I know you'll want to hear this!"

Her special announcement was a surprise only to Caddie, not to anyone else. Everybody had already heard the news that, independent of her will, Thea had gifted Wake House with a new piano, and tonight was its formal unveiling. Caddie hadn't noticed the bulky shape, obviously a piano, covered with green felt and a gold ribbon bow in the back of the room, or if she had noticed it, she'd thought it was some unfinished Christmas decoration, the base for a train set or something—she didn't know what she'd thought. She wasn't thinking too clearly now, either. But it was a piano, and after a short speech, Brenda whipped the green cloth away with a flourish and said, "Ta-da!"

An Ellington classic grand, polished mahogany, magnificent. Stunned, Caddie joined in the clapping and cheering until Cornel stepped in front of the instrument and called for quiet.

"I have something to say. Don't worry, it won't take long." He scowled and stuck his head out, raptor-style. "I've been here three and a half years. Feels like home, that's the best I can say about it. Now I got somewhere else to go, and we'll see how that works out. Some people I'll miss. Other people, like Bernie . . . haw-haw." Luckily they knew Cornel well enough to laugh with him, even sad-faced Bernie, who would probably miss him the most.

"I want to make two toasts," Cornel resumed. "First one's to Brenda. You put up with a lot, and not just from me. Thanks for everything. You're a good person and I wish you all the best."

"Hear, hear." Everybody who had a drink took a sip.

"And . . ." He hesitated. "You new folks, you'll have to take my word for it that there's somebody who's not here tonight that was much loved. We lost her last summer, and we're still . . . well, we're not going to forget her. She brought us a lot of happiness. She warmed us up. If there's a heaven, which I doubt but who the hell knows, she's up there and she's looking down on us now." He coughed. "To Thea."

"To Thea."

Brenda took Cornel's arm and leaned against him. "I know

something that would've made Thea very happy tonight. If Caddie would play some Christmas carols on our brand-new piano for us. Will you, Caddie?"

"Of course. I'd love to."

It was true. She wasn't shy or nervous, just anticipatory. She played all the standards, and when somebody requested "The Little Drummer Boy," a song she'd never played in her life, she ad-libbed the drum sound with catchy bass notes that had people clapping their hands in time. *Gosh*, she thought, *I'm good at this.* Realizing it made her joyful, but the two people she wanted to thank were gone, Thea forever. Magill, too, probably, because Caddie had broken his heart. Twice.

29

At eleven o'clock she started telling a lie: that Nana's teenage sitter had to be home before midnight, so she had to leave soon. "Oh, *stay*," they said, her sweet friends—the ones who hadn't gone up to bed already themselves— but Caddie couldn't bear the thought of all the gaiety that would be required of her at midnight. When twelve o'clock came, she wanted to be home.

She held Cornel too long, saying goodbye to him at the door; he backed out of her arms and coughed, embarrassed by her affection. She hadn't noticed till tonight how much he was like Finney. "You take care, Cornel, and be *happy*." He looked skeptical. "Try not to be miserable," she amended. "Promise me you'll try not to be miserable."

"Okay. What I can't figure out is what they want me down there for anyway."

"Because you're *family*."

"Oh, yeah."

"Incorrigible."

"*You* try not to be miserable. And don't forget you're coming to visit. I heard you, you can't take it back."

"Then I guess I'll have to come visit." She stole a quick kiss on his whiskery cheek. "Safe trip. Love you, Cornel."

Maybe he heard that, maybe not. He executed a stiff military salute and pivoted. Before she went down the porch steps, she glanced back and saw his hunched-over, hungry-bird figure in the hall, peering at the photograph of Thea when she was a little girl.

There wasn't much traffic on the roads. By now most people were where they wanted to be at midnight. A carful of inebriated young people stopped beside her at a traffic light; a girl rolled down the back window. Caddie expected anything, including vomiting, but the girl stuck out her arm and offered her an unopened can of beer. "No, thanks," she mouthed. The girl shrugged while her friends laughed uproariously. The light changed and they roared away. *Be careful!* she wanted to call after them, like a mother.

She drove through town and, without thinking much about it, made a right on Antietam instead of going straight. She'd driven past Kinesthetics, Inc., a couple of times since that day with Thea—not on purpose, just because she happened to be in the neighborhood— and the small parking lot had never been this crowded with cars. Except for the restaurants and places like the Elks Club or the VFW, downtown was dark and deserted, but all the lights were on at Magill's foot factory, and when she stopped at the curb and rolled down her window, she could hear the driving bass of dance music. Office party.

She pulled into a no-parking space in front of the building and turned off the motor. In the dark, she found a comb in her purse. She freshened her lipstick more by feel than sight. Best not to know the details anyway, she decided.

The farther she went up the concrete walk, the louder the music got. She was on a mission, an experiment in personal courage, but it wouldn't be cowardly to peek through the modern glass doors first, check out the lay of the land. That would just be prudent. Too bad the black glass was opaque. What if the doors were locked? Well, that would be fate. Not to mention symbolic. She put her hand on one of the brass knobs and pulled.

She was in a small reception room, brightly lit but empty. No point calling out "Hello?" because the music, coming down a corridor to the left, boomed in her ears like her own heartbeat amplified. The corridor was brightly lit, too, and she kept wanting a dark place, a vestibule where she could gather herself, see before being seen.

From here she could see the party in progress in a large room at the end of the hall. A woman and a man danced past the doorway with their arms in the air, and behind them other people gyrated in couples, groups, and by themselves to an old Tom Petty song. She'd been expecting to see fake feet, Full Speed Feet, in some context or other, she realized, maybe on a production line, but the party room was just an office with desks pushed against the walls. Plates of food and snacks covered a long, candlelit conference table in the back; under it a copper washtub bulged with ice and bottles. Except for candlelight, the only other illumination came from a Christmas tree and a string of twinkling white lights over the long back window.

Magill was nowhere.

A man saw her, an Asian man about her age, with a glossy ponytail and a gold stud in his nostril. He popped the caps on two bottles of beer and zigzagged nimbly through the dancers to where she stood half in, half out of the doorway. "Happy New Year," he shouted over the music, and handed her a beer.

"Happy New Year."

"I'm Otis."

She'd heard of Otis. He was a biomechanical engineer, like Magill, and he was "brilliant." In his spare time he designed toy electric trains. "Hi, I'm—looking for Magill," she said instead of her name. "Is he here?"

"He just left. But he'll be back, he and Minnie went for more champagne."

"Oh."

"You're Caddie."

"No, I'm not." It just popped out.

Otis's black eyebrows came together. "You're not? Sorry—I thought I saw you once at Wake House."

"At what?" She was terrified. She never lied, and she was doing it so *well*.

"Uh, nothing." Otis looked baffled. "Come on in. They'll be back soon, because it's twenty of twelve." He backed up to let her in. The people behind him, dancing and yelling at each other over the bluesy music, looked just the way she'd imagined people who made feet with Magill would look, funny and serious, young, sort of nerdy, sort of hip. Nobody had on a tuxedo, but a woman with wavy red hair down to her waist had on a slinky silver evening gown and a tiara. Other people wore jeans and sneakers or cocktail dresses or suits.

"Is there a ladies' room?" Caddie asked.

"Yeah, you just passed it."

"Great, I'll be right back."

"Want to leave your coat—"

"No, that's okay. Be right back."

By the time she got to the ladies' room door, Otis had melted back into the party; he didn't see her keep going, put her beer bottle on the receptionist's desk, and leave the building.

Well, at least she didn't feel ashamed. Lonesome, unlucky, unwanted, foolish, but not ashamed. She could have waited for Magill and Minnie, and embarrassed everybody instead of just herself, but she didn't see how that would've been brave. It would've been stupid. And she could have told Otis who she was, but what difference did it make? Magill would figure it out anyway. Besides, in some weird way, lying to Otis had been the best part. She'd broken a rule.

"Home already? It's not even midnight." Rayanne got off the couch and stretched. The TV was blaring rock music, but she looked half asleep.

"How's Nana?" Caddie asked, taking off her gloves.

"She went to bed. She was going to stay up and watch the ball drop, but she crashed about an hour ago. Hey, if you're back—you know what, I think I'll run. My folks are having a party, and if I hurry I can get there before twelve."

"Sure, go—no, wait, I'll drive you." It was five of twelve, but Rayanne only lived in the next block.

"Nah, I'll just run, it'll be faster." She grabbed her coat off the newel post. "See you next week. Happy New Year and all."

"Bye—thanks—happy New Year!"

On television, Dick Clark stood outside someplace over Times Square in his overcoat, talking about how many people were down there in the crowd, how many minutes were left before this year ended and the new one began. Why did people think that was a cause for celebration? It seemed to Caddie like a made-up holiday, as authentic as Secretaries' Day. The second hand hits the twelve, so it's time to jump up and down and blow horns and kiss each other?

"It's bogus," she told Finney as they trotted up the stairs to check on Nana. Dirges should play at midnight, priests should say solemn masses, people should stay in their houses and be quiet. The passage of time only signified one thing, when you got down to it, and any moment that marked it was the opposite of a joyous occasion.

Nana stirred when Finney jumped up on the bed. "Did you bring me those?" she murmured. The dog nuzzled her cheek and she opened her eyes. "Oh, hey. You're home."

"I'm home." Caddie sat on the edge of the bed. "Sorry we woke you. Were you dreaming?"

"You were a little girl and you brought me a bouquet of dandelions. You thought they were flowers."

Caddie smiled. The light from the hall illuminated half of her grandmother's face, left the rest in shadow. She looked dreamy and insubstantial. "Did you have a nice time tonight, you and Rayanne?"

"Who? Oh." She yawned. "We watched an old movie, something about a ship. Claude Rains. Where'd you go?"

"Wake House."

"Have fun?"

"Yes. Everybody asked about you."

"That's nice." She closed her eyes. Caddie thought she'd fallen back to sleep, but a moment later she mumbled, "Happy New Year. You making any resolutions?"

Caddie thought. "Yes. I'm going to join the orchestra again. I'm going to get out more."

"That's a good one," Nana said. "I will too, then."

"And I'm going to keep writing people's life stories at Wake House. I just decided."

"Good for you."

"Happy New Year, Nana."

"Gonna be an excellent one."

"It is?"

"Yes, sir."

"How do you know?"

"We're due."

"That's for sure. G'night," Caddie whispered, and tiptoed out of the room with the dog under her arm.

She took him for a walk. It was after midnight, but she kept the leash short in case somebody set off firecrackers. Besides thunder, firecrackers were the only things Finney was afraid of. Cars lined the streets bumper to bumper on both sides, no empty spaces. A listless flurry of snow had whitened the grass but melted on the pavement. It was bitter cold. None of the parties had spilled outside, but she could hear them through windows and walls, the shouts and laughter and the muffled, thumping music. *I ought to be more depressed*, Caddie

436

thought. She *was* depressed, but it felt more active than passive, so it wasn't as bad. She had an invigorating sense of failure.

Early Street was quieter; if anybody was having a party here, it was a sedate one. What they had a lot of on Early Street was Christmas decorations. Her neighbors had that in common with Dinah and Earl. *I have an aunt and an uncle*, she thought, to cheer herself up. And a second grandmother she didn't think about very often. Probably because Nana was enough of a grandmother for several people.

"Business, Finney. *Business.*" He'd pulled her around the block twice but he hadn't done anything. She switched leash hands to warm the freezing one in her pocket. In front of Mrs. Tourneau's house, he began to pull hard on the leash, like a horse within sight of the stable. "No, you don't. First you have to go. Hey—"

Somebody was in her yard. Somebody was sitting on the bottom step of the porch. All she could see was a shadowy outline, big and silent and not moving. It scared her to death. But Finney wasn't barking—that should've tipped her off. Hauling her behind him like a sled dog, gasping and strangling, he took a shortcut to the house through the frozen mud. Caddie let go of his leash and went the long way, up the snowy walk.

Magill stood up before the dog could tackle him. He had on his coat but no hat, no gloves. Finney jumped on his legs, yipping, begging to be picked up, and he leaned over and hoisted him into his arms. Poor black overcoat, thought Caddie. All those white hairs, stuck like glue.

She stopped on the walk a few feet shy of Magill. "He liked Christopher, too," she said. "He has really bad taste."

"It's not so much bad taste as superior tolerance." He had to lean his head back to keep from getting licked on the mouth. "I remembered 'Indian Love Call.' Shall we sing it?"

"What did Otis say?" Caddie asked.

"I'll be calling yooooou . . ."

"What did he say, how did he put it?"

"Otis?"

He didn't know what she was talking about. He really didn't. His complete incomprehension made her put her hands on her arms and hug herself. "You didn't talk to him."

He took a deep breath and grinned. "Excuse me?"

"You didn't even know I was there."

"Where?"

She just had one more question. "You're not in love with Minnie, are you?"

"*Minnie?*"

That was the right answer. "It's freezing out here, let's go."

"Caddie, about tonight."

"Wasn't it a great night? Don't you *love* New Year's?"

Finney was scratching at the storm door, anxious for his after-walk snack.

"No, I hate New Year's," Magill said, following her up the steps. "Everybody's faking. It's the worst night of the year."

"Oh, no. We have to mark time. We're human beings, we need the ceremony. Look—we got through *that* old year, now we get a new one. It's a gift."

"You think so?"

"Absolutely."

And if not, it ought to be.

POCKET
BOOKS

FLIGHT LESSONS

By Patricia Gaffney

Fox sixteen years, Anna has studiously avoided her Aunt Rose. Exchanging cards at holiday time – that's as far as Anna is willing to go with the woman she once loved more than anyone else in the world. That love died the night Rose betrayed Anna and her mother – and Anna can't forgive or forget.

Years have passed since she's been back to her hometown on Maryland's Eastern Shore, where Rose still runs the family restaurant. Anna has built a life elswhere with a job she likes and a man she loves. Or so she thought.

Another betrayal, another loss. Needing an escape, Anna has only one place to go: home to the family, to the restuarant, and to Rose who has been trying for more than a decade to regain Anna's trust. And right now, Rose needs her more than ever . . .

'A rich, rewarding read . . . will interfere with all other life until you finish it' Cathy Kelly

ISBN 0-7434-5055-8
PRICE £6.99

**POCKET
BOOKS**

This book and other **Pocket** titles are available from your local bookshop
or can be ordered direct from the publisher.

Please send cheque or postal order for the value
of the book, **free postage and packing within
the UK,** to: SIMON & SCHUSTER CASH SALES
PO Box 29, Douglas, Isle of Man, IM99 1BQ
Tel: 01624 677237, Fax 01624 670923
bookshop@enterprise.net
www.bookpost.co.uk

Please allow 14 days for delivery. Prices and availability subject
to change without notice.